The First Time I Died

Jo Macgregor

VIP Readers' Group: If you would like to receive my author's newsletter, with tips on great books, a behind-the-scenes look at my writing and publishing processes, and notice of new books, giveaways and special offers, then sign up at my website, www.joannemacgregor.com.

First published in 2018 by Jo Macgregor
ISBN: 978-0-6399317-2-2 (paperback)
ISBN: 978-0-6399317-3-9 (eBook)

Cover design by Jenny Zemanek at Seedlings Design Studio
Formatting by Polgarus Studio

"The past is never dead. It's not even past."

— William Faulkner, *Requiem for a Nun*

Prologue

July 2008

The covered bridge crouched open-mouthed on the road ahead. Bushes grew densely on either side of the opening. Vines sent tender shoots and tendrils around the weathered timber sidings and through the lattice truss work to probe the dark interior.

I reduced my speed, checked for oncoming traffic, and drove into the tunnel. The wooden slats creaked beneath the weight of my car, and the roar of the Kent River rushing over the rocks ten feet below reverberated in the confined space. I crawled along, torn between the fear that the floorboards would give way beneath me if I went faster and the irrational dread that the low, arched beams and wooden walls would close in on me, trapping me in their dank grip.

I shivered and gooseflesh tightened the skin on my arms — a sure sign, my mother would say, that a ghost was walking over my grave.

I hunched over the steering wheel, gripping it with both hands as the shadows wove a deep gloom behind me. On and on the tunnel stretched, for far longer, surely, than its two-hundred-and-seven-foot length. I kept my eyes on the square of light glimmering ahead, accelerated over the last twenty feet, and popped out into the muggy warmth of the July day on the other side.

My eyes were watering — possibly due to the dazzling summer sunshine, but probably because that's just what they did these days. Tears flowed even when I wasn't thinking about him, about what had happened. They just came, and sometimes they went.

I snagged my Ray Bans from the glove compartment and fumbled them on. The rest of my clothes and possessions were stuffed in the suitcases now packed in the trunk, along with my week-old high school diploma. In a few hours, I'd be in Boston, ready to unpack and start a new life.

I spared a brief glance for the rusted town limits sign as I whizzed past. The pole listed sideways as if it, too, was unable to bear the weight of its burden. It was stuck there, keeling over in slow-motion surrender, but I was getting away. Leaving the last year far behind me.

And if I had my way, I'd never come back.

1

NOW
Saturday December 16, 2017

Afterward, whenever anyone asked me to tell them about what happened, I never knew *when* to begin the story. I think it all started when I went back home, but maybe it was when I died. Or when *he* did. Or even the year before that, when we had all the rain. Perhaps it was the meeting with my faculty supervisor that started the chain of motion — I'd like to be able to blame him.

I knew *where* it started, though — in a small Vermont town tucked into the cleavage between the Green Mountains and Kent Hill, ground zero of several dying businesses, multiple illicit affairs, endless dull gossip and one grand mystery. The last time I'd driven this highway, I'd been eighteen years old and headed in the opposite direction, determined never to return.

And yet here I was, headed back to my hometown.

A new wooden sign, complete with painted crest and brick pillars on either side, materialized out of the mist at the town limits. In fancy hand-lettering, the sign proclaimed: *Welcome to Pitchford, Vermont. Chartered 1767. Population 2826.*

The welcome sign wasn't the only change. A few hundred yards after the turnoff to the old Johnson farm with its weather-beaten barns and herds of Holstein dairy cows, and on the other side of Kent Hill, was the new and improved home of Beaumont Brothers Spring Water Company. *Pure water, pure life*, their tastefully subdued signage announced. According to my father, who occasionally updated me on town news, the new bottling plant had been built the year after I graduated high school.

By then I was already in Boston, flunking my first year of premed. My second year wasn't any better. I spent nights in my room, lost in the oblivion of sleep. I struggled to get out of bed in the mornings, couldn't concentrate in lectures, didn't care enough to study, refused to talk to anyone about it. I was in limbo, waiting for my new life to begin, or my old life to let go of me. When neither happened, I dropped out and ran away to the other side of the planet. For over a year, I worked as a volunteer on conservation programs in South Africa — tagging rhinos, cleaning cages in a primate sanctuary, caring for wild dogs and cheetahs in breeding programs, and drinking enough of the cheap local beer to anesthetize an elephant's memory. My own, however, remained stubbornly persistent.

Back in Boston, I began the long journey of studying psychology, intending to understand the faulty minds and repair the wounded hearts of the world. Although if my master's faculty supervisor, Professor Kenneth Perry, was to be believed, then even back then my true — albeit unconscious —

goal had been the impossible task of understanding and repairing myself.

At our most recent monthly progress meeting, Perry had studied me over the top of his spectacles, as if trying to fathom the depths of my motivations. "Your Statistical Methods II credit is still not complete. More importantly, your thesis is still nowhere bloody near done, despite you buggering around with it for years. *Years!*"

Perry was a Brit, originally from Exeter, and he used words like bugger, bloody and bollocks all the time. I'd caught the habit from him.

"I know, I know," I said. "It's just that I keep falling down the rabbit hole of research and finding more interesting side topics."

He raised an eyebrow, and I hurried on.

"I'm thinking of changing the focus to look at how the social construction of grief is mediated by support on social media. What do you think? I could look at how the memorialization of the lost one on social media sites both fixes *their* identity and changes the identity of the survivor."

I rubbed a thumb against the tip of my forefinger, where a thin filament of skin was peeling away. I wanted to nibble it off, but knowing Perry, he'd interpret that as a regressive oral gesture — a substitution for thumb-sucking.

"And as for stats — my brain just doesn't work that way."

"Bollocks," he said.

"You'd think I'd get a little sympathy from the Psych department."

He gave me a wry smile. "Sympathy? If I was your therapist,

I'd be more likely to interpret your endless delays."

"Oh, yeah?"

"I'd explore whether you really want to do this."

"You think I should dump grief altogether and find a whole new topic?"

"I'm not talking about your poxy thesis. I'm talking about all of this." He spread his arms wide. "About psychology."

"You're implying I don't really want to be a psychologist?" I said, outraged. "After I've spent so long studying it?"

"I'm asking *because* you've spent so long studying it. You should be finishing your doctorate by now. And instead, you're still mucking about with your Masters."

"That's not because I don't *want* to be a psychologist."

"Isn't it?" He tilted his head and contemplated me shrewdly. "You've heard of the concept of 'the wounded healer'?"

"The theory that people study psychology as a roundabout way of dealing with their own issues, instead of getting therapy for themselves?"

"That's the one."

"You think that applies to me?"

"Don't you?"

Bloody shrink. Answering a question with a question. I tried to pinch off the irritating bit of skin with what remained of my nails.

"You've had some difficult things happen in your life," he said. "Issues with your family of origin."

"We've *all* had those," I muttered.

"And a tragic, traumatic loss."

That was a low blow. I shifted my gaze away from him and

stared out of the window, across the university lawns. On this early December evening, no students lingered on the icy stone benches to debate Nietzsche or the reality of experience. Oak trees stretched arthritic limbs — bare of all but the most tenacious leaves — up to the sullen gray sky.

"Garnet?"

I turned back to face him.

"I think it might be useful for you to take a moratorium."

"You don't think I can finish. You don't believe I've got what it takes," I accused.

He snorted. "Really? That's your best attempt at derailing me?"

I shrugged. "It was worth a shot."

"Take a break. Spend some time thinking about what you really want to do with your life."

"What — I'm supposed to hang around my apartment making pro and con lists?"

"Go home."

"This *is* home."

"Get some country air. Make some decisions. Visit your family."

His tone — concerned, gentle even — made me uncomfortable. I didn't want to go home, particularly at this time of year. Keeping my hands in my lap, out of his line of vision, I worried at the loose skin on my finger.

"When did you last see your parents?" he asked.

"A few months ago."

They visited me twice a year, every year without fail — for the fourth of July and for Christmas — but my mother wouldn't be up to travelling to Boston this December.

"Didn't you say your mother had a stroke?" he asked.

"A transient ischemic attack," I corrected.

"Close enough."

It had been close enough to scare the crap out of Dad. He'd said her face had drooped on one side and that for several minutes she'd rambled on confusedly — more so than usual, apparently. Then she'd lost her balance and broken her left ankle, and she'd had to spend three weeks resting with it elevated. It was still in a knee-to-toe cast.

"She's recovered well," I said. "And she's on blood pressure meds and blood thinners, so it shouldn't happen again."

"Even so, the TIA may be a warning of things to come. Your parents are never going to be physically healthier or mentally sharper than they are now. How old are they, anyway?"

"My father's sixty-three and my mother's sixty-four, and apart from this latest episode, they're in great health."

"No one's immortal. Spend the holidays with them, drink eggnog or whatever your favorite festive tipple is."

"Irish coffee, served extra hot. No one ever serves it hot enough. Although I did find this great place in Beacon Hill that—"

"Garnet," he said, interrupting my attempt to change the subject, "how many Christmases with them do you think you have left?"

Not realizing what I was doing until it was done, I tore the filament of skin off with my teeth, leaving a thin strip of raw skin. Damn, that was going to hurt later.

"You can let me know your decision in January," Perry said.

His suggestion wasn't entirely without appeal. My parents had pleaded with me to spend the holidays with them in Pitchford, plus my father had privately begged for my help in persuading my mother to close her sandals-and-candles shop in town. If we got her to agree, then he'd be grateful for my help in sorting, clearing and purging the contents. And there was a part of me that wanted in on that action, that longed to toss all the crystals, dream catchers, incense sticks and astrology charts into the trash, where they belonged.

"And if you decide to continue, I want your completed thesis by the end of May," Perry said. Although I didn't always get his dry, British sense of humor, I was pretty sure he wasn't kidding.

"You're giving me a deadline? An ultimatum?"

He nodded.

"Bastard," I said, just loud enough for him to hear.

"I've been called worse."

"Is that all?"

"One more thing — and you're not going to like this either. If you decide to complete your master's, I'll require you to enter therapy."

"*What?* For myself — like, as the patient?"

"Yes."

"Why?" I demanded.

"To address your social adjustment issues, and to treat your excoriation disorder."

"I do *not* have excoriation disorder. I just bite my nails."

"Please, Garnet, I've seen you draw blood picking at the skin on your fingers and your lips. Do you pick or peel anywhere else, or do any other kind of self-mutilation?"

I scowled at him. "And I do not have social adjustment issues."

"So you've started socializing with friends in the evenings and on weekends? You have a boyfriend?"

"For your information, I went out on a date just last week. Had sex afterward, too!"

"Spoken to him since?" When I didn't answer, Perry added, "You're afraid of intimacy, Garnet. You need to work through that. How can you help others unless you've dealt with your own stuff?"

"I'm going now." I grabbed my bag. "I'll see you in January."

"You have a very merry Christmas, now!"

Which was how, a week later, I came to be driving down the icy highway that cut through the woods, headed back to my hometown for the holidays. My Honda's headlights picked out the details along the road — the picnic site at Flat Rock, the tall pines and firs looming in the mist like gray giants, their boughs already heavy with the season's first real snow, and up ahead, the covered bridge that straddled Kent River. I tried to stare it down. Blinked first.

A shadow broke from the dark mass of trees to my left and bounded into the road ahead of me. I slammed on the brakes, wrenched the wheel. Tires squealed. The car lurched, spun sideways, slid across the road and came to a juddering halt with the nose a hand's breadth away from the rough bark of a tree trunk. Heart hammering at the base of my throat, I cursed my stupidity. I knew how to drive on these icy roads. Dad had drummed it into me as a teenager. Drive slowly, pulse the brakes, turn *into* the skid.

And be on the lookout for moose.

Wiping cold sweat off my upper lip with a trembling hand, I started the stalled car and began backing up. A loud horn sounded. I snapped my head to the side to see a black Suburban snaking out to avoid hitting my reversing rear as it sped down the highway.

Damn. I'd almost killed myself twice in two minutes.

I took several calming breaths to damp down the adrenaline and cortisol racing through my veins, then inched back into the road, checking each direction repeatedly before setting off in the direction of town at half my previous speed. I slowed down even further as I approached the covered bridge. It had a new roof and reinforced concrete abutments — repairs made, so a small information sign said, after storm damage sustained during Hurricane Irene in 2011.

Inside, it was still dark and claustrophobic. And it still took way too long to drive through. As my car rumbled over its boards, I resisted the crazy sensation that the wooden sides were closing ranks in the darkness behind me, sealing off the route out of town. If I were a therapist — and despite my protestations to Prof. Perry, I was far from sure I wanted to be — I'd have been tempted to interpret the tight tunnel as a symbolic birth canal.

But this time, I realized, I was going *back* to Mama.

2

The day of the picnic was the first clear day in ages. After what felt like a year of thick clouds and heavy rain, the sun emerged triumphant in a cloudless, turquoise sky, and the message went out on Myspace and in texts: *Spring Break! Picnic today, noon, Flat Rock, bring food and drinks. Seniors and juniors only.*

We arrived in small groups, peeling out of cars and claiming spots on the grass, benches and boulders at the site. Someone hooked up their iPod to a pair of mini-speakers, and The Fray wondered how to save a life. We dumped our offerings of soda and snacks on the lichen-covered, flat-topped boulder, like supplicants at a stone altar to an ancient god. My friend Jessica Armstrong and I had caught a ride with her handsome brother, James, whom everyone called Blunt because he was always stoned. Though he'd been out of high school for a couple of years now, Blunt's stash of weed was his ticket to any gathering of teens in our town.

Jessica hoisted her clinking backpack onto the rock and extracted a tower of red Solo cups and three bottles of wine. Everyone standing nearby cheered.

Pete Dillon, captain of the football team and never one to deny his appetites, gave her a wink and said, "Suh-weet, Armstrong! How'd you get your hands on the weineken?"

Jessica blushed, but tried to play it cool. "I lifted it." To me she whispered, "From my father's liquor cabinet," and, at my look, added, "*What?* He won't miss a few bottles."

My contribution to the food consisted of an enormous bag of my favorite Fiery Habanero Doritos and another of popcorn, a tube of Pringles, and a few bottles of Coke and Sour Apple soda — all legitimately sourced from my father's grocery store in town. Hot, salty, sweet and sour. I had all my extreme taste bases covered.

Others had brought hot dogs, goldfish crackers, more chips and enough candy to get everyone smacked off their heads on sugar. Colby Beaumont, I noticed — and I always noticed Colby Beaumont — had brought several six-packs of bottled spring water in a range of flavors, which he'd probably collected from his family's bottling plant just a mile down the way. He was wearing faded Levis and an old Red Hot Chili Peppers T-shirt, and his fair hair shone in the sunlight. Even Judy Burns — who was all over him like salmonella on steak — couldn't dim his gorgeousness.

Jessica elbowed me in the ribs and tilted her head in Colby's direction. She was always trying to get me to make a move on him, telling me, "You two would be perfect for each other." She regarded the fact that Colby was currently dating Judy as inconvenient, but irrelevant. "That won't last, you'll see. What's she got besides beauty?"

We both stared enviously at the long legs, big boobs and sleek, strawberry-blond hair of our fellow senior. By comparison, I was boring. Average height, medium-brown hair. The only non-regular things about my appearance were my boobs, which were smaller than the norm.

"Colby strikes me as the kind of guy who likes, you know, brains. And personality."

"She's not stupid," I conceded begrudgingly.

"Plus," Jessica continued, undeterred by my pessimism, "I heard from Stef that they're really rocky. But you've got to make him *notice* you. Like, starting now."

I made myself consider it logically. If I spoke to him, one of two things could happen — either he'd blow me off, or he wouldn't. Fifty-fifty odds weren't bad. I pulled my long braid of brown hair around to the front, because Jess always said it looked cuter that way, and made myself smile as I walked over to Colby. Judy narrowed her eyes territorially at me and held onto Colby a little tighter.

"Hey Colby, can I try a bottle of the lemon and lime water?" I asked.

"Sure, help yourself."

He fished a few bottles out of the cooler of ice beside him and held one out to me. I took it, hyper-aware of the brush of his fingers against mine. I offered him some of my prized hot chips. "Want to try these? Since you like chilis."

"He doesn't like chilis," Judy said. "Why would you think he does?"

Colby looked confused, and I inwardly cursed my sucky social skills.

"Um." I pointed to his shirt.

"Oh, right, I get it." He grinned and took a few chips and popped them in his mouth.

"Well?" I asked him.

"They're not bad at all. Spicy, but not too hot."

"Wait for it ..." I said.

Judy gave me a why-are-you-still-here look, but Colby's eyes widened as the slow burn kicked into higher gear. Then he went red and coughed, while Judy slapped his back with a manicured hand.

"I *told* you he doesn't like hot things. Are you okay, Colbs?" she asked, fussing over him and handing him a cup of soda.

"The heat is murdering my face," he rasped. He gulped down the soda, then pulled a face. "Too sweet!"

"Here." I handed him the bottle of lemon and lime water I'd just taken. "Sorry."

"You eat those things?" he asked when he could breathe again.

"All the time," I admitted, fiddling with the end of my long braid, feeling the spiky tuft of hair against my fingertips.

He raised his eyebrows at me and rubbed a hand across his chest. "Respect. I think I'll stick to musical peppers."

Judy placed a fingertip on his jaw and turned his head to face her again. "Let's hike to the top of the hill, Colbs. Maybe we can get some privacy that way."

Colby chugged the rest of the water like his throat was burning before giving me a quick grin. Judy muttered

15

something about irritating interruptions as they walked away. I stood like a dope, watching him go, admiring the fine sight of his denim-clad butt until Jess joined me again.

I sighed. "I'm such a moron. Why didn't I offer him Pringles? Or popcorn?"

"Consider the upside," she said. "At least he won't forget you."

We hung around, soaking up the sun, while some of the others trailed after Colby and Judy. It was always like that — wherever Colby was, others wanted to be. Jess gave a snort of disgust, and following her gaze, I saw Pete lying on a patch of grass with a girl from my class called Ashleigh Hale. He had his tongue down her throat, and she had her hands under his shirt.

"Come on, you don't want to watch that," I told Jess.

She had a soft spot for Pete. But he had a hard one for every girl in town. He'd even tried putting the moves on me a couple of times, but his bulky muscles and frat-boy-style charm couldn't compare to Colby's lean frame, fair hair and slow smile. Pete was loud and funny. Colby was deep and intense. I knew which one I preferred.

Jess and I headed up the trail that snaked through the trees and around the side of the hill, all the way to the source of the spring near the top. Halfway up, Jess and I stepped off the path to catch our breath. Thirsty from the hot, salty chips, I finished my water while I took in the view. Come the end of September, the scene would glow with the ruby, russet and flame yellows of a New England fall, but now the hills were an endless vista of green stretching to the distant ridge of mountains. The woods ended, like the curve of a frothy wave on a beach, where old Elias Johnson's dairy farm began on the lower slopes of the hill.

From this distance, the black-and-white cows looked like a kid's picture book drawing of cows in a green pasture. But I'd done deliveries from my father's store to that farm, and I knew that up close the cows were gross, their faces and udders raw and red with eczema caused by a toxin that flourished in the warm, wet weather. The poor creatures got severe sunburn and had bare, bleeding patches where they rubbed against trees and poles, and my father's store did a good trade in the zinc ointment that helped the condition.

"Ready to go on?" Jess asked.

I nodded, and we were just about to get back onto the path when Pete Dillon came striding up. Ashleigh was nowhere in sight.

"I didn't think you were going to join us on the hike," Jess said, looking happy at Pete's change of plans.

"I just wanted to give you guys a head start, else it wouldn't be a challenge. Watch me get to the top first," he said and took off running up the trail.

"Why is everything a competition with him?" I said, as he disappeared around a bend.

Jess sighed. "He likes winning."

"He likes beating Colby, you mean." As popular as Pete was, everyone knew that Colby was top dog at Pitchford High.

"That, too," she conceded.

We set off again, each in a haze of unrequited adoration.

"Hey," I said, trying to shrug off the mood, "time for a bet."

"Lay it on me."

"Which girl from school gets pregnant first?"

"Good one!" Jess said. "I'll put five bucks on you."

"*Me?*" I squeaked, nearly face-planting in the mud as my feet slipped on the pine-needle mulch. "What the ...? Why would you say that?"

"It's always the ones you least expect."

"How d'you figure that?"

"I watch movies. I know things," she said, sagely.

"Well, you're wrong." I picked a wildflower and plucked off its petals as I walked. Most flowers had an odd number of petals, so as long as you started with *he loves me*, you were good. "Ten bucks says it'll be Judy."

"Not altogether unlikely. You think she and Colby have gone all the way?"

"I do." It pained me to think of it, but statistically speaking, it was highly probable.

"Can't your mother make you a Judy voodoo doll? And a Colby-Garnet love potion?" Jess said, giggling.

I threw the stripped flower head at her.

When we got to the top of the hill, everyone was already clustered around the spring. The way Pete was slapping hands with the guys around him made me think he'd alpha-dogged his way to the top and got there first after all. Colby was explaining how the spring — which, honestly, looked kind of unimpressive as it bubbled out of a crack in the granite and disappeared back underground a foot or so later — was the source of Beaumont Brothers' spring water, even though it was harvested and bottled at the plant down the hill, near old Johnson's farm.

Judy sat on a rock nearby, examining her fingernails and looking bored. Maybe she'd heard the story of the Beaumont brothers' discovery before, but I was fascinated. Though, to be honest, I would've been enthralled by Colby reading the ingredients list on the back of a bottle of hot sauce. Nearby, Pete talked loudly about the changes he planned to make to the football team's strategy in the next season, all the while shooting not-so-surreptitious glances at Judy. I guessed the ultimate win for him would be to score a touchdown with Colby's girl. Boys were so strange.

After a while, Colby and Judy headed off into the woods alone — to do the deed? — while the rest of us lazed about in the dappled shade. Jess passed around a bottle of wine she'd lugged up the hill, while one of Pete's teammates passed around a roach no doubt purchased from Blunt. Sleepy from the wine, I lay down with my head against Jess's backpack and dozed, only opening my eyes when Jess kicked my ankle.

"Look," she said, pointing at me, but I followed the direction of her thumb, as per our secret code.

Colby was emerging from the trees, running a hand through his thick blond hair and looking … sheepish? Oh, they'd done the deed alright. I closed my eyes again, but another, sharper kick had me sitting up and blinking.

Mouth pursed, face red and eyes swollen, Judy stormed across the clearing, muttered something to a group of her friends, grabbed her bestie by the arm, and took off down the hill almost at a run. Within minutes, the news had spread amongst the rest of us — Colby and Judy had fought and broken up.

Judy's friends were volubly scandalized, loyally accusing Colby of all kinds of nastiness. Pete looked hopeful as he pushed himself off a rock and strolled onto the path after Judy, a hound dog following the scent. Colby splashed his face with water at the spring and avoided everyone's eyes, while Jess gave me a knowing smile.

"You," she said, rounding her hand over her flat belly. "And twenty bucks says by the end of the year."

I was still busy telling her not to talk out of her rear end when Colby strolled up to us.

"Hey, Jess," he said, "can I give you two a ride back to town? I'm guessing Blunt is pretty blazed by now and shouldn't be driving."

He spoke to her, but he was looking at me.

3

Church and state still stood sentry at the top of Main Street, Pitchford. The Bethel United Methodist Church faced the perky red door of the Town Office across the street, as if to say, "You aren't rid of me yet," and the old black bear weather vane which still crested its steeple angled this way and that in the gusting wind, as if sniffing at the nearby woods for a hint of coming snow.

Founded in 1772, the town had been abandoned by many of its more ambitious or distractible denizens several times over the years — in the mid-nineteenth century by desperate hopefuls headed out west for the gold rush, and again during the Great Depression when the mills ceased their grinding, and the screaming blades of the logging companies fell silent. In the 1990s, young people left their cash-strapped farming fathers and cheesemaking mothers in the fertile valley and set course for New York and Philadelphia and other places where your neighbors might not know your name, but didn't know your private business, either.

I preferred the anonymity of living in Boston. My apartment was small and the walls were thin enough for me to hear the baby next door crying, but I felt a sense of space and freedom there that was missing in Pitchford, even though the houses here were set far apart on large lots, and my eyes could stretch over the uninterrupted view to drink in the sight of mountains and forests.

At the stop street, I lowered my window and was hit by a blast of frigid air and a rush of the kind of country silence that made a city-dweller's ears reverberate. It would take me a day or two to get used to the absence of constant noise. I closed the window and set off slowly down the hill, amazed at the changes visible all around me.

Towns in this part of the state tended to be either dying or thriving. Ours used to be the moribund type, with a long-dead sawmill, a few small, dusty stores clinging stubbornly to their patch of land on the main drag, and a decommissioned stone-works where local kids risked broken bones leaping into the murky water at the bottom of the deep marble quarry.

You didn't have to live in this neck of the woods to know that over the last decade or two, many of the small towns here had succumbed to massively rising rates of drug abuse and accompanying crime; it was all over the daily news. First prescription opioids, then crystal meth and now heroin — Vermont formed a lucrative corridor for dealers hopping between the big cities of New York, Chicago, Boston and Detroit on their way to Montreal.

But Pitchford hadn't died. In fact, it appeared to have miraculously transformed itself in the years I'd been gone.

There were signs of the metamorphosis everywhere. I drove beneath the Christmas lights draped across Main Street, trying to figure out if the old-timey lampposts they hung from were new, or if they'd always been there. What definitely *was* new was a rash of businesses with quaint storefronts and cutesy names: Granny Smith's Craft Cider Company, Adirondacks Antiques, and The Granary Gristmill and Bakery, which advertised a variety of artisanal breads in gold vintage-style lettering on its window.

Artisanal was a hot new word in Pitchford, it seemed. I could purchase Green Mountain Blue at the Artisanal Cheese Company, and across the way, The Vermont Syrup Emporium offered tastings of artisanal maple syrup. Judging by the luxury SUVs with skis and snowboards strapped on their roof racks that were parked outside the Emporium, maple syrup had become a popular tourist attraction.

I cruised past an art gallery, pottery studio, woodwright and cabinet-maker, chic boutiques, and a specialty chocolate store called New England Nibbles. Farther down the street was Dad's old mom-and-pop grocery store, now a Best West supermarket cunningly hidden behind a country store facade. Dad had done well out of the sale to the chain and had urged Mom to sell her neighboring New Age store, but she'd refused. Big surprise. She said helping the customers was what kept her alive, and vowed that the only way we'd get her out of Crystals, Candles and Curiosities was in a coffin.

The store's name was a pun, because my mother's name was Crystal. An embarrassing tradition on my mother's side of the family ensured all daughters were named after gemstones and crystals — which was how I got saddled with my ridiculous name. I had one aunt named Beryl, another called Ruby, and my grandmother's first name had been Emerald. If I ever had a kid, I'd be sure to call her something like Mary or Sue.

With my mother resting up at home, the store windows were dark, and a "closed" sign hung forlornly on the inside of the glass door. The thought that Windsor County's alternatively-minded would have to buy their tarot cards and angel charm bracelets somewhere else brought a grim smile to my lips.

At the bottom of the hill, where Main Street ended, the Tuppenny Tavern and Chop House was still open for business. The old-timey name wasn't new, though the neon sign in vintage-style script glowing through the mist was. I wondered if the nearby pier which jutted out into Plover Pond was still a favorite hangout spot for the town's teens.

I took a right, turning away from the bar and the pier and the memories, but there was no getting away from the pond. It lay on my left, sulking coldly in the dead center of the village, circled by the prosaically named Pond Road, with the town's streets radiating out from it, like the concentric arcs of a spider's web.

The surface of the pond was frozen, but the dark water beneath showed through cracks in the ice like veins of blue blood beneath the surface of white New England skin. A *No Skating* sign was stuck on the sandy bank near the little bay, deterring adventurous souls from venturing onto the treacherous ice — something I was in no way tempted to do.

In spring, the gazebo-style bandstand located in the waterside park would be draped with heavy bunches of lilac wisteria blossoms, and in summer, couples would sit on the mown green grass, or paddle with their toddlers at the water's edge. In fall, the maples, oaks and birches would fire up in a blaze of copper, brass and gold leaves, but on this dull winter afternoon, the scene was a palette of monochromatic colors. Snow covered the ground, the naked tree limbs were black against the iron-gray sky, and the gnarled bare vines of the wisteria strangled the pale ribs of the empty bandstand. A lone jogger ran along the trail beside the pond, puffing out clouds of frosty breath. The strip of reflective fabric across his sweatshirt flashed amber against the bleached scene and then was gone.

I pulled my gaze away from the pond and took in the other side of the road as I drove on. I passed a house with a twenty-foot Douglas fir out front, trimmed with a necklace of soft white lights. That had been Jessica Armstrong's home. We'd been so totally out of contact that I didn't know whether her family still lived there, or even whether Dr. and Mrs. Armstrong were still alive.

Like many of the houses on Pond Road, the old Armstrong house looked like it had been renovated in recent years. This was now prime real estate. Front doors wore stylish wreaths made of fir, holly, pinecones and ivy and garnished with supersized ribbons, but no inflatable snowmen or garish Santa Clauses decorated the front yards of Pitchford's wealthiest citizens. Even the old Frost Inn — a real dive back when I'd lived here — had a new slate roof, paved parking lot and forest-green window boxes.

The whole town seemed to have been given a facelift, but I

wondered if the veneer of charming good taste and discreet affluence extended beyond Main Street and Pond Road to where the real folks lived. At the turnoff to the road headed out the other side of town, a cluster of matching signs pointed the way to hiking and biking trails, a berry farm and the Beaumont Golf Estate and Hydrotherapy Spa. Yup, nearby towns may have fallen on bad times, but good times had fallen on Pitchford.

Approaching the next intersection, I hit the signal to turn right onto Algonquian Street, then hesitated, scraping my front teeth over a rough edge of skin on my lower lips. Three blocks up and to the right, at the house on Abenaki Street where I'd spent the first eighteen years of my life, my father would have swept the path and driveway in anticipation of my arrival and would no doubt be anxiously checking his watch and peeping out of the front window every ten minutes. My mother, wearing her St. Christopher medal to ensure travel blessings, would have said a prayer even as she laid out a crystal grid on her altar in the living room — she liked to hedge her bets with all the deities. Both would be full of news and questions. Instead of taking the right, I made a U-turn and headed back in the direction of town, keeping my eyes averted from the pond and the pier.

Some things couldn't be faced on an empty stomach or a caffeine deficit.

4

Most of the usual crowd were already partying under the pier near the Tuppenny Tavern by the time Jess and I arrived late that summer evening. My gaze immediately zeroed in on Colby Beaumont, who was chilling out in a large group of seniors, including two girls called Kathryn and Taylor who were leaning up against each other. Jess and I had a bet going that they'd be the first gay couple to attend the senior prom in the history of Pitchford. Pete Dillon's best friend, Brandon Nugent, sat cross-legged and swaying slightly, eyes glazed and a doofus smile on his face. I was surprised to see that Colby's older sister, Vanessa, was also there, along with a big guy who was a local police officer. They'd both graduated high school years ago, and word was she was studying at school in Boston or New York. Maybe she'd come home for her summer break.

"If, once I've blown the popsicle stand that is this town, I can think of nothing better to do with my summer vacation than come back home and hang out with a bunch of teens under the pier, please stage an intervention. Kidnap me and put me on a bus headed out of town," I told Jess.

"Okay. Permission to slap you in order to bring you to your senses?"

"Permission granted."

"And where should this bus be headed?"

"Anywhere but here."

As if they'd heard my judgy opinion, Vanessa and the R-guy stood up, dusted the seats of their pants, and walked off in the direction of the Tavern.

My gaze locked back on Colby. He wore baggy shorts and his blue tee with the hole in the shoulder. The group of girls seated close to him, giggling and exclaiming at his every word, wore bikinis and the alert, eager expressions of hunting dogs.

"Kill me now," Jess said.

My thoughts exactly. But Jess's gaze was, as usual, fixed on Pete, who stood to the side of the main group, pinning Judy Burns against a wooden piling. They were making out hard enough to earn an R-rating, but by the way both of them kept cutting glances at Colby, I figured they were more interested in his reactions than licking each other's tonsils. For different reasons, both of them wanted him jealous.

As soon as the cop was gone, beers were pulled out of bags and coolers, and Blunt ambled up to us, holding a baggy of weed out to me.

"Hey Jess, and Jess's friend. Can I interest you ladies in something to take the edge off?"

I shook my head. I'd smoked pot once and had felt nothing except irritable and tired.

"Something stronger, then? I've got Oxycontin, Vicodin, Percocet?"

A regular pharmacy, was Blunt.

"How about serrano, bird's eye or devil's tongue?" I asked.

"What are those, man? Mushrooms? Meth?"

"Fuck off, Blunt. She's not interested in your merchandise," Jess said, her gray eyes — so like her handsome brother's — filled with contempt.

He stood still and stared at me for several moments, as if trying to figure my angle, then shrugged and strolled off.

"He's dealing pills now?" I asked Jess softly.

"He's dealing whatever he can get his hands on."

"How? I mean, where does he get them?"

"He steals pages from my father's prescription pads and fills them at drugstores in nearby towns."

"Jeez. That's kinda … hardcore."

"Yeah," she said grimly. "I think he's coming off the rails. He came home the other day bragging to me that he'd beat up a pharmacist in Rutland because the guy had refused to fill the script and threatened to call the cops."

"Shit." I began nibbling on my pinkie nail.

She automatically pushed my hand away from my mouth. "But maybe he was just talking smack, you know? I don't believe half of what he says anyway, he's always out of it."

"Do your parents know?"

"About him using? Yeah. About him dealing and stealing? I don't think so."

"Are you going to tell them?"

Jess sighed. "I don't know. I don't know what they'd do

about it, to be honest. It's not like they can ground him or confiscate his cell phone."

Blunt had moved out of home more than a year ago, and now lived in a trailer park just outside of town. Rumor had it that he farmed weed in a clearing up in the woods.

Jess kicked at the damp sand with a toe of her sandal, dislodging a rusted bottle top. "Besides, you can't report your own kid to the cops."

"I guess not," I said. "What about rehab?"

She gave me a sad smile and sang, "They tried to make him go, but he said, 'No, no, no!'"

I gave her a long hug. She hated what her brother was becoming, but I knew she still cared about him.

The group of Colby fangirls ran screaming and laughing into the pond, splashing water at each other and angling their bodies, some lithe, some curvy, to maximum advantage. The display was wasted on Colby, though, who scanned the faces under the pier, caught my eye, and waved Jess and me over.

Jess told me to go without her. "You don't need me there, playing third wheel."

I perched myself on the damp sand right next to Colby, in the space the girls had vacated.

"Beer?" he offered.

I took the longneck and sipped, shuddering a little at the icy bitterness, conscious of his warmth beside me.

"How's your summer going?" he asked.

"Okay, you know, nothing wildly exciting. I help my dad out some at the store and hang out with Jess. And yours?"

"It's had its ups and downs."

Had he classified breaking up with Judy as an up or a down?

"You've got a job at the town clerk's office, with Jessica's mom?" I said, and then silently cursed myself for letting the question slip out. I had no desire for him to know how I tracked his every move.

"Yeah." He laughed. "She's a piece of work, that woman."

She was? "In what way?" I asked.

"Colby! *Colby!*" the girls in the water yelled. "Come on in!"

He glanced at them and then stood up, offering me his hand and pulling me to my feet. "Go for a walk?"

"Sure," I said, trying to look casually cool rather than super enthusiastic.

I tried even harder when he kept on holding my hand as we walked away from the pier. His hand was warm, and much bigger than my own, yet our fingers laced comfortably. When we passed Jess, I studiously avoided making eye contact, sure she'd be giving me a *you-go-girl!* look. We strolled along the narrow fringe of sand at the water's edge and passed by the little bay that was a favorite swimming spot. The sounds of shouting and laughter faded behind us, swallowed up by the warm air and the water.

The setting sun reached fingers of light across the sky to touch the patchy clouds with shades of peach and plum, and burnished Colby's blond hair with gold. A dog ran up and down in the shallows, barking at waterfowl landing on the pond further out. A kayaker pulled his craft onto the sand and hoisted it onto his shoulders to carry it back to his car, whistling to the dog to follow him. On our right, picnickers were shaking their blankets, packing their baskets, and corralling their sticky kids. An old homeless guy sat himself down on the steps on the bandstand and sucked on a bottle wrapped in a brown paper bag.

"You were telling me about your job?" I prompted.

Colby picked up a pebble and threw it sideways so that it skimmed across the surface of the water, bouncing four times.

"Well, my dad and uncle wanted me to take a summer job at the water company — you know that's the Beaumont family business?"

"Sure." Everyone knew that.

I picked up my own pebble, threw it crossways at the pond. It merely sank into the water.

"But I told them no. It didn't seem right, you know?"

I nodded, understanding. "Everyone would know you're the boss's kid. It would be ... awkward."

"Yeah, and not fair. Especially not with jobs as scarce as they are around here. But my father and uncle were pretty pissed that I turned them down. I think they intend for me to take over the business one day." He skimmed another stone. Six bounces. "They've got my whole future laid out for me." He didn't sound enthusiastic about it.

"Your uncle doesn't have kids?"

"No, he never married. Not sure why. So, if the Beaumont brothers want to keep it in the family, it'll have to be Vanessa who steps up. She'd have the head for it — even though she's studying political science at Boston U. Or if they want someone who has the heart for it, they can wait for my baby sister, Cassie, to grow up. She loves the water better than any of us do."

"So, you don't want to go into business?"

He mimed cocking a gun and firing it into his temple.

"What do you want to do then?" I asked.

"You first."

"I don't know. I can't decide. I like math and science stuff — physics, chemistry."

"You do?" He looked surprised. "Why?"

I'd never thought about why. "I guess because it's ... definite. There's a truth to math. You can count on it. Two and two are always four. And if you have three apples and I have one less than you, then we're always going to have five in total. I like that. It's solid. Comforting."

"You like logic."

"Yeah, I do." Maybe because it was in such short supply in my home life.

"So, you're going to be a scientist, or an engineer?" he asked.

"Maybe. I haven't decided."

We walked further, until we were past the bandstand and alone at the edge of the pond, watching the last sliver of sun setting behind the dark copse of trees on the far side. The night was perfectly still and the water smooth except for the ripples sent out by a lone green-headed mallard paddling toward the bank of tall reeds to our right.

"So, what do you want to do when you leave school?" I asked again. My voice sounded too loud in the evening hush.

He ran a hand over the back of his hair and smiled at me ruefully. "You'll laugh."

"I won't. Promise."

"I want to be a cop."

The duck laughed then — a low, raspy quack — as if in response to Colby's words.

33

"A *cop?*" I asked.

"Yeah. I want to be a cop, right here in Pitchford."

Because there was something vulnerable about him in that moment, and because I'd promised, I didn't laugh. But I wanted to. Who in their right mind would want to stay in Pitchford, let alone as a cop?

Keeping my voice neutral, I asked, "Why?"

"I love this place, you know? The pond and the woods and the people. But I think it's going downhill. Most of the kids ditch town when they leave school, and never come back."

That was certainly my plan.

"So, there's no new blood or energy. The drug problem is getting bad, thanks to assholes like Blunt."

After Jess's story about Blunt's violent temper, I wanted to warn Colby to steer clear of confrontations, but I didn't want to interrupt him. He was passionate about this, I could tell. His face was earnest, and his eyes glittered in the dim light.

"And where there's drugs, there's crime. I can just see this town going to shit. First the petty stuff — theft, shoplifting, prostitution. Then the more serious stuff — rape, assault, even murder. And white-collar crime — shady land deals, corrupt representatives. It snowballs, you know? I want to stop it. Frank Turner won't be chief for much longer; he's past retirement age already. He's careless and forgetful. This town deserves better."

Everyone knew Chief Turner was useless. My father said he was as idle as a toad in the bottom of a well. My mother said that he was a typically lazy Leo, and that what this town needed was a heroically brave and suspicious Aries.

I didn't know what star sign Colby was. Didn't ask. Didn't

care. My mother's theories were seriously dumb, and I wanted nothing to do with them.

"What about the new cop — Ray? Roy?" I asked.

Colby grinned. "Ryan. He's totally into my sister — maybe he'll follow her to Boston and there'll be a vacant post soon."

"Well, if anyone can do it, you can," I said, kicking off my sandals and wading into the water.

"Will you come back to Pitchford once you graduate college?" Colby asked me.

I was delighted to see that he looked hopeful. Still, I said, "Not if I can help it."

He nodded, seemingly unsurprised.

"I can't wait to get out of this town," I said. "The same people doing the same things, the gossip, everyone knowing your business." Not to mention wanting to leave home.

He took a step closer to me, brushed a stray strand of hair back from my cheek, curled it around his finger and gave it a little tug.

"It's not all bad, surely? There must be something here you like," he murmured.

The air shifted around us, pushed us closer. I couldn't find my voice.

"I guess we'll just have to make the most of our time together," he said, which was as good as straight-up saying "I like you."

Smiling at him, I whispered, "Okay."

He pressed his lips to mine for a fleeting second. I smelled cola lip balm, and felt my cheeks flush and a goofy smile curve my mouth when he stepped back and tucked the curl of hair behind my ear. Then he took off his T-shirt in the funny way guys do, grabbing it at the back and pulling it over their heads. Wait. He was undressing?

Not sure whether to panic or to fling myself at him, I just stared, enjoying the sight of his chest and flat belly.

"Let's go for a swim," he said.

"A swim? Now?"

"Yeah, the water's warm, the company's good, and the stars are coming out. What would you rather be doing?"

"I'm not wearing a bathing suit."

"Neither am I," he said and ran into the pond in his long shorts.

I hesitated a moment and then stripped off my sundress and followed him, wearing only my bra and panties.

"You lied," I gasped, shivering. "The water's not warm."

But he was. And as he pulled me into his arms and kissed me — slowly at first, tenderly touching his lips against my shoulders, my temples, my lips — I thought I'd never be cold again.

5

NOW
Saturday December 16, 2017

Dillon's, on Main Street, had once been a greasy spoon, infamous for old man Dillon's wandering hands and old lady Dillon's temper. It now grandly declared itself to be *Dillon's Country Store and Café*. Well, this should prove interesting.

I parked directly outside, beside a lamppost with a sign announcing a Carols by Candlelight gathering scheduled for the following evening down at the bandstand by Plover Pond. I would *not* be attending that event, no sir, no ma'am, no matter how hard my mother tried to strong-arm me into holly-ing and holy-ing. Just the idea of cheerful carolers singing merrily of silent nights, baby boys and joyful tidings in that particular spot raised a fierce prickle of anger behind my eyes.

Grabbing my handbag, I climbed out of the car, slammed the door behind me and, gasping at the shock of freezing air and buffeting wind, set the remote lock and alarm. At the double beep, a nearby man walking a dog on a lead turned in surprise. He smiled indulgently at my foolish big city ways and patted his pet, which was shivering despite being swathed in the absurd canine equivalent of a holiday sweater.

"You don't need to lock your car here, ma'am. We don't have criminals in this town."

I recognized the old man at once as my one-time high school chemistry teacher, but he clearly didn't remember me. "I know exactly what kind of town this is, Mr. Wallace."

Enjoying the look of surprise on his face, I spun on my heel and took a step toward the café, but something brushed up against my legs, tangling my feet, and the icy sidewalk slipped out from under me. I fell hard, slamming flat on my back and banging my head against the lamppost. White lights popped in the blackness behind my eyes. I couldn't breathe.

I heard pants and grunts. Someone was crouched beside me, asking me something. I wanted to tell them to back up out of my space, but there was a weight crushing my lungs flat and no air to speak. Hands helped me into a sitting position, and a voice said, "There now, stay calm. You'll feel better in a moment or two. You just got the wind knocked out of you."

The grunts were coming from me, not the dog, I realized. Embarrassment superseding panic, I forced a small breath in through my nose, and then pushed a slow breath out through my mouth. That helped. Uttering a curse on my next exhalation helped even more.

"There you go," the voice encouraged.

I opened my eyes and saw Mr. Wallace bending down to peer at me solicitously. His dog sat beside me, licking my hand, and a small group of people had gathered around to watch my growing relationship with the sidewalk. I waved them away.

"Give her some space, folks. She'll be fine in a minute, just let her catch her breath."

Face hot, and still trying to steady my breathing, I glowered down at my feet to see what had tripped me up. A broadsheet of the *The Bugle* was twisted around my ankles, its headline urging me to support the campaign to rename Pitchford. As I snatched the crumpled newspaper off my feet, my gaze was snagged by a black-and-white photograph of a face. Then a blast of wind whipped the paper out of my hand, and it was gone, flapping down the sidewalk and into the afternoon mist like a pale bat.

"Here, let's get you to your feet," Mr. Wallace said.

Accepting the proffered hand, I allowed myself to be pulled upright.

"Thanks," I wheezed. My chest ached like I'd been kicked in the ribs by a mule.

"Can I help you somewhere?"

"I'm fine. Just need to sit for a bit." I indicated the café with a jerk of my chin.

Mr. Wallace insisted on lending me a steadying arm for the few steps to its entrance. I was uncharacteristically grateful for this chivalry; I still felt a little faint and dizzy. At the door, I glanced back over my shoulder, but there was no sign of the newspaper. Thanking my escort again, I entered the café.

"Well, look at what the cat dragged in," said the man standing just inside, under a hanging branch of mistletoe.

I stepped aside smartly. Time had not been kind to Pete Dillon. He'd been in the same year as me in high school, but back then he'd been six-foot-one of solid quarterback muscle. And he'd had more hair. Now he had a small paunch, his features were more smudged than chiseled, and his hair had receded to deep widow's wings at the top of his temples. His smirk was the same, though, as was the assessing look he gave me from top to toe. Pete had always been a player, and good-looking enough to have his pick of the girls. I'd never been interested, which had annoyed him no end even though I don't think he ever truly wanted me. He just wanted me, and everyone else, to want *him*.

"It's you, Crystal's daughter. Gina ... something," he said.

"Garnet."

"Yeah, right," he said, like I was having him on. "Long time no see. It must be, what — seven or eight years since you were last here?"

"Nine and a half."

He nodded. "That's right, yeah. Because didn't you leave town the year after—" He cut himself off, grimacing.

"I left right after I graduated high school."

"You've changed. You cut your hair. And didn't you used to be a blonde?"

"No."

In high school, I'd worn my hair long down to the middle of my back because Colby had loved it that way. I cut it short when I moved to Boston, and now it just brushed my shoulders. But it had only ever been chestnut brown.

"And didn't your eyes used to be brown?"

My eyes were blue. "I think you're confusing me with someone else."

"Here, let me take your coat."

I looked around. The café was mostly full, but there were still a couple of empty tables.

"Can I sit anywhere?"

"Sure. You look kinda pale. You okay?"

"I just need coffee." And to sit down.

"We got coffee. All kinds."

I headed to an empty table at the far wall, rubbing my aching hip where, no doubt, a bruise was already blossoming. Pete trailed behind me, rattling off the options.

"Our special today is a Christmas spiced cinnamon steamer, but otherwise we have all the regulars — cappuccino, espresso, latte, macchiato."

The place was a regular Starbucks. Back when old man Dillon ran the joint, you could get your cup of joe black or white; both had tasted the same, and neither had tasted much like coffee. I sank into the chair with my back against the wall. A tight knot of pain was gathering behind my eyes. Was it due to the blow I'd taken to my head, or was it just caffeine withdrawal? It could also just be a tension headache brought on by being back in Pitchford — I could feel my shoulders hunched up tight, inching toward my ears.

I cricked my neck and rolled my shoulders, telling Pete, "I'll have a large regular coffee. Extra, extra hot."

"One Americano — *grande*, extra hot — coming right up."

"Extra, *extra* hot," I said to his departing back.

With a sigh, I leaned back and looked around. Surprisingly, *Dillon's Country Store and Café* was charming. The enameled tables, with their drop sides and tops decorated in a variety of country motifs — black-and-white floral edging, cream with blue windmills, pink roses on pale green — looked to be originals. One wall was dominated by a huge Hoosier cabinet, complete with threaded glass drawer knobs and shelves laden with decorative sugar canisters, spice jars, striped milk jugs and flour sifters. Artfully arranged beside the antique cash register on the counter up front were handcrafts, maple sugar candy, and cotton sacks of Dillon's Own Finest Arabica coffee beans.

The young couple at an adjacent table got up and headed out, leaving a neatly folded copy of *The Bugle* lying on their table. Had I seen what I thought I had back outside, or had my brain been rattled by the encounter with the lamppost? I was about to grab the paper when a tall mug of coffee was plonked down on the table in front of me by an attractive woman in an old-fashioned waitress uniform.

"Garnet McGee, as I live and breathe!"

"Judy Burns," I replied.

"It's Judy *Dillon* now." She tapped the wedding band on her ring finger as she sat down in the chair on my left, blocking the newspaper from my view.

I wasn't surprised to discover that Pete and Judy — or Punch and Judy, as we'd called them back in the day — had wound up together.

Judy gave me an appraising look, taking in my heavy, lace-up Doc Martens, black jeans and turtle-neck, my unstyled hair and bitten nails. "Are *you* married?" she asked.

"No."

"Any kids?"

"Tell me about yours." Clearly, she was eager to.

"We have three." Judy wriggled in her chair, preening.

"Congratulations," I said. She seemed to expect it.

"There's Deanna, who's nine, Dallas, who's seven, and our baby, Dayle, who's just turned three. That's Dayle spelt D-A-Y-L-E, because she's a girl. They're all girls."

Bet Football Pete loved that. I touched the side of the coffee mug with assessing fingers. It was warm, not hot and definitely not extra hot, let alone extra, extra hot. Why did they never believe me?

"So you live in Boston now?" Judy asked.

"Uh-huh."

"Your mother misses you terribly. Every time I visit her store for a reading she tells me how she longs to see more of you."

I had nothing to say to that.

"You shouldn't leave it too late to catch a man, you know. Your face starts sagging and your eggs start rotting after thirty-five."

"Judy, you always were a charmer."

I dug a finger into the pad of flesh at the base of my left thumb and rubbed hard, a process, so my mother always said, that was supposed to alleviate headaches. The old white scar on my palm stretched and crinkled in tandem with the movements.

"And you're how old now — thirty-one, thirty-two?"

"I'm twenty-seven, same as you. We were in the same year at high school," I snapped.

It wasn't that I feared getting older, or that I envied Judy her husband and all those rug rats. It just wasn't a part of my plan to get married. On the contrary, as Perry had seemingly noticed, it was my modus operandi never to get too close to anyone, to leave them before they could leave me. But I *had* thought that, by this age, I'd already be qualified and running my own practice in a charming Victorian-style brick townhouse in South End or Beacon Hill. It was never part of the plan to still be struggling to complete my thesis while working as an assistant in the university's psychology department, *and* still accepting financial help from my father to pay for my apartment. I might no longer live in my parents' house in my old home town, but I wasn't independent, not really. And that rankled.

I tore the tops off three sugar packets, poured them into my coffee and stirred.

Judy eyed this with a critical eye, no doubt thinking I'd find it even harder to snag a husband with a diet that was sure to thicken my waistline. Hers, I noticed, was as trim as it had been a decade ago, and her breasts, if anything, seemed both larger and perkier. But there was a tightness around her eyes and mouth that made me think life with Pete and the three D's wasn't all sunshine and roses.

Tilting back my head — a movement which made it throb — I gulped the lukewarm coffee down in one continuous swallow. I gingerly explored the tender lump on the back of my head. I'd better not mention my fall to my parents, or my mother would tip six kinds of remedies into my mouth and no doubt spout some nonsense about the incident being an omen of bad luck presaging a drop in my fortunes. My father would insist I get a doctor to check me out. Was Doc Armstrong still practicing, I wondered.

"I'm so sorry to interrupt your gossip session, but could you possibly get Garnet's order in?" Pete had returned and was scowling down at his wife.

I fully expected her to put him in his place — she'd never been one to keep her mouth shut — but she stood up hurriedly, smoothed her apron, gave me a smile which didn't quite reach her eyes, and asked, "What'll it be?"

She hadn't brought me a menu, but I didn't like to point that out in front of Pete.

"Something hot." I was still feeling chilled after my stretch on the icy sidewalk.

"Soup of the day? Our Saturday special is—"

"Sure."

"I'll be right back." She stepped around Pete and headed back to the kitchen.

"Good coffee, huh?" he asked me.

"The best," I said, straight-faced.

"Yeah." He nodded, smirking as widely as if I'd just complimented him on the size of his dick, before the bell on the door summoned him to welcome a new family of customers.

Judy reappeared, told me my soup would be just a couple of minutes, and began clearing the cups and plates from the table next to mine, putting the folded newspaper on her tray.

"Can I have that?" I asked.

"Sure."

I took it and held it against my chest for a long moment, unsure whether I really wanted to check inside, then placed it flat on the table in front of me. There, on the front page beneath the banner, was the headline I'd seen about renaming the town. Delaying the moment of opening the paper, I read the short article beneath.

The move to rename Pitchford in line with its charming New England identity was being spearheaded by Michelle Armstrong, Pitchford's town clerk and treasurer. So, Jessica's mother, at least, was still alive and living in town. She'd moved up in the world since the days she was a mere committee member, regularly coming to the K12 school shared by the handful of towns in the surrounding area to do "inspections," and embarrassing her daughter by being overly friendly to the kids, acting as if she herself was still eighteen.

Armstrong argued that Pitchford's old name didn't adequately convey its tourist potential and caused endless confusion with Pitchfield over in Washington County. She was pushing for the town to be renamed Pitchford Springs "in a fitting acknowledgment of the importance of the natural water springs in the town's economic resurgence." My father said that, these days, the Beaumont Brothers Water Company employed half the town — and almost all the newcomers — and contributed generously to its improvements.

Reading between the lines of the article, the town clerk's quest to reinvent Pitchford as the cutest little village in all New England was meeting with considerable resistance from older residents. Nevertheless, she'd no doubt still get her way. My mother always said Michelle Armstrong was as bullheaded as a Taurus, as vindictive as a Scorpio, and as petty as a Pisces. My father said she was a woman he never wanted to cross. I didn't care one way or another what they called the town. Giving it a new name wouldn't change its true nature, any more than sticking a mahogany veneer on a coffin changed that it was a cheap pine box for a corpse.

"Here you go." Judy placed a bowl of soup down in front of me. This time she didn't linger.

Bracing myself for what I was about — or not about — to see, I opened the newspaper and glanced down. And there it was, in the bottom right corner of page two.

Seeing the photograph of him was like getting winded all over again. I focused on the headline above the picture instead.

Tenth Anniversary of the Disappearance of Colby Beaumont.

6

A blizzard set in on the night Colby never came home.
I twisted myself into a sick knot of fear while it raged
for two days — dumping a foot of snow over the town,
freezing the pond, closing the school, preventing a search, and
blowing away any clues that might have been left behind.

I startled awake on the third morning, alerted by the sound
of silence after days of shrieking winds. The world outside my
window was shrouded in white, and a feeble sun strained half-
heartedly to raise its head above the horizon.

As I hurriedly dressed in my thermal clothes and snowsuit,
the rough purr of the snow blower started outside — my father
must already be clearing the path and driveway. I grabbed my
phone and ran downstairs, only to find my mother was still in
her bathrobe and slippers.

"Why aren't you dressed yet? They said the search would
start at sunrise."

She handed me my snow boots and gave me what I think

was supposed to be an encouraging smile. "I'll be staying here, Garnet, where I can do more good."

"Doing what precisely?" I asked, thrusting my feet into the boots and yanking on gloves and a beanie.

"I've already lit a candle and—"

"We need searchers, not candles."

"Perhaps I'll use a pendulum and map."

I snorted. Under the best of conditions, I had limited patience for her drivel. Today, with Colby's life at stake, I was tempted to slap her.

"And even though the signs are bad—"

I didn't want to hear this. "*Signs*? Have you been studying bird entrails, or consulting the dead?" I snarled, heading for the front door.

"And I'll keep praying for St. Jude to intercede. He's the patron saint of lost causes."

"It's not a lost cause. It's *not*!" I yelled at her as I slammed out of the house.

My father took one look at my face and said, "She'd get in the way more than she'd help, you know that."

"Let's go. Please let's just go," I said.

Dad had fitted snow chains to the tires of his car the day before, but he still inched with infuriating carefulness down our street, ignoring my orders to go faster. Plow trucks had already cleared and salted the way on the bigger streets, and down on Pond Road an emergency truck was parked beside an old oak where a fallen limb had taken down the power line. The screams of the power saw tore through the snow-muffled silence, setting my teeth on edge.

A search party was gathering at the bandstand, stamping their feet, blowing into gloved hands, and sipping on steaming cups of coffee. We immediately walked over to Colby's father and uncle — Philip and Roger Beaumont. With their identical graying blond hair, brown eyes and thin noses, they looked so alike, they could've been twins. That day their faces were pale and pinched tight with worry. Colby's father had their young Dalmatian on a lead; perhaps they'd brought him in the hopes he could help track Colby, but surely even a champion bloodhound couldn't detect a scent buried under a foot of snow. The dog yelped in recognition and came over to leap up against me.

"Down, Domino. Sit!" Colby's father said.

"Any news?" I asked, rubbing the spotted dog behind the ears.

Mr. Beaumont shook his head. His eyes were red and puffy.

"Why hasn't the search started yet?" I was impatient to get going.

"We're waiting for instructions from Chief Turner," he said. "Roger thinks we should search the woods north of town."

"Why there?" I asked.

"Get me a cup of coffee, will you, Garnet?" my father said.

A refreshments table had been set up in the bandstand and was being manned by Jessica's mother and father. Mrs. Armstrong, wearing skintight jeans, high-heeled boots and a determined smile, was serving the volunteers hot drinks. Beside her, Doc Armstrong handed out donuts.

"Thank you for your community spirit," she said to me, as she said to everyone. "Coffee or hot chocolate?"

"Two coffees, please." I stirred three sugars into mine and left my dad's plain.

"Give her a donut, Alan," she told her husband.

From the smell of Doc Armstrong's breath, he'd already added a shot of something stronger than half-and-half to his morning coffee.

"We'll have chicken soup and rolls by noon," Mrs. Armstrong assured me. "That should warm you all up."

I had no intention of eating lunch at the bandstand. By midday, if not sooner, Colby would be wrapped in a blanket, sitting beside me in the back of his father's BMW or maybe an ambulance, on his way to the hospital for a checkup. He'd be holding my hand tightly and wearing a smile on his chapped lips as he told me all about how he'd ridden out the monster storm — perhaps in a garden shed, while eating turnips and sleeping under old dog blankets. I'd kiss the tip of his cold nose and promise never to let a mad word escape my lips again, and he'd fall asleep with his head on my shoulder. At the hospital, the doctors would pat him on the shoulder, tell him he was a lucky man, and declare him free of any lasting damage. We'd go home together and lie on his bed with him curled around the back of me, his lips against my neck. That was what *would* happen today.

"We'll have found Colby by then," I told Mrs. Armstrong.

She hesitated, then said, "Of course, dear."

"Is Jessica around?"

"With the school group, over there." She pointed to a gang of teens behind the bandstand.

As I strode over to my father to give him his coffee, Police

Chief Frank Turner gave the horn on a megaphone a quick blast to get everyone's attention. Standing on the top step of the bandstand, he laid out plans for the search.

"We don't want any more kids going missing, so I'm going to ask that anyone eighteen or under stays in town and searches the streets and yards, sticking together in groups. Mrs. ... Mrs. ..." He gestured in the direction of Jessica's mother.

"Armstrong," she said, looking peeved that he hadn't remembered her name.

"Yeah, Mrs. Armstrong has a pile of missing-person posters for you to attach to lampposts."

Mrs. Armstrong switched on her practiced smile and held up the posters with Colby's photograph. A squeeze of fear tightened my insides. I looked away from the picture, studying my feet, focusing on the patterned footprints crisscrossing each other in the snow all around where I stood.

"Roger and Philip Beaumont will be searching the woods north of town."

"I'll go with them," my father told me.

I thought this was a stupid idea and told him so. "Colby didn't set out for a hike through the woods at night!"

"Officer Ryan Jackson will lead the search down at the pond, walking the strip between the Tuppenny Tavern, where Colby was last seen, and here, then searching the perimeter of the pond wherever access is possible," Chief Turner continued.

My father shook his head at this. "Waste of time. Why would he be at the pond?"

"Why would he be in the woods?" I retorted.

Why would he be anywhere except at home, texting me

happily about school being closed because of the snow?

The chief explained that he'd be keeping an eye on proceedings, while patrolling the highways leading in and out of town, searching for signs of an accident or any indication that Colby had hitchhiked out of Pitchford. You didn't have to be a genius to know that he was just too lazy to join the search on foot. Probably the only time he'd get out of his cozy cruiser would be to top up on coffee and donuts at the bandstand.

"Do not search in groups of less than three. Do not wander off alone. Do not stay out after dark." Turner sucked on his teeth for a few moments. "Mrs. Armstrong has the missing-person posters."

"He's repeating himself," I grumbled under my breath. "We're wasting time. We need to get going."

"Call me if you find anything," Turner ordered. "Check in with Officer Jackson every hour and meet back here by three-thirty. The forecast predicts clear conditions, but if the weather turns, get back here immediately. Good luck, people. Let's end with a prayer."

While Turner prayed for God's help in locating Colby, I finished my coffee and looked around at the bowed heads. I had no time for prayers. If God existed and cared enough to help find Colby, why hadn't He stopped him getting lost in the first place? We should already be out there, searching.

"Where's Mrs. Beaumont?" I asked my father, not bothering to keep my voice down.

"She's at home. Apparently, Cassie's not well and can't come out in the cold," he whispered back.

I noticed Colby's older sister, Vanessa, had joined the small group of searchers by Ryan Jackson. Clearly, she also thought the woods were a waste of time.

"Amen," Turner finally concluded, and the volunteers split into their groups and splintered off in all directions.

I found Jessica, and we followed a group of seniors toward the part of town where Colby and I lived, while the guys from Colby's swim team opted to search Main Street. Nothing would have kept me from searching the woods or around the pond if I thought Colby might be there. But I knew he was most likely to be near his house or mine because I'd texted him on Sunday night begging him to come see me, so we could talk. He'd ignored my message, so I'd sent more, getting madder and madder, telling him it was urgent and not to be a jerk. But he'd never replied, and he'd never arrived.

The last time I'd seen him had been on Friday at school. He'd seemed as distracted and worried as I'd been, but it couldn't have been about the same thing, could it? As I trudged up the hill, scanning the streets for any sign of him, the thought occurred to me that maybe he'd noticed something, put two and two together, and developed a strong desire to avoid me. An instant later, I felt guilty for doubting him.

Colby being Colby, it was much more likely that he *had* set out to come visit me, so we could talk, and when the storm suddenly hit, he'd taken shelter somewhere. Or perhaps fallen into a ditch, or been knocked over in a hit and run. It didn't seem very likely; things like that didn't happen in Pitchford. But then again, disappearances didn't happen in Pitchford.

7

THEN
Wednesday December 19, 2007

"Colby! Col-by!" I yelled.

A group of guys — including Pete Dillon and his sidekicks Dave and Brandon, and most of the football team — walked ahead of us along Algonquian Street, bitching loudly about the cold and doing a poor job of hanging the posters on the street lights. Jessica and I went after them; she maneuvered the posters higher up on the poles, and I tightened the strings even though I had to take off my gloves to do so. Pete and his fellow asshats kept their gloves on, and their laughs and shouts echoed above the dull silence of the snow-covered streets, making me angrier by the second. When they all cracked up at some joke Pete made, I stormed up to them and shoved him in the back, sending him stumbling.

"Stop screwing around!" I said.

Brandon made a mocking *oooh* sound, and Dave said, "Chill, McGee," but Pete gave me an unreadable look and then nodded.

"Let's go check Pequot Street," he told his crew, and they jogged off down the road in the opposite direction.

I marched on, sweeping my gaze left and right, squinting against the glare reflecting off the snow.

"You okay?" Jess asked me.

"No."

I grabbed a long stick from a downed tree limb and gently poked it into snow drifts, testing for the resistance of human flesh.

"Are you … I mean, have you started your period yet?"

"No."

I tramped around the side of the Ingram house, where they had a tool shed. A bank of snow was piled up against the door, resisting my attempts to yank it open. Under my rough treatment, a daggerlike icicle dislodged from the eaves and plummeted down, narrowly missing my foot.

"Watch it!" Jessica said. "Here, let me."

She was taller than me, and stronger, and she managed to work the door open a few inches. I peered inside. Lawnmower, axe, gas can, saw, rake, snow shovel. No Colby.

Breaths misting the air and noses dripping from the bitter cold, we returned to the street and walked on, checking every yard, combing the hedges and bushes, plowing through the mounds of snow on either side of the road. Calling for Colby.

When we reached the big stormwater pipe where kids sometime hid to drink and smoke, I hopped down into the gully and burrowed into the slope of snow covering the opening.

"*Garnet?*" Jess said, like she strongly suspected I'd entirely lost the plot.

"Maybe he fell and took shelter here from the storm," I said, digging and scraping until I broke through the snow and looked inside the pipe. In the dim light, I could just make out the crumpled shape of a body curled in on itself.

"There!"

"Is it him?" Jessica demanded.

"I think so!"

Heart jumping like a jackrabbit, I crouched down and crawled into the pipe, scrambling toward the dark heap ahead of me. I was within touching distance of the shape when I saw what it was — just a big garbage bag stuffed with trash, spilling empty cans and plastic bottles.

"He has to be here. He has to," I said, my voice a rough sob.

I plunged my hands into the bag and scrabbled around, crying out as a sharp pain burned my left palm.

"Garnet? What happened?" Jess called from outside.

I had to find him.

"Colby," I cried. "Colby!"

I pulled out handfuls of potato peelings, a clumped mass of paper towel wet with dark stains, candy wrappers, and soggy newspaper which disintegrated between my fingers, then collapsed and lay sobbing in the bottom of the pipe.

"I'm calling Chief Turner," Jessica yelled. A few minutes later she crept into the pipe beside me and hauled me into a sitting position. "It's okay, shhh, it's okay. Just hold onto me," she crooned, holding me against her while I wept.

"It's not okay. He isn't here. He isn't anywhere, I can feel it. He's gone, he's dead, I know it."

"Shhh." She hugged me tight. "You don't know that. We've

still got the whole town to search."

"He's gone and died and left me alone."

She held me against her, rubbing my back and whispering words of false hope. By the time Chief Turner arrived, I had subsided into hiccups.

"Garnet McGee, is that you? Come on out."

I shook my head and clung to Jessica.

"She doesn't want to, Chief."

"Look, don't make me come in and fetch you. I'm not a slight little thing like you girls — I'll get stuck and they'll need dynamite to unplug my sorry ass. Come out. We need your help. Don't you want to help us find Colby?"

I crept out, shivering and dripping a strand of blood beads onto the snow from the cut on my hand. The small crowd gathered around the pipe gaped at me.

"Stop staring and go find Colby!" I cried.

"Jessica, you go on searching with these folks. I'll have a chat with Garnet and dress that cut on her hand," Turner said.

"There's paper towel with bloodstains on it back there," I told him, pointing at the pipe.

"I'll get it checked out. You come with me, now."

At his cruiser, he retrieved a medical kit from the trunk and said, "What say we take care of your wound inside the comfort of the vehicle?"

He was red-faced and puffing from the exertions of climbing into and out of the gully, and I figured he'd drop dead of a heart attack directly if he had to chase me, so I climbed into the passenger seat. He eased himself inside, sniffed, then started the engine and let it idle with the heater blowing at full blast.

"Colder than a witch's tit out there," he grumbled. "Now, let me see that hand of yours."

I stuck my throbbing hand out to the side but stared silently ahead. The windscreen was misting up and the interior getting muggy with the heat and damp. The rotten, decaying smell of the filthy stormwater pipe rose off my muddy clothes.

Turner examined my hand, asking, "So, Garnet, you're Colby's girl?"

"Yes."

"Do you know where he is?"

"No." *Obviously.*

"Sure 'bout that?"

"If I knew where he was, I wouldn't be creeping around storm water drains where he *isn't.*"

"Hmm," he said, and sucked his teeth loudly.

I felt a cool stinging sensation on my hand and a tugging pain as he wiped it with something. "This might need a stitch or three."

I rubbed a forearm against my window, clearing a circle through which I could check outside.

"Know of any reason why he might have run away?" Turner asked.

"He didn't run away."

More sucking of his teeth.

"His car is still parked at his house, and his mother says none of his clothes are missing," I added.

"She told me his phone and his laptop are, though." Turner rubbed ointment onto the cut. "She also told me it's all happy families at home, no fights. That right?"

"He … He maybe mentioned some stuff, but nothing that would make him run away, just like a few arguments with his little sister, disagreements with his parents about what he'll do when he leaves school. The usual stuff."

I felt him stick a bandage over the burning cut.

"Did he fight with *you*?"

"No." I rubbed at my hand, pressing the edges of the Band-Aid down hard.

"Uh-huh." More sucking of his teeth. "No problems between you at all?"

No way was I going to tell Turner about any problems Colby and I may or may not have had.

"Look," I said, "shouldn't you be out there searching for him, instead of sitting here asking me dumb questions that have nothing to do with his disappearance? Something's happened to him."

Turner's phone rang just then, startling me with its loud claxon sound.

I studied his face intently as he took the call, trying to divine whether it was news about Colby.

"Yeah … Yeah. Is that right? Uh-huh. Hmm. And where exactly? … And it's definitely his? … I see. I'm on my way."

"What? What is it?" I demanded as he slipped the car into gear and we pulled off.

"That was Richard."

"Who's Richard?"

"The boy's uncle."

"Roger. His name is Roger."

"Of course. It seems that search party north of town found

a blue woolen cap belonging to young Colby."

"They found his beanie? In the *woods?*"

"They found it alongside the highway." He cut me a sideways glance. "Right where a hitchhiker in a hurry might accidentally drop something on his way out of town."

"He *didn't* run away," I repeated.

"Uh-huh. And was he into drugs?"

"No. He didn't even smoke pot."

"You sure 'bout that?"

"I'd know."

He sucked his teeth in a way that conveyed extreme skepticism. I was about to explain how Colby felt about drugs, about dealers like Blunt, when the radio on the dashboard crackled.

"Frank? Ryan here. I'm at the pond, at the little bay about three hundred yards north of the Tavern. You need to come down here, quick as you can."

"I've got the McGee girl with me. We're on our way to the boy's father and uncle. They found his knitted cap beside the highway. I'll come down to you just as soon as I've checked with them."

"You need to get here *now*, Frank. We've found … something."

8

Saturday December 16, 2017

I read the headline in the newspaper again.

Tenth Anniversary of the Disappearance of Colby Beaumont.

Ten years ago today — could that be right? I'd been bracing myself for the nineteenth. But yes, he'd gone missing on three days before.

My gaze returned to the photograph. The grainy black-and-white picture didn't do him justice. Colby Beaumont had been golden. Tall, with fair skin and honey-colored hair, eyes the color of maple syrup in the sunshine, and a wicked grin. He'd shimmered with life and joy.

The picture blurred. I dashed a quick hand across my eyes and read on.

Colby Beaumont, eighteen years old at the time, went missing on the evening of Sunday, December sixteenth, 2007, on his walk home from the Tuppenny Tavern in Pitchford, and was never seen alive again.

A severe snowstorm impeded initial search efforts, and it was only when the weather cleared that Pitchford's residents could join local police in combing the town and surrounding areas. On December nineteenth, Police Officer Ryan Jackson found Beaumont's body submerged under a cracked section of thin ice near the shore of Plover Pond.

The state's chief medical examiner conducted the autopsy at the Burlington Mortuary and confirmed the cause of death to be drowning, while the manner of death was declared to be undetermined. According to the autopsy report, Beaumont had been assaulted and severely beaten immediately prior to his death. It could not be established whether his attacker willfully drowned him, or whether, disoriented by blows to the head during the savage beating, he had inadvertently staggered into the pond and drowned accidentally.

Despite a thorough investigation with the assistance of state police, the identity of his attacker was never discovered.

At the time of his death, Beaumont was a senior at Pitchford High School, where he participated in debating, hiking and swimming. He was survived by his two sisters, Cassandra and Vanessa, his mother, Bridget, and his father, Philip, co-founder with elder brother Roger Beaumont of the Beaumont Brothers Spring Water Company.

Asked for comment by The Bugle *this week, Philip Beaumont stated: "My grief is as fresh today as it was ten years ago. No parent should outlive their child. A father's role is to protect his children."*

Someone was calling my name. I looked up to find Pete standing beside my table.

"Sorry, what?" I asked.

"Is there something wrong with your soup?" Pete said. No smile this time.

I wished he would get lost so I could finish the article, but he seemed set to stay until he got the thumbs-up. Distractedly, I grabbed a spoon, plunged it into the thick, creamy liquid and had the first taste at my lips when the smell registered. I dropped the spoon back in the bowl.

"Is this clam chowder?" I asked him.

"New England's finest. It's my mother's recipe."

"I'm allergic to shellfish."

My stomach turned. That close. I'd been that close to anaphylaxis.

"Can I bring you something else?"

I shook my head and regretted it instantly. The headache was getting worse. Perhaps I *should* get my head checked out by a doctor.

If my mother was here, she'd say that after my fall, the near collision with the moose and the close call with chowder, it would be safe to order something else off the menu because I'd had my three-things run of bad luck. But I didn't believe in her superstitions. Or the safety of Pete Dixon's kitchen.

"Just the check," I told him.

I returned my attention to the newspaper and read the final paragraph in the commemorative article.

> *Anyone with any information should contact the Pitchford police department. "The case may be cold, but it is not closed. Someone knows the truth of exactly what happened to Colby Beaumont, and I will not give up on the investigation until the perpetrator is brought to justice," Police Chief Ryan Jackson said yesterday.*

I closed the newspaper and dropped it onto the table.

Ryan Jackson — so the department's young officer had become the chief. That had been Colby's dream. Most kids grow out of playing cops and robbers, but not him. He wanted to be a cop, to be *the* cop in this town. It was one of the few things we disagreed on. I'd wanted to get out, to find a bigger life in a better city, but he'd wanted to stay right here in Pitchford.

I guess we both got our wish.

I left Dillon's and drove through the gathering gloom of dusk toward my parents' house, swallowing down nausea, wincing at the pain burying its claws in my head, and aware of a rising sense of dread. Was this concussion, or perhaps even the aura which precedes seizure activity in the brain? Or was I merely suffering from the psych student version of med student-itis — getting paranoid about my own symptoms and hypochondriacally diagnosing myself with the maladies I'd studied? It was probably just a migraine.

Plover Pond lay at the bottom of Main Street, milky as a

dead eye in the mist. I automatically averted my gaze, but a flash of red in my peripheral vision made me do a double-take. Someone was out on the pond, and it looked like a kid.

I turned right into Pond Road, scanning the area, looking for someone who might be there to fetch the kid, someone who could do something, but the park was deserted and the bandstand empty. Where was an adult when you needed one?

The figure was over on the far side of the pond. I could drive around, but a dense thicket ran between the road and the pond on that side, and it would probably take me longer to get to the kid that way. The darkness was deepening; I needed to get to the kid quickly.

I pulled over, parked and got out of the car. The icy gusting wind had me reaching back inside for my trench coat and scarf. The coat — knee-length wool with brass buttons, purchased at an army surplus store — was my favorite for the streets of Boston, but it was no match for this weather. I fastened the buttons with fingers made clumsy by the cold, then found my mittens and beanie tucked in the pocket and yanked them on as I ran across the road and through the park. The ice was muddy at the edges of the pond but felt solid enough. I gave another glance around, saw no one else. Reluctantly, I stepped onto the ice. And immediately slipped forward onto my knees. Great, more bruises.

Cursing the pond and the biting cold, I eased myself back onto my feet and cautiously half-walked, half-slid across the slippery surface. When we were kids, we'd done this all the time, but I'd lost the knack, and my boots weren't made for walking on ice. Arms out for balance, like a tightrope walker, I moved unsteadily across the pond.

"What are you doing?" I shouted at the kid when I was about halfway to him, but the wind snatched my words and hurled them north.

The kid didn't move — maybe he was literally frozen in place, stuck to the ice. My eyes watered in the wind, and beneath my feet, the ice creaked. I'd forgotten the mesmerizing quality of that sound, how it made you simultaneously want to hear it again and run the hell away.

As I neared the kid, the ice got sketchy. A thin layer of water covered the surface, and forked white lines, like frozen lightning, flashed out from where I placed my feet. I stepped carefully, steering a crooked course to avoid the bigger cracks. Then I saw it, realized why the kid wasn't moving.

Oh, crap.

9

NOW
Saturday December 16, 2017

The little kid in the red jacket was standing on a chunk of floating ice about the size of a door. It was fractured with cracks, the largest of which ended at his feet. The boy was young, maybe only seven or eight, and too small to make the jump across the dark water to the more solid section of ice on my side. His nose, burnt red by the cold and wind, stood out lividly against the stark white of his face, and beneath his panic-widened eyes, ice glistened where tears had frozen. He was trembling violently.

"You okay, kid?" I asked.

"I– I was too scared to move," he said, through frosted, quivering lips. "In case I fell."

"That was a smart decision. But I'm here now, I'll help you." I took a step closer to him, testing that the ice was solid enough before I eased my full weight onto it. "What's your name?"

"N– N– Nicholas."

"Okay, just take it easy, Nicholas. We're going to get you home safe, okay? Are you alone? Was there anyone else out here with you?"

"Kate. Kate was here. W– we were playing tag."

"And where is Kate now?" Please tell me she's not under the ice.

"She ran away."

"She got away safe?"

He nodded.

Relieved, I unwrapped my scarf from around my neck and tried to estimate whether it would be long enough to reach him, but I'd always been useless at anything visual-spatial. I *could* tell it was too light; the wind would blow the end back at me before it ever got near the kid. I wrapped one end of the scarf around my right hand and made a noose at the other, tightening it around my beanie to give it some heft. Then I tossed the scarf toward him, testing the length. Immediately, the boy made a convulsive grab for it. The ice splintered beneath him, and he waved his arms frantically to regain his balance.

"Don't move!" I yelled. "Hang on a sec, okay? It's too short. I need to get closer. I'll tell you when to catch it."

I took another step toward the end of my section of ice. With a loud snap, the ice cracked beneath me. Nicholas squeaked in fear, and my heart kicked hard in my chest.

"I know it's scary, but I need you to stay calm, okay? Just stand still and breathe as slowly as you can."

I eased myself down onto the ice, lying on my stomach to spread my weight out, and inched forward toward the kid.

Awkwardly, I flung the scarf in a sideways arc across to him.

Again, it landed short. I pushed myself forward another few inches. The ice creaked in protest beneath me. Lined fissures like dead white fingers reached up toward me, and the cold penetrated my coat, chilling my skin. If I didn't hurry, we'd both die out here from exposure.

I threw the scarf again, and this time the end landed near enough to the kid's feet for him to reach.

"Slowly, now," I cautioned him. "Move real slow, and try to get onto your knees, or even onto your belly, like me. That's right, just like that, Nicholas, you're doing great."

"Can you pull me now?" he asked as soon as he grabbed the scarf. His voice was high, and now that rescue was within reach, he was starting to panic.

"Hang on, Nicholas, stay cool. You need to get that end tight around your wrist. Pull the beanie out of the knot and stick your hand inside instead. Then pull it tight. Can you do that?"

When his hand was secure inside the noose end of the scarf and he was flat on his belly, I said, "Right, Nicholas, hold the scarf tight with both hands. I'm going to pull you over to my side. It's going to feel too slow, but I promise it'll happen real quick. You start counting from one, and by the time you get to fifty, you'll be safe over those cracks and on this side with me. Okay?"

He nodded rapidly.

"Let me hear you counting."

"One … two … three …"

I started pulling on the makeshift rescue rope, trying to keep the pressure steady and fighting the temptation to give one almighty yank to get this over with.

The boy slid slowly across a few inches of ice. "Eleven ... twelve ..."

"That's great. You're doing fine," I said, as much to reassure myself as the kid.

Another steady tug and he slid farther forward. This was going to work.

"Nineteen, twenty, twenty-one," Nicholas said quickly.

"Almost there." We were flat on the ice, a foot apart. I needed to sit up to pull him all the way across, to a safe spot beyond me. "Keep counting while I pull you farther back."

"Twenty-four-twenty-five-twenty-six," he gabbled quickly as I pushed myself up onto my haunches, dragging steadily on the scarf.

"There you go!" I announced, as I dragged him alongside me. "We did it!"

I'd half expected him to sag in relief or perhaps burst into tears the moment he felt safe. I had *not* expected him to launch himself into my arms. His weight slammed into me, knocking me over and whacking my already-bruised head against the ice.

Things happened fast, then. With a crack like a gunshot, the ice fractured and split beneath me. As I fell, ass-first, through the widening crack, I gave the boy an almighty shove, propelling him back onto solid ice.

"Run! Get help!" I yelled at him even as I sank into the blackness below.

The water was ice and fire, scalding my hands and face. I kicked powerfully several times, pushing myself up to get my head back above the water, where — stunned senseless by the breath-robbing, heart-stopping cold — I gasped and flailed around for a few panicked seconds.

I grabbed at the edge of the ice, trying to catch my breath, but my mittens gave me no purchase on the slippery wetness. I released my hold to pull them off and immediately started sinking back down into the water. Seizing the ice just as my head went under, I pulled up with all my might, drew in a breath, and then edged sideways, hand over hand, to a drier section where I could get a better grip on the ice shelf.

"Help!" I screamed, even though I knew it was futile. This far out, in this wind, no one would hear.

The water was soaking into my clothes, creeping up through my heavy coat, tugging me down. I needed to shed weight. My heavy boots were laced on tightly and didn't budge when I attempted to kick them off. I tried to let go of the ice to undo the buttons on my coat, but my fingers were frozen to its surface.

Shit, shit, shit. Screw this pond and everything about it.

I struggled to get a grip on my rising panic, to think through my options. Which would be better, which would buy me more time — wrenching my fingers free, or staying stuck? In the end the pond made the decision for me, inexorably tugging me back into its icy maw like a monster dragging down its prey. I felt a tearing sensation, but no pain, as my fingers ripped free of the ice, and then I was sinking through the scorching water.

Air. I needed air.

Kicking, and pushing my hands against the dragging grasp of the water, I propelled myself upwards, thrust my head above the surface and sucked in a breath. I needed to rid myself of my waterlogged coat. Treading water with tired legs, I tried to undo the buttons, but my fingers were numb and clumsy, and the wet wool refused to give. I gave up, reached for the ice again, but the pond sucked me back down into its black embrace.

One part of my mind detached from the rest and scientifically reminded me that if I didn't get more oxygen within seconds, I would drown. But the dark was deepening, and I no longer knew which way was up. It was getting harder to move my legs and arms. My limbs were deadening. Everything was slowing down, shutting down. Stopping.

I held my last breath through the agony of burning, bursting lungs. The rest of me no longer felt pain, no longer even felt the cold. A warmth was stealing through my body and with it, a growing feeling of peace.

The pond clamped its claws over my lips, relentlessly pulled them apart, and breathed water into me. In an instant, my throat constricted, spasmodically shutting tight against the invading fluid. Lights popped in the spreading blackness of my vision.

This is it. This is how I die. The pond gets me, too, in the end.

There was no fear left in me, no struggle. It felt inevitable. Destined, even.

The detached part of my mind noted with satisfaction that I didn't, in the hour of my death, pray to a god I didn't believe in. And there were no thoughts of uniting with Colby on the other side. But I did think of him, wondering if this was how it had been for him — this calm surrender to the pond's enfolding arms. Had he thought of me in those last moments?

Warm now, and strangely comforted, I welcomed the euphoria blossoming inside me. The last pinpricks of white in my vision expanded into glowing halos of golden light.

My heart thudded one last time. And stopped.

Outside myself, I saw my body drifting in the black water, still as death. The silence was so deep it had its own music. The darkness enfolding my body was so intense I could almost touch it. And the light filling me was so radiant that it obliterated everything.

10

A flash of blue-white light.

Black nothingness.

The lightning again.

Darkness.

11

L ight — soft and constant — penetrated my eyelids, and
pain nudged me awake.

I blinked my eyes open, tried to clear my throat
against the obstruction there.

"Hey, kiddo."

"It's a miracle!"

Dad. And Mom.

A third voice said, "Garnet, can you hear me? I'm going to
remove the breathing tube now. When I say 'cough,' cough as
hard as you can, okay?"

A cough and a scrape later, my throat was clear. I blinked again
and looked around the room. White walls, a window, beeping
machines, a nurse in uniform, a drip stand with a line entering my
arm. My father and mother sat beside my high metal bed, and a
huge arrangement of flowers rested on the bedside cabinet.

"I'm in a hospital?" I croaked. My throat felt raw, and it
hurt to breathe.

"You're in the County General hospital, in Randolph, and I'm Sarah Henshaw," the nurse said.

Dad patted my hand. "You had us a little worried."

"A little worried? I was out of my brain with it! But I've had a prayer chain going for you the whole night," said Mom, who, I now saw, was in a wheelchair, her right leg in a knee-to-toe plaster cast.

"Thirsty," I rasped.

The nurse — a compact woman with a firm grip and a no-nonsense attitude — helped me to sit up and passed me a cup of water. The tips of several of my fingers, I saw, were bandaged. I sucked on the straw, swallowed and winced.

"Your throat and chest will hurt for a good few days," she explained.

And the rest of me? I felt stiff and sore all over, like I'd been run over by a steamroller.

The nurse made some notes on the chart at the bottom of my bed and then fitted an automatic blood pressure cuff around my right arm and a clamp on my left forefinger. The cuff tightened and then deflated, and behind my head a machine beeped its results.

The nurse frowned. "Well, that can't be right."

I craned my neck upwards to see her tapping the machine with an impatient finger, then switching it off and on again. She repeated the procedure of taking my blood pressure but seemed no more satisfied with the results.

"Sorry, it's on the fritz. We'll have to do this the old-fashioned way. I'll be back in a minute," she said and left the room.

Loud voices and the rattle of a trolley sounded from the hallway outside, but inside it was quiet. The only other bed in the ward was empty. Bright sunshine streamed in through the window beside my bed. *Sunshine*? How long had I been here?

"What time is it?" I asked.

"It's just after ten-thirty in the morning," Dad said. "You slept the whole night through."

I could tell I'd had more sleep than he had; there were dark rings under his eyes.

"What happened?" I asked.

"You fell through the ice. You can thank your lucky stars—"

"Jupiter," Mom interjected.

"—that help got to you so quickly. The boy's friend had run to get help, and Chief Jackson was already on the way and calling the paramedics when you went into the water. Plus, you weren't too deep down; he found you floating just beneath the surface."

That was surprising. It had felt like I'd been in that water for ages, and that I'd sunk to the very bottom of the pond. But I knew that the norepinephrine secreted during the body's fight-or-flight reaction could mess with time perception and memory. There was a name for it. Something like tachypsychia, or maybe temporopsychia. My foggy brain struggled to dredge up the term.

"So, we don't know exactly how long you were under, but it couldn't have been too long," Dad said.

My mother tutted. "It was long enough. Your heart stopped. You had to be brought back from the dead."

"*What*?"

"You drowned! You went into the life beyond," she said, sounding both excited and impressed.

"They did CPR on you," my father explained. "Chief Jackson first, then the paramedics on the ambulance journey here to Randolph."

"They shocked you with that machine of theirs — twice. And you came back!" My mother said. "It just wasn't your time to go."

"God wasn't ready, and the devil didn't want you," Dad said with a gentle smile.

The nurse returned, wrapped a manual blood pressure cuff around my arm, inflated it and lifted my hand, fingers over the pulse point on my wrist. A strong wave of fatigue swept through me; it was all I could do to keep my eyes open.

"That all seems normal," she said, noting her results on the chart. "How are you feeling?"

"Exhausted. Like I've been on my feet for twenty-four hours."

"Spiritual jetlag," my mother murmured.

I gave her the look that deserved. "And my head hurts."

My mother pressed something into my left hand. "Here, you just hold onto this." It was a white stone with a striated, crystalline surface.

"What the …?"

"That's selenite, for healing. It'll help with the headache."

I handed it to Dad and said to the nurse, "I think I'm going to need something a little stronger."

"Sure, honey. I'll bring you meds for the pain, but what you really need now is rest." She looked at my parents. "You can visit again tonight."

"Tonight? Can't I go home? I feel—" I wanted to say "fine," but the word that came out was "okay." Truth was, I felt a little weird. Kind of spaced out and not myself.

"We'll see what the doctor says after his examination. He'll probably want to keep you in for another night, just to be safe."

"We've got a room at an inn in town," Dad said. "We'll stay another night if you have to, then drive you back to Pitchford tomorrow."

"The boy — is he okay?" I asked, ashamed that I'd only just remembered him.

"Nicholas? He's as fine as a fiddle. The Coopers are very grateful to you," Mom said. "They sent those beautiful flowers. And a lovely note, too."

My father beamed at me. "You're a hero, kiddo. You saved his life!"

Part of me felt proud. Part of me wondered if he would have been saved anyway, without my clumsy efforts. Without me having to go through all of this.

"And my car?"

"Already at home," Dad said. "Don't you worry about anything."

"Time to go, folks," the nurse said firmly, taking hold of the handles of my mother's wheelchair. "Are you hungry, Garnet?"

I nodded, suddenly realizing I was ravenous. When had I last eaten?

"I'll bring you some soft food. Any dietary requirements?"

"She's allergic to shellfish," my mother said quickly.

"No lobster bisque, then," Nurse Henshaw said with a wink at me, and expertly wheeled my mother out of the room. My father kissed me on the forehead, promised to visit again later, and followed them. In the silence left by their departure, I felt a pang of guilt. I hadn't asked my mother how her foot was.

They'd only just left when the neurologist — a tall beanpole of a man, with a circle of graying hair like a monk's tonsure — came to examine me.

"To begin with, I'm going to name four objects, and I want you to say them back to me," he said.

I nodded.

"War, orange, north, duck."

The duck made me think of the pond. Everything made me think of that damn pond.

"Can you repeat them back to me?"

"War, orange, duck, and ... uhm ... north."

War, orange, duck, north, I repeated them silently to myself, while, at his instruction, I stood up, balanced on each leg and walked in a straight line, like a field sobriety test. I was familiar with the mini mental state examination he put me through — I'd learned it when we covered traumatic brain injuries in neuropsychology — and was glad to discover I knew the day and date, and remembered both my own and the president's full names.

I could waggle my tongue, lift my arms above my head, smile, follow his moving finger with my gaze and feel it when he lightly touched my arms, legs, feet and face with a Q-tip.

"War, orange, duck, north," I repeated when prompted.

The doctor seemed satisfied with my reactions and responses, but he frowned when he shone a light into my eyes.

"Have your eyes always been like this?"

"Like what?" I asked, worried that my pupils weren't constricting, which I knew could be a sign of brain damage.

"Heterochromic."

"Hetero-what now?"

"Your irises are slightly different colors."

"No, they aren't."

"Take a look for yourself."

I walked over to the basin at the end of the room and peered into the mirror above it. Above my unusually pale face, my left eye did indeed look a little darker than the right. Almost as if it had a hint of brown running through the blue.

"That's new," I said. "And bizarre. Should I be worried?"

"It's unusual but not unheard of for eye color to change following injury. The iris is like a layer with loose pigmentation scattered along its sides, and trauma can sometimes disperse the pigment, leaving lighter or darker areas. Of course," he added, "that's usually following a direct blow to the eye region."

"It's not a bleed in my brain, or something?"

"We did scans last night, and there's no bleeding and no fracture of the skull. How are you feeling?"

I shifted my attention away from the mirror and considered. "My chest and throat are sore, and I have a headache, but otherwise I feel okay. Maybe a little … dizzy?"

It came out sounding like a question, because *dizzy* wasn't the right word, but I didn't know how to describe what I was feeling. Dissociated maybe. Like when they dragged me out of that pond and pulled me back into the land of the living, not all of me came back. Like there was a part of me still outside my body.

"It's possible you have some concussion; there's an area of swelling and contusion at the back of your head. Sit down, let me examine it."

I climbed back into the bed and winced as the doctor's fingers felt around the tender lump.

"How did you injure it?"

An image flared in my mind's eye. Someone swinging a fist at the side of my head. Pain exploding in a shower of sparks. Involuntarily I flinched away from the doctor.

"Someone hit me." Why did I say *that*? "No, I mean, it felt like someone punched my lights out, but actually I just fell on the ice and knocked my head. And before that on the sidewalk."

"Hmm." He contemplated me with an assessing gaze. "I think we'll keep you in for another night's observation."

At my sigh of disappointment, he added, "If all goes well in the night, and you're feeling ... clearer ... about what happened, we'll release you in the morning."

He wrote up his notes on the chart, and after he left, the nurse returned, placed a tray of food on the table at the end of my bed, and wheeled it up closer to my head. She injected a clear substance into the drip, saying, "There you go, you'll feel better soon. Now eat up."

Though it hurt to swallow, I did as she said, finishing half the tasteless, mud-colored soup and all the luminous pink jello.

"What's the matter with my fingers?" I asked.

"The surface skin is ripped off, so they're raw. But they should heal up nicely within a week or two."

I remembered the pond, my fingers frozen to the ice, and shuddered.

"Now you get some rest," she said. "I'll pop in later and check on you."

"Thanks," I said, lying back on the cool pillows, and sighing with relief when she closed the window blinds against the light. I shut my eyes, hoping to drift back off to sleep, but images of the past day flashed through my mind.

I tried to piece together what had happened in some kind of coherent order, but it was all a muddle. The kid in red on the ice. His friend — the little girl running — panicked and crying. I hadn't seen that, of course, but I could imagine it clearly in my mind's eye. The pond, the creaking ice, the dark night. No, that wasn't right. It had been afternoon, not night.

I recalled the water — the shocking cold of it, the sensation of being pulled back into it, hands holding me under. No, that was wrong, too. I hadn't been held under. It had just felt that way, like between them, the pond and the dead weight of my coat had forced me down.

With a pang of intense feeling that felt almost like longing, I remembered the part at the end — the warmth and the musical silence, the golden light. What the hell had *that* been? Probably a consequence of lack of oxygen to the brain, I reasoned, trying to remember if anoxia could cause visual and auditory hallucinations. Whatever its cause, it had been eerily calm and peaceful, such a contrast to this place with its banging and clanging, and a nurse coming in every hour to check on me and to complain about the equipment, most of which didn't seem to be working properly. A bit like my brain.

12

That night, I got a visit from Police Chief Ryan Jackson.

"Hey, Garnet."

"Hey, Ryan."

For a few moments we stared at each other, taking in the difference the years had made. He had to be four or five years older than me, but he looked good. Unlike Pete, he still had a full head of thick black hair, and his waist was as trim as it had been back when he dated Vanessa Beaumont. Had he married her eventually?

"You're looking good," he said.

"No, I'm not."

"Well, you're looking alive, which is kinda the same thing. It was still touch and go when they took you away, so I wanted to see for myself that you made it."

"My father tells me that you saved my life."

He shrugged. "I did CPR until the paramedics arrived. But they're the ones who brought you back."

"Thank you," I said gruffly.

"You're welcome."

"No, seriously — I'm super-glad I'm not dead. Thanks for not giving up on me."

"Anytime. Thanks for saving the kid." There was a moment's silence, then he fished a plush toy out of the paper bag he was holding. "I bought you a get-well gift."

It was a blue bear, wearing a cheerful *It's a boy!* T-shirt.

I raised an eyebrow. "I know I'm a little confused, but I think I would have remembered having had a baby."

"The options in the gift store downstairs were limited."

"They don't sell beer there, do they? I could kill a beer."

Where did that come from? I didn't even like beer.

It was his turn to raise his brows. "You probably shouldn't be drinking right now."

"Yeah, you're probably right."

He sat the bear on the tray table at the foot of my bed and said, "When you're up and about, maybe we could have coffee?"

"Sure," I said, unenthusiastically.

My plan was to persuade my mother to shut up shop, help my father to clear it out, spend Christmas with them, and then head back to Boston directly after. I had no desire to hang around town socializing with the locals.

My parents arrived at that moment. My mother thanked Ryan loudly and effusively, and my father headed straight for me, frowning in concern.

Saying he needed to get back to work, Ryan wished me well and headed out. As he left, the blue bear toppled over and fell to the ground.

"Oh, look, it fell. Bob, hand that to me, will you?" my mother said. "Thank you, dear. Isn't it just *darling*, Garnet? Where should I put it?"

I gestured to the empty chair on the left side of my bed, but she tucked it into the bed beside me.

"It's so cute! And so is Ryan, I must say. I do like tall men, and he has a calm and steady aura. And he gave you the kiss of life!"

I ignored her. I was good at that. Dad spoke softly about the weather. The intense cold had lifted, and we were in for a warmer spell.

Just like a decade ago.

Mom stroked my hand, wondering out loud whether her peonies and asters would think it was a false spring, and whether I knew that asters were an enchanted flower that symbolized love and patience. I must have drifted off because when next I opened my eyes, the room was dark and quiet, and my parents had gone, although there was someone behind me on the other side of the bed. I was lying on my side, facing the doorway, and by the crack of light coming in from the hallway beyond, I could see that the blue bear had fallen again and lay on the ground well out of my reach.

I shivered as a rash of goose bumps tightened my skin. Snuggling deeper under the blankets, I asked, "Would you mind picking up the bear?"

There was no response. I glanced over my shoulder and saw that no one was there. Funny, I could've sworn someone was with me. Maybe I was still asleep and dreaming.

I dreamed more after that — a pleasant mishmash of scenes

of Colby and I together, laughing, talking and kissing. Then we were squatting side-by-side on our haunches, in the grass beside the bandstand down by Plover Pond, facing a row of purple asters. We had small gardening trowels in our hands, and we were digging in the dirt, planting something.

Or perhaps digging something up.

"You go on upstairs, I'll fetch your suitcase from your car," my father said as we arrived at my parents' house in Pitchford the next day.

"I'll get lunch ready," my mother said, swinging herself into the kitchen on her crutches.

My old bedroom looked exactly as it had on the day I left — cherrywood pencil-post bed, patchwork quilt in shades of forest green, braided rug on the floor, and a free-standing oval mirror in the corner. The large corkboard on the wall above my desk was still pinned with the sentimental scraps of an eighteen-year-old's life — concert ticket stubs; a strip of photo booth shots of Jessica and me wearing witches' hats from the time we went on a school outing to Salem; a faded magazine picture of Robert Pattinson in full Edward Cullen mode; and a printed quote reminding me that where there was love, there was life.

Nothing in the room had been changed. Had my parents been waiting for me to return, to step back into my old life all this time?

My father came in, carrying my suitcase and the flower arrangement from the kid's parents. "Where do you want these?"

I took the flowers and said, "You can put the suitcase on the bed, thanks, Dad."

"Welcome home, kiddo. Hope you stay a long while."

Not if I could help it.

He gave me a tight hug and then left, saying over his shoulder, "Don't be too long unpacking, okay? I'm starving."

I wondered if he'd had anything to eat today; he and my mother had been at the hospital bright and early to check on me. After a problem-free night, I'd been given a more-or-less clean bill of health and discharged with painkillers, sleeping tablets ("Just in case,") and a warning to take it easy and keep a lookout for symptoms of concussion.

I felt stiff and sore, but more than that, I felt *strange*, not wholly myself. Safe and alone in the comfortable familiarity of my old room, the realization finally hit me that I had nearly died. Hell, I *had* died. My knees felt suddenly wobbly, and tears pricked my eyes. Screw this bad-luck, pimped-up, no-good excuse for a town, and especially that damned pond that lurked like a malevolent spider at the center of it. And at the center of my life.

I dumped the flowers on one side of my dressing table, trying, and failing, to keep my gaze from straying to the cluster of framed photographs set out on the other. My throat tightened painfully as I took in the frozen memories of Colby and I staring at each other in picture after picture. We'd been so in love. I remembered feeling it like a dazzling light in the core of my being, an ignition of my senses, a spark of awareness electrifying my skin, a gravitational pull toward him. I hadn't felt anything near half as strong since.

My gaze traveled over the photographs. Colby and I smiled out from a snapshot of us at our lunch table in the school cafeteria. Jessica, I recalled, had been behind the camera, urging us to keep straight faces, which had only made us laugh more.

I leaned closer to examine a picture taken on the day of the school trip to the old Beaumont Brothers bottling plant. It was after Colby had broken up with Judy, but before he and I had started dating, which would've made it sometime in May 2007. I'd wanted to take a photograph of Colby without making it obvious, so I'd wandered around snapping shots of groups of kids I had no interest in before taking his. He was looking directly into the camera, grinning widely. He'd probably seen right through my schemes. Pete and Judy, who'd already hooked up by then, were in the background. Pete looked bored, but Judy was smiling, and — was she looking at Colby? Could be. She'd never wanted their breakup, and in anyone's book, Pete was a poor replacement for Colby.

Rubbing the bandaged edge of my thumb across my lips, I studied a photo of Colby wearing new khaki chinos and a neatly pressed blue shirt and standing, hands on hips, in front of the big sugar maple tree in his back yard. Mrs. Beaumont had taken it on the first day of his summer job at the town clerk's office, and later printed off a copy for me to keep.

Colby shone out of the pictures — vital, glowing with life and joy, ready to take on the world. I stretched out a finger to trace his face on one close-up, murmuring, "I miss you, Colby. Always and forever."

Though I'd touched it lightly, the framed photo fell over. I placed it upright again, shivering at a cold breeze on my neck.

I was about to check my bedroom windows for the source of the draft when I saw the family photograph of the Thanksgiving dinner at the Beaumont House. I picked it up and scrutinized it. Colby's mother stood between her husband and his brother at the head of the table. Colby's younger sister, Cassie, sat on one side of the table, along with his older sister, Vanessa, and Ryan Jackson. Colby and I sat opposite them, him hugging me, our heads tilted toward each other. Everyone, except Cassie, was smiling. That would have been Colby's last Thanksgiving, I realized, just weeks before he died.

A wave of nausea surged in me, and I ran for the bathroom.

13

Thursday November 22, 2007

On the ceiling above us, sticker stars, moons and planets glowed in pale luminescence. Colby and I lay in darkness on his bed, light-headed with desire as we kissed and slid hands beneath clothes, impatient for the feel of each other's skin. Colby groaned and pulled me closer, like he could merge with me, flesh onto flesh, bone into bone. I opened my shirt, unclasped my bra and pulled his head down between my breasts. Trembling, he pressed kisses along the curves and drew a puckered nipple into his mouth. Beneath the ripples of pleasure, I felt something deeper, a primal and ancient connection to all women who had ever felt this bewildering combination of power and vulnerability, who had ever gazed down on the head of a man nuzzling them and felt a fierce urge to protect, intertwined with an overwhelming urge to be held, loved, possessed.

Sudden bright lights made me blink. Colby cursed. I yanked the duvet up to cover us.

His ten-year-old sister, Cassie, stood in the doorway, her hand still on the light switch. "Gross me out!" She wrinkled her nose at us and shook her head until her blond pigtails swung.

"Don't you ever knock?" Colby yelled, throwing a pillow at her.

"Mom says it's dinner time. So, you can't do sex now."

"We're not having sex!" Colby said, which was true for the state of affairs that night, but no longer true for our relationship as a whole.

Instead of leaving, so I could get dressed, Cassie stepped into the room and began inspecting the items on Colby's desk.

"We're having roast turkey with stuffing, and buttered mashed potatoes, and pumpkin pie. And also minty peas and slimy zucchinis" — she shuddered at this — "and cranberry sauce. And cornbread, because Mom says Uncle Roger will 'not be happy' if he doesn't get cornbread and gravy. And gravy! We're also having gravy. What's this?" She held up some stapled papers.

"It's none of your business, that's what it is," Colby said.

Rubbing her lower back, and peering at the page, Cassie looked, for a brief moment, like a little old lady. "Beaumont Golf Estate development contract," she read.

"It's from work."

Why'd he brought a contract home from work?

"Now put it down and get out of my room. And stay out," Colby said. "And stop taking my stuff all the time."

"I don't."

"Oh, yeah, so if I search your room right now I won't find my chemistry set?"

"You won't *find* it, no." She beamed an angelic smile of innocence at him.

"Brat!" Colby said, but I could hear the laughter in his voice. "I need that for my project. You bring it back tonight, and don't mess around with those chemicals, Cas. Some of them are toxic."

"Toxic, schmoxic." She tossed the contract back onto his desk. "Goodbye. I'm off to eat gravy and to tell Mom you two were making sex."

She stepped quickly out of the room, and we heard her run laughing down the hallway. Muttering that I didn't know how lucky I was to be an only child, Colby bounced out of his bed and went to close the door.

Looking down at the still-evident bulge in his jeans, he said, "Say something to get my mind off your ..." — he waved a hand at my chest — "because I don't have time for a cold shower."

I grinned. "Um, okayyy ... So, you've started your chemistry project?"

"Yeah, though I can only do the experiments when my brat of a sister returns my test tubes. Have you started yet?"

I fastened my bra and shirt. "Just with the theory. I'm going to test the sugar content of supposedly healthy drinks like fruit juices and sports drinks, and compare them to sodas to see which is the sweetest."

"Let me check something." He gave me a long, deep kiss. "Uh-huh, thought so. *You're* the sweetest."

I play-punched him on his arm. "Bet you say that to all the girls."

A barrage of knocks rattled the door. "Mom says if you

don't come now, you won't get any turkey, you'll just have to eat vegetables. And all the zucchini," Cassie shouted gleefully at the keyhole.

By the time we got to the dining room, Colby's parents and sisters were already seated at the table, along with his uncle Roger, and Ryan Jackson, who was dating Vanessa. Domino sat under the table, thumping his tail in anticipation of dropped scraps or sneaked treats.

Mrs. Beaumont dished up the food, but before giving us the go-ahead to start eating, she said the grace, and then insisted we each say something we were grateful for.

"I'll start," she said. "I'm thankful for my beautiful family."

"I'm grateful for the land development deal we're putting together. It's going to bring a much-needed injection of money to this town," Roger Beaumont said.

Vanessa rolled her eyes.

"I'm thankful for the stars and moon above us, which allow me to see the things below," Colby said, with a wicked grin and a squeeze of my thigh under the table.

I giggled, while Mrs. Beaumont said, "Lovely!"

"I'm grateful for Colby," I said.

Mrs. Beaumont beamed at me; Vanessa snorted.

"I'm not grateful for my sore back or these gross zucchini," Cassie said, making a face at her plate. But at a look from her mother, she added, "But I'm grateful for potatoes and gravy."

"Ryan?" Mrs. Beaumont prompted.

"I'm thankful I'm not on duty today. I'd much rather be here than manning the phones at the police station."

Vanessa, who — by her expression — seemed to think we

were all being way too sappy, said, "Well, I'm extremely grateful I'm not at Camp David having dinner with George Warmonger Bush!"

"Vanessa," her mother said in a warning tone.

"Who found time between pardoning and eating turkeys," Vanessa continued, "to call some servicemen in Iraq and thank them for their service to our great nation in a war without basis—"

"*Vanessa*," her father said. "Please don't."

"—in a country we should never have invaded, and from which we now seem unlikely ever to withdraw!"

Colby grinned. He was used to his sister's politics ruffling the feathers of his parents.

"That will do, young lady," her uncle said sharply. "It's rude to discuss politics at the table."

"*You* can't tell me what to do," Vanessa protested. "You're not my father!"

"Well, I am," Mr. Beaumont said. "And I agree with your uncle."

"Don't you always?" Vanessa muttered under her breath.

"*Bon appetit*, everyone! Tuck in," Mrs. Beaumont said, and we all began eating.

Cassie hid her vegetables under a slice of turkey breast, poured herself a glass of Beaumont's *Very Berry* water, and blew bubbles into it through her straw.

"Stop that, please," her mother told her.

"Vanessa says you work at the town clerk's office every Saturday?" Ryan asked Colby.

"Yeah, just back-office admin. My father says I need work experience."

"We *wanted* you to work at the bottling plant," Colby's father said.

"And how's the job going?" Ryan asked.

"It's okay, a little boring."

"What's it like working for Michelle Armstrong?" Vanessa asked.

"She's very energetic and enthusiastic," Colby said, sounding like he was choosing his words carefully.

Smiling inscrutably, Vanessa exchanged a quick glance with Ryan.

"The best place for you, Colby, would be working alongside your father and me in the family business," Roger said.

Colby cleared his throat. "Yeah, about that ..."

"It's our legacy to this family and to the town. Do you know that we employ almost thirty-six percent of Pitchford's residents and contribute majorly to the taxes which support the town? And now that we're taking it nationwide, why — the sky's the limit!"

"The thing is, I don't want to go into business." I could tell Colby was making an effort to keep his voice calm. It wasn't the first or even the twenty-first time he'd had this discussion with his father and uncle.

"You know, not everybody subscribes to the exploitative economics of capitalism, Roger," Vanessa said.

"*Uncle* Roger," her father said.

Obviously hoping to forestall an argument, Mrs. Beaumont turned to Cassie, whose straw was making loud slurping noises as she sucked the empty bottom of her glass. "Cassie, why aren't you eating your food?"

"I'm not hungry. Can I get more water?"

"*May* I," her mother corrected. "And you're probably not hungry because you're always filling up on water."

"*May* I?" Cassie said.

Her mother sighed. "Of course."

Cassie bolted to the kitchen. Colby, meanwhile, stared his uncle straight in the eye. "I want to go into law enforcement. I want to do what Ryan does."

Ryan raised his eyebrows at this, but Roger shook his head as if the very idea of wanting to be a cop instead of taking over the reins at Beaumont Brothers was absurd.

"Want doesn't always get, Colby," he said. "Being an adult means you need to make the occasional sacrifice."

"Occasional sacrifice? I'd be giving up on my dream." Anger was creeping into Colby's voice now.

Mrs. Beaumont, wearing an increasingly forced smile, offered Roger the serving dish. "More turkey? Or perhaps another spoon of creamed potatoes?"

"Your father, for example, wanted to be a veterinarian," Roger persisted. "But he let that pipe dream go in the interests of serving the family and the town."

Mr. Beaumont nodded, but I thought he looked kind of sad. Cassie returned to the table, where instead of eating her peas, she began surreptitiously flicking them at Colby and me, in between feeding her turkey to Domino.

"I *would* be serving the town and its citizens — including this family — if I became a cop," Colby pointed out fiercely.

"So, you want to put me out of a job?" Ryan teased, clearly trying to defuse the growing tension.

"I guess so," Colby replied.

"Then you should definitely investigate the water business!" Ryan said, grinning.

Everyone laughed, except Colby. I could tell he was still mad.

Under the table, I took his hand and placed it back on my thigh, then moved it higher. A smile teased at the edges of his mouth. Staring straight ahead, I placed my hand between his legs and rubbed. His smile widened.

"Wait! We need a family photograph. Squash together, everyone," Mrs. Beaumont said. She set her camera on the sideboard, fiddled with the timer and then hurried to take her place between her husband and her brother-in-law.

I cuddled up closer to Colby, keeping my hand between his legs.

"Everybody lean in and say, 'Cheese!'" Roger Beaumont said.

"Or *squeeze*," I whispered into Colby's ear, suiting the action to the word as the flash went off.

14

Monday December 18, 2017

I leaned over the toilet, ready to throw up, but the sick feeling settled as quickly as it had come. Was transient nausea another symptom of concussion?

At the basin, I switched on the light above the mirror to check my eyes. The iris of my left eye was unmistakably darker than the right. The contrast — more marked than it had been yesterday — changed my whole appearance. I didn't look like me.

I washed my hands and splashed cold water on my face. Immediately I was back in the water, sinking, thrashing, drowning. Feeling the pull of the pond, its frigid, watery kiss, the embracing darkness. And then the radiating light and sense of peace.

I bunched my hands into tight fists, and the sharp pain in my fingertips brought me back to the present. I made a mental note to go online and research near-death experiences. In the meantime, I'd be careful not to mention a word of the golden glow, the pervading calm or the beautiful music of silence to my mother. No doubt she'd believe the light was a bridge to the beyond, plus she'd have a host of hunches about why I'd been returned to my life, and I had less than zero desire to hear any of them.

The light above the basin buzzed and flickered and then went out. I tapped the fluorescent tube a few times, but it was dead. Switching on the main bathroom light, I stripped and took a long shower, making the water as hot as I could stand it, and losing a few of the fingertip bandages in the process. The skin underneath was raw and red, and one still oozed blood.

Drying myself, I took stock of the damage. There were bruises on my hip and knees, a long scrape down the underside of one arm, and my head still ached dully, but all in all, I reckoned I'd got off lightly. I stuck new Band-Aids on the worst of my fingertips, swallowed a couple of Tylenol, and got dressed. When my father called impatiently that the food was ready, I gave my unbalanced eyes a last glance and headed downstairs.

The food — vegetarian chili with bread rolls — was already on the dining room table.

"I thought we should eat here, rather than in the kitchen, since it's a special day," my mother said, smiling at me. "It's such a treat to have you back with us!"

I didn't know if she meant my being back at home, or back in the land of the living, and I didn't ask, just took my old seat at the table.

The dining room hadn't changed much, either. A low basket of dried flowers still gathered dust on the chestnut sideboard, and the old spinning wheel sat in the corner as it always had, though now my mother's crutches rested up against it. A large cut crystal, dangling from a ribbon near the window, refracted shards of rainbow light around the room.

"Please get rid of that revolting thing, Bob, it's bringing bad energy to our meal," Mom said, frowning at the book lying on the table beside Dad's place setting.

I glanced at the title as, with a resigned sigh, Dad picked up the book and took it through to the living room. *Richard Ramirez: America's Night Stalker.* Robert McGee was a mild and gentle man, but you'd never know it from his reading tastes, which ran to the brutally violent and macabre. The bookshelves to the right of the fireplace in the living room were packed with true crime volumes and biographies of all the famous serial killers — Jeffrey Dahmer, Ted Bundy, John Wayne Gacy — plus a host of more obscure murderers. My father could tell you more than you ever wanted to know about dreadful ways to die, and the only time he'd ever gone overseas had been to attend RipperCon in London's East End with like-minded obsessives from around the world.

The bookshelves to the left of the fireplace were filled with my mother's tomes on the tarot, crystals, intuitive psychics, "true-life" hauntings and mediumship. On their London trip, while Dad had attended seminars on the possible identity and motivations of the Ripper, Mom had taken day-trips to Stonehenge, Glastonbury and Tintagel.

I buttered a roll and took a big bite. There was no trace of the nausea I'd felt upstairs, but I couldn't resist a huge yawn.

"Tired?" Dad said.

"Nah," I said, although I was. "That was just a silent scream for coffee."

"I'm on it." He hurried back to the kitchen and returned with a pot of the good stuff, plus three mugs.

"My old cup!"

Delighted, I grabbed the large red mug printed with a Turkish proverb: *Black as hell, strong as death, and sweet as an angel's kiss* — just how I liked my coffee. I poured myself a large cup, declined Mom's offer of cream, and stirred in sugar.

Dad frowned at me. "Three spoons, kiddo?"

"Garnet always was excessive," Mom said, apparently ruminating to herself. "Extra chili, more salt, ice even in winter. And way too much black eyeliner."

Irritated, I waved a hand in front of her eyes. "Sitting right here, Mom."

"I've read up on it — well, you have to when you get to my age," Dad continued. "They say sugar is the new fat. Seems it's a bigger factor in heart disease than cholesterol!"

I took a sip of the brew and almost shuddered because it *did* taste very sweet. "I don't think I need to worry about lifestyle choices, Dad. The way yesterday went, bad luck will kill me before cardiac arrest does."

Immediately, Mom perked up. "Why? What happened yesterday? Apart from your dying in the pond, I mean?"

"She didn't die, Crystal, stop saying that, will you?"

"Oh yes she did! She was as dead as a doorknob."

"Nail," I said.

"What's that, dear?"

"Dead as a doornail."

"I don't think that can be right. What's a doornail, anyway? The point is, you absolutely, positively left this life, and I want to hear all about what that was like, too."

"I don't remember."

She pulled a tragic face.

"First-time nerves. Next time I die, I'll be sure to take detailed notes for you," I said sarcastically. Then, because she looked ready to apply thumbscrews to hear about my adventures in the world of spirit, I threw in a distraction. Pointing to my eyes, I said, "Notice anything different?"

"Well, will you look at that!" Dad said, his gaze switching between my eyes.

"Holy mother of earth! I don't know what that means, but it must mean something. I'll call my friend Bettina — she does tarot *and* iridology — and get her expert opinion," Mom said.

"Please don't," I retorted. "The doctor says it sometimes happens after accidents."

"Is it permanent?" Dad looked worried.

I shrugged. "Don't know yet. We'll have to wait and *see*. Keep a close *eye* on things." I elbowed him in the ribs, and he laughed, as I'd hoped he would. My father worried too much.

"What are your plans for today?" Mom asked between mouthfuls.

"To start clearing out your shop."

"I haven't decided whether I want to close it."

"Yeah, well, we need to have that discussion sometime soon."

"There's no rush."

But there was; I wanted to get out of town as soon after Christmas as possible.

"Besides," Mom continued, "you should take it easy today. The doctor told you not to overdo it. And tomorrow you could visit some old friends, catch up with Jessica. She still lives in town, you know. She'd want you to touch base."

"And you'll want to visit Colby's family, I suppose," Dad added.

I felt a pang of something, guilt maybe. Or dread. Politeness dictated that I visit them to pay my respects, but I knew it would depress me and stir up things I'd rather leave be.

I sipped my coffee. "How's Cassie doing?"

Through my father's updates, I'd learned of her struggles with kidney disease over the years, poor kid. Poor family.

"Still in remission," he said.

"Remission? So it was *cancer*?" Somehow I hadn't grasped that.

Dad nodded, Mom tutted and I grimaced, even less enthusiastic now to pay that visit.

Dad patted me on the shoulder and said, "Eat the frog, kiddo. Do the hardest thing first—"

"—and the rest of the day will be easier," I finished. The saying was one of Dad's favorites. And it was good advice.

"Alright, I'll go see them. Tomorrow."

I spent the rest of the day resting, drifting in and out of naps, watching reruns of *Law and Order* on TV, and catching up on my parents' news while I helped them dress the Christmas tree in the living room. Apart from her broken ankle, my mother seemed to have no lingering effects from her ischemic attack. Her face looked fine to me, and I hadn't noticed any neurological deficits other than the ones she'd always had – a belief in the impossible and a habit of getting words and sayings mixed up. But for perhaps the first time, I was aware that both my parents were getting older. They moved more slowly and carefully, had more liver spots on their hands, and reminisced about the past more than they spoke about the present. They took a nap that afternoon, and apparently it was a daily habit.

Perry was right — they weren't getting any younger.

That night I had a series of such bizarre dreams that I wound up taking a sleeping tablet and didn't wake up until ten the next morning, with dread for the scheduled visit to the Beaumonts a heavy weight in my stomach. Realizing that it was the nineteenth of December — the anniversary of the day they'd found Colby's body — I wished I'd gone the day before after all.

My mittens and scarf had been lost in rescuing the kid. Worse, my trench coat was a bundle of shrunken wet wool draped over a rail in the laundry room, and one of my Doc Martens had gone missing — swallowed by the pond or lost en route to the hospital. So I dressed in the only other footwear I'd brought — my running shoes — and grabbed my parka for warmth. On my way out, my mother called me over to where she sat, foot up on an ottoman, in the living room.

"Here, dear, this will help," she said, handing me a small bottle.

"I'm not interested," I said, glaring suspiciously at the label.

"It's Rescue Remedy drops, Garnet. Goodness, you'd think I was trying to poison you! It's just a little essence of Rock Rose, Star of Bethlehem—"

"What's it supposed to do?"

"It'll settle your nerves and help if you're feeling teary."

I gave her a skeptical look.

"It's a very popular and powerful homeopathic remedy."

"Then it's the opposite of powerful, Mom. Homeopathic stuff is so diluted that it has no detectable active ingredients in it."

"It retains the *memory* of the ingredients, the patterns. And the more diluted it is, the more powerfully it works."

"Well, that makes complete sense."

"It works!" Mom said mulishly.

"It's a placebo," I replied. "It's just expensively packaged, plain old water."

"Then you won't mind having a sip. Of plain old water," Mom said, smiling triumphantly.

Clever old devil, she'd outmaneuvered me.

"Ten drops, straight onto your tongue."

Perhaps there was something to my mother's remedy, because I felt calm as I arrived at the Beaumont Golf Estate just outside of town. The housing development was located on a hill that sloped gently down to a golf course at the bottom and the Kent River beyond, and was crowned with a forest of tall firs, spruces and pines. Enormous two- and three-story houses — different enough to give a semblance of individuality, uniform enough to ensure a cohesive look — were set at generous intervals. Discreet signage advised residents to stick to the speed limits, keep their noise levels down, be on the lookout for stray deer, and to pick up their dog's poop. A gardener clipping a hedge in the front yard of the Beaumonts' new residence — more mansion than house — nodded a greeting as I walked up the path. What would Colby have made of all of this?

At their old house in town, there'd been a doorbell which had played a cheerful ding-dong, but here a big brass knocker in the shape of a lion's head was mounted in the center of the oak door. At my rap, loud barking sounded from inside. Mrs. Beaumont, alerted to my arrival by the security officer at the estate's gate house, opened the doors almost at once.

Mom! The word was in my head.

Yes, this was Colby's mom, even though she looked very different than the last time I'd seen her.

A bunch of emotions surged through me at the sight of her. Surprise, relief, anxiety. And something that felt a lot like love.

Mom!

"Garnet McGee — goodness me, you're all grown up!"

"Hi, Mrs. Beaumont."

"Please, call me Bridget. Come in, come in. This way," she said, leading me through an entrance hall with Persian rugs scattered on its marble floor, a wide staircase sweeping up to the second floor, and what looked to my untrained eye like superb modern art on the walls. The Beaumonts' fortunes had clearly prospered in the last decade.

"I put on a fresh pot of coffee, and there's still half a rhubarb cheesecake left that we can tuck into."

I followed her into a kitchen which was probably larger than my entire Boston apartment. And brighter, too. Burnished copper pots hung from a rail along one wall, a lavish crystal chandelier hung above a central island, and stainless-steel appliances gleamed their promise of gourmet food.

I trailed a hand over a black granite counter top which sparkled with flecks of blue. "This is lovely."

"It's called Blues in the Night — it comes from Angola, in Africa. The granite from Pitchford's quarry is a little dull."

A lot like the town.

She extracted a steaming coffee pot from a hi-tech machine and placed it on a tray, along with cups, plates, forks and the promised cheesecake.

An old Dalmatian dog limped into the kitchen, barking frantically at me. Its hackles were raised and its ears flattened.

"Is that– That's not still Domino?" I asked.

Baring its teeth, the dog gave a low, menacing growl, and then it rushed at me.

15

With a squeal of fright, I leapt onto the central island, bringing my legs up to my chest, out of the way of the dog's snapping teeth.

"Domino! *Domino!* Be quiet!" Bridget Beaumont grabbed him by the collar and dragged him to a corner of the kitchen, ordering him to "Stay!"

"He used to like me," I said, speaking loudly above the dog's continued protest at my presence.

"Don't take it personally. He's an old man now, aren't you, Domino?" She rubbed behind the Dalmatian's ears, and he calmed down a little. "He's half blind and mostly deaf, and he's probably forgotten you. It *has* been a while since we saw you."

"Yes, I'm sorry about that," I said, suddenly uncomfortably aware that I'd abandoned this family as suddenly and completely as Colby had left me. "I was just …"

Just what? Utterly smashed by grief, too cowardly to face

the Beaumont's pain, too set on forgetting the past to risk coming back to Pitchford?

"I understand, truly I do," she said, with more compassion in her voice than I deserved.

"Here, let me get that, you lead the way." I took the laden tray from her hands and carried it through to the living room, because she didn't look strong enough to carry it.

Bridget Beaumont had aged. Although she'd always had a trim figure, now she was so thin she looked frail. Her hair, swept into a neat chignon, was entirely gray, and she looked bone-tired. Dark smudges the color of my bruises cradled her eyes. Shockingly, she looked older than my mother even though she must've been a good ten years younger.

I was flooded by a sudden and completely inexplicable urge to hug her, to lift her right up off the ground and swing her around in the air and tell her I loved her. I squashed the crazy impulse and carefully placed the tray on the low coffee table in the living room. When I looked up, I saw that she was studying me. What changes in my appearance struck her, I wondered.

"Please, help yourself," she invited, gesturing to the coffee and cake.

I poured myself a cup, and my hand automatically went to the sugar bowl, hovered over it for a moment, and then withdrew. It seemed like I'd lost my sweet tooth in the pond yesterday, and I was in no hurry to reclaim it.

"Cake?" Bridget offered.

"Maybe later."

I took a seat on the right-hand side of a long leather sofa. At least my seating preferences hadn't changed. I'd always preferred to sit on the right side of other people. Whenever Colby and I had sat side by side, he'd always been on my left. Colby, who was left-handed, said that suited him just fine. Back then, when the two of us sat together on a couch in his house, Domino would jump up and try to squeeze between us, eager for a tummy rub. Today, the dog stayed in the doorway to the room, growling at me.

Bridget whistled and then called, "Come, boy. Come have a piece of cake."

Domino took a step forward, barked once, and then retreated to the doorway with his ears flattened and his tail between his legs.

"I don't know what's gotten into him," Bridget said apologetically. "*Domino*, quiet. Down!"

The dog lay down, rested his gray muzzle on his paws and kept his rheumy eyes fixed on me.

"How are you, after your accident on Saturday?"

"You heard about that?"

"My dear, this is Pitchford. Everybody heard about it. There was a 'local heroine' write-up in *The Bugle*. What a blessing for Nicholas Cooper that you were there to save him!"

"I'm just grateful Ryan Jackson was there to save me."

She glanced at my bandaged fingers. "And are you fully recovered? They say it could have been serious."

She didn't say, "You could have died," or "I believe you almost drowned." *Died* and *drowned* are words that she no doubt took care to avoid.

"I'm fine. How have *you* been these last years?"

"It hasn't been easy."

A psychologist, or even someone temperamentally suited to be a psychologist, would surely have known how to respond. But I could think of nothing to say. I sipped my coffee while Bridget cut a tiny bite off her slice of cake and ate it without any sign of pleasure. Over in the doorway, Domino whined softly.

"Mrs—" I began, just as she said, "There's a box—"

"Go ahead," I said.

"I have a box with some of Colby's personal belongings. I donated his clothes to Goodwill some years ago, but I didn't know what to do with his other things. I couldn't just toss them in the trash." She looked down at her plate, mashing cheesecake with her fork so that creamy ridges squeezed up between the tines. "I thought you might like to look through it. Maybe there'll be something you'll want as a keepsake? You can take the whole box home with you and go through it in your own time. Keep whatever you'd like and then let me have the rest back."

I *so* did not want to open a box of painful memories, but I could tell it was important to her. She wanted me to want something of Colby's.

"Sure, that's very kind, thank you," I said.

"I'll get it after we've had our coffee."

I looked around the room, not letting my eyes linger on the framed photographs of Colby. My gaze instead rested on a picture of his sisters, Vanessa and Cassie.

"How are the girls?" I asked, forcing brightness into my voice.

"Vanessa got her master's in politics and philosophy at BU,

and now she works for Amnesty International. She lives in Boston with her husband and their darling baby daughter. I'm a grandmother, can you believe that?" Bridget said, smiling.

"Wow."

In my memories, Vanessa was a young college student, eager to debate politics with the older generation. But now she was married and a mother. And though Cassie must be about twenty years old, I still pictured her as young and mischievous, her hair — the same blond as Colby's — swinging in pigtails as she chanted, "Garnet and Colby sitting in a tree, K-I-S-S-I-N-G!"

In my mind's eye these last ten years, everyone in Pitchford had stayed the same as the day I'd last seen them, like the villagers in Brigadoon. But coming back had broken that spell. Everyone here had changed almost beyond recognition.

"Vanessa's coming home for the holidays. I'm sure she'd love to see you. Why don't you join us for dinner on Christmas Eve? Tell your parents we'd love to have them, too."

"I'll do that, thanks. And how's Cassie doing? I was so sorry to hear about her health troubles. But my father says she's in remission?"

"You don't know?" Bridget asked, her face grave.

"Know what?"

"It's back."

I stared at her, uncomprehending.

"The cancer's back," she said.

No!

That's when the first flash of color happened. Like an explosion of mustard gas, a sickly yellow clouded my field of vision. No, not my vision, precisely. It wasn't happening in my eyes, but rather inside my mind. Another symptom of concussion? I shook my head, trying to clear the yellow haze.

Bridget must've thought I was rejecting the fact of Cassie's condition, because she said, "I'm afraid it's true. She's been fighting this for years, but ... she's not winning."

I blinked several times as the yellow faded, and tears welled up instead. How much tragedy could one family endure? I wiped my eyes with the heel of a hand. I didn't want to cry, I wanted to rage. I blew out a slow breath, trying to calm myself down.

"That's just terrible. I am so sorry to hear that," I said, all too aware of the inadequacy of the words.

She set her plate of mashed cake down on the table. "When it started, all those years ago, we didn't know for the longest while. It's a silent disease in its early stages. You feel tired and more thirsty than usual, but Cassie always loved drinking water, so we never thought anything of it when she drank more. It was only when she complained of serious back pain and smelly urine that we had her tested. She's had the whole gamut of treatment — surgery, targeted therapy, radiation. Even a transplant when she was seventeen."

I already knew some of this from my parents, but I listened without interrupting. It seemed like she needed to tell me the whole sad story.

"For about a year and a half, she did really well on the new kidney, but then her body rejected it, and it had to be removed. She went back on the waiting list, but then they discovered the cancer had spread to her lymph nodes, so she no longer qualified for a transplant. It's been one kidney and dialysis ever since."

"And ... now?"

"The cancer's at stage IV, and it's metastasized to her lungs and liver."

"That must be so hard for her. And for you, too."

"Philip handles the medical side of things; he has since the beginning, thank God. After losing Colby, I was very depressed — 'out of it,' I think you young people call it. A hopeless mother to my girls. But then Cassie got sick and she needed me, and that pulled me out of my funk of self-pity. I didn't have the energy to deal with doctors and medical insurance, so Philip took care of all that, while I took care of Cassie. I try to make sure she doesn't suffer more than she can bear."

From the pain in Bridget's voice, it was clear that her own suffering was almost more than *she* could bear. I nibbled on the Band-Aid on one of my fingers, biting lines into it, pinching the sides together to form a sharp corner.

"Soon she'll be free," Bridget murmured, as if to herself, then she pinned me with an unexpectedly intense gaze. "I wish I could be free, too. I can't stand this place, this house, this town. And most especially do I loathe that pond," she said bitterly.

"I hate it, too."

"Having to drive past it all the time ... Why, it just about kills me."

"Then why did you stay?" I asked. "Why didn't you just leave town after — after Colby?"

Turning her palms up in a helpless gesture, she gave me a

desolate smile. "I feel closer to him here."

I nodded. I could understand that, sort of. I felt closer to him here, too. At every turn there was a reminder of him, or us. But that wasn't something I wanted — it hurt more than it consoled. Maybe, if you immersed yourself in the space where the person had been and welcomed the memories, then perhaps you got used to them after a while. Perhaps you grew desensitized, and the shock of it didn't wind you or hurt as much. But looking at the woman opposite me, broken and crushed despite her erect posture and neat hair, I thought maybe that was a crock of shit. Maybe the pain never left you.

"And, of course, there's my husband's business," Bridget continued. "After we lost Colby, Philip was overwhelmed by grief. He threw himself into the water company, drove himself like a demon building the new bottling plant, marketing the new flavors, growing the business. It became his life, his everything."

I realized she hadn't lost just her son; she'd lost her husband, too.

"But it's given us the income we needed." She caught my involuntary glance at the luxurious surroundings and quickly added, "Oh, not all this. I could live without the finer things. But it's funded Cassie's treatments. Much of it, especially the newer treatments and experimental trials, weren't covered by insurance, so we needed a lot of money, and Beaumont Brothers provided. And so we stayed." She leaned over to pat my knee. "But I'm glad you got out, dear. It would please Colby to know you're happy."

Happy? It wasn't the word I would've chosen.

"I keep busy and stay out of mischief."

"Your mother tells me you're studying to be a psychologist?"

"Yeah, trying to. Although I'm not sure it's what I want anymore."

"I imagine it's a tough job, listening to everybody's tragedies and problems."

"Yeah, I guess so."

"And you volunteered in Africa, she said?"

"Yup. If you ever need to bottle-feed a baby cheetah, you know who to call."

I swallowed the last bitter sip of cold coffee and set my cup down on the table.

"Would you like to say hi to Cassie?" her mother asked.

Honestly? No.

But it couldn't be avoided. Trying not to venture too close to Domino, who was still whining plaintively, I followed Bridget up the sweeping staircase to the upper landing, which had a wall of photographs on one side and a bronze statue on a narrow table up against the railings on the other. The piece was arrestingly beautiful — heavy, yet elegant, a sweeping abstract form of two lovers merging into one, their exposed ribs blending into rough, arced sweeps, their faces devoid of features but tilted toward each other. This was the sort of thing normal people decorated their houses with — real art and photographs — not dream catchers and pictures of chakras.

I rubbed a hand over the patina of a smooth curve. The statue made me think of Colby and me. Everything here did. The town was sinking its claws into me, dragging me back. As

I turned to follow Bridget, I came face-to-face with a large, framed photograph of Colby. In an instant, I was back in the Bethel United Methodist church.

16

I waited until the last minute before going inside. Keeping my back to the buffeting wind, I traced patterns in the snow with the tip of my boot while everyone else scurried inside.

"Hey, stranger, how're you doing?" Jessica had just arrived, along with her parents.

She enfolded me in a tight hug while I stood, unmoving, as she murmured words intended to comfort me. I hadn't seen her since the day of the search.

I'd been standing behind the police cordon set up where they'd dragged Colby out of the pond, when Jessica ran up to me. My gaze travelled up and down the length of the body stretched out on the snowy bank, taking in the bleached, wrinkled hands, the split lip and bruised, scraped face, the swollen, broken nose, looking for some sign of Colby. But though the plaid shirt and jeans were his, though the hair was his exact shade and the height was right, there was nothing of the boy I loved in that pale, waxy figure. Instead of the presence of Colby, there was only a deep absence that echoed the cold emptiness inside of me.

I still felt like that. Numb. Too frozen on the inside to return Jessica's embrace.

She let go of me and peered into my eyes. "Why haven't you answered my texts or called me back?"

I shrugged. How to explain?

The sight of Jess, even the thought of her or any of the other kids from school, brought back the picnic at Flat Rock, parties under the pier, and sitting together at our school lunch table, laughing at my addiction to peanut butter, bacon and pickle sandwiches. And Colby was in each of those memories. Allowing them back was painful, like my heart and throat were being crushed. I didn't want to remember any of it. Everything before now needed to be blank, as void of details as a layer of newly fallen snow.

I'd spent the last week in my room, crying, desperate for the oblivion of sleep, waking from the horror of nightmares, my thoughts on an endless shuffle of what-ifs and if-onlys. Music — heavy metal, nothing that reminded me of Colby — played loudly through my earbuds had helped deafen the chaos inside my head and my parents' entreaties to "talk."

A bunch of girls from our class arrived at the church and drifted over to Jess and me.

"Hey, Garnet, sorry about Colby," Ashleigh said awkwardly.

"Yeah, sorry. It's so bad," Taylor added.

An invisible line divided them from me. On their side was the world as it had been until a week ago, but minus Colby. I was in a whole other place and so separate from them, we might as well have been strangers. We *were* strangers. I was no longer who I'd been, and they didn't know who I was now — I could see it in their eyes. I didn't want to be with them. Not even Jess. Especially not Jess, who was so entangled in my memories of Colby.

"How's your hand?" she asked, taking my hand in her gloved one.

I pulled it back. "Why don't you go inside, where it's warm? I'd rather be alone, right now." My voice sounded flat and brusque.

Jessica cast me a wounded look, but I didn't feel bad. I didn't feel much of anything.

Nose dripping from the cold, I stayed outside, staring up at the blue sky slashed by contrails, listening to the melancholy notes of an organ drifting out of the church. Standing beside the open doors with a clipboard in hand, Jessica's mother loudly asked each new arrival to sign up for a spot on her schedule of meals to be made for the Beaumont family.

"We need to continue giving them our full support at this very difficult time," she repeated between exclamations of delight at promised deliveries of baked lasagna and meatloaf. Doc Armstrong must have been inside, keeping warm.

Eventually my father came out to fetch me. "They're starting, Garnet."

I trudged up the steps, took the white rose handed to me by the usher at the door, and walked down the aisle. The rose stem was bare of thorns, which struck me as all wrong. They should have left the thorns and lopped off the bloom. Front and center on a table ahead, standing in a pool of the roses, was a large, framed photograph of Colby. He was smiling into the camera, his eyes alight with life and joy. He looked ready to grab hold of life by the feet, turn it upside down, and shake the riches out of it. Beside the photograph stood a small marble urn.

My feet faltered. My breath wheezed out as if I'd been punched in the gut. So that was Colby? That small container of ashes was all that remained of him. He was gone. No more smiling eyes, no laughter. No hands around my waist or lips touching mine. No more dreams of righting wrongs, or persuading me to stay in Pitchford. Whatever he'd ever thought, hoped, felt or experienced was gone now, burned into nothingness. Smoke on the air.

Never again, I vowed. I will never allow myself to be hurt like this again.

My father's hand at my elbow urged me forward. I put a lid on my horror and desolation and pushed down hard to seal it inside of me. At the altar, I dropped the rose on the others scattered there. What were they for, what was it supposed to mean? And how could he have been cremated already? The whole scene felt surreal; Christmas decorations still hung from windows and pillars, and a festive red-and-green floral arrangement had been shoved into a corner to make way for the white funeral wreath.

I turned my back on the ashes and petals and went to Colby's family, who were seated in the front pew. Cassie, her shoulders shaking with her sobs, had her head in Vanessa's lap. Sitting on the other side of Vanessa, Mrs. Beaumont cried silently. Tears leaked out of her eyes, trickled unchecked down her cheeks and dripped down to form wet patches on her gray dress. Vanessa, her own eyes red and puffy, wiped her mother's tears with a tissue and stroked Cassie's head. Colby's father sat unmoving and expressionless beside his wife, staring straight ahead. In the row behind, Roger Beaumont leaned forward to lay a hand on his brother's shoulder and gave it a squeeze, as if transfusing strength into that shell of a man.

I took Mrs. Beaumont's hand — cold and limp — and murmured my condolences. My voice was toneless, my face felt wooden, my eyes were dry. I repeated a variation of the same inadequate words to each member of the family. *Sorry, sorry, sorry.* If you repeat a word enough times, it loses all meaning, becomes a mere collection of letters. *Sorry.*

Mr. Beaumont nodded numbly, but the rest didn't respond. Was I bringing back painful memories for them as Jessica had for me? I left them to their grief and went to sit with my parents.

The minister greeted the congregation, prayed and asked us to rise for the singing of the first hymn. Despite my mother's disapproving tuts, and my father's reproachful look, I stayed seated and stonily silent. Amazing Grace? Nothing about Colby's death was amazing, and there was no evidence of grace. After the hymn, the minister started talking. Odd phrases caught my ear — "so short a time" and "meet again in the hereafter" and "the comfort of God's mercy and everlasting love." All lies. Colby was gone, and he'd taken the best of me with him.

I looked around the church while the minister droned on, recognizing the faces of the searchers — those who'd checked the streets, the yards, the woods and the pond until they'd gotten the result no one wanted. Mrs. Armstrong sat erect, perhaps ready to bolt for the door the minute the service ended to catch any delinquents who hadn't yet volunteered offerings of tuna casserole. Beside her, Doc Armstrong had nodded off. Chief Turner sat in the row in front of us, sucking his teeth. Every few minutes he shook his head, as if again rejecting the reality of the tragedy that had happened in his little town, on his watch.

It seemed like most of Pitchford High was here, including the principal and several of the teachers. Jessica sat near the back with the girls from earlier, while Judy Burns had her head on Pete Dillon's shoulder and was weeping loudly. Pete, wearing an ugly tie that he'd surely borrowed from his father, tugged at the tight collar of his shirt. By the look on his face, he'd rather have been anywhere but at that service. Yeah, join the club, buddy. Vanessa's boyfriend, Ryan Jackson, stood at the door, feet apart, hands behind his back. He was wearing his police uniform and surveying the assembly of town folk with a keen gaze.

For the first time, I registered that not only was Colby dead — possibly murdered — but that someone in this very congregation might have killed him. Someone had beaten him badly, and they might even have held him under that cold black water until he drowned. I studied the faces around me — some crumpled in sadness, some impassive, a few frowning.

Did you do it? Did *you?*

I'd done it. Or, at least, I was the reason it had been done to him. Colby had left the Tuppenny Tavern at ten o'clock after having dinner there with his father and uncle, but he'd refused a ride home, saying he needed to have an important conversation with someone. That someone was me. He'd been headed to my house, and on the way, he'd died. Or been killed.

I fiddled with the dressing covering the cut on my left palm, peeling it back, peering at the angry red gash beneath. I'd refused to let my dad take me to get stitches. Somehow this raw wound connected me to Colby's wounds, and I wanted to be like him. I wanted to be with him.

After another monotonous hymn, Colby's father got up to do the eulogy. His face was white, his lips gray, and he looked gutted, like someone had taken a sharp spoon and hollowed out the heart of him. Sighing, he took his place behind the podium up front and lifted a piece of paper like it was the heaviest thing in the world.

He cleared his throat. "Thank you for coming. Bridget and I …"

His voice petered out as he stared out at us and then looked down at his notes in a puzzled way. He turned the paper around and upside down, seeming utterly bewildered.

"I– Bridget and I…" he began again, and then stopped.

Roger Beaumont made his way out of the pew and down the aisle, put an arm around his brother's shoulder and led him back to his seat. He took Colby's father's place at the podium and began eulogizing his nephew as a fine man, lauding his sporting and academic accomplishments, and speculating about what a magnificent leader of the family business Colby would have made.

It was my turn to be bewildered. Who was he talking about? Not the Colby I'd known and loved. He was talking about

Colby's achievements, but he should have been talking about Colby's nature. His strong sense of justice. His kind and generous heart.

One summer, when I was about eleven or twelve years old, I'd gone down to the pier at Plover Pond to swim. Colby Beaumont had been there with a group of other boys, doing dive-bombs off the end of the pier, dunking each other in the water while they yelled insults. They ignored me; I still lacked the budding boobs and curves which would one day draw their interest. Colby, hair slick and skin tanned the color of a glossy hazelnut shell, was performing graceful backflips off the pier. The way he balanced on the balls of his feet, heels off the edge, then rose up on his toes and paused for a moment, muscles tensed, before bending his knees and flinging himself backward in a flexed ball that cannoned into the water — I could've watched him all day.

When I tried to get a turn at the end of the pier, the other boys jostled me aside.

"Get lost, shrimp," one said. The name stuck for years.

But Colby, glistening wet with drops on the ends of his lashes, called them on it. "Let her have a turn."

"Thanks," I told him. And then, because I would have regretted it if I hadn't, I asked, "Will you teach me how to do a backflip?"

"Sure, if you teach me how to dive. You know how to dive?"

I nodded eagerly, glad I could teach him something, too.

Later, of course, I realized that he was just being kind. Of course he knew how to dive. He just didn't want me to feel he was doing an annoying girl a favor out of pity. *That* was Colby

— kind, thoughtful, fair. I think it was on that day, repeatedly doing untidy, sprawling flips into the water and teaching Colby to dive when he already knew how, that I fell in love with him.

In the church, Roger Beaumont was still going on about the other Colby. I became aware that my finger was stinging. I saw I'd bitten it down to beyond the start of the nail bed, exposing raw pink flesh. Suddenly, I couldn't stand being inside that coffin of a church any longer. I stood up and walked out, past Mrs. Armstrong's disapproving face, past Pete and Judy and Brandon, past Jessica, now whispering into Ashleigh's ear. At the exit, Officer Jackson stepped aside to let me pass, and the door closed behind me with a faint creak.

Outside, the air was brisk and smoky with the scent of log fires. I stretched my sleeves over my hands and folded my arms, tucking my hands under my armpits. I was staring at the distant ridge of blue mountains, debating whether to wait for my parents or to start walking home through the cold, when someone called my name. Blunt was standing in the lee of the stairs, smoking. I joined him and asked for a drag.

"Didn't know you smoked," he said.

"I don't."

I drew in a deep breath, rejoicing in the almost-pain of the smoke inside my lungs, coughing out the white mist, visible proof that I was still alive, even though I felt dead.

"Would you like something stronger?"

"Dealing at Colby's funeral, Blunt? Really?"

He blinked his bloodshot eyes and frowned at me. "No, man. I wasn't going to ask you to *pay*. I was offering you something to dull the pain. To, like, switch off feeling, you know?"

"I think I'm capable of switching it off on my own, thanks," I said.

And right at that moment, I did.

17

NOW
Tuesday December 19, 2017

The photograph of Colby on the landing wall held me frozen, pulling me in, tugging me back. For so long I'd kept a lid on the past and a tight rein on the present. Keeping my distance, keeping my head. But it was all bubbling up and coming out now.

My eyes slid to the collage of Beaumont family pictures beside and around it: the family gathered on the porch of their vacation home at Oak Bluffs, in Martha's Vineyard, and another of them packing suitcases into a car outside the old house in town; pics of the kids — a gap-toothed Colby on his first day of school, Cassie dressed in a Princess Leia Halloween costume, Vanessa in graduation cap and gown; an old wedding photo of Philip and Bridget Beaumont, and one of them standing on either side of an adult Vanessa, who was cradling a red-faced baby in a lace christening gown.

"Garnet?" Bridget was waiting outside a door at the end of the hallway.

"Yeah, right with you."

Bridget opened the door and peeped inside. "Oh, good — you're awake. There's a visitor to see you, Cassie." To me she added, "You two can visit together, while I go get the box of Colby's things."

Knowing that I wouldn't like what I was about to see, I hesitated a moment, then almost stumbled into the room. It felt like a hand on the base of my spine had urged me forward, but I'd surely imagined that.

Cassie was worse than I'd expected. Much worse. She looked as fragile as a dried fall leaf, and much younger than her twenty-odd years. Her cheekbones were sharp arcs in her sallow face, and below puffy lids, the whites of her eyes were yellow.

A deep wave of sadness swept through me.

Regret. Fighting. Love.

Old memories flickered behind my eyes — Cassie alone on a swing hanging from the sugar maple in the backyard, Cassie tearing tufts off a whirl of blue cotton candy, Cassie denying she'd raided my room again.

No, those were Colby's memories, not mine. Had he told me about them? Must have.

I stepped closer to the bed. "Hey, Cassie."

She looked confused for a moment.

"It's me, Garnet McGee. Colby's old—"

"Girlfriend. Yeah, I remember," she said in a hoarse voice. "How're you doing?"

"Better than you, kid. I've got to say, you look like shit."

She grinned at that. "Always were a straight-talker. What happened to your fingers?"

"It's a long story."

The table beside her bed was topped with a forest of pill bottles, tonics, vitamins, supplements, a glass of water — Beaumont Brothers, no doubt — and a small vase of purple, pink and red sweet-peas.

"Enough medicine for you?" I asked.

"If you shake me, I rattle."

"And sweet peas in midwinter? Impressive."

"Mom got them for me specially. I'm guessing she doesn't think I'll see another spring."

Unfair!

I was seized with an urge to bellow my rage and punch the wall until my knuckles bled, only I wasn't the sort of person who bellowed and punched. I sat on the edge of her bed and took her hand in mine. It was cold. Again, I felt that surge of helpless fury and misery.

"I'm so sorry, kiddo," I said. "This is ... there are no words for what this is."

"Yeah. Someone needs to invent stronger curse words."

"Can I get you anything, do anything for you?"

"Could you scratch my back? I itch all over and I can't reach."

I eased her forward off the pillows and gently scratched, aware of ribs and vertebrae beneath my tender fingers.

"Thanks," she sighed and lay back. "So, you've come back?"

"Hell, no. I'm just visiting."

"After all this time?"

I gave her hand a remorseful squeeze. "I'm sorry, I should have visited sooner. I'm a coward."

"So why now?"

"My mother's closing up her shop and needs help clearing it out."

"Tell her to cast a spell or summon the fairies for me." Cassie's soft laugh caught in her throat and became a rough cough.

I passed her the glass of water, and she took a sip. Letting her catch her breath, I gave her the low-down on my life in Boston, my struggles to finish my studies.

"When you qualify, come practice here," she said. "This town is full of crazies and sad-sacks. You could make a mint."

"What did you want to be, before you got sick?" I asked.

"A scientist."

"I remember! You were always doing experiments with vinegar and baking soda, or throwing matches on pool chlorine, and didn't you have a seriously scientific microscope?"

"No, that was Colby's," she said, and her face was so sad in that moment that I felt I could tell her, at least. It was safe. She'd understand.

"I still miss him so bad, Cassie. More than I can even allow myself to know."

"Me, too. But I'll be seeing him before you," she said, and with a pale flash of her old spirit, stuck her tongue out at me.

"Cheeky monkey."

"And then I'll finally know what happened to him."

"I wish I knew, too."

"Why don't you try to find out, then?"

"Me?"

"Why not?" A spark of enthusiasm lit her eyes. "Do it! The not knowing … it's a killer. I think it killed me, the stress of it.

My mother got this woman in to try to help me. She called herself a faith healer — though, clearly," she said, indicating her thin frame, "she wasn't a very good one. Anyway, she said she was also psychic. She told me that I was 'locked in a limbo of unknowing,' and that maybe Colby was, too. That neither of us could move on or heal until the truth came out."

"Cassie, you know those people all talk pure baloney. Trust me, I'm the daughter of one. I've heard those kinds of predictions all my life. They're always vague and ambiguous; they say nothing definite and only give you false hope. It's all a steaming pile of—"

"But what if it's not?"

There was an expression like panic in her eyes at the thought that Colby might be trapped in some limbo between worlds, and that she might soon be, too. I cursed the charlatan who'd planted the ridiculous fear in such a vulnerable girl.

"Sure, I'll do it," I said. "I'll try to figure out what happened and come tell you, so you can relax, okay?"

"Promise?" she said fiercely, gripping my hand with feeble strength.

"Promise," I said, already regretting my rash commitment.

She demanded I capture her cell number in my phone and, when she was satisfied I had it right, said, "Hey, were your eyes always different colors?"

I shook my head but was spared the necessity of explaining because Bridget stuck her head around the door just then.

"Cassie, I think you should rest now."

"I should be going," I said, suddenly aware of how tired Cassie looked.

"Five more minutes," Cassie begged.

"Okay, but no more than that," her mother said. "See you downstairs, Garnet."

Cassie waited for the sound of her mother's footsteps to recede, then said, "There's something of Colby's I want you to have."

Damn. More stuff to trigger memories.

"You'll need to get it. It's in my closet, on the top shelf, in my old jewelry box."

I rummaged between the sweaters until I found a mauve jewelry box, patterned with silver butterflies. "This one?"

She nodded.

I opened it. A tinny melody from *The Nutcracker* played, while a miniature ballerina in a pink tutu, with a solid blob of gold hair, twirled around on a spring, admiring herself in the mirror set in the lid. A couple of ribboned medals from dance exams nestled in the velvet-lined tray.

I held them up for her inspection. "These?"

"Look underneath, in the bottom section."

I lifted the inner tray and gasped at what lay beneath. "Is this Colby's phone?"

It was the original model iPhone; he'd gotten it as a birthday present that year, when they first came out. I touched the screen with a tentative finger, half expecting it to vanish like my other hallucinations.

"What the hell, Cassie? *You've* had it all these years?" I asked, flabbergasted.

"I *know*. I'm sorry!" she said, and burst into tears.

Immediately I felt bad. This was a dying girl — I couldn't

yell at her, no matter how much I wanted to.

"We all thought it must be at the bottom of the pond."

I picked up the phone, a thrill of excitement pulsing through me. I transferred it to my left hand so that my fingers might even now be covering the places his own had held it. I closed the lid on the ballerina, trapping her in prostrate silence, and shoved the box back on the shelf, then returned to sit by Cassie.

"How?" I asked, as gently as I could.

"I took it, that last night, and hid it. Switched it off so he couldn't call it and find it."

"*Why?*"

"To spite him. He'd accused me of stealing his chemistry set again, and I hadn't. He was always accusing me of taking his stuff. It never occurred to him that it might be Vanessa, or someone else. I wanted to teach him a lesson. I thought it was so funny when he stomped around the house, searching everywhere for it, before he left for that dinner with Dad and Uncle Roger. He came looking for me, of course, but I hid under the bed, and he didn't find me. Then he disappeared, and I felt so guilty and ashamed ... I still do." She wiped her eyes on her sleeve and cleared her throat, looking miserable. "And then Chief Turner came to question each of us, and I was terrified. He said I'd better tell him anything I knew or I'd be in big trouble, and it kind of had the opposite effect on me, you know? I was too scared to say anything about the phone. And the longer I didn't tell, the bigger the secret became, and the harder it was to even think of coming clean. I was sure the cops would stick me in prison if they found out." She gave me a look that pleaded for my understanding. "I was only ten years old, Garnet. I didn't know any better."

"But afterward, when you were older, you didn't think to hand it in then? I mean, it could have information about Colby's last days, might even have a clue as to what had happened to him."

"I knew it was locked and password-protected, so no one would be able to get anything off it. Besides, I figured the cops got all the information from the service provider at the time." She sighed. "Anyway, I'd hidden it away back then and kind of blocked it out of my memory. You shrinks have a name for that?"

"Repression."

"That's the one. For years and years I forgot it even existed. But recently I started going through my stuff, giving some special things away to friends because, you know ... And I found it again, and I didn't know what to do with it. I'd be so relieved to get rid of it. Do you want it?"

"Yes!"

I wanted it alright. Because, unless Colby had changed it, I still knew what his password was.

18

Tuesday December 19, 2017

On the way home from the Beaumonts', my eyes kept straying to the rearview mirror. The box of Colby's stuff sat on the back seat, along with my handbag, which now held his phone. I was impatient to know what information it might contain, but also wary. My casual promise to Cassie to investigate the mystery of her brother's death now felt like a solemn vow — I guessed a deathbed would do that to you. I had no idea how to conduct an investigation, and I couldn't think what I'd be able to discover that had eluded the Pitchford police department for a decade, but Colby's possessions seemed like a good place to start.

I turned on the car radio, but static interference obscured the news bulletin on WBTN-FM. I hit the button to scan through available stations, but each one hissed and crackled. My radio must be on the fritz. Great — just another thing to add to the list of things that had gone wrong since I hit Pitchford's town limits.

Though I'd intended going straight home, I found myself drawn to the pond instead. Without knowing why I was doing it, I pulled into a parking spot near the picnic area at the bandstand, killed the engine, grabbed my bag and parka, and got out of the car.

Plover Pond waited at the bottom of the rise — a still, empty expanse of white so brilliantly reflecting the winter sun that it dazzled my eyes. It should have been beautiful. The only sounds were of passing cars on the road behind me, and the forlorn call of some bird that ought to know better than to be in Vermont in winter. As should I.

A cold quickening in my solar plexus unnerved me. My mind urged me to turn and leave, but the pond had a hook stuck in my gut, and it reeled me in closer and closer still, to the wrongness that was Plover Pond. My breathing shortened and shallowed, and a cold sweat beaded my top lip. I wanted to run away. I needed to get nearer.

I told myself to get a grip. I was merely experiencing some post-traumatic stress — autonomic hyper-arousal, anxiety, distress in response to similar cues — and avoidance of this scene of my trauma would only make the condition worse. I needed to confront it. If Professor Perry was here, he'd tell me to give myself a dose of systematic desensitization.

I forced myself to walk right up to the edge of the water, at about the spot I'd stepped onto the ice three days ago, and waited for flashbacks to hit. Nothing. I made myself run through the memory of what had happened — the walk across the ice, the boy in red, my fall into the water. Dying. But even that didn't set off any flashbacks or send me into a panic attack.

Relieved, and even a little proud of how well I was coping, I gave myself a metaphorical pat on the back. Job done, time to go.

Instead, obeying an irresistible compulsion, I found myself walking along the water's edge in the direction of town. My pace picked up, and soon I was striding, then jogging toward — what? I tripped over a small snow-covered rock, righted myself and gave in to the urge to run flat out.

Get there.

Where? What was happening to me?

When I got to the little bay where the Tuppenny Tavern first came in sight, I stopped abruptly.

Here.

Now what? The banks here were as deserted as the ones at the bandstand had been, the pond just as empty, the growing dusk of the afternoon just as silent. I had no clue what I was doing here. Running through a mental checklist of PTSD symptoms, I concluded that I must just have experienced a fight-or-flight reaction, even though I didn't feel panicky at all. I felt … impatient.

Waiting. Cold. Wind.

The words were in my head, settling like snowflakes into my thoughts. But they weren't my words, or my thoughts.

Dark.

Water. Water.

I stepped right up to the pond where the water's edge peeked out like a liquid petticoat beyond the white frock of ice. A glint of light beneath the water caught my eye. Crouching down on my haunches, I saw it was a stone — purple at one end, fading to the color of frost at the other. I stuck my fingers into the chilly water, plucked the stone out of its muddy resting place, rinsed it, and brought it up close to my eyes.

Night.

Hands pin my arms behind my back. Blows rain down on me. A fist crushes my nose, crashes into my temple. Lights explode in my head. A fist in my stomach fells me like an axed sapling, robs me of air.

Stop. Please. Help!

I crumple onto the sand, spitting blood. The toe of a boot kicks my ribs; I hear the inside crack of snapping bones.

"Enough, man, you'll kill him!"

Dark faces.

I curl into a ball, hands and legs up to protect against the blows. A vicious thud into my hip, another into my lower back. A lightning strike of pain spirals me into darkness.

I wake up, groaning. The taste of copper and fear is in my mouth. Blood smears my vision. Panic fills all of me. So much pain.

Help!

A touch at my neck. Someone bends low over me. I try to flinch away, but I've forgotten how to move. Hands slip under my arms, start dragging me backward over the sand.

They've stopped hitting me. Maybe they'll save me.

Help me.

Icy water against my jeans. Pulling me the wrong way, dragging me into the water!

No. Stop!

Blood in my throat. Cold water. I twist to see who's dragging me.

Too dark. Deeper water. Up to my chest. Every breath hurts. Bursts of pain with every lurching tug deeper. Must get free! I struggle, fight against the dragging grasp. The hands release me! I push myself up onto my hands and knees. Dizzy, wobbly, confused. I must get away. Must crawl out of the water.

A foot stomps onto my back, presses down between my shoulders. Pushes me under the water.

Freezing water on my face pile-drives shock into me. My thoughts clear. Breathe, must breathe! I lift my head. Can't get it above the surface. I'm in too deep. Pressure on my back and shoulders holds me under. My arms flail, try to reach around. Oblivion beckons. Must ... breathe ... Another shove. My face is in the mud. Dark, dark—

"Garnet? Garnet!"

Someone was shaking my shoulder. I sucked in rapid breaths, opened my eyes, and blinked in the sharp daylight, confused and disoriented. I was lying, curled up in a tight ball on the damp sand by the water's edge, with a shape looming over me. Ryan Jackson.

"What happened?" I asked him.

"You tell me."

Drowning. And getting beat up by someone. And ...

More than one.

The words pricked at me, sharp as pins. I blinked hard, trying to clear my head.

"Here, let me help you up. Are you okay?"

No. That was the honest answer. I wasn't okay at all. I was seriously spooked. Because what I just saw and felt — those weren't my memories. They weren't even my imaginings because I had never, not even right after it happened, allowed myself to think about what Colby had experienced when he was attacked. Crazy as it sounded, even to myself — hell, especially to myself — I thought I'd just had a flashback to Colby's death. And I felt sick to my stomach now that I knew how he'd suffered, how filled with fear he'd been in those last moments, how his death had been nothing like my calm descent into light.

Silently reminding myself that I knew nothing of the sort, I dusted sand off my knees and the seat of my pants, buying time to compose myself. Something bizarre and scary was happening to me; I hadn't been right since this man had fished me out of the pond three days previously, and breathed life back into me.

"I had ... flashbacks. Of drowning," I said, omitting the disturbing fact that they weren't flashbacks of *my* drowning. I might have been going crazy, but I wasn't stupid enough to alert the world to that fact.

"Some flashbacks. You were full-on fetal, trembling and moaning. And your eyelids were flickering. Like you were dreaming. Or maybe having a seizure."

"That wasn't a seizure." I might have been confused about a lot of things, but I was clear on that.

"You look like you need a drink. Can I buy you one?" Ryan jerked his chin in the direction of the Tuppenny Tavern.

"Yeah. An Irish coffee would be great."

I was suddenly aware that I was freezing cold, chilled through from the tip of my nose to the very marrow of my bones. My body felt unfamiliar, too. On every step, I expected my broken ribs to protest, my back to ache. I wiped my lips with the back of a hand, checking for blood. Nothing. My head felt like it was stuck inside a clamp and being winched tighter with every step, but that pain felt familiar and thoroughly my own.

"How'd you find me?" I asked as we walked slowly away from the bay, putting yards and minutes between me and those images. And the disorienting sense that I was in someone else's body.

Or that he was in mine.

19

"I was on Pond Road and saw your empty car," Ryan said, tucking his hand under my elbow as we climbed the stairs by the pier. "Figured I should check on you. When I couldn't find you, I followed your tracks in the snow."

"You can't seem to stop helping me," I said.

"You can't seem to stay away from icy water. What's with you and that pond?"

Good question.

The parking lot of the Tuppenny Tavern was filled with SUVs topped with skis and snowboards; the bar was clearly a favorite with the après ski crowd. Ryan held the door open for me, and I entered first, welcoming the enveloping hug of the warmth inside. I found us a small table in a quiet corner, while Ryan went to order our drinks at the bar.

"Extra, extra hot," I called after him.

The interior of the Tuppenny looked like a fresh and clean version of a decorator's idea of a Ye Olde Tudor Inn. Logs crackled and sizzled in a vast stone fireplace, and red velvet cushions topped spindle-legged stools at the bar counter. I'd bet that the paintings of fox hunts and the blackened beams crisscrossing the ceiling above were fake, but the polished brass railings and old saddles hanging on the far wall looked real enough, and the scrubbed wood floor may well have been from another century. I eyed the laminated menu lying on the table, half expecting to see offerings like steak and kidney pie or blood pudding, but there were only the usual burgers, steaks and pizza.

Ryan returned and put my Irish coffee and his chilled longneck down on the table.

"The bartender gave us these on the house, because you saved the Cooper kid." He sat down opposite me and asked, "Feeling better?"

"I'm fine." I was no longer trembling, but I still felt shaken. And as tired as if I'd just run a marathon. I rubbed my temples with my knuckles, trying to massage away the pain behind my eyes, and felt grit under my fingers.

"You've got sand ..."

Ryan brushed my right cheek, sending grains sprinkling onto the table, then leaned forward and studied me intently for several long moments with slate-gray eyes. My mother was right about one thing — he was attractive.

"Your eyes," he said. "I don't think they used to be different colors."

"It's a recent development."

"It's ... uncanny."

I broke contact with his gaze, took a sip of the whiskey-laced coffee and frowned.

"Not hot enough?"

For once, it was. But I found myself not enjoying the taste.

"May I?" I reached for his beer.

"Be my guest."

I swallowed half the bottle before pausing to catch a breath and give a satisfied sigh. I only just curbed my urge to burp.

Ryan grinned. He lifted the cup of coffee, clinked it against my bottle, and took a small sip. Making a *not-half-bad* kind of expression, he resumed his unsettling perusal of me. "And no lingering problems after your dip in the pond the other day?"

I downed most of the rest of the beer and signaled a waitress to bring me another before I spoke. "I saw your appeal for information in *The Bugle*, in that commemorative piece about Colby Beaumont. Did anything come in?"

"Nope." He sipped his coffee, checked his top lip for cream. "Not that we really expected anything. That case is as cold as Plover Pond."

"You never discovered anything more, never got any tips that could help solve it?"

"Not a peep. And we looked, believe me. Especially with Vanessa Beaumont breathing down our necks."

"She kept your feet to the fire?"

"Yeah, especially in the first few years. She still calls every sixteenth of December to check if there's been any progress. But the case file is this thick" — he held his thumb and forefinger a couple of inches apart — "and full of nothing."

The waitress delivered my beer. I waited until she left before asking Ryan, "Bottom line?"

"Colby Beaumont, age eighteen, died by drowning after

having sustained a serious assault at the hands of a person or persons unknown—"

"Person*s*," I said. *More than one.*

"That was never established. According to the Medical Examiner's report, it could have been done by one person."

I gestured for him to continue.

"And occurring at a location unknown."

"At the pond," I said. "In that little bay."

It wasn't a question, but he replied as if it was. "Probably, yeah, given that's the part of the pond where he was found, and the medical examiner concluded the assault occurred shortly before death. Plus, forensics found a tooth there — one of his."

Noticing the wince I tried to hide by taking a swallow of beer, Ryan said, "Let's talk about something else. You don't want to hear this."

"I do," I said fiercely.

"Okay, then. Following the beating, Colby either made his way into the pond where he drowned, or he was taken there and drowned by the said person or persons unknown. His body was recovered three days later, and the responsible party has never been identified."

I'd lost another Band-Aid in my pondside incident, and now I picked at the label on my beer bottle with what remained of the exposed nail. "Did you have any suspects?"

"Back then? Sure. Well, 'suspects' may be overstating it. We interviewed some persons of interest, but nothing ever panned out into anything solid. Over the years it just got older and colder."

"Who?"

"What?" he asked.

"Who were these people of interest? And what made you interview them?"

"We did a thorough job. They either lacked motive, or opportunity, or both."

"*Who?*" I pressed.

He swallowed the last of his coffee, looked into the bottom of the mug as if reading tea leaves, and then said, "We looked at the Dillon boy."

I leaned forward at this unexpected information. "Pete Dillon? Why?"

"There was some gossip at the time about Colby and Dillon's girlfriend, Judy Burns."

"Well, Colby and Judy *were* an item for a while, but they'd been over for" — I did a rapid calculation — "around eight months by the time he died."

"You were dating him at the time."

"I was," I confirmed, ignoring the ache that always accompanied that thought. "And Judy had been dating Pete for a while already."

"Yeah, so no motive," Ryan said. "Unless …"

"Unless?"

"Unless Colby was seeing her again, on the side? She denied it when we questioned her, but people lie, so maybe—"

"No," I said flatly.

"Are you sure?"

"I would have known." Wouldn't I?

"Every couple has its secrets, and its problems."

I nodded, conceding the point. We'd had at least one big

one, but it hadn't been Judy Burns.

"Colby wasn't a cheater."

"You ever think maybe you idealized him?"

I returned my attention to the beer label, repeatedly digging the edge of a nail into it all the way around, leaving a scalloped border.

"We tend to do that, with the dead — idealize them, I mean," Ryan continued. "If we go by statistics, then even if Colby hadn't been killed, chances are that the two of you wouldn't still be together for a happily ever after."

I've never considered that, never wanted to. For me, Colby was frozen in time, and he'd always been perfect. Would we eventually have drifted apart, started fighting about flaws in each other, gone our separate ways? I couldn't imagine it. But then again, I couldn't imagine Colby as a thirty-year-old with maybe a beer paunch and receding hairline like Pete's, snoring in the bed beside me, while I yelled at the kids to shut off their lights and go to sleep already, resentfully contemplating that other life, the one outside of Pitchford, that I'd never explored because I'd been fool enough to marry the first guy I'd slept with.

What do you say, Colby, I thought, *would we have stayed in love?*

Always, forever — the words blossomed in my head, so clear and intense that I startled, knocking over and spilling the remains of my beer.

Oblivious to my inner crazy, Ryan merely tossed a paper napkin on the puddle. "Anyway, he had an alibi."

"What? Who did?"

"Pete Dillon. Judy Burns said he was with her all night."

"Oh. So, who else was a suspect? Sorry, 'person of interest.'"

"I'm going to need another drink to admit to this one. You want one?"

"Better not. I need to drive home, and you never know when a cop might be watching."

"Hah," he laughed, signaling to the waitress to bring him a beer. "Well, one of our crazier suspects was Michelle Armstrong."

I gaped. "Jessica's mother? *Why?*"

"At first we interviewed her routinely as one of Colby's circle of contacts. He'd been working for her at the town clerk's office."

"That's right, he had a summer job there."

"And afterward he worked there most Saturdays."

I nodded. "I remember."

"Did he ever tell you much about it?"

"Not really. I got the sense he didn't much like her — Mrs. Armstrong. But we didn't discuss it in detail."

An image flashed into my mind right then — a big golden cat. A mountain lion?

"See? I told you every couple has secrets," Ryan said, grinning again. He had a dimple — just the one — in his right cheek.

The waitress arrived then, deposited a longneck on the table in front of Ryan with a flirty smile and a flash of cleavage, and then collected my empty bottle. I snatched it back off her tray.

"Not finished," I told her, and resumed my attack on the damp label. "What are you trying to say about Michelle Armstrong?" I asked Ryan.

"During the course of our interviews with her and the other staff, we discovered that she was rather *fond* of your boy, Colby."

I let my confusion show on my face.

"Bit of a cougar, is our town clerk," Ryan said.

"A cougar!" Not a mountain lion.

"Yup. *MILFy Michelle*, they called her. I guess even back then Doc Armstrong didn't have the wherewithal to service her engine."

"Are you saying that she and Colby … that they …? No way!"

"Nah. I think maybe she came on to him, though. According to staff, they had a shouting match in her office the day before he died. She said he quit, but maybe she fired him."

Why hadn't Colby told me that?

"So, she was under suspicion because he didn't … welcome her advances?" It sounded like a flimsy motive to me.

Ryan shook his head. "I told you, it wasn't a serious hypothesis. Clearly *she* couldn't have given him that beating."

"She might have hired a couple of thugs," I said crossly, Jessica's mother at an all-time low in my estimation.

"We questioned her thoroughly, but nothing."

"She had an alibi?" I asked.

"Not really. She said she was home with her husband, but that he was sleeping. Probably passed out." Ryan tilted a thumb to his mouth, as though hitting the bottle hard. "But it was a flimsy motive. If MILFy Michelle went around murdering all the young men who didn't return her favors, this town would be short a score or more of men."

"She put the moves on you, too!" I said, amused.

"Oh, yeah. If it wears pants, she wants in 'em."

It had always been a bit of a joke around town how friendly Jessica's mother had been to young men, but I'd never suspected she'd come on to *teenagers*. On to Colby.

I tore the wet label off the beer bottle. Irritated that it hadn't come off in one piece, I grabbed a knife from the canteen of flatware on the table and scraped at the narrow strip left adhering to a line of glue.

"Who else?"

"Why do you want me to tell you about who we already know *didn't* do it?"

"Humor me, okay?"

Ryan took a long swallow of his beer. "Chief Turner questioned Colby's family — you always have to. And, of course, I knew them personally. They seemed a normal-enough bunch. No abuse or anything like that, no motive to kill their son. And his parents were absolutely devastated by the loss. Still are, I reckon."

"Yeah, I saw his mother and younger sister today."

"Cassie? How's she doing?"

"I think she's dying."

Ryan blew a long sigh. "That family has suffered more than any family should have to."

I pushed the bottle, now satisfyingly clear of any remnants of label, away from me. "So, did you identify anyone else who may have wanted to assault and murder him?"

"Nope. We couldn't find anyone apart from the Dillon boy and Michelle Armstrong who had a bad word to say about him. He was a good kid."

"Yeah." I cleared my throat, trying to dislodge the frog stuck there, and signaled for another beer.

"Chief Turner figured it for a robbery gone wrong, because Colby's wallet, laptop and cell phone were missing, but it turned out he hadn't taken his wallet with him — we found it in a drawer in his bedroom when we searched there a couple of days later. We never did find the cellphone, though, or his laptop."

For an instant, I considered telling Ryan that the phone was, right at that moment, in my handbag, but I held my tongue. I planned to hand it over to Ryan — of course I did — but I wanted to check it out myself first. No doubt once the police had it, I wouldn't see it again.

The waitress brought my beer and placed a bowl of peanuts close to Ryan. He immediately scooped up a small handful and tossed them into his mouth.

I wrinkled my nose in disgust. "You really shouldn't eat those. Don't you know that studies have shown they're full of urine and bacteria from all the unwashed hands dipping in and out?"

"I like to keep my immune system primed and fit by inoculating it with germs regularly."

I couldn't tell if he was being serious or not. I said, "If Turner thought it was a botched robbery, what was *your* theory?"

"Did you know that there was a serial killer operating in New England at the time?"

I tucked my chin back in surprise.

"It took us a while to link the deaths, to see the pattern,

because he used different M.O.'s — stabbings, slitting the vic's throat — plus, he killed in different towns across a few states. In Vermont at Montpelier and Manchester, and in Concord and Meredith in New Hampshire. There was even one in Maine, if I remember right. Eventually some special unit at the FBI got on it and connected the dots. Based on the location of where the victims' bodies were found, they did some geographical profiling and predicted the unsub probably lived in Vermont."

"The 'unsub'?"

"Unknown subject — the suspect. Back then, I thought Colby might have been one of the killer's victims."

"Did the FBI do a profile of the suspect?"

"It was very vague and generic — they invariably are. A load of crap often as not."

I looked at him, waiting.

"White male or males — they said it was most likely a single operator but couldn't one hundred percent exclude a pair — probably between twenty-five and forty-five, but with a margin of error of ten years on either side. See? Vague. It could have applied to most of the men in this town, including me."

Including my father, I realized, and those of my friends — they would all have been in that age range.

"Oh, and probably employed in his own business, with a reason to travel around a lot — like maybe a trucker or sales rep," Ryan added.

"If the victims were all murdered in different places and in different ways, what made the FBI think the deaths were connected?"

"They were all beaten badly before being killed. And they were all young men around Colby's age. The victims were gay, so we figured it was either some homophobic freak taking out what he saw as deviants, or that the killer himself was gay. That he picked up these boys and then got his kicks killing them."

"Colby wasn't gay," I pointed out.

"No, but he sure was pretty. Say the perp was out cruising that night. He sees Colby strolling along alone, thinks maybe he's looking to be picked up, so he stops and offers a ride. A storm was coming in, remember? The temperature was dropping fast. Maybe Colby accepts the offer, thinking that's all it is, and then when things turn sexual, he refuses. The perp feels rejected and enraged, and beats him unconscious."

I remember that darkness blossoming across my — no, *Colby's* — field of vision.

"And then dragged him into the water and drowned him, or Colby could've crawled there himself in his confusion," Ryan said. "That's what I thought at the time, anyway."

"And now?"

"Now, I think it's unlikely it was the serial killer. His M.O. was to beat his victims, then kill using a knife, so why would he drown this one? Besides, an assault like I described would've happened in his car. And it's a long way between the side of the road and the pond — too far, I reckon, to carry the deadweight of an unconscious eighteen-year-old male. We checked, once the snow had melted, and found no drag marks from the road to the water. Anyway, it's all moot," Ryan continued. "At the time, I sent all the details through to the FBI, and they ruled out the possibility of it belonging to their serial killer case."

I took a sip of beer. "Did they ever solve those murders, find the murderer?"

"No, but that's not unusual. Often, serial killers don't have a clear motive for killing *this* particular person, rather than someone else like him. The victim is just there, at the wrong place and wrong time — the *type* of victim might be carefully chosen, but the specific identity of the victim is often random. That makes it hard to trace a connection between victim and killer."

"So, he's just gone on murdering young men all this time?"

"Nope. The murders stopped the year after Colby's death."

"Could it have been someone in this town who quit when the heat got too much?"

Ryan looked unconvinced by my theory. "There would have been other — probably more likely — reasons."

"Like what?"

He shrugged. "A bunch of things. Maybe the perp got arrested for auto theft or assault or rape, got sent to prison, but never confessed to his other crimes. Or he dropped dead of a heart attack, or moved to Mexico, or hit his late fifties — that's like the male menopause for serial killers."

I knew that from my psychopathology courses. Increasing age brings infirmity and a drop in testosterone levels, leading to decreased aggression. Violent assaults and murders tend not to be an old man's crimes.

I swept the scattered bits of beer label up into a small mound while I thought back to my experience at the pond that afternoon.

More than one.

"Just to double check, Colby's attack — could it have been more than one person?"

"The medical examiner said the marks on his body were 'not inconsistent' with him being restrained by one person and beaten by another, so, yeah, we considered that as a possibility at the time. What makes *you* ask that, though?"

"Just a feeling," I said.

20

By the time my parents and I sat down to dinner that night, I was utterly exhausted. I wanted sleep much more than I wanted my mother's honey-baked chicken, and had little patience for her rambling explanation of how she thought she'd rather not close Crystals, Candles and Curiosities after all.

Seeing me roll my eyes and take a breath to argue, my father quickly asked about my day. I updated them on my sad visit to the Beaumonts.

"I feel for that poor woman," said Dad.

"I'll light a candle and say a quick novena to St. Raphael. He's the patron saint of healing," my mother said.

I shoved chicken into my mouth and refrained from pointing out that Raphael was not a saint, that Mom wasn't a Catholic, and that as far as I understood, novenas took nine days.

"Bridget has invited us to dinner on Christmas Eve."

"How lovely! I'll call her later and tell her we're coming."

"Where were you this afternoon?" Dad asked.

"I had a drink with Ryan Jackson in the Tuppenny." I had no intention of expanding on the nature of our conversation, or what had happened before, at the pond, while Mom was present.

"Some folk complained that he was too young to be police chief, but he's good. Better than Frank Turner ever was," Dad said.

"And he's handsome and single," Mom added.

I dropped my knife and fork onto my plate. "I think I'm ready for bed."

I packed the dishwasher while Dad made three cups of chamomile tea at Mom's instruction. Then she shooed us out of the kitchen, saying she had some cleaning to do, though how she planned to do it while on crutches, I didn't know and didn't ask. In the living room, I flopped onto the couch with a deep sigh.

Dad placed the tray of tea cups on the low table in front of me. "You look tired, kiddo."

"It's been a long day. And a strange one."

"How so?"

"A bunch of things. My eyes are getting more and more different. I needed to throw up this morning, but as soon as I ran to the bathroom, the nausea vanished. I keep—" I'd been about to say, "hearing words in my mind," but stopped myself. That sounded simply too crazy. Besides, I didn't precisely *hear* them. It was more like I felt them. They were just *there* — present and intense, like pebbles dropped into a pond.

"I have words coming to mind over and over again," I said. Electing not to mention the assorted strangenesses at the Beaumont house, I added, "And at the pond this afternoon, I felt ... *compelled* to walk down to the water. And then I saw these violent flashes. It felt like I was drowning. Ryan Jackson found me lying near the water, twitching and groaning."

"I'm no shrink — that's your bailiwick — but it sounds like flashbacks to me," Dad said.

I picked up my cup and took a sip of the hot, fragrant tea. "Okay, yes. Only ..." I hesitated, but I needed to tell someone. Needed to hear a reassurance that I wasn't losing my mind. "The thing is, Dad, they weren't *my* flashbacks. I mean, the images and sensations weren't of me, of when *I* drowned. I think ... I think they were Colby's — of the attack on *him*, and *his* death."

A gasp from the doorway let me know that my mother had overheard me. Crap.

My father merely stared at me, a worried expression on his face, but my mother, crutches wedged under her arms, clapped her hands like a delighted child presented with a gift-wrapped birthday present.

"You're getting messages from the other side of the veil, because you've been there now," she said, eyes round with excitement as my father helped her into a chair and handed her a cup of tea.

I rolled my eyes. "The other side of the veil, really?"

"This happens, you know! People who have NDEs often suddenly develop their psychic powers," she continued, undeterred. "Or is it mediumship you've been gifted with?"

"I'm certain I have neither — because they don't *ex-iissst!*" I almost sang the last word, and then, in spite of myself, asked, "What's an NDE?"

"A near-death experience! Haven't you studied the phenomenon in your courses?"

"No."

"What else have you noticed?" she continued, undeterred. "Electrical disturbances? Strange reactions from animals? Heightened emotions, sensitivity to light and sound, a drop in temperature or cool breeze in a closed room?"

I forced myself to keep a blank face, but my staying silent must have tipped Mom off, because she exclaimed, "You *have*, haven't you?"

"I think maybe I have a concussion," I said, and began running the edge of a fingernail over my lower incisors, searching a rough edge I could tear off. Pity I hadn't lost this habit in the pond.

"Well, *I* think you're finally in contact with your *Gift*." She said it like that, as though the word took a capital letter. "You're developing your psychic abilities."

"That's bullshit. I don't have psychic abilities." What was I saying? "*Nobody* has psychic abilities."

"Garnet," my father said, a pleading note in his voice. He must be as tired of these arguments as I was.

My mother smiled at me in an infuriatingly smug way. "The truth exists whether you believe in it or not, Garnet. The world isn't limited to what you can see and measure. People once thought x-rays and infrared light and auras didn't exist, but they do!"

My dad groaned. "Not this debate, *again*."

"You watch. I predict we'll see a full blooming of your latent abilities," Mom said.

I snorted. "*What* latent abilities?"

"You were born in the caul," she said, with the air of someone delivering an argument-clincher.

"Born in the caul? What the hell is that?"

"It's when the baby comes out with the membrane covering its face."

"Oh. Well, I'm sure that's perfectly normal. It probably happens all the time."

"No, it doesn't. Caul-bearers are *very* rare, and very lucky. I knew from the moment I saw you with that membrane that you'd have supernatural abilities. I watched you carefully throughout your childhood."

"You must have been very disappointed then."

"Not at all. You were special from the get-go."

"All children are special, Crystal," Dad said.

"Not in the way Garnet was. Don't you remember how she just *knew* things?"

"*I* know things," Dad said. "For example, that Jeffrey Dahmer killed and dismembered seventeen victims but was found to be legally sane at his trial, and that his father taught him how to bleach and preserve chicken bones! People know things because they hear them, or see them, or read them. It's not a metaphysical mystery." He opened one of his true crime books and ostentatiously tuned out of the conversation.

"Robert John McGee" — my mother always used our full names when she was angry — "you are such a ... a *muggle!*"

That set me laughing, which in turn made Mom become more earnest. Her face grew red.

"It's not a joke. It's real. Even when you were little, you knew what I was thinking before I said it and—"

"Everyone can do that, Mom. When you know someone well, you can tell what they're thinking, and finish their sentences for them. That's not proof of anything."

"*And ...*" — she paused, as if for dramatic effect — "you had a friend no one else could see. When you were about four or five, you played and spoke with a presence called Johnny!"

That, I actually did remember.

"So?" I said. "I had an imaginary friend. What's that got to do with anything?"

"If you *knew* anything about anything important," she said, waving a hand to dismiss the entire field of psychology and anything else I may have learned in my life, "you'd know that 'imaginary' friends are actually *spirit guides!*"

Dad lifted his book high enough to block us out of his line of vision and muttered something that sounded like, "Thirty-five years!"

"No, they are not spirit guides," I said to my mother. "They're fantasy companions invented by imaginative children, from a desire to have a playmate. It's not an uncommon phenomenon, especially for only children. I had no brothers or sisters, and I did have an active imagination."

And a self-serving desire to score two ice creams when the truck came around, and I conned our neighbor Mrs. Ellis to buy one for me and one for "my friend Johnny in the back yard."

"I'd often walk in on you chatting away to him, laughing or nodding. Maybe he's back!"

"Of course," I replied. "He said he would be."

"He did?" she asked, in a thrilled voice.

"He did. He said, 'I'll be back,'" I said, in perfect imitation of Arnold Schwarzenegger's Terminator.

Dad's shoulders shook. He was sniggering behind his book, but Mom was overjoyed.

"There you are then," she said. "A prophecy fulfilled."

Common sense was a flower that didn't grow in my mother's garden. She never listened to reason, and logic may as well have resided on a different planet for all the notice she took of it. Come to think of it, she'd probably have given it more credence if it came from the mouth of an alien. How was it possible that half my genetic makeup came from her, that I'd come out of her womb — apparently dragging a membranous bit of her with me?

"I thought you said you had some cleaning to do," I reminded her.

"I was so excited, I got distracted! I'd forget my own head if it wasn't bolted on," she said, making her clumsy way back to the kitchen.

"You shouldn't tease her; it only makes it worse," Dad chided me.

"It couldn't possibly be worse."

"Now, about your symptoms, kiddo."

I yawned widely. "Yeah?"

"Don't you know someone at the university you could consult? Find out what might be happening with you? You might discover that this is completely normal for someone who's been through what you have."

At least I had one sane parent. "That's a good idea. I'll call my supervisor first thing tomorrow. Right now, I need my bed."

"Sleep tight, don't let the bugs bite. Or the nightmares!"

I kissed him on the forehead and left him to his killers. Just then my mother came into the hall, awkwardly holding a plastic bucket that banged against her crutches, sloshing water over the sides with every step.

I quickly took the bucket before she could slip and break the other ankle.

"Thank you, dear."

Piled in the bottom of the bucket was a small mountain of stones of different shapes, sizes and colors, covered by water.

"What on earth is this?" I asked

"My crystals, of course." Mom opened the front door and said, "Will you just put them over there, in a clean patch of snow in the moonlight?"

"*Why?*"

"It's a full moon tonight, so I'm bathing them. The light and the distilled water purifies them of negative energy and recharges their healing and metaphysical properties."

I opened my mouth to argue, thought better of it, and put the bucket in the snow outside.

"A little to the left, so they're all in the moonlight. Lovely! Just there is perfect."

"That reminds me," I said as I came back inside, locking the door behind me. "I found a pretty stone down at the pond. I thought you might like it."

"That's very thoughtful, dear. Thank you!"

My mother sounded so surprised at this small kindness that I immediately felt guilty. Really, it wasn't hard to make her happy. I didn't do enough for either of my parents. It wouldn't kill me to call more often, or send the odd bunch of flowers or a bottle of whiskey. Mentally committing to spending lots of time with them while I was in town, and Skyping more regularly once I was back in Boston, I patted the pockets of my parka where it hung on the coat rack in the hall and pulled out the purply-white stone.

As soon as she saw it, my mother sucked in an astonished breath.

"What is it?" I asked. "What's the matter?"

"You picked this up *just* before you had the visions of Colby, didn't you?"

"Maybe," I said warily. "Why?"

"It's a quartz. Amethyst quartz on this side" — she touched the lavender-colored end — "and clear quartz at the other. It's very unusual to find both colors in one piece like this. And *very* significant. Would you like to know why?"

"I'm sure you're about to tell me." I was already regretting giving her the stone.

My mother sat in her chair, lifted a heavy book off the small table beside it, and flipped through the pages until she found what she was looking for.

"Here we go." She passed the book to me, stabbing her forefinger at two entries on a page headed "Quartz."

I read them quickly.

Clear quartz: Quartz amplifies and helps transfer one form of energy into another. For example, it transmutes mechanical forces into the electrical signals of information, enabling psychics to receive communications from the spirit realm more clearly. Use quartz to clarify communication and to intensify the energetic properties of other crystals, so as to channel stronger, clearer vibrations.

Amethyst quartz: This violet quartz also amplifies energy, plus it opens and intensifies intuitive gifts. Use it for protection, to clear and stimulate the third eye of the sixth chakra, and to kindle the crown (seventh) chakra so as to maximize intuition and clairvoyance, and allow a powerful connection to the metaphysical universe.

When amethyst and clear quartz bind in a single crystal, their separate effects are combined and magnified. A good mantra for the possessor of such a stone is: "I trust myself. I see what I need, and what I need to see will come to me."

I didn't believe a word I'd read. So why did I feel so rattled?

Telling myself that any similarities were mere coincidence, I slammed the book closed and handed it back to my mother.

"I think it belongs on the fiction shelf," I said and tried to give her the crystal. "Here."

But she shook her head and closed my hand around the quartz, enfolding it in the old scar in my left palm. "Oh, no, dear. It found *you*. It's yours."

21

My body was exhausted, but my brain was not yet ready for sleep; too many questions and what-ifs bounced around the trampoline walls and floor of my mind. I fired up my laptop, replied to a couple of the most pressing emails and then, hoping to prove my mother wrong, asked Google to give me the lowdown on being born "with the caul." Immediately I discovered that my mother was right about it being a rare event — occurring in only about one in every eighty thousand births.

According to longstanding beliefs in many cultures, being born with the remnants of the amniotic sac covering my face meant I was destined for greatness and good fortune, and would be the lucky possessor of psychic abilities and … immunity from drowning.

Superstition and coincidence, that's all it was. Nothing more.

I killed the crazy caul sites and began researching the

phenomenon of near-death experiences; it wasn't a topic that had ever even been mentioned in my science-heavy psych courses. Although what I read raised more questions than it answered, I must have drifted off eventually, because when I startled awake just after six the next morning, my laptop was on the bed beside me, its screensaver showing me the red sands of a distant desert.

Remnants of my disturbing dreams — vivid enough to be the products of a hallucinogenic trip and featuring a scantily clad Michelle Armstrong, former Chief Frank Turner, and my father wearing a butcher's apron — evaporated like mist in the sun, and I was left with a vague sense of unease. From now on, I'd just take the damn sleeping tablets.

A bleary-eyed glance at my face in the bathroom mirror showed that my eyes were now two distinctly different colors — my right eye was the usual blue, while my left eye was mostly brown. It looked like I was going to be stuck with a permanent reminder of my trip below the ice.

The house was dark and quiet when I stole down to the kitchen in my bathrobe and socks to put on the coffee machine. I stuck two slices of whole grain bread in the toaster and, yawning, thought about the day ahead. Priority number one was to find a charger for Colby's old phone.

I turned my bread over in the toaster and pushed the lever down again — I liked my toast well done and hard enough to crack a tooth — and poured myself a cup of coffee, thinking about where in this house old phone chargers might be stored. Hadn't my father once owned an iPhone?

Under the counter to the right of the fridge was a double-depth drawer that we McGees called "the drawer with the answer to everything" into which were crammed loose odds and ends that might, with luck, include a charger. Rummaging through the contents — most of which were tangled up in the stretched tape of a disemboweled cassette — I found a bottle opener in the shape of a leprechaun; several fridge magnets in the shape of the US states; some papers held together with a binder clip (including a takeout menu from Pitchford's only pizzeria and a pamphlet about the Beaumont Golf Estate); an almost-empty bottle of arnica oil; a coaster from an Irish pub in Montpelier, and a mulch of loose batteries, elastic bands, bamboo chopsticks, tarnished coins, loose keys, corks, and tiny takeout packets of hot sauce and chili salt that I suspected were still from when I'd lived here.

Nestling right at the back of the drawer, under a stack of orphaned Tupperware lids, was a bird's nest of electrical cords. I disentangled these and separated out three phone chargers, and then ran up to my bedroom and tried each of them on Colby's phone. None of them fit. Damn.

Back downstairs I shoved the chargers back into the drawer and then struggled to get the damn thing closed again — the contents seemed eager to make a break for freedom. Perhaps there might be more old chargers in the basement, where Dad kept his electric tools and stuff.

Spreading a thick layer of butter on my hot toast, I sprinkled it with salt and white pepper and took both it and my coffee with me down the stairs that led to the basement and garage. It was freezing down there. My socks were a flimsy barrier against the cold of the cement floor, and my breath made white puffs in the musty air.

The basement light — an unshaded globe dangling from the ceiling — threw sharp shadows across a workbench and shelves untidily stacked with Dad's tools and fishing tackle, and the overflow of Mom's crap from the house. I munched on my toast as I took in the mess. A bundle of dried herbs — "white sage for smudging" according to the label tied to it — lay beside a power drill; dusty porcelain fairies stared blankly at an incomplete set of spanners, and a fist-sized jade Buddha with the lobe of one ear chipped off sat atop a stack of sandpaper.

Two cardboard boxes packed with old magazines teetered precariously at the edge of the workbench, and a pile of Dad's old leather-bound planners, one for each year stretching back to 2005, were wedged on the shelf above.

Dad's narrow workbench was littered with pliers, hand- and hacksaws, screwdrivers, a hammer and other unidentifiable tools that looked like they might belong on a tray of torture instruments. A kitchen stool, fuzzy stuffing escaping a rip in the leather seat, stood beside the workbench, and on the floor underneath it, I spied a couple of large Rubbermaid storage containers. The one closest to me bore a strip of masking tape on which was written, in my father's hand, "electrical".

Bingo.

Gripping the remaining half of my toast between my teeth, I dragged the container out and delved in, but although I found electrical flex, plugs, fuses, spare globes in a dozen different shapes and sizes — though none that looked like replacements for my bathroom mirror light — a snarled string of Christmas lights, and several old TV remote controls, I found not a single phone charger.

Shivering, I sat back on my heels, drank some coffee — already more than halfway cold — and then ferreted through the contents of the other container, which was labeled "miscellaneous." Inside I unearthed several rolls of duct tape, an economy-sized pack of rubber gloves, wrinkled and twisted tubes of superglue, a spray-can of silicone lubricant, a flashlight, a bundle of zip ties of different lengths held together by a thick rubber band perished with age, an old jelly bottle filled with different-sized screws, a padlock and keys, a disposable raincoat, an ancient-looking canister of pepper spray, a roll of black trash bags, a coil of green nylon rope, and a vicious-looking box-cutter. But no phone charger.

I replaced the lid, musing that the contents of Dad's miscellaneous storage box could easily equip a serial killer or two. I laughed out loud at the crazy thought, then stopped abruptly and peered back inside — the hodgepodge of items now appeared sinister. The last bite of toast tasted like sawdust in my suddenly dry mouth. I washed it down with the remains of the cold coffee and chided myself for being ridiculous. I was just spooked by my father's awful books and Ryan's killer theories, that was all. Time to go back upstairs — I wouldn't find anything useful here.

As I shoved the containers back under the workbench, I remembered that the box of Colby's belongings was still in my car. I retrieved it and turned to head back to the kitchen, but with a soft pop, the lightbulb above me went out, stranding me in a darkness so complete, it felt solid. My savage expletives fell into the cold silence like pebbles into a bottomless well. Clutching the box against me with one hand, I stuck my other out ahead of me, groping blindly for obstacles.

I touched a soft, smooth surface which yielded beneath the pressure of my fingertips. Sliding my hand sideways, I felt fluffy softness. Skin and hair! I gave a terrified yelp, then immediately cursed myself for being six kinds of stupid. It was the stool that I'd touched — the leather seat, the fleecy stuffing — nothing more.

Taking tiny steps, I shuffled over to where I thought the stairs must be and, fumbling, eventually found the bannister. I clung on tightly as I climbed. No claws dragged me back, no teeth nipped at my ankles. Of course they didn't.

22

Wednesday December 20, 2017

Back in the brightly lit kitchen, I poured myself another cup of coffee, even though caffeine was probably the last thing my rapidly beating heart needed. I briefly contemplated spiking it with a calming shot of whiskey, resisted the urge, and carried the box of Colby's stuff up to my bedroom, still chiding myself for my silly, childish fears.

Professor Perry had what he called an "open house" every weekday morning between seven-thirty and eight o'clock, when he took unscheduled calls and allowed pop-in visits at his office at the university. I still had fifteen minutes to kill before I could call him and be reassured that I wasn't being visited by the ghost of Colby past, and also — a more likely but equally scary possibility — that I wasn't experiencing the visual and auditory hallucinations and thought delusions consistent with a diagnosis of psychosis. That I wasn't, in other words, either being haunted or going crazy.

I sat cross-legged on my bed, contemplating the box,

wondering what monsters of memory might lurk inside, ready to drag me back into the pain of the past. Taking a deep breath, I opened the lid a fraction and closed it again — Pandora slamming the lid on the box of evils afflicting humanity. Then I gave myself a mental pep talk. *It's just old stuff. Colby's not in his things. You have to do this, so you may as well get it done. Eat the frog. Just do it, already! If you do this, you can have as much chocolate as you want today.*

What finally gave me the motivation to open it was the thought that maybe his old iPhone charger might be in among the contents. I opened the lid again, paused, and sniffed hesitantly. Smelled only stale air, leather and paper. Lying on top of the contents were Colby's old school notebooks for AP Chemistry, English, and World History. What had happened to his notes for the other classes?

I opened his English notebook and stared down at the familiar angular handwriting, tracing a finger up and down the spikes of his capital A's. The first exercise was a descriptive essay on the history of the town of Pitchford — we'd all had to write it in our first week of senior year. This was followed by various fiction pieces, some angsty poems that an objective reader might call hilariously bad, but which brought tears of sadness to my eyes, and a letter to the editor of *The Bugle* urging the law enforcement agencies of Vermont to take a tougher stance in the war against drugs, alleging that incompetence and indifference were allowing the rampant spread of the problem. We'd all had to write a letter to the press and send it to the local newspaper as part of the exercise. *The Bugle* had printed Colby's, but not mine, which, if I remembered correctly, had urged parents and teachers to put more effort into encouraging girls to study STEM subjects.

Jessica's had been a diatribe about the dangers of alcohol and drug abuse, but the spineless editor of *The Bugle* called her mother for permission to publish it. Mrs. Armstrong refused and then tore a strip off her daughter for airing the family's dirty laundry in public. Jessica's mother had always been set on preserving the family's reputation. Between Blunt's drug abuse and her own escapades, it must have been a full-time job.

Colby's English notebook was only half-filled; the last exercise was a review of the movie *Michael Clayton*, dated December thirteenth. Three days later, everything had stopped. One by one, I turned the blank pages, the tangible emptiness of the life unwritten, until I got to the last page. And there it was, in blue ballpoint on the bottom right corner — a pair of interlinked hearts crested with two words in my handwriting: *Always. Forever.*

We'd had a habit of writing miniscule messages to each other on the inside back covers of our notebooks. I was pretty sure that if I still had mine — which I didn't, I'd tossed everything from that year — I'd find the same words inscribed by him in the back of at least one of them. Always and forever. That phrase had been our thing, how we'd signed off texts, what we'd tattooed on our arms in felt tip pens, what we'd promised between heated kisses.

I checked the inside cover of the history notebook and found a Nietzsche quote I'd written there: "There is always some madness in love. But there is also always some reason in madness." I grabbed the last notebook — AP chemistry —

keen to see if I'd written anything there. There were only a couple of blank pages left in this one. It looked like Colby had written his class in the front and then started filling up from the back with his research and experiments for the research project we'd all been so busy with that semester.

The fine hairs on the back of my neck prickled, and once again yellow saturated my vision. Groaning in frustration, I rubbed the heels of my hands hard against my eyes, pushing back the yellow until pinpricks of lights popped behind my eyelids. When the color receded, I checked the inside back cover of the notebook, read the handwritten exchange between the two of us.

Don't go, read Colby's.
Don't stay, read mine.
This is my world.
My world is bigger than this.
Promise you'll come back?
I promise I'll come back for you.

I recalled that exchange, how I'd crossed the fingers of my free hand when I wrote the last line, because although I had truly intended to return, I'd planned that it would be solely to persuade him to join me in leaving forever.

Had Bridget Beaumont kept these particular notebooks, rather than all of them, because of these personal notes? Already cursing myself for being a sentimental fool, and knowing I'd regret it, I set them aside to keep along with a black fountain pen which brought back memories of me buying it, getting Colby's name printed on the side in gold lettering, and giving it to him on his birthday.

Sifting through the pile of stuff left in the box — a jumble of old CD's, paperclipped pay slips from his job at the town clerk's office, swimming goggles, a couple of books, and a worn baseball mitt — I found myself looking into Colby's eyes. The photograph of him, the same one that had been in the church the last time I'd set foot in it, the same one that now hung on the upstairs wall in the Beaumont's new house, was reproduced on the front of a blue leaflet.

Damn. Why would his mother have kept the funeral program? It was nothing but a reminder of Colby's death, of that unspeakable day, and the bleak days on either side of it. I wanted to toss it into the trash can but found I just couldn't. Dropping it onto the detritus of used tissues and candy wrappers would be like admitting it, too, was just worthless trash.

Ah, so that was how it worked, this limbo of hanging onto the relics of the dead. It hurt to keep them, but you couldn't let them go.

I picked up the funeral program, ready to drop it back into the bottom of the box, and at once an image — a series of images — flickered behind my eyes. Jessica, collecting the blue programs left behind on pews, gathering them into a pile and depositing them on the table by the door; her mother roughly shaking Doc Armstrong awake with low imprecations muttered through gritted teeth; Chief Turner, kneeling at the altar, praying; Roger Beaumont helping his dazed brother down the outside stairs of the church; Blunt Armstrong leaning against a wall around the back of the building, passing a baggie to the town's homeless guy; Vanessa, holding her sobbing mother in a tight hug; and Cassie, solemnly walking down the aisle into the bright light outside, her hands carefully cradling the urn of Colby's ashes.

It was happening again. I was "remembering" something I'd never experienced. I couldn't have seen those things — I'd been out of that church and walking home long before the service even ended. I felt dizzy with disorientation and unable to fill my lungs. Either the inside of me was filling up with expanding bubbles of air, or I was teetering on the edge of a panic attack.

I grabbed my phone and called Professor Perry.

"It's Garnet McGee. Do you have a few minutes to talk?"

23

NOW
Wednesday December 20, 2017

"Well, hello there," Professor Perry said, sounding more cheerful than any normal person should at such an early hour. "What's up? Have you reached a decision?"

"A decision?" I said, confused. Then I realized he was talking about me reevaluating my future career choices. Had that discussion occurred only two weeks ago? "Uh, no. A lot has happened since I got here."

I filled him in on my fall and head-bang, and on how I'd apparently drowned in the pond and been brought back to life.

"Good God, that sounds ghastly! Not the part about saving the boy, obviously, that was positively heroic. But what you went through must have been an ordeal. Are you okay?"

Define okay. "The doctors have said I'm fine."

"I can hear an unspoken 'but'."

"Yeah. *But* I've been having some strange … symptoms."

"I'm listening."

"I get these bouts of nausea and exhaustion, and chills that give me goose bumps, and bad headaches all the time."

"That could all be due to concussion."

"One of my eyes — the iris, I mean — has turned brown."

"Bugger me! Anything else?"

I hesitated, reluctant to put my crazy into words.

"Hello? You still there?"

"Okay, so this is going to sound weird," I warned him.

"I'm a shrink. I'm good with weird."

"Right. So ... I've had flashbacks of drowning and dying. And random waves of emotion that aren't related to what's happening at the time."

"Those are bog-standard post-traumatic stress symptoms, Garnet, you know that."

"Yeah, except ... You remember I told you about my boyfriend's death back when I was in high school?"

"I do."

"Well, the flashbacks are of his death, *his* drowning. Not mine."

There was a long silence on the other end of the phone. I could just imagine Perry's expression of surprise and disbelief. I tugged off one of my socks and ran a hand over the underside of my foot, feeling the wrinkles in the skin, the roughness around my heel.

"I had an– an *episode,* I guess you could call it, where I saw him being assaulted," I continued. "But it was as if I *was* him. I could feel the blows on my body, and I heard someone talking in the background, yelling at the attacker to stop."

Perry cleared his throat. "And this isn't something you witnessed at the time?"

"No! No one did. Apart from the attacker, obviously."

More than one.

"Attacker*s*. There was more than one of them," I added, obediently taking direction from the words in my mind.

"But there must have been reports, from the police or in the news? Perhaps you picked up some details that lodged in your subconscious, and now they're bubbling up to the surface?"

"I guess." My fingers picked at the ridge of hard skin between the pads on the ball of my foot, searching for an irregular edge. "But I've also had other memories that aren't mine. Like of things that happened at his funeral after I left. And of his younger sister. I feel a little ..." What — haunted? Accompanied by a presence? Not myself? I settled on a clinical term: "Dissociated."

"That must be distressing," Perry said. "Sorry to ask you this, but I do need to check: have you been taking any drugs?"

"Just painkillers for the headaches. Not even anything that contains codeine."

"And have you had any trauma debriefing?"

"No," I admitted. What could a counselor tell me that I didn't already know? "And another thing, when *I* drowned, that was also some crazy stuff right there. White light, euphoria, floating out of my body — the whole nine yards. What was *that* about? I've always believed, I've always *been sure,* that dying would be merely a lights-out-and-then-nothing kind of experience. But it wasn't like that at all."

"Perhaps not, but neuroscientists have found biological explanations for most of what people claim to undergo in near-death experiences," Perry said. "Should I fill you in on the details?"

"Sure. Hang on a sec while I find some paper, so I can take notes." I got my notebook from my handbag, found a clean page and pressed the nib of the fountain pen down until the ink started flowing. "Right, shoot," I told Perry.

"First off, we know that the fight-or-flight response to impending death causes abnormal functioning of dopamine and a huge release of noradrenaline in the locus coeruleus," Perry said, "Which may account for the sensation of seeing one's life flash before one's eyes."

"I didn't experience that."

"Depletion of blood and oxygen flow to the eye can cause tunnel vision — literally."

"I didn't have that, either."

"How about hallucinations, disorientation and confusion?"

"Now we're cooking."

"Those are also caused by a lack of oxygen in the brain. And that euphoria you mentioned?"

"Yeah?"

"The stressed brain can trigger a rush of endorphins, causing a sense of bliss or peace. And damage to or misfiring in the temporoparietal junction could arguably cause the sensation of being outside your body."

"Right, that makes sense."

I capped the pen and tossed both it and the notebook aside. Perry wasn't telling me anything I hadn't read in my research session the previous night. The neurological explanations were plausible but not conclusive, and there wasn't definitive proof for any of it. From what I'd read, the science didn't always line up with people's near-death experiences. For example, many of the people who described visiting heaven (and sometimes hell — I'd been amazed to discover that nearly a quarter of NDEs were deeply unpleasant experiences), or encountering long-deceased relatives had not been suffering a lack of oxygen at the time.

"Okay," I said. "I'm playing devil's advocate here, so please don't think I've gone over to the dark side, but what about patients revived from death who know what happened while they were supposedly dead — like what music was playing, or what was said in the room?"

I was thinking about an apparently famous case in which the patient recalled that Hotel California had been playing while she was brain dead, a fact later verified by the surgeons working on her.

"Those are probably cases of anesthesia awareness — those patients weren't actually dead, merely heavily sedated but not fully unconscious. It's not an uncommon phenomenon."

His explanation didn't match what I'd read. I began picking at my foot again, trying to tease a shred of tough skin away from the sole with nails bitten down to the quick. Slipping automatically into the habit of a decade ago, I opened the drawer in my bedside table and rummaged through the remains of my teenage essentials until I found what I was looking for — my old pair of tweezers, a tube of Neosporin and a bottle of pink vitamin E oil.

"What about when they've been dead, and I mean verifiably flatline, but have seen things in the room that they *couldn't* have seen from their position on the bed?" I asked Perry. "I think it's called nonphysical veridical perception."

"Ah, you've been doing some research?"

"I have," I admitted. "There's this case where a woman who died in a hospital resuscitation room claimed she floated outside her body and saw a tennis shoe on a third-floor window ledge. Afterward, they found the shoe exactly where she said it was."

Tucking the phone between my ear and shoulder, I bent over my foot, gripped an edge of skin with the tweezers, and pulled steadily down. Peeled off a thin strip. Sighed with relief.

"I'm not familiar with that specific case," Perry was saying, "but you'll probably find there were some errors or inconsistencies in it. These are, after all, the subjective reports of people who *want* to believe, rather than double-blind objective scientific studies. We can't vest too much significance or validity in their so-called 'findings.'"

I tore a page out of the notebook and dropped the shred of skin onto it then began feeling for the next uneven edge of skin, while Perry continued, "I do seem to remember there was a huge and scientifically rigorous study recently where they placed pictures of symbols on specially installed shelves up near the ceilings of operating and emergency rooms, so that supposed NDE experiencers could float up and take a look. And not a single subject reported seeing them."

Cognitive bias — remembering only what agreed with your worldview or what you wanted to believe — didn't just govern oddballs like my mother. Professor Perry, ultra-rational scientist that he was, apparently also had selective memory. Because I'd read up on that very study the night before and discovered that there had been some serious methodological problems, including that the sample size had been so small that any findings were statistically insignificant.

Although the experiment ran for over four years and across fifteen hospitals, and included over two thousand cardiac arrest victims, only three hundred and thirty of those patients survived. Of those, a mere nine individuals claimed to have experienced an NDE, and just two of those described having an out-of-body experience. One was too ill and exhausted to participate in the study, which left a total sample of one single subject. And, as luck would have it, that particular patient had not been treated in one of the hospital rooms with the ceiling-height picture installed, so the whole point of the experiment was never tested. Even so, the patient's account of what had transpired in the three minutes while both his heart and brain were in total flatline matched what was verified to have happened in the room at the time.

Also, having been through the experience myself, I'd put good money on the probability that the experiencers were concerned with other things during the time of their NDE, not floating about the top of the room checking out pictures on shelves. Certainly, *I* hadn't been paying attention to fish or patterns on the surface of the pond ice at the time I'd been dying.

But I didn't tell Perry any of this — I wasn't on a mission to convert him to the reality of NDEs. On the contrary, I wanted *him* to convince *me* that they were merely the glitches of a dying brain.

I picked up the tweezers again.

24

NOW
Wednesday December 20, 2017

I peeled another strip of skin off the sole of my foot and then forced myself to replace the tweezers in the drawer. It would be all too easy to drop back into the deep end of my old habits.

"What really bothers me," I told Perry, "is the uncertainty of it all. Explanations are plausible, but not proven. Connections between brain activity and NDE features are probable, likely, possible, but not definite."

"Garnet, if you become a therapist, you're going to have to get a whole lot more comfortable with ambivalence and uncertainty," Perry said.

"So, we don't know anything for sure?" I challenged. It was infuriating.

"The fact is, we simply don't have enough accurate NDE data to establish definite correlation, let alone causation. And in the absence of proven scientific explanations, phenomena such as pseudoscience, religion and mysticism rush in to fill the information breach."

"You're telling me. You wouldn't believe some of the bizarre stuff people believe."

It seemed to me that near-death survivors were so convinced of the mind-blowing reality of their personal experiences that few felt the need for reductionist scientific explanations. Meanwhile, most scientists regarded the whole field of NDEs as nonsense. They ridiculed any attempts at explanation and denied it was a suitable field for serious enquiry. So, each camp went about believing what they chose, with very few attempting to bridge the gap between faith and evidence.

"But that's always been the path of scientific progress," Perry said. "First there's a mystery, then cultures generate a mystical explanation to account for it, and then science hypothesizes a different truth and eventually proves it, whereupon that becomes the new, commonly held view."

One commonly held view was that one shouldn't use expired medicines, and the tube of Neosporin had kicked the bucket back in 2010. But how bad could antiseptic ointment truly go? Deciding to risk it, I rubbed a little of the cream into the raw strips on the sole of my foot.

"Fortunately," Perry continued, "science is always curious and always advancing. In rat studies, for example, they've identified a sudden spike in brain activity just prior to flatlining, which might explain the vivid sensations and images these people report experiencing. It's arguably—"

Might. Arguably. Again with the inexact, tentative language.

"—just a hyperactive spasm of the brain resulting in sensations which feel hyper-vivid. And then survivors create some order from the chaos of their experience by assigning it meaning. Plus, there's a mass delusion effect because we've all seen movies and TV shows where people die and 'go into the light,'" he said, in a mocking tone. "So, we're primed to experience what you called 'the whole nine yards.' We may even collude in *adding* the visuals because we've been exposed to them in the media."

I didn't tell him that NDEs weren't a modern cultural construct. There were records of what sounded a lot like what I'd experienced dating back to medieval times, or even further back — some of those biblical visions matched modern descriptions of NDEs.

I crumpled the paper holding the skin filaments into a tight ball and lobbed it across my room into my trashcan. Then I opened the bottle of vitamin E oil and sniffed the familiar rose-scented aroma. I squeezed a small puddle into the palm of one hand and massaged it into the sole of my foot. First you scratch it, then you peel it, then you fix it.

"Besides," Perry continued, "people *want* to believe in something more, that they have a spirit, that there's a life beyond death, and that the process of popping their clogs will be somehow mystical and transcendent. When they're brought back to life they need to believe there's a possibility for redemption, for a second chance at living according to a better set of priorities."

I had to admit there was something to that. Since the drowning, I'd felt restless, irritated at many of the trivialities of daily living. Perhaps some of my desire to find out what happened to Colby, for myself and for Cassie, was an attempt to give my survival meaning. It was a shock to discover that, despite what I'd always believed about myself, deep down I also apparently thought I was more than just meat.

"Have you had any other unusual experiences that can't be explained by what we've discussed?" Perry asked.

I wanted to believe the logical explanations he'd given me, so I made no mention of my hair standing on end, cold breezes in sealed rooms, malfunctioning electrics, words and colors blooming in my mind, the strangeness of a clearly terrified old dog growling at me, or the metaphysical meaning of a piece of quartz. I could chalk them up to coincidence, an overactive imagination, and the degenerative effects of age on a dog's brain and senses. And I'd always known my mother's theories on stones — on most things — were complete and utter bullshit.

So, I merely said, "No."

A glint of light off a shiny object in the box of Colby's belongings caught my eye. It was a medal from the only time he'd ever placed first in a swim meet. As I picked it up, a succession of images ghosted through my mind: diving off a board into a pool, cold water, burning muscles, touching the far wall with both hands, a flood of joy, looking down at the medal lying on the pecs of my chest. My wet, hairy, *male* chest.

I dropped the medal as though it burned.

"It's happening again, right now!" I babbled into the phone. "I just picked up a medal Colby won for swimming, and I relived the whole race. What's happening to me? My mother" — I blew out a frustrated breath — "I can't believe I'm even saying this, but my mother, who's a certified kook, says that I've become psychic, and I'm picking up on Colby's vibes or something."

"I see. And do you agree with her?"

"Of course not! But how can I know things I never experienced, or saw, or read about? Your neurological theories may account for what happened in my near-death experience, but they don't explain what's happened since."

He paused for a moment, as if collecting his thoughts. When he spoke, it was in calm, measured tones. "Memory is a funny old thing — notoriously inaccurate and unreliable. It can be bloody hard to tell the difference between what you yourself have truly experienced, and what you've seen in old photos or videos, or even what you've been told, imagined or dreamed. The mind often mixes these up, mistakes one for another. Are you sure these 'memories' are real? Have you checked their accuracy with others?"

"No."

"Is it possible that some of them may be things you've previously been told, and your subconscious has added elaborating pictures or a soundtrack, to the basic facts?"

"I guess."

"For example, were you at that swim meet where Colby won the medal?"

"No, I missed it."

My mother, I recalled, had insisted I help her out in her shop that day. I'd been furious with her for making me sell joss sticks when I could've been supporting Colby.

"But you knew he'd swum and won his race?" Perry said. "And you must've had a good idea of what swim meets looked like in general? Maybe you'd attended some previously or seen him swim on other occasions?"

"Yeah, that's all true."

"From there, it's a short jump to imagining what it must have been like that day. If you imagine it with enough sensory detail, you can fool the brain into thinking it was real. You've heard me say it many times: at its deepest levels, the brain cannot tell the difference between what's real and—"

"—what's sufficiently vividly imagined," I completed the phrase for him.

I knew this. I'd studied it. The phenomenon accounted for why hypnosis worked, and why it felt so *real*; for why we screamed at the movies when the killer raised his chainsaw, even though we knew full well, in our conscious minds, that it was all make-believe. It was how we terrorized ourselves into panic attacks by imagining the humiliation of a failed examination or a flubbed speech.

"So that's what this is? I'm just imagining things, not actually hallucinating?" I asked, feeling relieved.

"I think it's the most likely explanation. Perhaps being back in your home town is bringing it all up for you. Do you think you dealt with your grief thoroughly at the time of your boyfriend's death?"

"Probably not."

Definitely not. I'd shoved it all down into a box of my own labeled "do not open", locked and buried it deep in the mausoleum of me, and never returned home or exhumed the memories again.

"What might have shaken your memory tree?" Perry asked.

"My near drowning, I guess. And probably also visiting Colby's family. They're not doing well."

"How did seeing them again make you feel?"

"Sad. Angry." I popped the cap of the fountain pen and began doodling on the back of my hand. "Guilty."

That surprised me. I hadn't realized I'd been feeling guilty.

"What do you feel guilty about?"

I mulled it over for a few moments. "That I'm alive and he's not. That my family's okay and theirs isn't — my mother has a broken ankle, but Colby's sister is dying of cancer."

"Survivor guilt — it's the pits. Any unfinished business from way back then that may be making you feel guilty in the present?"

"We'd had something important we needed to discuss, Colby and me. I'd asked him to come over so we could talk. That's why he wasn't at home safe with his family. He was out alone, on his way to me. That's why he got killed."

"You have to know that it wasn't your fault, Garnet."

Did I?

"Sure," I said.

"I suspect these symptoms may be your psyche's way of punishing yourself. Your subconscious is creating graphic images of Colby's death, and of the life he no longer has, to remind you of the guilt you feel you deserve."

That made sense. "So, you reckon I don't need to go back to the hospital to get myself checked out?"

"You say the scans were clear? There were no bleeds or other pathological findings?"

"They said it was all normal."

"Give it a couple of weeks to settle down," Perry advised. "Take it easy, get lots of sleep and rest. That's on the physical side. And on the psychological side ..."

I stopped doodling and pricked my ears. "Yeah?"

"Forgive yourself. Do whatever it takes to deal with your guilt and appease that part of you that's accusing and possibly punishing you."

"Okay. So, what do I need to do?"

He chuckled. I should have known better than to ask a shrink for specific answers.

"Only you can know the answer to that, Garnet. Perhaps you already do."

I thanked him and ended the call. Then, feeling like a fool, I closed my eyes and made a deal with myself. *Listen up*, I silently told the supposedly punitive part of me, *I'm going to investigate Colby's death properly. I'm going to find out exactly what happened, and who did it. And then my debt will be paid. I'll have done what I can for you, and you'll need to let me go, okay?*

It didn't escape my notice that while I'd started off speaking to myself, it now felt like I was talking directly to Colby.

I replaced the cap on the pen and read the three words I'd scribbled on the back of my hand.

Always
Forever
GUILT

25

"Still nothing?" Jessica asked.

"Still nothing. It's freaking me out," I whispered back furiously.

"Good morning, future scientists!" Mr. Wallace greeted the AP chemistry class in his usual way. "Please get out your notes for your research projects; I want to do a progress check with each of you."

Jess, sitting on a high stool on my right, plonked a binder on the lab table and sighed. The stool to my left was still empty; Colby was late.

Like me.

While Mr. Wallace droned on about control samples and accurate measurements, I picked at the scab on the back of my hand — a result of my hurried flight out of the house this morning. I'd been desperate to escape my mother and the stupid prediction her tarot card reading supposedly prophesied for my life, and in my rush, I'd scratched my hand on the holly bush growing beside the front door.

Now I swore under my breath as a bead of blood appeared on my hand. "What am I going to do, Jess?"

"Good morning. Or, should I say good afternoon, Mr. Beaumont," Mr. Wallace said.

Colby had arrived. His face was thunderous, and when he apologized for his tardiness, I could hear anger in his voice.

"Let's start with you, Miss Hale." Mr. Wallace was old — fifty-five at least — and old-school. He always addressed us by our surnames. "What are you measuring, how far are you, what have you found?" he asked Ashleigh.

Colby took his seat beside me, slammed his notebook on the lab table, and gave me a tight smile.

"You okay?" I said, eyes on the muscle pulsing in his jaw.

"What's up?" Jess asked.

"Your brother, that's what!" Colby snapped back.

"Whoa, there! Him James, me Jessica. Don't take your beef with him out on me."

"I walked Cassie to her class today because she's not feeling well," Colby said. "And who do you think I found hanging around, chatting to the kids? Blunt, that's who!"

"Maybe he just—" Jess began.

"Just what? They're middle-schoolers, Jessica. Middle school! What's he doing hanging out with them if not getting an early stake in the market?"

"You three," Mr. Wallace said, frowning at us, "settle down. And get ready, I'll be checking on your progress next."

Rubbing his wrist as if it was hurting, Colby whispered, "I've got a good mind to report him to Chief Turner."

"For *reals?*" Jess challenged him, and then muttered, "Snitch."

"When it comes to saving lives? You bet I'll snitch."

I was stuck in the middle of their fiercely muttered conversation, with each of them cutting me glances that demanded I weigh in on their side. I was glad when Mr. Wallace interrupted the argument.

"Mr. Beaumont, how is your project coming on?" he asked.

Beside me, Colby drew in a long breath as if trying to calm himself. "It's okay. I've finished the theory section."

"And the experiments?"

"I got an impossible result on one of my tests. But I think it's because my little sister's been fiddling with my chemistry set. I'll repeat the experiments."

"Fine, let me know how it goes. Miss Armstrong?" Mr. Wallace turned his attention to Jessica. "You're focusing on acid rain, is that right?"

"Yes. I'm comparing the PH of rain in Pitchford last month to the annual averages to see if it's increasing. And I'm comparing to national averages to see if we're better or worse. I've done the measurements, but I haven't finished the statistical analysis yet."

"What's the matter with your wrist?" I asked Colby. "Did you get into a fight with Blunt?"

"It's nothing, don't worry about it. Listen, I need to talk to you," Colby murmured to me. He looked serious, worried even.

"What about?"

Colby leaned closer to me and murmured, "It's ... big. I want to run it by you before I decide what to do."

"Me, too," I whispered back. "I mean, I need to talk to you, too, about something big."

Mr. Wallace came to stand directly in front of us, effectively cutting our conversation short. "The last two years have had exceptionally heavy rainfall, Miss Armstrong; don't forget to factor that into your discussion and analysis."

Colby scribbled something in his notebook. A reminder to call me later, perhaps.

"And how about doing a retest in a few months' time, just for the fun of it?" Mr. Wallace said.

"I'll schedule it in my planner right away," Jess replied. I could tell she was being sarcastic, but he looked pleased at her diligence.

"Right, then. Miss McGee? How are you coming along?"

I had no patience for this now. I had bigger things to worry about than the sugar content of fruit juice. "Not well. I mean, I'm feeling sick. May I be excused to go to the restroom?"

Mr. Wallace looked taken aback but he gave me a hall pass, and even allowed Jessica to accompany me in case I needed help.

As we walked through the hallways, Jess asked, "What's got Colby so bent out of shape? He's not usually so hostile."

"I don't know."

I was too preoccupied with my own problem to worry much about anyone else's. In the girls' restroom, I went to the farthest stall, locked the door, pulled down my jeans and underwear and sat down, trying to summon the courage to look. I took a quick glance, then leaned forward and looked harder. Every inch of my panties was spotlessly white.

Jess's head appeared above the top of the partition. She must've been standing on the toilet in the next stall. "Well?" she demanded.

"Nothing. Not a speck. How is this possible?" I wailed. "We've only had sex five times. And we used a condom."

"Did you use it right?"

"I don't know!" It wasn't like I had a whole lot of experience.

"Maybe it tore. Maybe God's punishing you."

"I don't believe in God," I retorted, unraveling a long piece of toilet paper and wadding it up into a ball.

"Doesn't mean *He* doesn't believe in *you*. Doesn't mean He hasn't got it in for you."

I gave her an irritated look. "Him Colby. Me Garnet. Don't take your beef with him out on me, Jess!"

"Sorry."

I wiped myself, hard. Backward and forward, and pushed inside a little for good measure, then inspected the toilet paper.

"Fuck!"

I'd never wished as hard for anything as I wished for my period to arrive that day.

"I swear, if I start, I'll never ever complain about the curse again," I said.

"Do your boobs feel tender?" Jess asked.

I gave them a few experimental squeezes. "Yes."

Jess winced. I moaned.

"Don't worry – it's also a symptom of PMT," she said hurriedly.

I yanked up my clothes and flushed, watching the water swirl around the bowl. If I was pregnant, it would be my life going down the toilet. What the hell would I do? If I kept it, I'd be stuck in this town living with my folks forever. I didn't see how I could trot off to college in Boston ready to pop a baby into the world, or how I'd cope trying to get a degree while being a new and single mother. Maybe I'd have to stay and get married. At seventeen! Good guy that he was, Colby would surely pop the question if I told him, but I didn't think a teen marriage would be a good start to the rest of our lives. He'd surely feel trapped and resentful. I know I would.

I could terminate it. I didn't want to think about that — not the process, and not how I'd feel afterward. And what would Colby's opinion on abortion be? My gut told me he wouldn't want me to do that, but it was ultimately my choice, right? Only, that would mean I'd have to keep the truth from him, and keeping such a big secret didn't seem like a great start to our happily ever after, either.

There was no good solution to this, except that I wasn't pregnant. Anything else would be catastrophic. At the basins, I washed my hands furiously, rinsing away the smear of red around the picked scab on my hand. I wanted blood in my pants, dammit, not anywhere else.

"I think I'm going to win my bet about who gets pregnant first," Jess said, inspecting a pimple on her chin in the mirror beside me.

"Don't even put those words into the universe, Jess! You shouldn't even have said them in the first place back in the summer."

"Because now they're manifesting? You sound like your mother," Jess said, laughing.

"Don't say that either!"

I had no desire to sound like my idiotic mother who, while I'd eaten breakfast that morning in the kitchen, had dealt her tarot cards for me and drawn one with a lightning-struck tower on it.

"Ooh, it's the chaos card," she'd announced. "It's the card of upheaval, of being blindsided. Dramatic and cataclysmic change is nigh."

"Well, at least it's not the end that's nigh," I snarked.

"Have you been feeling fear and anxiety recently?"

"No, not the least bit."

The truth was, I always felt anxious. That was how these stupid fortune-tellings worked. You were always worried about something and going through change in some part of your life, so the "predictions" were always true at some level.

"Well, you will. Hopes and promises may be shattered." My mother gave me a concerned look. "Of course, it's not *necessarily* a bad thing. Bettina says the tower card signifies a cosmic kick up the ass! Now, in numerology, chaos is number sixteen" — she tapped the number on the bottom of the card — "which reduces to seven, and that's all about change and options."

"Are those bodies falling out of the tower?" I asked, peering more closely at the picture.

My mother nodded grimly. "A male and a female, conscious and unconscious, contemplation and action. They've been shaken out of their ordinary existence. That means a loss of control. And see these giant waves and the climbing fire? They signify that the signs have been around you. This storm has been brewing for a while, but you've been too blind to see it while living in a tower of illusion."

"So basically, you're saying some shit is about to go down in my life."

"Honey, please don't curse."

"Well, this was a delightful experience. I can see why people pay good money to get tarot readings," I'd said, and banged the door shut on my way out.

Hours later, with all signs pointing directly to cata-freaking-clysmic upheaval in my life, I was still trying to convince myself that her reading had been mere coincidence.

"You've got to relax, though," Jess said, rubbing my back in what I guess she thought was a soothing way. "I read online that extreme stress can delay the onset of a period. So, the more you worry about it, the less likely it is to come."

"Then I'm screwed, because I can't relax *until* it comes! I need to know, but no way can I just march into the drugstore and ask for a pregnancy test."

"Hey, I just remembered! My mother has one hidden in her underwear drawer. I could swipe it for you."

"Your mother has a pregnancy test?" I asked, momentarily distracted. "For *herself*?"

Mrs. Armstrong must've been in her mid-forties, and if she and the doc were still doing it — and just the thought of that totally grossed me out — they'd surely be using contraception.

"I don't know. Maybe she had a scare, and then before she could use it, she got her period? Maybe she's keeping it for the day I need it. I can't ask because she's told me to keep out of her private stuff."

"Why were you looking in there?"

"She's got such hectic lingerie. Like black lace-up bustiers and lacy red thongs. There was even a pair of crotchless panties in there! Is it for her and my dad? It weirds me out. She's too old for sexy," Jess said, looking deeply uncomfortable.

For perhaps the first time I realized that other people were also embarrassed by their mothers. We walked back to chemistry class in silence, each lost in thought. I needed to talk to Colby, but not yet. I'd give it two more days. If my period didn't arrive by Sunday, I'd tell him.

As Jess passed Colby, I heard him say to her, "Give your brother a message for me: He'd better stay away from Cassie. If he goes near her, I'll knock his block off."

26

Wednesday December 20, 2017

After breakfast with my parents, I drove into town, and scanning the old-timey facades of the stores on Main Street, I eventually found one selling computers and cell phones. When I showed the guy behind the counter Colby's phone, he snickered at the idea that they might have a charger to fit it.

"That phone is ancient, man. I suggest you try Hugo's on Cabot Street — he stocks loads of museum pieces."

Hugo's Hardware didn't have an old-fashioned storefront, at least not in the way that Michelle Armstrong and those who wanted the town to have a cutesy feel for the tourists would define it. But none of the snow-blowers, window scrapers and snow shovels in the window display looked like recent models, and the knee-high-sized plastic reindeer nestling in a bed of Styrofoam-ball "snow" was covered in dust and faded tinsel.

Bells jingled as I opened the door and stepped inside, and a man's voice called out from the back, "I'm comin'. Just give me a minute!"

I made my way past a clutter of Christmas lights and tinsel trees, plastic sleds, an old-fashioned wooden toboggan and, bizarrely, a life-size pink plastic flamingo. It was musty and stiflingly warm inside the store. I slipped out of my parka and took in the eclectic collection of wares displayed on every available surface.

Barrels stuffed with tiki torches, rakes, brooms, mops and fishing rods bookended isles of shelves that were jammed with all kinds of supplies arranged in no discernible order: BB guns, sealed packs of hinges, rolls of chains and nylon rope in different thicknesses, DIY equipment, and jars of zinc cream and hand degreaser.

An old man emerged from a door at the back of the store and limped over to ease behind the counter, where shelves of hunting rifles and ammunition were cheerfully, if incongruously, interspersed with Christmas cards featuring nativity scenes and doves of peace. He had a narrow face as brown and deeply grooved as an old hickory stump, a full head of snow-white hair, and a beard long and luxurious enough to be the envy of any Boston hipster. He wore a holiday sweater psychedelically patterned with red snowflakes and green reindeers.

"Hi, hi," he said, the words sounding like *hoi hoi* in his old Vermont accent. "Sorry to keep ya waiting. I was just having a bite of breakfast. I'm Hugo, what can I do for ya?"

As he spoke, an overpowering odor of garlic wafted across to me. I took a step back and switched to mouth-breathing.

"I'm looking for a charger for this." I handed over Colby's phone.

"Well, let's see if we can help ya," he said, making no move to do so. Instead he studied me for a few seconds with faded blue eyes, then snapped his fingers and announced, "You're Bob and Crystal's kid, ain't ya? Name of … don't tell me, don't tell me — Mandy!"

"Garnet," I corrected.

"Fer sure? It's a very unusual name."

"So they tell me. Do you have a charger for that?" I pointed to the phone.

He spared it the briefest of glances before returning his gaze to me. "Haven't seen you around here in years."

"I live in Boston now."

"Is that right? And what d'ya do over there in Boston?"

"I'm studying psychology."

"Studying psychology!" he exclaimed — like it was the oddest thing to be doing over there in Boston — and cackled more pungent fumes in my direction. "Married? With a couple of ankle-snappers?"

"No."

"Lonely, are ya?"

"No! Look, do you—"

"Now you were the girl who dated poor Colby Beaumont, weren't ya?"

I sighed. All roads inevitably led to Colby.

Hugo rubbed his hands together gleefully and gave himself a small round of applause. "I never forget a face. And nor a name, either." He tapped a gnarled finger to his temple. "I store them all up here."

"Good for you," I said. "Do you know where you store your phone chargers?"

He stroked his beard. "Hard tellin'. Could be in a few places. That's an old piece of equipment. We don't get much call for such."

He scrunched up his eyes and scanned the countertop, as if he might find just such a charger there. That part of the surface not stacked with goods — boxes of batteries, key rings, lighter fluid, and a pyramidal stack of bottles of kosher dill pickles — was covered by a huge laminated sign, its corners curling up against the yellowed, peeling tape holding it in place. To go by the services advertised, Hugo's was a wondrous emporium of services: *We sharpen knives, scissors, axes, machetes, garden tools; We fill gas bottles; We pierce ears (only!); We repair screens and replace windows; We Cut Keys! And Pipes!*

Could they tighten the screws coming loose in my head, I wondered?

Hugo poked about in a few drawers under the counter but seemed more intent on extracting news from me than unearthing the item I needed. "Why are ya back in Pitchford, then?"

"A couple of reasons."

"Visiting your folks, I betcha. How's your mother's hip?"

"It's her ankle, and it's healing well, thank you. Could we look for the chargers now?"

"And you'll be seeing the Beaumont family, fer sure?"

"If you tell me where you think the cell phone accessories might be, I could help you look."

"Hmmm," he said, rotating on the spot as he stared around the store for inspiration. "Can you hand me that box up there on the top shelf? No, not that one, the one next to it. That's it."

I placed the cardboard box on the counter, and he blew dust off the top — or perhaps it voluntarily took flight to escape his noxious breath — then opened it.

"This looks hopeful," he said, tilting the box to show me the jumble of old phones, wires, adaptors, plugs and screen protectors. "Now, the Beaumonts ... Their little girl is very sick, did ya know that?"

"Yes."

"Cancer's a right son of a bitch. Let's see, how about this one?" He tried to disentangle one charger from a knotted bundle, gave up, and handed the whole bunch to me. "One of these should be the ticket."

"I don't think so," I said, seeing nothing that looked like an Apple product.

"Cassie! That's the little girl's name, eh?" He tapped his head knowingly again.

"Yes. But look, the ends of these are the wrong shape to fit into this phone."

He squinted at the cord then handed me back the phone. "Ah, just give 'em a try. You never know."

I got the distinct impression he was keen to prolong my visit. Perhaps he got lonely in this old store away from the buzz and business of Main Street and just wanted some human company and a chat. It wouldn't kill me to indulge him. Besides, if I wanted to be a psychologist, I should practice my underdeveloped skills in empathy and patience. So I made a show of trying each of the chargers, shaking my head sadly each time one failed to fit.

"It's too bad, you know," Hugo said. "First the boy and now

the girl. Their mother, now — Barbara, is it?" He shot me a glance, his untamed eyebrows undulating like hairy caterpillars inching across the surface of a branch.

"Bridget," I said.

"I'd have got there without any help," he said, sounding offended. "Now she, *Bridget*" — he gave me a look — "was real bad after the boy's death. I reckon losing another child will lay her so low she won't ever get up again. Now the father ..." He paused, eyeing me.

"Philip," I suggested tentatively.

"Yes, Philip — as I was *just* about to say — he took it hard, too, but he's done well since with that water company of theirs. Water!" Hugo shook his head in bemusement. "They put it in bottles now, and folks buy it instead of turning on the faucet. Made them a pile of money, mind. So did that housing development just outside of town that never ought to have been built."

My ears pricked at that last bit. "Do you mean the Beaumont Golf Estate?"

"You betcha bub, I do. Those Beaumont boys made millions off of that, didn't they?" He frowned down at the tangle of cords in my hands. "You're wasting your time there, my girl. I don't believe any of those are going to fit your telephone."

"That's what *I* said."

He stuffed the cords back into the box, closed it and patted it fondly.

"What do you mean, the estate should never have been built?" I asked.

"That land isn't right for building humungous houses on,

that's why it was always a trailer park. A darn nice one, too. Neat and tidy, with a great view of the valley, and folks put up little porches and flower boxes outside their trailers. But they just bought the land, turned most everyone out on their ass, and that was the end of that. I had the whole story from Lyle Wallace, who used to live in the trailer park back when he worked at the Johnson dairy farm. They wanted to buy up Johnson's land, too, you know, but he held out. Anyhow, now he's homeless, poor man."

"Farmer Johnson?"

"No, *Lyle*." He gave me a look that suggested he doubted my mental acuity, and checked a wall clock with a small garden fork and spade for hands. "Should be coming in soon. I make him a packed lunch, every day, see? And something for his cat."

"What's wrong with that land?"

He tapped the box. "Can you put this back in its place for me? My arms and shoulders don't work as smooth as they used to. Arthritis."

I grabbed the box and shoved it back into position on its shelf. "The land?" I prompted again.

"It's wetlands, ain't it? The ground is soggy. Lyle says those houses are going to subside and send cracks up the walls, you mark his words. I don't know how they got permission to build there — must have greased the town clerk's palm, if you ask me," he said, rubbing fingers and thumb together.

I dusted my hands off on the seat of my jeans. "Michelle Armstrong?"

"The one and only. She's riding the high horse in this town, trying to rename it and change all the stores, pushing old folks like me out. 'Rebranding' she calls it. I call it filling her coffers, because she's an investor in that development syndicate, did ya know *that?*"

"I did not."

Hugo parked himself on the stool behind the counter, all thought of finding me a charger seemingly forgotten. "Well, I'm not one as likes to gossip—"

Could have fooled me.

"—but I don't reckon town clerking pays Lady Muck-on-toast enough to keep her in the manner she thinks is fit for herself. I remember when she was a snotty little kid who stole whatever she could fit into her pockets. You ask your father if she wasn't always filching gumballs and little knick-knacks."

"So, she invested in the new development and made good money?" I asked. Trying to keep the old man on track was like herding cats.

"Oh, yah. Because by then Doc Armstrong had retired. Had to, didn't he? So he wasn't bringing in any money, and that good-for-nothing boy of theirs was costing them a small fortune; somebody had to top up the family fortunes."

I held up a hand to halt the flow. "Wait, wait. Why did Doc Armstrong have to retire?"

"Well, I'm not one as likes to spread stories, but the good doc always did have an inordinate fondness for old Johnny."

"Johnny? Johnny who?"

"Mr. Walker, if you catch my drift." Hugo mimed tipping back a bottle into his mouth and made chugging sounds in his throat.

"Ah."

"Got to a point where he couldn't doctor anymore."

"And his son, James?"

"You kids had another name for him."

"Blunt."

"That's the one, Blunt. I never forget a name." He nodded in satisfaction. "He's another one with whatchamacallit—? Substance abuse problems. The apple don't fall far from the tree, eh? But how come he got to keep his trailer in the woods back of that development, that's what I'd like to know. Lyle wants to know, too. Course, his pigeons are coming home to roost now, ain't they? Hasn't got long, I hear."

"Lyle?" I asked, struggling to keep track of the conversation.

"Lyle? No, Lyle's as strong as an ox. He sails through summer and spits in the eye of winter."

"So, who's dying — Blunt?"

"No, not the boy," Hugo said impatiently. "His father."

27

Wednesday December 20, 2017

"**D**oc Armstrong is dying?" I asked, shocked.

"Cirrhosis of the liver, as I heard it," Hugo said.

"Jeez, you leave a town for a decade and everyone gets ten years older and sicker," I muttered.

"Not me, I'm healthy. Want to know my secret?"

"Sure."

"I eat a garlic sandwich for breakfast every morning."

That explained the awful odor.

"It keeps the bugs away," he said.

Customers too, I'd bet.

"You said Blunt was a good-for-nothing. Drugs?" I asked.

"You betcha. If it ain't the liquor that's been the death of Doc Armstrong, then it's his boy, because that one never could clean up his act, and he tries to take some of our youngsters down his path, from what I hear. The official story is he does construction work out of town from time to time in Bangor and Portland and such, but everyone knows it's the boy going into rehab out of state. He comes back looking shiny pink and clean, and flies right for a month or six, then he starts up again. That kind of treatment costs a family a wheelbarrow of money and a whale of tears."

"Poor Jessica."

"Oh, yah. But now that's a girl as done well for herself, even if she did—"

The bell on the shop door interrupted, and Hugo looked over my shoulder, nodding.

"Hi, hi, Lyle, come in. I'll just go fetch your lunch," Hugo said, and disappeared to the back of the store.

The man who walked up near to where I stood at the counter moved so slowly and carefully that his steps made no sound. He was tall and had dark eyes, but I could make out little else about his appearance because he was wrapped in sweaters, a coat, two scarves, mittens and an ice-frosted khaki balaclava. A stuffed backpack was slung over one shoulder, and a mean-looking marmalade cat rested in his arms. I nodded a greeting, and the wool-swathed head nodded back. So this was Lyle.

He gently placed the cat on the floor, where it sat beside his feet, yellow eyes fixed on me. No, not quite on me — its gaze appeared to be focused to the left of me. I glanced over my shoulder to see what it was staring at and saw nothing. Lyle pulled off his mittens to reveal hands clad in fingerless gloves. He rubbed the fingertips, with their dirty, overgrown nails, over his lips.

"Your eyes are different," he said in a pitch so rough and

deep, it was more vibration than voice. "Which one is real?"

"Both of them."

"I don't know which one to focus on."

I lifted my hands in a can't-help-you-with-that-problem kind of shrug.

"And I don't know you," he said. "You're a stranger."

Not as strange as you, buddy.

"I grew up here. But I left many years ago," I said, wondering why I was telling him anything.

"Now you're back."

They were innocent words, but something about his gruff tone and the way the cat was tilting its head and squinting off to the empty side of me, was unnerving.

"I'll be going home soon," I said.

"This *is* home." The words sounded like a threat.

"Right. What's your cat's name?" I asked, reaching out to stroke it and pulling my hand back rapidly when it hissed at me.

"Cat," Lyle said.

"Your cat's name is Cat?"

"You have a problem with that?" he said, taking a step closer.

"No. Uh-uh, not me. No problem at all," I said, backing up.

"Here you go," Hugo called from behind me.

He handed Lyle a brown bag and a travel mug, and placed a bowl filled with what looked (and smelled) like mashed tuna on the floor beside the cat. It ignored the food and continued its unnerving examination of the space beside me, its eyes

216

flicking from side to side, and up and down.

"That's not like Cat, to ignore her food," Hugo said, frowning at the animal.

"She doesn't like to eat in front of strangers," Lyle said. "She doesn't *like* strangers."

"Well, if I could just get—" I began, but Lyle stowed the bag and travel mug in the capacious pockets of his overcoat, then scooped up the cat in one hand and the bowl of food in the other and left without another word.

"Not very sociable, is Lyle," Hugo said. Then he held up a bulging black trash bag. "Look what I found in the back!"

He spun the bag around to unwring its twisted neck and then plonked it on the counter. Inside, I could see all manner of junk, including some cords and wires. I began sorting through them.

"So, Jessica Armstrong was your friend way back when. Who else was in your class at school?" Hugo asked.

"Katherine Kehoe, Judy Burns, Taylor … something, Ashleigh Hale." They were names I hadn't thought of in years.

"Hale! I remember her — a shy little thing. Wouldn't say boo to a goose. She left years ago. California, or Colorado. Something with a C. Callicoon, maybe. Who else?"

"Pete Dillon, and his friend Brandon Nugent."

"That Nugent boy enlisted right after high school and was killed six months later in Afghanistan, did ya hear about that?"

I shook my head, a little shaken by that piece of news.

"Pete Dillon, now — he pulled his life together many years back. He runs old man Dillon's store with that pretty little wife of his, did ya know that?"

"That, I did."

He raised his eyebrows at me, as if surprised I knew anything. "Very fancy eatery and doing nicely, they tell me. Still, it doesn't stop the rumors." He fished a silver badge out of the bag, breathed essence of garlic on it, and buffed it against his trouser leg before pinning it onto his lurid sweater. "Vermont Wrestling Champion, 1957," he said, beaming proudly.

"What rumors?"

"Take your pick: that he don't treat his little lady well, that he has a piece on the side over in Randolph, that he poisoned the old man to inherit the store, that his expensive Ethiopian coffee is really just repackaged Folgers."

Startled, I looked up from the tangled contents of the bag. "Poisoned his old man?"

"Could be. Could well be. Way I hear it, Randolph Dillon was in the process of changing his will, but he gave up the ghost before it was finalized. Very convenient for *someone*, I think. And I have it from the horse's mouth that he died frothing at the mouth. Cyanide, if you ask me. Or a tot of weed killer would've done the trick — we've got some deadly ones in stock right here," he said cheerfully, pointing at a nearby shelf as though I might be in the market for some toxins. "Now, Samuel Wallace — he was a teacher at the school back in the day. Was he one of yours?"

I nodded. "He taught me chemistry."

"He's a strange one. I could tell you some stories about him. He's Lyle's father, did you know that?"

"No," I said, very surprised.

My return of ignorance brought a gleeful smile to Hugo's face. "He's the principal now."

"Do you have some kind of a light?" I asked. "I'm battling to see inside this bag."

"Here you go," he said, fetching a lamp with an extendable neck from the far end of the counter. "Now Mrs. Jorgensen would have been principal back then, but she's retired now. Spends her days fishing for pike and carp." He pronounced the word *kerrup*. "And teaching her parrot to speak. Damndest thing! That bird says, 'Would you like a hall pass?' and 'You may be seated,' and rings like the school bell!"

I remembered Jorgensen. Wouldn't have guessed she'd had a sense of humor. I made to angle the light so that it shone into the bag, but as I touched the shade, the bulb blew. *Again.* Really?

"Son of a bitch," Hugo said mildly.

I snagged my own cellphone from my handbag, activated the flashlight function, and shone it into the bag.

"If you have a fancy phone like that, what do you need this old thing for?" Hugo asked, pointing at Colby's phone.

"Reasons," I said.

"Me, I like a phone that's a phone and a flashlight that's a flashlight, but you can't fight change, can you?" he said sagely, though his store seemed a monument to precisely the opposite sentiment.

I spied a charger with the right sort of connector head and eased it into the socket of the iPhone. It fit.

"We have a winner!" Hugo said. "Now you just need to free it from its bedfellows."

I started picking at the knots and tangles that entwined the charger with other cords and wires, thinking about the rest of the old guard in town, and about what else had changed.

"What happened to Chief Turner?" I asked.

"Retired. Soon after your fellow died. He was never the same after that. He's still around — lives at the Roseacres Nursing Home. Doc Armstrong is there, too, now. Guess Mrs. Armstrong is too busy running the town to take care of her husband at home." He barked a laugh and gave me a broad wink. "She never did like the old ones."

Hugo gusted out a deep malodorous sigh. "He's completely off his rocker, of course — Turner, I mean — old-timer's disease. They all seem to get it these days, but it won't ketch me. Want to know my secret?"

"Let me guess, garlic?"

"You betcha."

I wondered just how bad Frank Turner's dementia was, because he'd be a useful person to interview about Colby's death. I'd pay him a visit just as soon as I got the wretched charger freed.

"And the new police chief?" I asked.

"Eh," he cackled, "all the young ladies want to know about that fella, and I guess you're no exception! He's divorced."

Interesting.

"He had a lovely wife, mind, with golden hair and cornflower eyes, but she was a Southerner, and I don't think she ever took to our Yankee ways. Or maybe she just couldn't stand the winters. Anyhow, she ran off with some Texan fella. That must've been three or four years back."

"Got it!" I said, finally freeing the cord and handing it to Hugo. "Can we check whether it works?"

He plugged the charger into an electrical outlet on the wall. Holding my breath, I leaned over and stared at the phone, willing it into life. For long moments, nothing happened. Then a battery charging icon appeared in a corner of the blank screen.

"We did it!" Hugo said, smiling widely. "For sure, you'll be wanting an adaptor that fits into your car's cigarette lighter?"

He found one with such alacrity that I immediately suspected he'd been drawing out the whole process of finding the charger to prolong our chat. The old codger named a price at least triple what the charger could have been worth and encouraged me to pop around again soon, so we could chew the fat.

Outside the air was cold and odor-free, the sky crowded with steel wool clouds. I slipped behind the wheel of my car, plugged the charger in and connected it to the phone, and then I started the engine and cranked up the car's heater.

My stomach rumbled. I'd kill for a burrito with extra-hot tomatillo salsa and an icy margarita on the side, but I was pretty sure Chipotle hadn't yet staked a foothold in Pitchford. I found a half-crushed packet of chips in the glove box and ate them on the way to the Roseacres Nursing Home. Hugo had said both Turner and Doc Armstrong lived there; perhaps I could pop in and pay my respects to Jessica's father, too.

Yes. The word washed through me like a powerful wave.

Whatever this thing I was experiencing was, it wanted me to talk to the doctor.

28

Roseacres Nursing Home smelled of urine, pine disinfectant and the flat, dead-skin odor of old people.

"Are you family?" the attendant behind the front desk asked around her wad of gum. She had a hypnotic way of chewing that wrenched her jaw to the side on every pass, like a cow working its cud.

"Yes," I said. "I'm his niece from Boston."

She studied me for a few seconds with round brown eyes and asked, "Is this the first time you're visiting? Do you know what to expect?"

"I understand he has Alzheimer's Disease, yes."

"It's far advanced, I'm afraid. I'm not sure he'll even know you're there. His mind slipped away long since, but his heart keeps on pumping. Sad!"

I nodded.

"*Jesus!*" she yelled.

It took me a moment to realize she was summoning an

orderly, not cursing her patient's tenacious heart.

"Take Ms." — she checked the register where I'd entered my details — "McGee to the memory care unit. Visitor for Mr. Turner."

I followed the orderly down long hallways, past private and shared rooms, a dining hall, and a large, sunny room labeled "Recreation," where a bunch of old biddies were moving slowly, and completely out of time, to a song that enthusiastically urged them to touch their hands, shoulders, knees and toes. I remembered the ditty from Kindergarten, but back then we'd gyrated wildly to the music. The old ladies of Roseacres moved with the deliberate caution that accompanies an ever-present fear of slipped disks and broken hips.

The memory care unit was located at the far end of the home. Jesús keyed a series of numbers into a security keypad on the wall, and the closed door popped open. We entered the ward, stepping into a soft cacophony of off-key singing, disconnected murmurings, and moans from the patients inside. Some, like the woman singing that the hills were alive, were bed-bound, but several sat in a row of wheelchairs facing a long window which overlooked the snow-blanketed gardens beyond.

I swallowed hard, unnerved by the horror of the room. It was clean, warm, bright, and the patients had been given objects to hold for play or comfort — soft toys, small photograph albums, activity pillows with zippers, tied bows, and movable buttons threaded on a string. They seemed well treated, and their attendant walked amongst them, soothing, picking up dropped objects, holding plastic cups to drooling mouths to give sips of water. But still, it was a prison. They were trapped by their disintegrating brains as surely as by the ward's locked door.

Jesús wheeled one of the patients around and pushed him to a quiet corner of the ward where a few visitors' chairs sat waiting forlornly. I took one of the seats and examined Pitchford's old police chief. Frank Turner, shockingly thin, stared down at his right hand, where his fingers continuously worked a fidget spinner. From a tank mounted to the rear of his chair, oxygen whispered through a thin tube into his nose.

"Mr. Turner? You have a visitor."

Jesús gently lifted his patient's chin so he could look at me, but the effort was wasted; Turner's gaze was blank. His eyes moved over me as impassively as if I was another piece of furniture. As soon as the orderly removed the support of his hand, Turner's head sank again, as inexorably as a setting sun, to rest on his chest. His thumb and forefinger squeezed the central button of the spinner, and he gave an incoherent moan as the twirling blur resumed.

Whatever the one-time chief of police may once have known, it was now sealed in the impenetrable maze of his brain.

"The hills are alive. The hills are alive," the woman sang behind me.

"Would you like to stay and visit for a while?" Jesús asked me.

"No," I said, embarrassed at how emphatic my voice sounded. "I'm sorry, I guess I didn't realize he'd be this ... out of it."

Jesús nodded. Clearly it wasn't the first time he'd seen

relatives and friends enter this room all fired with good intentions, but after mere minutes of visiting, become eager only to get the hell away.

"Don't worry," he said. "It freaks everyone out."

Understandably so, but I was training to become a psychologist; I should be more okay with this. I should be able to face pathology with patience and equanimity. Was my reaction of distress — and even, I thought guiltily, revulsion — just a normal consequence of being confronted with something shocking and wholly unfamiliar? Or was it another indication that I was not suited to being in a care profession?

Back in the hallway, I asked Jesús if he could take me to visit Dr. Armstrong. "He's my best friend's father, and I haven't seen him in years."

"Sure, I'll take you to him. He's in the nursing care section because he's sick, but there's nothing wrong with his mind, and it'll be good for him to have a visitor for a change."

For a change?

Doc Armstrong's brain might still have been sharp as a tack, but his body, slumped against a pile of pillows, was wasted by age and illness. Like all of the Armstrongs, he'd been tall, but now he looked shriveled. His eyes and skin were jaundiced — no doubt due to liver failure — and his hands trembled. The only vital things about him were his eyebrows, which bristled with white hairs growing in every direction.

The orderly said he'd be back later to check on his charge, and when he left, I closed the door behind him.

"Excuse me, my dear, but do I know you?" Dr. Armstrong asked.

"It's me, Garnet McGee. Jessica's old friend from school?"

"Garnet McGee ... Ah, yes, I remember."

"How are you doing, Dr. Armstrong?"

"How does it look like I'm doing? I'm knocking on death's door. Or perhaps he's knocking on mine."

I tried to think of a comforting response to that, but came up with nothing.

"May I?" I indicated the visitor's chair beside the bed.

"Couldn't stop you even if I wanted to, which I don't. There's a chess set in here," he said, indicating a bedside cabinet topped with several varieties of medication and a glass of water. "If you get it out, we can play a game."

"Uh, okay," I said, extracting the set and placing it on the tray table above his bed. "But I should warn you I'm not very good at chess."

"Then maybe you'll learn something."

I fully intended to, but not about chess.

He helped me set up the pieces in their proper places and then said, "You can be white. That means you begin."

I moved a pawn two spaces forward. That much I remembered.

"Are you in town to visit Jessica, then?" Doc Armstrong asked.

"To catch up with everybody," I said untruthfully. "But mostly to spend some time with my parents."

I explained about my mother's fall and the plan to pack up her shop, while Doc Armstrong made a matching move with his pawn, so that our two pieces stared blindly at each other. Trying to remember anything from the handful of times I'd ever played chess in my life, I settled for moving another pawn.

"I don't know if you remember, but I dated Colby Beaumont back when I was in high school here."

He nodded. "That does ring a bell."

"It's been ten years since his death. And still nobody knows what really happened to him."

Doc Armstrong captured my pawn with one of his and moved it to the side of the board, staying silent.

"I wondered if you could shed any light on it?" I asked.

He raised his untamed eyebrows at me, and I hurriedly added, "I mean, I guess the town doctor knows a fair few of the town secrets?"

"Your turn." He jerked his chin at the board.

I grabbed a knight, which I vaguely remembered was allowed to move two blocks in one direction and one block in another — or was it vice versa? — and plonked it on a new spot. "Can I put it there?"

"You can," he said, and promptly captured the piece with another of his pawns.

At this rate, the game would be over before I got a single question answered. I stared at the board as if considering the consequences of a variety of possible moves, and said, "You were called to the scene when they found Colby. His body, I mean."

"Yes, I pronounced death. But I didn't do the autopsy — that was the state's chief medical examiner."

This being Vermont, there hadn't been an inquest, and while the main findings and conclusion of the Medical Examiner had been covered by the media, the full autopsy report hadn't been reprinted verbatim. Perhaps there had been something in it that I'd never known. Truthfully, until now, I hadn't *wanted* to know details.

I picked up my other knight and toyed with placing it on different blocks, playing for time. "Colby and the Beaumont family — they were your patients. So, were you copied on the autopsy report?"

"I was."

"And?"

"Are you going to play that piece or just wave it about?"

I replaced the knight in its original spot and inched a pawn forward one block. "What did the report say?"

Doc Armstrong shifted position, as if to ease his aching bones, and surveyed me with tired eyes. "Can I ask exactly what all this is about?"

"Being here, in town — it's bringing things up for me. Old memories and unresolved issues. A few days ago, I fell into Plover Pond and nearly drowned. In fact, I *did* drown. They resuscitated me."

"Goodness me! Is that how you injured yourself?" he asked, looking at the fingers that still sported Band-Aids.

"Yeah, but I'm fine now, more or less," I said, watching as he moved a slender piece with a pointed hat out diagonally across the board. A priest? Bishop? "But it's brought that whole time of Colby's death back for me, and I feel like I won't have any peace unless I find out what really happened that night."

"So, you're investigating his death?"

"I guess so. I mean, nothing formal. Chief Jackson seems to think it's a cold case, that there are no new leads to pursue, and no old ones that haven't been fully investigated."

"Yet you think you can do better?"

Heat rose in my cheeks. I looked away from his assessing gaze and randomly moved a piece shaped like a castle turret.

"You can't do that," Armstrong said.

"Who's going to stop me?" I retorted.

He pointed at my castle. "The rook can't move diagonally."

"Oh." I returned it to its spot and edged my queen out a few blocks. She could move in any direction, right? "The thing is, I knew Colby better than most. Maybe that gives me an edge."

He nodded as if conceding a point.

"So, about his body? The injuries?"

"Don't you know all this? From your father?"

I straightened in surprise. "My *father*? What's he got to do with anything?"

"He requested a copy of the autopsy report back then."

"He did? Why on earth would he do that?"

"He said it was for you. That you needed to know what happened." Armstrong took another of my men and added it to the steadily growing line of white pieces on the side of the board. "He didn't share it with you?"

"He– No. He must've changed his mind. I never saw any report."

"Could you not do that, please?" Doc Armstrong frowned down at my hands. Following his gaze, I saw I had one of my dead pawns in my hand and was scratching at the edge of the underfelt with a nail.

"Sorry." I replaced the piece on the board and pulled the

sleeves of my sweater down over my fingers. "Can you remember the autopsy findings?"

"I think so — the main points, at least. Death was due to drowning. The examiner found water in his lungs and stomach, which means he was still alive when he went under. The water was so cold that the soft tissues had largely been protected against deterioration. He'd been badly beaten shortly before his death, and he'd bled from both internal and external injuries."

The memory of Colby, lying bleached and broken beside the pond, reared up in my mind, kicking my heart into a rapid rhythm. I inhaled through my nose, deliberately trying to slow and deepen my breaths, and stared hard at the chessboard, burning the checkered pattern onto my vision to drive out the old images.

"Anything else?" I asked.

"They did a basic tox screen and found no drugs or alcohol in his system. He had lacerations consistent with being beaten by fists. No wounds due to a knife or other weapon. And there were cracked ribs — a good couple, I think."

"On his left side?" I said, rubbing mine, feeling an echo of the sharp pain where I'd been kicked.

No, not me. Him. Where *he'd* been kicked.

"I don't remember," Armstrong replied. "There was considerable bruising with, if I remember correctly, a concentration of contusions on the torso and shoulders."

Hands pushing me down. Holding me under the water. Can't see who.

"Could those bruises on his shoulders have been made by someone holding him under the water?" I asked.

More than one.

"They could have, yes, but the examiner couldn't be sure about that. They might have been a consequence of someone holding him in position while he was assaulted by a second attacker."

"On your knees, asshole!"

Hands holding me down, pinning my arms behind my back. Pain. Blood.

I struggled to stay present, to focus on what Armstrong was saying, even as a part of me wanted to slip into the past, to glean new details.

Cracking, shearing pain in my ribs. The agony of drawing breath. Dark faces.

"Enough, man, you'll kill him!"

I caught the tail end of whatever Armstrong was saying. "—could simply be where the blows landed. He'd been given a thorough going over."

"You just keep your distance. You hear me, dickhead? Keep your fucking nose out of other people's business."

"Let's go, man. Enough."

"No! I'm not done."

"He even had ruptured testicles." Armstrong's voice came from far off.

I shook my head, fighting the darkness that fluttered like moth wings at the edges of my vision, blotting out the light.

"Say again?" I asked, my voice hoarse with strain.

"I'm sorry, my dear, this must be hard for you to hear. Are you sure you want—"

"Tell me!"

"He'd been kicked in the testicles. One — or both perhaps, I can't remember — had ruptured."

An explosion of unbearable pain.

Darkness closes in, and I'm gone.

29

"Garnet? Are you alright?" Doc Armstrong said, sounding alarmed.

I opened my eyes and found myself doubled over a dreadful pain I no longer felt.

"Sorry," I croaked, rubbing a hand across my face, trying to clear the lingering dizziness. "May I?" I indicated the glass of water on his bedside cabinet.

"I think you may need something stronger, you've gone as pale as old bones. Here," he said, tugging open a drawer in the cabinet and extracting a bottle of Johnny Walker Blue and two shot glasses which clinked together in his trembling hand. "Would you do the honors? I'm likely to spill more than I get in the glass."

With hands that weren't much steadier than his, I poured a scant inch into each glass and handed him one. "They allow you to drink in here?"

"I've found that you can usually have, and do, the forbidden

— as long as you have money. Or power," he added, looking thoughtful. "Slàinte!" He chinked his glass against mine, slugged back the shot, and held out the glass for a refill.

"Should you be drinking, though?" I asked as I complied.

"You want to protect my health from the ill effects of alcohol? Very kind of you, Garnet, but you're thirty years too late. I don't think it's going to make much of a difference now." He took a sip and rolled it over his tongue, clearly savoring the taste. "And I'd truly rather drink the whiskey than the water."

I swallowed a sip, welcoming the burn which grounded me in the present and woke me up a little. Every time I had one of the episodes, I was left feeling drained.

"It's good, isn't it?" he asked.

"It's mighty fine." I finished it and poured myself another measure. Then I topped his up and returned the bottle to the drawer, which, I saw, was also filled with blister packs and bottles of pills. Feeling more alert, I asked, "Was there anything to suggest who attacked and murdered Colby?"

"In the autopsy report? No."

That seemed like a curiously specific answer.

"And based on anything else, perhaps on what you knew of the Beaumonts or other folks in town, any guesses who did it?"

He stayed silent for a few moments, making a meal of inhaling the bouquet of his dram. Eventually he said, "Aren't the nearest and dearest usually the main suspects?"

His tone was casual, almost flippant, but I locked my gaze on his. "What do you mean?"

"Don't we inevitably hate the ones we love? Aren't families the petri dishes of secrets and loathing?"

Was he talking about Colby's family, or his own? Or mine?

"Do you know something?" I asked.

"*Know* is a big word."

"*Suspect*, then."

He made a complicated move with his castle and king.

"Sir, isn't it time the truth came out?"

"*Truth*. Ah, now, that's an even bigger word. Whose truth? And what might happen if we all went about speaking the truth, possibly hurting others and doing more harm than good. And would it help anything at all — even if there was a hidden truth. And I haven't said there is, mind you."

He hadn't said there wasn't, either. He knew something for sure.

"Because the past cannot be changed one single iota," he said. "It's your turn, my dear."

I had my bishop retreat the few blocks it had previously advanced. "But we can change the *future*, if we expose the truth."

Armstrong glowered at me, his eyebrows knitting into a single white line above his nose. "Maybe that's what got Colby killed — his nosiness. Now you're going around waking sleeping dogs instead of letting them lie. It would be safer to let the past be."

What the heck did *that* mean?

"Are you threatening me?" I demanded.

"Not at all." He looked like he regretted saying anything.

"Tell me what you know!" I almost yelled the words in my frustration.

"Hand on heart," he replied, "I know nothing more about how Colby died than you do."

He moved a knight, protecting his queen from my bishop, and then closed his eyes for a minute. Was he merely resting, or trying to blot me out?

I could see I wouldn't get anything else out of him, so I fished my notebook out of my handbag and, rummaging for a pen, came up with Colby's — the one with his name on the side. Had I put that in my bag? I had no recollection of it.

"Here." I wrote my name and number on a page, tore it out and handed it to him. "If you think of anything else or remember something, will you let me know? You can trust me to do the right thing with the information."

Armstrong fingered the piece of paper thoughtfully before dropping it into his bedside drawer. "One of the consolations of death is that one isn't here to see the fallout afterward."

"Huh?" I said, confused.

"Forgive me, I was just pondering the nature of life, death and families. Your move, I believe?"

I pushed one of my few remaining pawns forward a block, but Armstrong shook his head. "You're putting yourself in check."

I moved it back, tried to figure any move that wouldn't get more of my army obliterated.

"Have you visited the Beaumonts?" he asked. "How's little Cassie doing?"

"Not much better than you, I think."

"It's an unspeakable tragedy," he murmured. "And have you seen Jessica yet?"

"No, but I plan to. Soon. How is she?"

"She can catch you up on all her own news herself. You still have her contact details?"

"No." I'd deleted all the old numbers, cut the old ties.

"Hand me your notebook and pen," he said. In a shaky script he wrote a name and number. "She's Jessica Mantovani, now."

"She's married?" I asked.

"Indeed. She has two kids, too."

"Wow."

I took the notebook and stared down at the unfamiliar name. The last time I'd seen Jessica, she'd been throwing her graduation cap in the air and hugging her new group of friends. I couldn't imagine her married, let alone being a mother. I was beginning to realize that most of my cohort had moved on. I was the odd one out, single, childless, not yet even settled in a career — a case of fixated development if ever I saw one.

Armstrong gestured to the chessboard and our all-but-abandoned game.

"My turn, *again*?"

He nodded. "The only way to stop playing is to surrender."

Screw that. I moved my queen to the side of my knight; they made a handsome pair. "And how is Mrs. Armstrong?"

"Oh, I'm sure she's fine; she always takes good care of herself," he said, bitterness creeping into his voice for the first time.

So, MILFy Michelle clearly wasn't big on visiting her dying husband.

"And Blunt? James, I mean. How's he doing these days?"

Doc Armstrong blew out a long sigh. "I don't see my boy as often as I'd like to." He took my queen and said, "Check."

"Oh, dear."

"Who told you where to find me if it wasn't Jessica?" he asked.

"Hugo."

Armstrong looked blank.

"From the hardware store?"

"Ah, yes. Hugo."

I moved my king a space to the side, tucking it behind a pawn. "He had lots of interesting things to say about Pitchford folks."

"Hugo is an incorrigible gossip."

"He said James has a trailer out at the new golf estate, that he was given special permission to stay when everyone else was evicted. Is that true?"

"Evicted? Ha!" Armstrong smiled wryly. "They were well-paid for their land."

Which, I noticed, didn't answer my question.

"Did he also tell you about bright lights hovering over the development? That it's being surveilled by government drones or UFOs?" Armstrong asked, chuckling.

"Nope, he just said that James lives up there."

Armstrong gave the smallest of shrugs. "That much is true." He swept his queen across the board, placing her on a clear diagonal path to my king. "Checkmate, I believe."

"Well, I lasted longer than I thought I would. I suspect you went easy on me."

He smiled enigmatically. "Would you help me put these away?"

I shot him an appraising glance. His face looked drawn and tired, and his breaths were shallow pants. I should have felt guilty for exhausting a sick man, but Doc Armstrong was right — it was too late to save him now.

Frustrated that he'd held back on possibly critical details, I helped him pack away the game, slotting every piece into its designated slot and folding up the board. "Hugo also said that old man Dillon died foaming at the mouth. Implied that he'd been poisoned by Pete."

Doc Armstrong gave a short bark of laughter. "The foam was due to pulmonary edema. Randolph Dillon died from an ordinary heart attack. And it wasn't his first, I might add — that man's arteries were more clogged than the drains in this place. If you value truth, Garnet, then take my advice and don't believe half of what that old crackpot tells you."

I said: "Sure."

But I thought: *which half?*

Back inside my Honda in the Roseacres' parking lot, I checked Colby's phone. I'd left it plugged in, but it seemed like no charging had occurred while the engine was off. Was that usual, or had Hugo sold me a dud adaptor? Either way, the iPhone was as dead as a dodo. I started the car's engine, and a minute later the charging icon appeared on the phone's screen. I sat with the engine idling, eyes on the phone, willing it to suck up power faster so I could explore whatever information it held.

While I waited, I mused on everything I'd heard that day. Professor Perry's theories on my mental health (or lack of it); Hugo's gossip about the dodgy land deal and his suspicions about some of the town's finest citizens; Doc Armstrong's warning, and the way he'd told me a little and withheld much more.

He was clearly on the way out and seemed lonely. His wife appeared to have abandoned him, and he'd given up on his son. I didn't know the state of play between him and Jessica, but I knew it was past time for me to speak to her directly. I keyed the number Armstrong had supplied into my own phone, hesitated a moment, then tapped the call icon. She answered on the third ring.

"Hi, Jessica, it's Garnet," I said.

"Garnet? Garnet McGee?" She sounded more astounded than delighted to hear from me.

"The one and only."

Silence.

"I'm back in town visiting my parents, and I wondered if we could get together and have a chat? Do coffee or something, and catch up on old times?"

The other end of the line was quiet for so long that I wondered if she'd hung up on me, but she was probably only debating whether to play nice or to advise me to go jump in the lake. Again.

Finally, she said, "When?"

"Today?"

"Well, I'm at the gallery, getting things ready for the opening tonight. It's my husband's latest exhibition. You can come around, if you don't mind talking while I set up."

It wasn't an enthusiastic sure-I'll-drop-everything-to-accommodate-you sort of invitation warmly extended to an old friend, but rather a polite, reserved offer to a remote acquaintance. It was what I deserved.

"Sure, okay. Um, the gallery?" I asked.

"Art on Main," she said. "It's on Main Street."

"You work there?"

"I own it."

Awkward.

"Wow, that's great," I said, trying to remember if I'd ever heard Jessica express any interest whatsoever in art.

Almost as if she could hear my thoughts, she said, "My husband is Nico Mantovani. The famous artist?"

"Right! Wow!" I'd never heard of him, but that meant nothing; my knowledge of art was limited to a fondness for Van Gogh and Monet. I'd have been hard-pressed to know the name of any twenty-first-century painter. "Should I come over now?"

"Yes, if you want some time alone with me. The guests will start arriving after five. You're welcome to stay for the exhibition, of course. Bring a plus-one, if you have one." Was there a sarcastic edge to the last words?

"I'm on my way," I said, and ended the call.

But I didn't put the car in gear and head back into town, to Jessica and my past. That would have to wait, because Colby's phone now showed one bar of charge in its battery display.

Holding my breath, I pressed the on switch. When the prompt to enter the passcode displayed, I typed 4EVA. And punched the air in triumph as the screen lit up.

30

With trembling fingers, I navigated to the call log on Colby's old phone. There it was, a record of calls received and made ten years ago. I scrolled through them slowly, trying to fit them into what I knew of his life in those last few days.

Missing were all the calls made to Colby's number after Cassie took the phone and switched it off, preventing any further updates on the phone. Had it been on then, or connected to a service now, it would have shown a barrage of calls from me, trying to find out where he was, why he hadn't come around. Then there would have been his family, friends and the cops' futile attempts to get hold of him. Last of all would have been the calls into the void that I'd made in those weeks between when his body had been found and his phone service had been cancelled, hopelessly calling over and over again just to listen to his voice on the voicemail message. I sighed, remembering those days of feeling adrift on a sea of deadness, not wanting to see anyone, unable to contemplate a future without Colby.

Colby's last outgoing call had been made to me, at just after four o'clock on the afternoon of December sixteenth, the day he'd disappeared.

Sadness settled in my heart like a fog. What had we spoken about during that call? I'd been panicked that I might be pregnant, and probably hadn't been very patient or loving. He'd been preoccupied with something those last couple of days, too. Could it have been something related to his death, or was it just the increasing pressure from his father and uncle to do college applications to business schools before the looming deadlines? We must have said we loved each other; we always did. And we would have ended the call with one of us saying "always" and the other "forever." Shit. Now it seemed to me that we'd been tempting fate, holding out a red rag to a bull universe every time we so blithely uttered those words. Nothing is always, no one is forever.

I wiped the heel of a hand across my eyes and redirected my attention to the activity log. On the same day, he'd received a call from his mother which had lasted four minutes, and he'd made a long call to his uncle Roger. Thumbing back in time through the list, I saw calls to and from his family, friends, people I'd either never heard of or had forgotten in the last decade — Seth, Antoine, John — and nameless numbers which meant nothing to me.

Had the cops checked these at the time? I'd ask Ryan when I handed over the phone — I planned on doing that soon. But not immediately. There was no guarantee I'd be allowed access to it once it became official police evidence, so I was first going to harvest every last bit and byte of information for myself before turning it in. The cops hadn't had it for ten years, another day couldn't make much difference.

I'd either find a way to download the contents of the phone, or I'd do it the old-fashioned way, writing down every incoming and outgoing call before going through it with a fine-tooth comb, identifying every person he'd had contact with, analyzing the data in the hope of gleaning some meaningful information. But that would take hours and was a task for later tonight or tomorrow. Right now I wanted to quickly check a few more things before the phone ran out of juice.

Doc Armstrong's comment about Colby's inquisitiveness landing him in trouble was niggling at me. What had Colby been nosy about? Nosy. The word triggered another memory. In the flashbacks Colby had sent me—

No, I had to stop thinking that way. In the vision-type episodes *I'd had,* I mentally corrected myself, one of the attackers had yelled at Colby to keep his nose out of other people's business. I could easily imagine Colby investigating something that offended his strong sense of justice — had it gotten him killed?

I navigated back to the phone's home screen and then to his internet browser, wondering whether his search history would still be stored and available even though the phone was offline. It was. The web browsing log comprised a simple list of sites visited, often with half the name and usually with most of the address cut off.

Maybe, before I turned the phone over to the cops, I'd buy

a new prepaid SIM kit, fire up the phone, and click on the links so I could see exactly where he'd been online. Then again, maybe installing a new chip and number would automatically erase the old call and browsing logs. I wished I knew more about technology. What the hell use was it to know the difference between transference and counter-transference, or regression and repression, instead of how cell phones worked?

It would be safer to manually capture Colby's browsing history, too, just in case. That would take quite some time — the list went back months — and it would take careful analysis to determine what might possibly have been relevant to his death, versus what was just the day-to-day surfing of a teenage boy thrilled to be the owner of the hottest new cell phone.

I read through the lines slowly, taking in what I could read of the truncated site names. In the last two weeks of his life alone, Colby had visited maybe a hundred sites, including YouTube and the iTunes music store a score of times, and Amazon twice. He'd visited Myspace and Funny Or Die every day, and regularly checked hockey results.

There were several visits to sites that I thought might have been related to his schoolwork: SparkNotes pages on Hamlet for his English Lit homework, and Wikipedia pages dealing with water quality and pollution as well as an FDA site about standards for bottled water for his AP Chemistry project. I was sure he'd visited at least one site for my benefit — the uses on zinc in dairy farming. The details were cut off, but I knew it would have been about using zinc ointment to treat bovine eczema. He'd seen how distressed I was by the sick cows I'd seen when doing deliveries for my father's store to the local dairy farms, and he'd no doubt been researching if there was anything else that could fix the problem.

Oh, Colby, you were the best, I thought. *I didn't deserve you.*

It looked like he'd also researched the admission requirements for a bachelor's degree in law enforcement at colleges in Boston; he'd been trying to find one there, so he and I could still be together after we graduated high school. I puzzled over the fact that he'd visited several pages dealing with financial assistance for studying the degree — had his family threatened to cut him loose financially if he didn't study business and take up his place at Beaumont Brothers? He'd also gone to the official FBI website, which made me wonder if he'd had ambitions beyond being a small-town cop.

The search history showed several visits to the Pitchford town clerk's website, specifically to pages with the words "budget" and "minutes" in the web address. Either he'd been an eager-beaver employee, or he'd been checking out official information related to the land deal Hugo was suspicious about.

I had no clue why he'd visited some of the sites, like one on heavy metal (I hadn't known his musical tastes ran in that direction), a wiki page on something, or some place, called Itai Itai, and another listing annual rainfall in Vermont. Perhaps he'd been helping Jessica with her project. He'd looked up the definition of the word hypophosphatemia; I'd need to look it up, too, since I had no idea what it meant. And he'd been researching street drugs — Oxycontin, crystal meth, heroin, Molly. Sticking his nose into Blunt's business?

With a pang, I saw that the final site he'd visited that last day had been a post titled "How to support your pregnant friend." So, he *had* known, or guessed, what I wanted to talk about that night. He'd been reading up on the options and resources available before we met to discuss it. Ten years after that date, I could still honestly swear that Colby Beaumont was the best and most decent human being I'd ever known.

God, but I loved him, still. And I missed him so badly, yearned for him from the marrow of my bones to the scratched and picked surface of my skin. I wasn't over him, not at all. Stubbornly and impossibly, I still wanted him back. Whether the words, images and sensations I'd been experiencing were visitations or hallucinations, I wasn't ready to part with them.

"Colby, are you there?" I whispered aloud. "Are you?"

Like an immediate reply, the words were in my mind. *Always. Forever.*

For the first time, I felt — or imagined I did — a real sense of his presence, as insubstantial yet undeniable as air. He was with me in the car, and it felt good, comforting.

Wait, what was I *thinking*? Like a needle-scratch on an old record, my inner scientist interrupted the irrational thinking, mounting a fight-back against my slide into the supernatural. I needed to stop this insanity. Colby was *not* with me in the car. Colby was nowhere. He was gone, had *been* gone for years and years. I simply had to accept that.

I needed to fight the delusions and hallucinations, not succumb to them. The images and sensations were merely products of my own fertile subconscious, which was determined to fill in the blanks of my memory, mollify my sense of guilt, and appease my long-denied needs for human intimacy. I wasn't in my right mind. I was, in fact, merely suffering from an acute adjustment disorder, co-occurring post-traumatic stress, and delusional thinking.

I turned the car heater down and opened my window a crack, breathing in the frosty air for several long moments to clear my head before turning my attention to the old phone. Immediately my eyes were drawn to the icon for messages. Even though there were no new notifications showing, it was an obvious place to look. Why hadn't I searched them yet?

Because I'd been too busy conversing with nonexistent entities?

I tapped to open the texts and started reading. There were messages between the two of us, sharing trig homework answers and agreeing to meet at my house that Sunday night, and a message from his father confirming the dinner arrangement with his uncle Roger at the Tuppenny Tavern. The first message that Sunday morning had been to me, just to tell me he loved me. I lingered on that text a few moments then scrolled back. My fingers stilled over a series of three texts received on the day before from someone called Jezebel.

I blinked, unable to take in what I was reading. Then I thumbed back to the first one and read them in sequence.

> *Dearest Colby, I didn't mean it about firing you. I was just a little mad. I'm concerned that you may have misinterpreted the argument you overheard in my office today. It wasn't what it sounded like. There is nothing untoward about that deal, but your uncle can be a difficult man at times, and he really is being absurdly*

obsessive about the details of the contract. You would think by now he would trust me, as I hope you do. Fond regards, Michelle

Michelle Armstrong was "Jezebel?" What had Colby overheard, how come she'd fired him, and why the hell did a text from his boss contain words like *dearest* and *fond*? The next text from her was even worse.

Let's get together tonight over dinner and a glass of wine so I can explain everything to you. There's a lovely private dining room at the Frost Inn. Shall I book it for us? Michelle

Mrs. Armstrong had been some piece of work! Offering an intimate dinner, with alcohol, to an underage employee. And one who'd had a girlfriend, moreover. Ryan had said she was a cougar; this was proof she'd been putting the moves on Colby. He, I was pleased to see, had replied to none of her texts, not even the one that read:

Don't sulk, Colby. I apologize for what I did in my office, ok? I was just trying to be friendly, to defuse the situation with a little humor. I see now that it was misplaced. Sorry!!!! Let me make it up to you. Michelle

Had Colby met with her? No, he wouldn't have. Would he? I hadn't seen him that Saturday night. And in our calls, he hadn't told me about being fired or said anything about her doing something that upset him. Feeling suddenly hot, I turned the car's heater off completely and lowered my window all the way down. My cheeks were burning, and I felt suffused by a sense of ... embarrassment? I got the distinct impression that whatever MILFy Michelle had done, Colby hadn't liked it, not one bit.

I scowled down at the phone but saw no more recent messages from Jezebel. But the next message in the list, also sent that Saturday, sent a thrill of excitement fizzing through my veins.

I need to talk to you privately. Tomorrow night, 10pm, at the bandstand by the pond? J

31

THEN
Thursday December 20, 2007

"She's not a suspect, Bob. We just want to ask a few questions, check if she has any information for us," Chief Turner said.

"Nevertheless, she's still a minor, so her mother and I will sit in on this interview," my father replied.

While they haggled, I slouched in a chair, allowing my eyes to drift around the room and my mind to wander to any subject but Colby. The walls of the police chief's office were pale green on the top and paneled with dark wood on the bottom, giving the room the look of a choc-mint popsicle. Two tall filing cabinets stood in one corner, and in the other, the state and national flags drooped from a plastic pole. A whiteboard planner, framed photographs of the police department staff posing with their marked cars outside the station, and a corkboard overflowing with notices, newspaper cuttings and business cards hung on the wall.

Turner's desk was similarly cluttered. A framed photograph

of the chief with his family and another of him receiving some award jostled for space with untidy piles of paperwork, a pair of Ray-Bans, a two-way radio unit, a goldfish bowl filled with red-and-white candy canes and, for some reason, a can of air freshener. Did he fart a lot?

Green tinsel with red bows festooned the doorframe and the non-opening window which looked onto the hallway, where two people sat slumped on a bench beside a water cooler. The tall man had the wild beard, rough, weathered skin and crazy assortment of clothes that identified him as homeless, while the dead eyes and facial sores of the emaciated woman next to him stamped her as a junkie.

Above their heads, posters chirruped warnings: *Stay alive, don't text and drive; Click it or ticket; Ice and snow — take it slow; Say nope to dope!* Someone in the Pitchford Police Department was a frustrated poet. I wondered if it was Vanessa's boyfriend, Officer Ryan Jackson, who now stood in front of the closed office door, arms behind his back, studying me.

His gaze moved from my unwashed hair, to my swollen eyes, bandaged hand and gnawed fingertips, but it couldn't see inside of me where the action was — where grief clenched my heart with cold fingers, aching rage throbbed behind my eyes, and dullness clouded my mind like the fog which hovered over Plover Pond.

"Chief Turner is talking to you, Garnet."

I shifted in the chair to ease my lower back, which hurt as badly as my head. "Yeah?"

"I asked you when the last time was you saw Colby — before his death, I mean?" Chief Turner asked.

"Friday, at school," I answered, and the interview began.

Turner sat behind his desk, fat as a tick, sucking his teeth as if he could extract an extra morsel of food from them, while I answered the same questions over and over.

Hadn't I seen Colby on Saturday?

No, he had a Saturday job at the town clerk's office.

Did I know who had attacked Colby? Did I know why he was at the pond that night? Did I know anything that might shed light on his death?

No, no and no.

Did he have any enemies?

No!

Did I know where his phone was?

No.

"His phone?" my father asked. "Wasn't it stolen?"

"Might have been," Turner said. "Or maybe not. All we know is it's missing, along with his wallet."

"So, it was a robbery, then?" my father said.

My mother leaned forward in her seat and asked, "How exactly did he die?"

Turner's tongue ran around the front of his teeth then settled behind his incisors and sucked. "It looks very much like he drowned."

"He didn't bleed to death?"

"I doubt it, ma'am. His lacerations didn't appear to be severe enough for that."

I clenched my left hand, aware of the pain in the cut on the palm, yet feeling separate from it. "What about those bloodstained paper towels in the storm water drain?"

"Juice from … those red, round jobs?" Turner said, and snapped his fingers when he got the word he was searching for. "Beetroot! It was beetroot juice."

My mother sat back, looking reassured. What about?

Ryan Jackson cleared his throat and spoke for the first time. "But there may have been severe internal bleeding."

My mother frowned, and Chief Turner looked irritated at the interruption. "What Officer Jackson means to say is that we won't know for sure until the medical examiner has done the autopsy." Directing his attention back to me, he said, "You mentioned yesterday that you and Colby had arranged for him to come around to your place Sunday night."

I nodded.

"Why? What was so urgent that it couldn't wait until you saw him at school the next day?"

"There was just something we had to talk about."

"I need to know the precise nature of that intended discussion, Garnet."

I hesitated, casting a glance back at Ryan. I didn't feel like discussing this in front of him, or my parents. Then again, I didn't feel like anything. And what did any of it matter now?

"Officer Jackson, go get us all some coffee, will you? Bring the cookie tin, too," Turner said. With an annoyed glance into the hallway, where the homeless man was chugging water from a paper cup and the junkie was pulling hard on a cigarette, he added, "And get rid of Lyle before he empties our water cooler."

"He said he had something to report."

"I don't have time for his crackpot tales about the CIA today. Tell him to clear off. And inform that … woman" — I had a sense he'd bitten back a harsher label — "that if she wants to smoke, she'll have to do it outside; this is a government facility."

Looking reluctant, Ryan opened the door and headed out. Turner's hand hovered over the candy canes a moment and then withdrew. He cleared his throat and said, "So, Garnet. Tell me what you planned to talk to Colby about on Sunday night."

Three pairs of eyes fixed on me.

I sighed. "I was worried that I was pregnant."

Turner smiled grimly.

My mother's eyes widened, and her mouth fell open. "*What?*" she said, looking first at me and then at my father.

He didn't look shocked at the news. He looked angry.

"Did you know about this, Bob?" she demanded.

"I guessed as much."

"Why? How?"

"Two teens who think they're in love — it's hardly a stretch to think they'd be sleeping together."

"Was there something more that made you suspect?" Turner pressed him.

My father blew out an irritated breath. "Doris, my sales assistant, told me Colby came in and bought a pack of condoms. Asked me, 'Isn't he the boy dating your daughter?' She thought it was a huge joke."

Dad stared down at his lap, opened the hand that was bunched in a fist, and massaged it as though it pained him. Becoming aware of Turner observing him, he stopped and folded his arms.

"So, Garnet, how did Colby feel—" Turner began, but my mother cut across him.

"Hold the telephones! *Are* you pregnant?"

I shrugged and glanced out of the window to the hall. The bench was empty now.

"Honey, why didn't you tell us?" she asked, her eyes moist with tears.

"I knew you'd be angry."

"I'm not angry," my mother said. "Not at all."

"I am," my father said. "Not at you, at him. He should have known better, used protection to keep you safe."

"He did. We did." I rubbed my aching lower back and sighed again. "Sometimes things just happen, is all."

Ryan returned then, with a tray laden with cups, a pot of coffee and a plate of festively frosted gingerbread men. I shook my head at the offer of refreshments and nibbled at an edge of hard skin on the side of my thumb instead, welcoming the sharp pain and the faint taste of blood.

"Why didn't you tell me about this yesterday?" Turner asked me.

"Because you would have assumed Colby had guessed, that he'd freaked out and left town. And then you wouldn't have searched thoroughly enough." I gave Turner a hard stare. "I *told* you he hadn't run away. He would never have."

As I shifted in my chair, I felt a familiar sensation deep inside. I closed my eyes against the welling tears and dropped my head onto my chest. This was what I'd wanted more than anything, right? But now that I had it, I didn't feel relieved. I felt empty. For a few hours, I'd thought I'd at least have something of Colby to hold onto, to keep and to love. But now I knew I didn't even have that.

I stood up, and as I walked to the door, headed for the restroom, I told my dad, "You can relax. I'm not pregnant."

32

NOW
Wednesday, December 20, 2017

S itting in my car, clutching Colby's phone with suddenly
sweaty hands, I read the message again. Slowly.

*I need to talk to you privately. Tomorrow night,
10pm, at the bandstand by the pond? J*

The hairs on the back of my neck stood up. Maybe, my logical
brain interjected, that was because the car window was open a crack,
and an icy breeze was blowing onto me. Whatever. This message
was something important, I *knew* it. Had someone lured him to the
pond, only to attack and murder him? Who was "J"?

Jezebel. But no, shameless as she was, Michelle Armstrong
surely wouldn't have called herself that. And anyway, the text
hadn't come from the number stored for her on Colby's phone.
Whoever had sent the message hadn't been saved with a name
in his contacts. I jabbed my thumb against the number, but
nothing happened. Of course not — the phone was no longer
connected to any service.

Colby had replied: *OK.*

I switched on my own phone and had just keyed in the first few digits of J's number when it rang loudly. Startled, I dropped Colby's phone down the side of the seat.

Who the hell was phoning me now? "Hello?"

"Hey, it's Ryan."

"Oh, hi. What's up?"

"I'd ... like to see you again. I thought we could have dinner together?"

This was unexpected.

"Would you like that?" Ryan asked.

Would I? He was a nice guy — smart, kind, and attractive enough to blip on my radar — but in the space of seconds I could see all the complications that would flow from a date with him. Sharing personal stuff. My mother's excitement. Local tongues wagging. Touching. Trusting. Leaving town, leaving him. Someone getting hurt. Nope, I would not like that.

"How about we do art instead?" I said and explained about the exhibition at Jessica's gallery.

He sounded keen to join me. "Should I come and pick you up at your parents' house?"

"No, I'll meet you there. Any time after five."

"I'll be there," he said, and added, "You sound breathless. Have you been running? Because I'm pretty sure the doctors told you to take it easy."

"No, I'm just ..." What — excited, nervous, uneasy? "I just found something that might shed light on Colby's last day."

"What? What did you find?" Ryan demanded.

"I'll tell you about it tomorrow. I just need to check a few things first."

"Garnet, if you have information or evidence about an ongoing murder investigation, you need to inform me immediately. Withholding anything is an obstruction of justice and can land you in hot water," he cautioned, his voice sounding a lot less friendly than it had a minute ago.

"I'm not obstructing anything. Quite the opposite."

"You can tell me tonight."

"It'll take too long," I said, playing for the time I'd need in order to save all the details from the phone. "I'll come into the station tomorrow morning, okay? And make a full statement with everything I know. Right now, I've got to go. See you later."

I ended the call and retrieved Colby's phone from under the seat, but when I pressed the button to activate the screen, I discovered it was stone-dead again, having disconnected from the charging cord when it fell. I tossed it into my handbag and headed back into town. If I was going to have some time alone with Jessica, I'd have to hustle — it was past four o'clock already.

A caterer's van was pulled up in front of the gallery, but I found a parking spot a little farther down Main Street. I ran a comb through my hair, applied a fresh coat of lipstick and stepped out into the cold, dark afternoon. Passing a clothing boutique on my short walk down to the gallery, I popped in and purchased a gray, knee-length cardigan with deep pockets and a brightly patterned silk scarf which I hoped would make my jeans and black turtleneck sweater look a little more stylish.

The assistant tutted at the casual way I draped the scarf around my neck, and insisted on tying it into an elegant knot. The deep yellow threaded through the gray-and-black paisley motif reminded me of the color that had twice flooded my vision. I told myself to forget about it. It was undoubtedly merely a neurological symptom, like the visual disturbances migraine sufferers often experienced.

At the gallery entrance, I slipped ahead of a bulky young man carrying trays of food and held the door open for him while I took in the interior. I wasn't sure what I'd expected, but it wasn't this classy space with large skylights set in a high roof above stainless steel rafters, and a polished concrete floor acid-washed in shades of nickel and verdigris green. The white walls were hung with Mantovani's paintings, and even my untrained eye could tell at a glance that his work was exceptional.

One piece caught my attention immediately. It looked like multiple black-and-white pictures of a woman's face, captured in a series of different profile orientations as if she was turning her head to glance backward, and emphasized with streaks of gold and scarlet. Examining it more closely, I saw that although they looked like photographic exposures, each of the faces was indeed finely painted. The information card beside the work informed me that the piece, titled "Echoes of Self," was a mixed media work in oil, cold wax, egg tempera and gold leaf.

"Garnet?"

I turned to see Jessica walking toward me, an uncertain smile on her face.

"Jessica!"

I opened my arms wide and went in for a hug, but instead

she air-kissed the space on either side of my cheeks. We exchanged the usual platitudes about not looking any older; mine, at least, were sincere. Jessica looked every inch the sophisticated adult woman I never felt myself to be. Her auburn hair swung in a shoulder-length bob, her makeup achieved the kind of naturally flawless look that only came with expert and time-consuming application, and she wore a snug-fitting dress of oatmeal cashmere that showed she'd lost a good ten pounds since high school. Her grooming was immaculate, but her face was taut with anxiety — in anticipation of this encounter with me, I wondered, or was she generally wound this tight?

"Can I offer you a glass of wine?" Jessica asked, gesturing to a back corner of the gallery where a young woman in a black tuxedo and baker boy hat was shoving a bottle of champagne into an enormous silver wine cooler, in which several bottles of wine already rested on a bed of ice. Stacked on the table beside it were glasses, bottles of red wine and, I was pleased to see, water.

"I'd better just go with water for now," I said. "I've already got two whiskeys under my belt."

She handed me a bottle of water — Beaumont's sparkling Eau de Café — and poured herself a large chardonnay. Touching her glass to my bottle, she said, "Here's to daytime drinking," and took a serious sip of her wine.

"Your father insisted," I said.

"You've been to see him?"

"This afternoon."

"That's how you tracked me down, I suppose. How was he?"

"Tired."

Also, cagey and not very forthcoming.

Jessica's erect posture slumped a little, and she took another swallow of wine. We moved into a corner near the bar, out of the way of the caterers who were placing tray after tray of food on a serried arrangement of three tables in the center of the gallery. My stomach growled, reminding me how little I'd eaten that day.

"How's your mother doing?" I asked.

"She's fine, still stays in the old house on Pond Road, but she's not up to taking care of my father now — well, you saw how ill he is. He gets great care at Roseacres, though, and I visit him as often as I can," she said, sounding defensive. "When he wasn't quite so frail, we'd have him and Mom over every Sunday for lunch."

"And Blunt? See him often?"

"We've never had him at our house."

"Oh."

"Nico wouldn't like it, and besides, I want nothing more to do with my brother." Judging by the fierce bitterness of her tone and the swig of chardonnay that followed, things with Blunt had been rough over the last decade.

"I hear he has a place in the woods?"

"Who told you that?"

"Hugo. The old guy who runs the hardware store on Cabot Street."

She gave a sharp bark of laughter that sounded very much like her father's. "That man's a terrible gossip, and he's more than a few colors short of a full palette. Did he tell you about the lights in the sky above the new golf estate?"

"Government surveillance?"

"Hmm. He told *me* it was aliens, and the farmers ought to lock their cows in their barns at night, so they don't get experimented on. Animal dissections and diseases — that's the agenda of the little gray men, according to Hugo."

"So, your brother doesn't live in the woods behind the estate?" I pressed.

She raised one shoulder in a half-shrug. "James struggles to function in society. That's why he lives in a trailer back up there."

"He has mental problems?"

"No. Maybe. I don't know — to be honest, it's hard to tell. He's pretty much fried his brain with drugs over the years."

"I remember he always used to smoke pot."

"And deal it — no need to be polite with me. He got into dealing prescription opioids, and when law enforcement cracked down on that, he switched to heroin." She avoided meeting my eye as she signaled to the bartender for another glass of wine. "Heroin is cheap and easy to use. Vermont's rotten with it. And now fentanyl, of course."

Had Colby's path crossed Blunt's, or had he perhaps tangled with a trafficker? There was big money in drugs, and people hyped up out of their right minds. Messing with them would have been dangerous.

"And sometimes I've wondered if he ..." Jessica's voice petered out as she stared into space, deep in thought.

I gave her a few moments and then prompted, "You were saying something about Blunt?"

"Was I? I don't remember now." She intercepted a woman placing a stack of laundered hand towels on the counter near the door and directed her to the bathroom at the back of the gallery.

"Catch me up on your life, and on how you wound up married to such a talented artist." I gestured at the works on the wall.

"He is great, isn't he?" she said, smiling complacently.

She had, she said, met Nico Mantovani just before she graduated with a business degree from the University of Vermont, in Burlington.

"It was his first ever exhibition, and it was held at the university's gallery, where I had a part-time job. He was eleven years older than me, and he wasn't famous yet, but I could tell he would be. He took me under his wing."

Listening to what she'd accomplished in the years since, I rather thought she may have taken him under *hers*, because it sure sounded like she'd been the force behind his rise to prominence and success in the art world. She'd married him, gotten a second degree, this time in the fine arts, opened this gallery to showcase his work and occasionally that of other local artists, and along the way found time to have a pair of twin sons. I was exhausted just listening to it all.

And also a little sad.

If Colby hadn't died, would he and I have married and had kids by now? I wondered if we'd still have been in love, or whether we would have gone the route of most childhood sweethearts — growing apart as we grew up. Always and forever, or older and colder?

"Twin boys! Will I meet them here tonight?" I asked Jessica.

"Goodness, no! They're really noisy and high energy. I

mean, they're three-year-old boys." She picked an invisible speck off the rim of her glass. "Nico likes peace and quiet. He finds they distract him from his work."

Not all wedded bliss in the Mantovani mansion, then?

"Oh, will he be doing work here tonight? Painting something for us?" I asked.

"No," she said stiffly, holding her glass out to the bartender for a top-up.

"You used to have a thing for Pete Dillon. I always thought" — when I thought about Pitchford and its citizens at all, which was hardly ever — "that you might wind up with him."

Jessica smiled, and a naughty glint lit her eyes. For a moment she looked like the friend I'd once known. "I always thought so, too. But duty came first."

"Duty?"

"Oh, finally!" she said, speaking to a man who'd just come in, carrying a tower of stacked boxes. "On the food tables, please, and wipe the platters before you transfer the sushi onto them. Come see, Garnet, what do you think of these stands?"

"They're … extraordinary," I said, eyeing the pewter octopuses which balanced glass platters in their writhing tentacles. In truth, I couldn't tell whether they were phenomenally stylish, or horribly kitschy.

Keeping one eye on the bustling caterers, Jessica asked me the question I'd been hoping she wouldn't: "So, what have *you* been up to all these years?"

33

Catching Jessica up on my life took less than a minute. While she'd been getting degrees, popping out babies, and growing a business, I basically hadn't accomplished a damn thing, either professionally or personally. As she grasped this, Jessica loosened up noticeably. Perhaps I was being unfair — maybe she was relaxing because the exhibition arrangements were clearly under her firm control, or perhaps it was because she was already well into her third glass of wine. A chip off the old Doc Armstrong block.

When the caterer presented her with an invoice for signing, however, she took it with a steady hand, inspected it with an expert eye, and immediately detected some error in the charges.

"Excuse me a minute, Garnet, I need to sort this out." She marched to the counter near the front door, whipped out a fancy stainless-steel calculator, and began adding figures.

"I'll just help set out the food," I said, moving over to the tables, where after checking over my shoulder that Jessica was still occupied in her calculations, I wolfed down several cucumber maki and one huge rainbow roll.

"Not enough wasabi," I told the guy still arranging food on the octopus platters.

He said nothing but stared at my mouth while brushing his top lip; I was just in time to wipe a few incriminating grains of rice off my own before Jessica returned.

"Honestly, you can't trust anyone!" She glared at me, and for a moment I thought she was mad that I'd made inroads into the food, but then I realized she was talking about the supplier. I wasn't off the hook, however, because she added, "I need to get something off my chest, Garnet."

I braced myself. "I'm listening."

"I'm still angry with you for what you did back then, in senior year. How you basically just stopped being my friend."

I was surprised to see that her eyes were moist. This obviously still mattered to her.

"Jessica, I'm sorry. It was such a bad time for me. I was …" How to put that confusing mixture of agonizing grief and necessary numbness into words? "Broken," I finished lamely.

"I could have helped you mend, but you wouldn't let me!" she accused. "You'd think that after Colby was gone, we would have drawn closer together, gone back to being the best friends we'd been before you two started dating, but you just locked me out of your life."

"You're right."

I tried to explain how I'd shut down on everybody, how I'd lost the capacity to connect with anyone, how I'd no longer trusted others not to disappear from my life without warning, taking the pieces they'd torn out of me with them.

Better never to have loved at all, than to have loved and lost — that had been the conclusion drawn by my seventeen-year-old self. I'd hurt Jessica, I knew that, but I'd needed to be alone, to depend on no one but myself. When she became friends with Ashleigh and Taylor and stopped trying to reconnect with me, I'd felt only relief, because there'd been one less thing to remind me of the past.

"You were so much a part of the happy times with Colby, and also so much a part of those awful days when he was missing..." Waiting out the storm. Tramping through the snow. Calling his name. Putting posters on poles. The pond. "I needed to block out those memories, you know? Which meant I couldn't hang out with people who'd been there. I wasn't strong enough to handle it. I was a coward," I admitted.

"I can understand what you must have been going through, it's just" — she blew out a long breath — "it really hurt to lose my best friend, you know?"

"I do know," I said, though I was thinking of Colby.

"Nothing was ever the same after that."

"I'm truly sorry." I gave her forearm a squeeze; I didn't think she'd welcome another hug. "You know, that whole time has been on my mind lately — Colby's disappearance, his funeral, how his death was never solved."

"Uh-huh."

"Did you ever remember anything that could shed light on it?"

"Me?" She looked startled.

"Yeah. Maybe something that in hindsight, or from the

perspective of your adult self, seemed odd or suspicious?"

"No, nothing. Why do you ask?"

"I just … It's not finished for me, you know? I've battled to get on with my life because it's still … open."

A flicker of sympathy crossed her features. It would no doubt disappear when I asked the questions I needed to.

"And did you send Colby—" I began, then stopped, trying to think of a way to find out what I wanted to know without tipping my hand. "Did you perhaps have any contact with him the day before he disappeared? Like, did you maybe call him, or send a text, or meet up with him that Sunday?"

"What the hell, Garnet? Are you accusing me of cheating with your boyfriend?"

Interesting. I hadn't said anything about *cheating*.

"Not at all. I'm just asking if there was any reason you'd have wanted to meet him. I remember you guys had an argument about Blunt, and I thought maybe …"

"Maybe — what, exactly? Are you accusing me of murdering Colby?" She slammed her glass down hard on the table. A little wine sloshed over the edge and puddled on the tablecloth.

"I'm not accusing you of anything, I'm just trying to figure out what happened, okay?"

Flustered, she left me to greet a cellist who'd just arrived and helped him set up near one of the front windows. Guests started trickling in a few minutes later. I was surprised to see Pete Dillon among the early arrivers. I would have said he was more the type to spend a winter's evening in front of the TV, beer in one hand, remote control in the other. It seemed like everyone except me had changed since high school. Jessica greeted Pete at the door, her cheeks pink and her face suddenly looking fully awake. I walked over to join them.

"Pete, you remember Garnet McGee from high school?" she said.

He nodded a greeting at me. "Yeah. She was in the coffee shop on Saturday."

"You've been here four days already?" Jessica said, clearly pissed that I hadn't made contact with her sooner.

"I did spend two of them in the hospital after nearly drowning in the pond!" I said.

"That was *you*?" Jessica didn't seem too worried at my brush with death. "I'd heard there was an incident, but I've been too busy organizing this show to read the papers."

I turned to Pete. "Where's Judy?"

"At home with the kids."

In a snippy tone, Jessica told Pete, "Inspector McGee here is trying to solve our town's grand mystery — Colby's Beaumont's death."

"Oh, yeah? Discovered anything yet?" he asked.

I gave a noncommittal shrug. "I may have found something."

Pete looked ready to ask me for details, but just then the great artist himself arrived, making a show of embracing his wife and greeting the guests loudly, and Pete melted away to grab a drink at the bar. Jessica introduced me to her husband, and it took me only five minutes to discover that Nico Mantovani was a douchebag. Attention-seeking, self-aggrandizing, and clearly uninterested in small fish like me who lacked either the funds to purchase his art or the influence to promote his fame. If this was the alternative to spending nights alone in my small apartment in Boston, Jessica was welcome to it.

The gallery was filling up quickly, and the noise level rising apace. I recognized many of the faces from back when I'd still lived in the town, but had no desire to reconnect with any of them. Jessica moved around the room, welcoming new arrivals and pressing food and wine on everybody. When Ryan arrived, looking even better in his smart pants, blue shirt and black blazer than he did in uniform, he made a beeline directly for me.

"What did you find out about Colby's death?"

"Can't a girl have a drink before she gets interrogated?"

"Fine. What would you like?"

Beer, but none was on offer. "White wine. With ice."

"With ice? Like, *in* the wine?"

"I like my cold things cold," I explained.

"Even in winter?"

"Even in winter."

"Whatever you say." He moved off through the throng to the bar while I edged over to the food tables and piled a plate with sushi.

Michelle Armstrong made her entrance in a flurry of loud greetings. I examined her with keen interest. Her figure was a little softer than a decade ago, but not much, and her face was, if anything, younger. She'd had it heightened, tightened and brightened — I'd put good money on that. In her tight-waisted, low-necked mini dress, her six-inch heels, and with her determinedly blond hair curled in ringlets around her face, she looked more than a little ridiculous. Mutton dressed as lamb.

Her eyes scanned the room, passing over me without a hint of recognition, and then returned to Nico. After fawning over him for several minutes — touching his hand, adjusting his collar — she turned her attention to a new arrival, Roger Beaumont. Colby's uncle was dapper in a navy suit, but he looked considerably older than the last time I'd seen him. I wanted to speak to both him and Michelle, to ask them about their calls and messages to Colby, but the room was crowded, and I couldn't seem to get near them. Instead, Ryan and I wound up chatting to Jessica, Pete, and Ashleigh Hale about how things had changed in Pitchford in the last ten years.

I sipped my wine which, sadly, had only two ice cubes bobbing about in it. I was only half-listening to the conversation; my thoughts were back on Colby's phone and that text message. The number had begun with the 802 Vermont area code and, if I remembered correctly, had a one in it somewhere. As soon as I got home, I'd charge the phone, note the number, dial it from my own phone, and identify who'd arranged that rendezvous with Colby.

There were several contenders for the sender, "J". It could have been Jessica — she'd certainly seemed overly defensive earlier — or her brother. I couldn't recall if James used to refer to himself by his given name or by the nickname we'd assigned him. The "J" could also have been Judy trying to worm her way back into Colby's affections. I didn't think she'd ever resigned herself to having Pete instead of Colby. Who would? Of course, the "J" might have referred to a surname, like — I cut a glance across at Ryan — Jackson. Suddenly, I was out of patience.

"It's too noisy here to catch up on everyone's news," I said. "How about we get together while I'm in town and do it properly? I'll book a table at the Frost Inn, and we can catch up on old times. Jessica, I have your number." I pulled my phone out of my handbag and looked at Pete expectantly. "But I don't have yours, or Judy's. Unless they're the same numbers as you had ten years ago?"

"No, they're different."

Damn. So much for my sneaky ruse.

Although I had no need for Pete and Judy's current numbers, I made a show of keying them into my phone and saving them as contacts when Pete rattled them off.

"Looks like it's time for an upgrade, there, Garnet," Pete said, curling his lip at my phone. "I can recommend this baby."

Smiling smugly, he showed us his phone — a sleek gold thing which may well have been worth more than my car.

"It's a thing of beauty, Pete," I deadpanned, wondering if overpriced phones were the new phallic symbols. Maybe I could do my thesis on *that*; it sounded like a lot more fun than grief.

"I bought one for Judy, too. I like to take care of my woman."

I couldn't be sure, over the loud hubbub in the room, whether he'd said woman or women — plural. Either way, it was the kind of patronizing comment that Jess and I would once have mocked, but now she said nothing. Her cheeks were high spots of color — from alcohol, heat or excitement?

"Can I have Blunt's number?" I asked her.

"You want to invite my brother to a reunion dinner?" she

said, looking and sounding incredulous.

"Sure, for old time's sake! So, can I have it?"

She rolled her eyes but sent the number to my phone as a business card. A quick glance confirmed it had a Vermont prefix, and that the second-last digit was a one. I needed to know if this had been his number ten years ago, what all of their numbers had been back then.

"Good thing my number's always stayed the same, else I'd never remember it," I said, pulling a comical face at my supposedly bad memory. "Do you all still remember your old numbers?" The question was clumsy, but I couldn't think of a better way to ask it.

"Why would we want to?" Pete said.

Feeling Ryan's assessing glance on me, I quickly changed the subject to the closing of the local school campus and was still lamenting the loss I didn't genuinely feel, when, of all people, my parents joined our group.

"What are you doing here?" I asked my mother.

"We were invited, dear, same as you, I imagine. Hello, Jessica! Long time, never see, Peter. Ryan!" She bestowed the smile of a mother with marital ambitions for her unhitched daughter on him, nodded politely at Ashleigh, and then continued, "We've just come from the hardware store."

"Getting new lightbulbs for the lights in your room," my father added. "I discovered this afternoon that your bathroom mirror light has blown."

What had my father been doing in my bathroom?

"I meant to ask you if you had a replacement for that; I couldn't find any when I searched in the basement."

My father frowned.

My mother continued talking as though there had been no interruption, "And what do you suppose old Hugo said?"

Uh-oh.

34

NOW
Wednesday, December 20, 2017

"Hey, Dad," I said quickly, trying to head my mother off at the pass, "maybe you should take Mom to get a drink and some snacks. The sushi's great."

"Hugo said you'd been in his store this morning, looking for a charger for a ten-year-old I-telephone," my mother said, loudly enough for everyone in the vicinity to hear. "What the hicky-dick was that about, Garnet?"

"Hicky-dick?" Ashleigh sniggered, but all other eyes in our group swiveled to me.

Ryan, of course, guessed immediately. "An iPhone from 2007. That wouldn't by any chance be related to Colby, would it? It wouldn't, for example, be the very phone that belonged to him and that's been missing all these years?"

Pete gaped, and Jessica narrowed her eyes at me. "Reunion, my eye! That phone is the real reason you wanted our numbers, isn't it?" she said.

I could feel the heat rising in my face.

"Where is it?" Ryan asked. "Do you have it with you right now?"

I involuntarily clutched my handbag tighter under my arm, cleared my throat and said, "If, hypothetically speaking, I did happen to come into possession of a phone which might contain useful information — and I'm *not* saying I have, mind you, and I *am* saying you shouldn't believe everything Hugo says, or *anything* my mother says" — I glared at her — "then I would be sure to hand it over to the appropriate law enforcement agency like a good citizen." Nobody smiled. "I just want to know what happened to Colby, *okay?*"

"Oh dear, did I put my mouth in it?" my mother asked.

Before I could give her a piece of my mind, I heard a loud voice behind me say, "I think it's time to get on with the formalities, Jessica, don't you?"

Turning, I saw Michelle Armstrong, Roger Beaumont and Nico Mantovani standing just behind me. Jessica joined her mother and husband, and we all shuffled over to the right side of the gallery while, with many giggles and the assistance of both Nico and an attractive young waiter, the closest thing our town had to a mayor climbed onto a footstool placed in front of the bar.

Though Ryan stood close enough to me for our arms to touch, I studiously avoided making eye contact with him, sure that his gaze would be disapproving. Pete and Jessica were right behind us, and judging by the sound of my mother's effusive thanks, someone had found her a seat up at the front of the crowd.

Michelle Armstrong introduced her son-in-law's latest collection of work with lavish praise and burbled on about how he added to the prestige of the town, and how she hoped Pitchford would become Vermont's own art-central. Then she declared the exhibition open and stepped off the stool, inclining her head in acknowledgement of the applause.

"Would you excuse me for a minute?" I said to Ryan.

"We need to talk about that phone."

"Yeah, of course. I'm not leaving town tonight, Officer."

Before he could say anything more, I made my way through the crush and descended on Roger Beaumont, who was contemplating the same painting I'd admired earlier.

"Mr. Beaumont?"

"Please, call me Roger," he said with a friendly smile.

"I'm not sure if you remember me. I'm Garnet McGee. I'm– I was Colby's girlfriend."

I extended my hand, and Colby's uncle shook it. I didn't like him, I decided at once. Was I getting the vibe via my supposed supernatural guide, or was it just because his grip was painfully firm? Men who needed to assert dominance through crushing the bones of a woman's hand? Dicks.

"I remember you very well," he said. "You were such a charming young thing."

"Really?" I'd never been called charming before. Perhaps he was confusing me with Jessica.

"Colby was very fond of you."

Patronizing jerk. Colby had been more than fond of me. I knew few things as certainly as I knew that.

"Yes, he was," I said, trying not to show my irritation. "May

I talk to you for a few minutes?"

"Of course."

Now that I had his attention, I wasn't quite sure what I wanted to ask him. And not at all sure where to begin.

"Um, I'm chatting to people about Colby. Trying to figure out what he was doing in the last days of his life."

"I see. To what end?"

"I, um, I'm hoping that finding out more about what happened will help me come to terms with his death. You know, get some closure." *Get closure* — I loathed that phrase. I didn't believe in the concept, and despised the way people thought grief was a time-limited process that you could shut down after a respectable period. "Not knowing exactly how he died, the case staying unsolved all these years, it's been hard for me. And for his family and you, too, I'm sure," I quickly added.

He nodded. "You think solving the case will bring closure?"

No, not really. "Yes, I think it might."

"And you want to be the one that solves it, that sets the world aright?"

"Well, I'd like to see if I can help in any way."

"I think perhaps a therapist would tell you to simply accept your loss."

"Don't tell me what a therapist would say," I said, losing the battle to keep my annoyance concealed. "I *am* a therapist, for crying out loud."

"*Are* you? Your mother told me you're still a student."

When I got home, I was going to kill her. Strangle her with one of her feathered dream-catchers.

"Colby called you, on the phone I mean, the morning of

the day he died," I said. Then, belatedly realizing that my anger had betrayed me into saying more than I'd meant to, I added, "According to the records the police obtained from his cellular service provider."

"The police let you read their case file?"

If Roger checked, he'd find out I was lying. But maybe he already guessed; both he and Michelle had been standing right behind me when my fool mother had spilled the beans about me and an old iPhone.

"I wondered what you'd chatted about?" I pressed.

He sipped his wine — white, no ice. "I'm afraid I don't recall exactly; it *was* a very long time ago. But we were having dinner together with his father that night — a sort of Beaumont Boys' night out" — he smirked — "so we were probably talking through arrangements for that evening."

"For over twenty minutes?"

"He was my nephew; no doubt we chatted about this and that, and things in general."

Bullshit.

I felt the word as a sensation in my gut, but I didn't need any paranormal nudging to know that Roger wasn't telling the truth. What eighteen-year-old guy calls their uncle for a twenty-something minute chat about "this and that?" When I checked the phone later, I'd examine the call log to see if Colby was in the habit of calling his uncle, or if that last call had been a suspiciously unusual event.

"*Ri-ight*," I said, skepticism coloring my tone as the mustard-yellow haze again began coloring my vision. I blinked my eyes several times and found Michelle Armstrong had joined us and was giving me an unflattering once-over.

"Garnet McGee! *You've* changed." Her gaze flicked between my eyes, but she made no comment about their differing colors.

"Hello, Mrs. Armstrong."

"You may call me Michelle. Here, you" — she caught a passing server — "take the lady's handbag and put it with the others at the back."

I handed him my bag then, realizing what I was doing, snatched it back again. Trying not to let Michelle and Roger see what I was doing, I took out Colby's phone and put it into my cardigan pocket. I wanted to keep that safely on me.

"Give him your cardigan, too, Garnet," she instructed. "You look unbearably hot in that thing."

"I don't feel hot."

Actually, I felt kind of chilly. Goosebumps tightened the skin on the back of my neck.

"You're sweating," she pointed out.

Was I? I raised a hand to my forehead. I was.

"I'm fine," I told the server, and watched him carry my handbag off to the back of the gallery.

"On behalf of the town, I'd like to thank you for assisting the Cooper boy at Plover Pond. Though, of course, help was already on the way." Michelle took a ladylike sip of her red wine and then smiled archly at Roger and me. "So, what were the two of you discussing so earnestly just now?"

"It seems Garnet here is looking into Colby's last days," Roger said.

"Why?" she asked.

"For *closure*, apparently."

Michelle pinned me with her sharp gaze. "What's this about?"

"Colby's death has never been fully explained. I just wondered if it was time to reassess the evidence."

"Oh, yes?"

"Yes." It came out more belligerently than I'd intended. Making an effort to soften my tone, I said, "Colby had a summer job as your assistant at the town clerk's office."

"He did."

"That was at the insistence of his father and me," Roger said smugly. "We wanted him to get some work experience under his belt before he joined the family business."

"As he told you more than once, Colby was never going to join the family business," I said.

"Why wouldn't he?"

I itched to wipe the supercilious expression off his face. "He wanted to do more with his life than sell bottles of water."

Roger's face reddened. In that moment, he looked like a man whose emotions could slip the bonds of control. But almost as soon as it appeared, his anger cleared. He merely chuckled and said, "Colby was still very young and idealistic, and a little bit foolish. He would have come to his senses eventually and realized that when all is said and done, family must come first."

"I also wanted to ask both of you about the Beaumont Golf Estate," I said, then hesitated, trying to think of how to ask the next question so it didn't immediately set their backs up even more. But I wasn't a trained detective or an experienced private investigator, and no one had ever accused me of being subtle. "There was some talk, at the time, about some aspects of that land deal not being entirely … aboveboard."

"I *beg* your pardon?" Michelle said, puffing up with indignation.

Roger gave a humorless laugh. "What possible business is this of yours?"

"Did Colby assist with the deal? Was he familiar with the contract? Might he have noticed any issues with it?" I asked quickly.

"What 'issues'?" Michelle demanded, and said something more which I couldn't hear.

My vision was starting to shimmer. Here we go again.

35

Michelle Armstrong's outraged face, Roger Beaumont's scowl, the entire gallery full of guests disappeared as the present slid into the past.

"There is no official report that documents any reason why that land should not be developed!" Mrs. Armstrong's voice sounds through her closed office door directly opposite my desk.

I stare down at my work, pretend to be absorbed. I listen hard but can't make out the words in the low reply.

"That's absurd." Mrs. Armstrong again. "Since when have you paid attention to gossip?"

Another urgent murmur.

What's going on? What's the problem with the deal?

"We'll use French drains and floating foundations. It'll be fine. I'll get you your damn clearance certificate."

This time I do hear the reply. "You do that, or the deal's off!"

The door opens. My father and uncle stalk out, faces angry.

Mrs. Armstrong comes to the doorway of her office, cheeks flushed, smiling. Nothing excites her like a good fight. Well, almost nothing.

"Be a good boy and bring me a cup of coffee, Colby."

I rubbed my hands over my face, scrubbing away the vision. Michelle and Roger were staring at me, as though waiting for a reply to a question one of them had just asked me.

Distracted and drained by what I'd just experienced, I blundered into my next question with all the tact and delicacy of that bull in the proverbial china chop. "Was the estate built on wetlands?"

Michelle's eyes widened, then narrowed. "No, it most certainly was *not*. There was nothing untoward or irregular about that development. I have the documentation to prove it, and you are welcome, as is any concerned citizen, to come inspect it at any time if you doubt the word of your elected town clerk!"

I thought back to what I'd overheard. What *Colby* had overheard.

"There were rumors …"

"There are always those who lack the brains or the balls to seize an opportunity when it presents itself, and who, in their envy, will try to cast aspersions on the successful people who do," Roger said.

Michelle smoothed her hands down the skirt of her short dress. Wiping sweaty palms? "Now if that's all …" she said, blurring away again.

I take the cup of coffee into her office. She stands behind her desk, leaning on straight arms, examining blueprints on the desktop in front of her. Her neckline gapes. Full breasts. Red lace. She looks up, gives me a smile.

That smile. The one I loathe.

"Come see. It's beautiful." Taps the diagrams, but arches her back to boost the display.

"I brought your coffee."

"Over here." Nudges a coaster on the desk.

I go around to her side, put the cup down, try to go. But her hand goes to my waist. Pulls me closer. Perfume, rich, sweet, turns my stomach.

"Take a good look. Don't you think it's exciting?" Her hand slides down, squeezes my ass, moves around my hip, cups my groin.

Revulsion.

"No!" I shove her hand away, back up three steps. I want to throw up.

Her face contorts — rejection, humiliation, fury.

"Get the hell out of my office." She pokes a red nail in my chest. "And keep walking. You're fired."

"You can't—"

"I just did."

Blood pulsed in my head and bile rose in my throat as the gallery shimmered back into view.

"You!" Shaking with anger, I pointed at Michelle and hissed, "You're a sexual predator, and you put the moves on Colby. You think it makes a difference because you're female and your victims are male? You're disgusting!"

She gasped and slapped my face with a loud crack that drew gazes from all around us. "How *dare* you?" she gritted out.

"And he rejected you. You fired him because of that. Did you also kill him because of it?"

She gaped, and then she hurled the ruby contents of her wineglass at me, and stormed off, declaring, "Never in my life have I been so insulted!"

All around me, people stared and tittered, while I stood, dripping Zinfandel, with a hand pressed to my stinging cheek. A server passed me a wad of paper napkins, and as I blotted my face, a pair of hands began removing my cardigan.

"Here, let me get someone to wipe this for you," Roger said. "Soda water will get the stain out if we move quickly."

"No!" I clamped my elbows tightly into my waist to stop him pulling it off. "I'm fine!" I patted my pockets, taking comfort at the feel of the phone still safely there.

Over Roger's shoulder, I saw Jessica slipping away to the private area at the back of the gallery, followed by Pete Dillon. The furtive look he gave to check who might be watching their disappearance told me everything I needed to know about the status of their relationship. I might not know art, or chess, but I sure knew guilt when I saw it.

Wiping myself with the napkins, I pushed my way through the crowd and headed out the front door of the gallery. I blew a plume of white breath into the frigid night air, wishing I smoked because right then I could have used something to soothe my frayed temper. I had calmed down only fractionally when Ryan exited the gallery and came to stand with me.

"I'd offer you some wine, only, you know, it looks like you've had enough," he said, grinning at my wet hair and stained clothes.

I forced a brief laugh. "Do people give *you* such a hard time when you investigate?"

"No, but then I have a badge. And a gun."

"I can see how that might help. Maybe I need to get deputized."

"I wish you'd leave the detecting to me. Tell me what you know and let me get on with it."

"*Know*? I know nothing, except that I might be losing my marbles."

"Have you been letting your imagination run wild?"

"Maybe."

But, increasingly, I didn't think I was.

He stepped closer — too close — tucked a wet strand of my hair behind one ear, and dipped his head to drop a soft kiss on my forehead.

No!

Had I thought that? Or had it come from that other voice? Either way, for me this was a no — with an olive and a twist of lemon. I was leaving town in a couple of days' time, and not up for any romantic complications. Plus, it would feel like cheating on Colby. Even though that was totally ridiculous. Always and forever didn't extend into the afterlife, did it?

I jerked my head back.

"Too soon?" Ryan asked.

I nodded. Explaining the real reasons would take too long and make me sound batshit bonkers.

"Can I at least give you a hug?"

"Sure."

I stood, awkward and stiff in his embrace, until he released me, saying, "Okay, then."

"Yeah, I better get home and freshened up before the local law enforcement mistakes me for a street wino."

I had my hand on the gallery door, ready to go fetch my handbag, when a car screeched into the handicapped parking bay outside the gallery, and Judy Dillon, together with three little girls in pink pajamas, nightgowns and overcoats, spilled out. Judy's hair stood out in a halo of wild frizz, she wore a mismatched assortment of clothes — like she'd grabbed whatever came first to hand — and she looked frazzled. The very antithesis of Jessica's well-groomed, overly thin elegance.

"Stay with me, girls," she said as she hurried toward the gallery.

Whining that she was hungry, the oldest girl deliberately stepped on the heels of her younger sister so that her over-boots came adrift, and the smallest one picked her nose and curiously examined the contents.

"Mrs. Dillon, you can't park there," Ryan said. "It's reserved for people with handicaps."

"What would you call having a missing husband, three kids under ten, and not a drop of booze in the house?" she snapped. "Is Pete in there?"

"Yeah," I said. Then I remembered where I'd seen him last, and with whom. "You've got your hands full with the girls. Stay here and I'll go get him for you."

"Fine," Judy said.

The smallest girl, who had climbed onto Judy's booted foot and now clung to her calf like a barnacle on a boulder, freed one hand to wave and say, "Hi!" to someone to the left of me.

I glanced sideways. No one was there. Maybe the kid was squint.

"What are you looking at, sweetie?" I asked her.

She transferred her gaze to me and opened her mouth, but before she could speak, Judy said, "Look, are you going to get Pete, or am I going to have to go in there and make a spectacle of myself?"

"I'll be right back."

Inside, the noisy crowd jostled me from every side as I made my way to the back of the gallery. I passed a closed restroom door and a small kitchenette, where I grabbed my handbag from the row of handbags neatly lined up on a counter. Right at the back was a closed door labeled *storage.*

Feeling like an idiot, I pressed my ear against it. The sounds I heard made me want to turn tail and run away, but Judy might grow impatient and decide to come find her man. I'd never been her friend, but I couldn't do that to her. I knocked on the door. No response. I opened it and peered inside. Pete had Jessica pressed up against a rack of shelves, his lips slanting across hers, his hands running over her ass. She had one hand behind his neck and the other inside his pants. Both of them were groaning loudly.

"Pete? Pete!" I tapped his shoulder. He spun around, already zipping his pants. "Your wife is here. She's out front."

"Fuck." Pete barged past me.

Looking embarrassed but also defiant, Jessica smoothed her hair and wiped a finger around her mouth, checking for smeared lipstick. "Don't you judge me, Garnet McGee. We don't all get what, or who, we want."

"I wonder if any of us do," I said to her departing back.

I got my car keys and phone out of my bag and, on my way

back through the gallery, pretended to be checking messages to avoid meeting anyone's eye. Ryan was waiting for me outside, watching the headlights of Judy and Pete's car disappearing down Main Street.

"Right. Now that I've pissed off just about everybody here tonight, I think it's time I went home and hit the sack. It's been a *very* long day, and I'm exhausted," I said, knowing full well I wouldn't catch a wink of sleep until I'd examined and made notes on every single bit of information in Colby's phone.

"Would you like me to drive you home?" Ryan offered.

"Thanks, but it's not necessary. I have more wine on me than in me."

"At least let me walk you to your car."

"Sure, it's a whole half a block away. You never know what might happen to me."

A minute later, we were at my Honda.

"So, can I take you out for a drink sometime? Maybe dinner?" he asked.

I opened the car door, held it between us. "Last time I knew you, back in 2007, you were dating Vanessa Beaumont."

He nodded.

"You and she didn't work out?"

"No. Things were different after Colby died. *She* was different."

I could relate to that.

"And now?" I asked. "Is there a Mrs. Jackson?"

"There was. We got divorced three years ago. She lives in Texas now."

Hugo had gotten that right, then.

"And a girlfriend?" Why was I even asking these questions? I didn't care about the answers. I did not.

"I'm a free agent, Garnet. Frankly, I'm a little insulted that you feel the need to check whether I'm cheating."

"No offense intended. It's just been that kind of night," I said, tossing my handbag into the car and getting ready to climb inside, but Ryan held out a hand.

"The phone, please. Now."

I looked him straight in the eye and lied. "I don't have it with me. I'll bring it in first thing tomorrow, I *promise.*"

He looked set to argue; a distraction was necessary. I stood on my toes, leaned over the top of the door and kissed him on the lips. Then, before he could recover from the surprise, I jumped into my car, backed out into Main Street and drove off. As soon as I was out of sight, I pulled over, keen to plug the old phone into the car's charger.

I stuck my hand into my cardigan pocket. And pulled out a stainless-steel calculator.

36

Thursday December 21, 2017

Pitchford Police Station looked much the same as the last time I'd seen it, except that the walls were a soothing putty color, rather than the old mint green, and Ryan Jackson now sat behind the desk in the chief's office. There were no photos on his desk; in fact, I saw no personal touches in the room at all.

"Colby's phone?" Ryan said eagerly.

Confession time.

"It's gone," I said.

Ryan's face fell; his eyebrows knitted across the bridge of his nose. "Gone? Gone where? What do you mean?"

"It's missing. Just like my own phone, which disappeared last night between the time I left the gallery and the time I got home. Seems Pitchford is a regular den of thieves!"

"Is yours a silver Samsung with a cracked screen protector?"

"Yes. What …?"

Ryan opened a manila envelope on his desk and slid out a phone. My phone.

I snatched it up and turned it on. "Where did you get it?"

"Someone found it, and because he *is* an honest and upstanding citizen" — here Ryan gave me a hard look — "he handed it in immediately."

"You need to work on that judgy attitude of yours, Chief," I said, relieved to see that my phone was still in working order. "And who was this paragon of honesty?"

"Samuel Wallace."

I tried to remember if my old chemistry teacher (and father of creepy Lyle) had been one of the guests at the gallery last night. He could have been. Or maybe he'd gotten my phone via his son.

"Where does he say he found it?"

"In a parking bay near the gallery — where you probably dropped it as you were getting into your car."

It was possible, I supposed. I'd been juggling my keys, bag and phone at the time, and I'd been focused on Ryan.

"I want to know about Colby's phone, Garnet. Now," he said, clearly pissed off with me.

"Keep your shirt on, Sheriff, I'm getting there."

I explained how I'd had the old iPhone in my bag and then moved it to my pocket, where I'd had it for the rest of the evening — or thought I had. At some point after that, someone had pickpocketed it and replaced it with Jessica's calculator, presumably in the hope that I wouldn't immediately notice the absence of its weight.

As soon as I'd discovered the switch, I'd returned to the gallery. Ryan was already gone, but Lyle had been lurking outside. Had he been there, somewhere in the darkness earlier, when I'd been outside drying off from my Zinfandel shower? When Ryan had hugged me.

"Hey, Lyle, we met in Hugo's store this morning, remember?" I'd said.

"I know who you are."

"Right. Did you happen to find a cell phone anywhere around? Mine is missing."

He stepped up to me, close enough for me to see the anger in his dark eyes, to smell the rank odor of his body. "You accusing me of stealing?"

"Me? No, I– I just wondered if you'd found anything. Or seen anything."

"I seen lots of things."

Me too, buddy. I was still baffled by the sight of Jessica getting it on with King Ding-a-ling. How could she possibly still burn hot for Pete? He no longer had the good looks he'd once had, and his personality had always been grade-A asshole.

"You seen Cat?" Lyle asked.

I shook my head. He turned and melted back into the darkness, whistling a low call.

Inside the gallery, I discovered some of the guests — Roger Beaumont and my parents among them — had already left, but I braved Jessica, Nico and Michelle's glares to ask around about the old iPhone. No one admitted to seeing or finding anything; I hadn't really expected anyone to.

When I left for the second time, I couldn't shake the feeling of being watched. I shivered, peering into the darkness beyond the street and gallery lights. Was Lyle still out there, or was someone else keeping an eye on me? Or — as Ryan had suggested — had I just let my imagination off the leash?

When I got home, I double-checked my handbag, on the remote chance that I'd put Colby's phone there and forgotten that I'd done so. But instead of finding his, I'd realized the absence of mine. Panicking, I searched the various zippered pouches and compartments, before tipping the bag upside down and shaking out every last penny and lint-covered cough sweet. Then I'd checked my car. But my Samsung was gone. I'd figured it had been stolen, too — that whoever had taken Colby's phone wasn't taking any chances that I might have stored information, or called numbers from it, or taken screen shots on my own device. If only I'd been that smart.

I felt really bad as I recounted the previous night's events to Ryan, because there was no doubt it was my fault that a crucial piece of evidence — possibly the first break in the case in a decade — was missing. If I'd handed it in immediately, or when Ryan had asked for it, this wouldn't have happened. But, just like Doc Armstrong had said, I'd thought I could do better.

Still glowering at me from across his desk, Ryan asked, "Any idea who took it?"

"It could have been anyone," I said.

It could have been you, I thought.

He'd known I'd be coming in this morning to hand in the phone. If he had some reason for not wanting the phone to be officially entered into evidence and examined, he'd have needed to get it last night. And he could have, as easy as winking. He might have dipped his hand into my pocket while we were outside, when he'd hugged me. That would have been the best opportunity. My lips twisted at the suspicion that it was the reason *why* he'd hugged me, that the affection had been faked — a mere ruse to distract me and get close enough to stick his paw into my pocket.

Men. You couldn't trust a one of them. If I never kissed another man, it would be too soon.

"Anyone," I repeated, trying to fathom whether the frustration that tightened Ryan's features was real or feigned. Surely someone truly cut out for life as a psychologist should be able to read people better.

"Like who?" he asked.

"A bunch of people heard or could've overheard that conversation about me having the phone and filched it later. Jessica was near me a lot of the time, and her mother seemed eager to separate me from my bag and cardigan. Roger Beaumont had a chance — he had his hands on my cardigan when I was distracted. But, honestly, it was such a crush, anyone could've done it. My folks could've done it."

I said the last bit in an attempt at levity, but I couldn't summon a laugh. Instead, unwanted thoughts about my father flickered through my mind. His obsession with murder, the storage container in the basement, how he regularly went out of town on fishing trips but always arrived back with no fish. He said he practiced catch-and-release, that the fun was in the hunt — in landing the fish, not in killing them. Now the unwanted thought that those trips could have been for entirely different reasons popped into my mind.

Suspecting your own father of being a stone-cold killer? Nice one, Garnet.

I was being absurd again. Dad was a kind and gentle person,

a good father, a patient husband. An absolutely normal man. I trusted him. I was just anxious — clinically so. The same anxiety that had me biting my fingers and peeling my skin also blasted me with crazy, intrusive thoughts from time to time. Especially when my stress levels were elevated, as they most assuredly were now.

"Any specific theories as to why any of those people would have wanted Colby's phone?" Ryan asked.

"It's a funny thing, but the last time I was questioned here" — I gestured to the office around me — "Chief Turner asked me if I knew whether anyone had a beef with Colby, and I couldn't think of a single person. I figured everybody loved Colby, because I did. But now it seems to me like half the town was upset with him."

"Go on."

"Suspect number one" — I held up a finger — "Michelle Armstrong. She'd put the moves on Colby and—"

"She's admitted that?"

"—and he rejected her. And she was angry about that. Seriously. Pissed. Off. And humiliated."

"When we chatted before, I mentioned that as a possibility, and you seemed surprised. But now you seem to know all about it. Who've you been speaking to?"

I ignored his question. "And methinks MILFy Michelle over-protested muchly last night when I confronted her about it. Maybe she even planned the wine incident with Roger Beaumont — who was certainly quick and eager to get his hands on my cardigan — because suspect number two, or *suspects* number two" — I held up a second finger — "are her and anyone else involved in that golf estate land deal. Including the Beaumont brothers."

Ryan gave a snort of laughter. "You think his own father and uncle killed him?"

"Someone did," I snapped. That shut him up.

I nibbled at the hard ridge of skin above my gnawed thumbnail.

"What's the golf estate got to do with Colby?" Ryan asked.

I explained about the rumors that the estate had been built on wetlands unfit for development.

"Who told you that?"

"Hugo," I admitted reluctantly.

"That old conspiracy theorist from the hardware store? Give me a break."

"Just because some of what he says is rubbish doesn't mean all of it is. Besides, Colby knew there was something fishy about that deal. He overheard Michelle Armstrong and Roger Beaumont arguing."

My vision was going funny, speckled with dots of light, like the start of a migraine. Images and words flickered behind my eyes.

"Get the hell out of my office. And keep walking, you're fired."

"You can't—"

"I just did. And you'd better remember that according to your employment contract, anything you've heard or read, any information you've come across in the course of your work, is confidential. Don't let me hear you've been telling tales outside of class, young man."

I bit down hard on the edge of my thumb, using the pain to pull me back into the present.

"And she *knew* he'd overheard stuff," I said. "She tried to shut him up. She threatened him!"

"How do you *know* this?" Ryan asked, looking bewildered.

"You wouldn't believe me if I told you."

"Garnet," he said, an edge of warning in his voice.

I held up three fingers. "Then there's Blunt — Jessica was definitely hiding something about him last night. Back then, Colby was angry that Blunt was maybe trying to sell drugs to the kids. He had a fight with Jessica about it that last day at school, so she was angry with Colby, too. Maybe she felt the need to protect her brother, or her family — they were always crazy-proud."

I showed Ryan four fingers, but he merely shook his head at me, like my theories were insane. Good thing he didn't know the *truly* weird things that happened in my head.

"And number five: that homeless guy, Lyle Wallace," I continued. "He was there last night, lurking around outside the gallery."

"Lyle's harmless, just a bit odd."

"That's what people always say about their weirdo neighbors — until they find the bodies in the basement."

"What possible motive could Lyle have had to hurt Colby, though?"

I had no idea. "A lot of other people were mad at Colby, too."

"Like who?"

Like my father.

"Like Chief Turner. Where are we up to — seven?" I said, wiggling my fingers.

"Six."

"Colby wrote a letter to *The Bugle* complaining about police incompetence in the fight against drugs — that would have angered Chief Turner."

"The cops are always being criticized in the media, but we don't go out and assault and murder the critics."

"You said he dragged his heels on the investigation; maybe that was deliberate? I remember that when we were all searching for Colby, Turner didn't even want to search the pond." I thought of something. "Neither did the Beaumont brothers!" Or, I realized with a sinking stomach, my father.

"But based on the lack of reports about Frank Turner busting out of his nursing home and racing his wheelchair down Main Street to the gallery last night, I'm hazarding a guess that *he* didn't steal the phone."

"Sarcasm isn't a good look on you, Chief."

"I ought to lock you up for obstruction of justice."

"Please don't. Orange overalls wouldn't be a good look on me."

His lips twitched, and I hurried on, "Pete Dillon hated Colby because everyone knew Judy preferred Colby to him. And maybe Judy was still pissed off about being dumped." I waggled all my fingers.

"Enough to kill him all those months later? C'mon, get real."

Listening to him say it loud, I couldn't deny that it *was* far-fetched. The thing was, I was getting increasingly accustomed to far-fetched.

37

NOW
Thursday December 21, 2017

"Where did you get the phone in the first place?" Ryan demanded, and then listened without interrupting as I explained who'd had it all these years and why. When I finished, he folded his arms across his chest and leaned back in his chair. "Losing the phone — that's a real blow to the investigation, Garnet. You should have turned it in as soon as you found it."

"I know, I'm sorry." I dug the edge of a nail into the cuticles of the other hand, circling the arcs of the nail beds, tugging back the cuticles, avoiding his accusing gaze. "Don't you have a log of the calls from back then, though?"

"Sure, but there might have been more information on the phone."

I didn't need to look up to know that he was scrutinizing me, suspecting that I already knew what that information might have been.

"But, you'd have records of that, too, right?" I asked.

"No. It took Turner several days to get his ass into gear and apply for a search warrant to get the information from Colby's cellular provider. He had difficulty keeping things organized, and he used to procrastinate. At the time, I thought he was just sloppy. Later I realized he'd been showing early signs of Alzheimer's. Anyway, by the time we received it, all we could get was call logs and metadata — the numbers, dates, times and lengths of incoming and outgoing calls. The details about voicemails, but not the actual recordings."

Crap. Like Cassie, I'd thought they would have retrieved all of that information in the initial investigation.

"We followed up on all of the numbers at the time. That was my job."

"Find anything?"

"Nothing suspicious. Most of the calls were to and from 802 numbers — friends and family."

"And the others?"

Ryan opened a worn folder lying on his desk and sifted through the papers inside until he found the records he was looking for. He scanned the list, refreshing his memory. "There were a few we never figured out." He flicked a finger at one of the numbers printed on the page. "This one, for example — outgoing, made on December twelfth."

I sat up straight, buoyed by relief and hope. Maybe some information could still be salvaged. "Who was the call made to?"

"That was the puzzling part. Any idea why Colby would want to call the FBI?"

"As in the Federal Bureau of Investigation?"

Ryan nodded. "It was to the main switchboard number, and he was put on hold for" — he glanced at the log — "two minutes and thirty-seven seconds. But we never knew who he wanted to speak to, or why."

"I have a pretty good guess," I said, my excitement extinguishing as quickly as it had kindled. "He wanted a career in law enforcement, but his family thought that wasn't good enough." Realizing I was talking to a cop, I puffed out a breath of air in a *go-figure* sort of way. "He probably called the FBI to find out about possible careers. It was one of the sites in his phone's search history, too, along with colleges offering degrees in law enforcement."

"Anything else in his search history?"

I told him about the homework sites, the visits to the Town Clerk website and searches on different kinds of drugs. "Oh, and he'd looked up the meaning of a word — hypo-something."

Ryan gave me a look.

"It was a very long word, okay? And I wasn't expecting the phone to be stolen before I could note all the details."

"Which it wouldn't have been if you'd—"

"Yeah, yeah. I plead guilty. Were there any other interesting calls in his log?"

"This one was made the day before he disappeared. I remember Turner got real excited about it — figured it was evidence that Colby was a troubled youth. Maybe that he had some psychiatric problems."

"Who did the number belong to?"

"A crisis counseling hotline."

I didn't need the word that popped into my mind —

pregnancy — to know why Colby had called that number.

"That was probably for me. I had a pregnancy scare."

"You told him?"

"I think he guessed."

"Hmmm." Ryan glanced back down at his list. "This one puzzled me. Also outgoing, to the department of Material Science and Engineering at MIT."

"Why would he have called them?"

"Good question. When I followed up, I found Colby didn't get through to the person he wanted to speak to, a Professor Harriet Linden. So, he left a message with the departmental secretary for her to return his call. Unfortunately, by the time she got around to doing so, Colby was … gone."

I swallowed. "And she didn't know what it was about?"

"Nope, said she'd never spoken to him in his life. So that was a dead end. The rest of the calls were nothing unusual."

"What about that long call to his uncle, the one on that last morning?"

Ryan consulted his notes. "He said it was to organize their dinner arrangement that night. That there was some to-ing and fro-ing on where they'd go and if they needed to make a reservation. And—"

"For twenty minutes?"

"*And* that they'd discussed Colby's future plans. The deadlines for college applications were approaching, and he wanted to give Colby guidance on his career choices."

"*Guidance*, hah! Wanted to choose for him, more likely. And what about the text messages on the phone?"

"I don't know what those are, Garnet, because I don't have

the phone," he pointed out, sounding irritated all over again.

"No, I mean, what did you find in the information you got from the service provider?"

"Sweet diddly squat. By the time the search documentation was submitted, that information had already been wiped. In 2007, unless you were a terror suspect on the NSA's watch list, that information wasn't stored for long — the metadata about texts was only retained for about a week, and the actual content of the texts, the message itself, for only three to five days."

"I'm sorry. I've really screwed this up."

"No argument from me," Ryan said. "So, if you saw something on that phone yesterday — and I'm thinking you did, and that's why you were asking about everyone's cell numbers at the gallery last night — you really need to tell me. Now."

"Okay. Just bear in mind that when I got it, the battery was stone-dead. As soon as I could switch it on, I did, but the power didn't last long before it died again. And the phone wasn't connected to any service. What I'm trying to say is, I didn't see much."

Ryan leaned forward, bracing his folded arms on his desk, drumming the fingers of one hand on the wood.

"Okay, there was a text message — incoming, sent the day before Colby disappeared, from a Vermont number. No name."

"You didn't recognize it?"

"No, but that doesn't mean anything, you know? Even then, the only number I knew by heart was my own. And Colby's."

"What did the text say?"

"I can't remember the exact words, but the sender wanted to talk to Colby privately, and suggested they meet at ten o'clock the next night, at the bandstand by Plover Pond."

Ryan's eyebrows rose in surprise.

"Yeah," I said. "He was meeting someone. That's why he was there. That's why he was late coming to see me — only he couldn't let me know because by then, Cassie had his phone."

"That works," Ryan said. "And no signature?"

"It was signed with a 'J'."

"'J' ..." Ryan said, and I could practically see the wheels in his head turning. "Like Jessica, and Judy?"

"And James Armstrong. Though I don't know if he would have signed off with a J. I mean, we all called him Blunt, but I have no idea how he thought of himself."

"Hmmm." Ryan looked up at the ceiling, thinking for a few moments, and then shot me a glance I couldn't read. "Or I suppose it could stand for John."

"John?"

"Your father's second name."

"In case you can't tell, this" — I circled my face with a finger — "is my rolling-on-the-floor-laughing-my-ass-off face."

"Some people call him RJ."

"But no one calls him J." I narrowed my eyes. "It's much more likely to stand for Jackson," I said tartly.

He merely laughed. "You think I'm a suspect in Colby's death now? Man, you don't trust anyone, do you? Tell me, how's that working for you?"

"I just want to know who killed Colby. Who the J is who sent him that message."

"Has it occurred to you that the 'J'" — he sketched quotation marks in the air — "could just be an emoticon?"

"Huh? You've lost me."

"Don't you remember how, back then, you'd type a smiley face, and it would appear as a J? Sometimes you'd get emails, or documents from other machines, and they wouldn't render correctly — the colon-parenthesis smile emoticons would show as J's."

I actually did remember that. At the time, I'd used Outlook as my email service, and it drove me crazy when it auto-converted my smiley faces to J's.

"But ... did that happen on phones, too?" My voice sounded plaintive even to my own ears; I could feel my grand theories slipping away.

"Yeah, I think so."

Ryan's phone rang then, and with a glance at the display, he indicated that he needed to take it. A moment later, the chief's office faded from my vision, replaced by Doc Armstrong's room at the nursing home.

"It's too late, there's no point in it now. Hell, there was no point when we first spoke about this all those years ago."

"There was always a point. I was just too cowardly to make it public." The lettering on the pen in my hands blurs as tears fill my eyes.

"Yes, well, in case you were planning on making any deathbed confessions, just know that I'll still bring the sword down on your son. I've got hard evidence, you hear? Footage! And this time they'll throw the book at him — he'll never see the outside of a prison

again. It won't make any difference to me that you're not here to see it."

The door slams. The room is empty. I sigh.

"But perhaps it will make a difference to me."

Vision shimmering, I blinked myself back into the present. Ryan was still on the phone — talking, by the sound of it, to someone about a car accident outside of town. With his back to me, he traced a red line on the route map hung behind his desk.

"How bad is it?" he asked the person on the other end of the call.

I was glad for the moment to recover my senses. What I'd just seen hadn't been a flashback of Colby's, but the pen in the vision had been his. It was the one I'd found in the box. The hands holding it had been old, and the voice belonging to them had been Doc Armstrong's. I searched my handbag, but the pen was missing. I'd used it when I visited him yesterday and must have left it behind.

For the first time, I'd received a vision of something Colby was not a participant in, or a witness to. It might not even have been a flashback. I might just have seen something that was happening right now, in the present. The thought came before I could stop it: had the pen somehow been a bridge for Colby to observe that encounter, and transmit it to me?

Crazy. I was losing more of my mind by the day.

All the same, I grabbed my notebook and a pen from Ryan's desk and quickly wrote down everything I could remember from the conversation, cursing the doc for having stared at the pen instead of at the person speaking to him. Whose voice had that been? It was male and had sounded familiar. But now, with the sights and sounds disappearing like the fading remnants of a dream on waking, I couldn't say for sure who it belonged to. They'd been talking about Blunt — must have been. Some man had been threatening Blunt so as to compel Doc Armstrong not to blab a secret he'd been keeping for years. What *was* it?

As soon as Ryan ended his call, I said, "I've got to go now. I need to go see Doc Armstrong."

"That'll have to wait," he said. "I'm afraid your parents have had an accident."

38

I didn't faint, or reel from the shock. Instead, my first reaction was a stupidly superstitious thought: *I did this. By thinking bad things about my parents, I caused a bad thing to happen to them.*

"Wait!" The alarmed expression on Ryan's face told me that my own face must've registered serious shock. "They're not hurt, or at least not seriously. But their car is stuck in a ditch and needs to be towed out to the repair shop."

I blew out a long breath. "Oh, good. That they're safe, I mean."

"Do you need me to go get them?"

"I'll do it. Where are they?"

"On the access road to the Johnson farm. Do you know it?"

"Sure, I used to help my father with deliveries there back in the day. What were they doing out there?"

Ryan held up his hands in a search-me gesture. "You'll have to ask them that."

When I arrived at the scene of the accident, my mother and father were keeping warm, waiting inside the cab of old Mr. Johnson's pickup. Their Ford sedan was indeed resting nose-down in the gulley beside the road.

"Are you okay?" I asked as I opened the pickup door.

"I am," said my mother, "but your poor father got hit on the pecker."

"Shit!" I craned across her to see him.

"She means beak," Dad said, pointing to a small cut on the bridge of his nose. "I banged it on the car door when I climbed out."

"Is it broken?"

"No. It's fine."

"Did either of you bang your heads?" I asked. One McGee with a malfunctioning brain was more than enough.

"The air pillows burst open, so we're both safe and sound," my mother said. "Though I would like to get home and have a warm bath and something hot to drink, because my goodness but it's cold enough to freeze the brass off a bald monkey!"

Dad and I exchanged smiles, then I helped them into my car — Mom in the front seat because of her cast — and thanked Mr. Johnson for his help. I'd driven just a few yards when a thought occurred.

"Did you get everything you might need out of the car? Leave any valuables behind?"

"My crutches!" my mother said. "They're in the trunk."

"And my emergency kit — it's in the trunk, too. I would hate for anyone to help themselves to that," my father said.

I braked, backed up, and braved the cold again. I transferred the crutches from the trunk of their car to mine and returned to get the large red box with a white first aid cross stamped on the top. It was big enough to hold the contents of an entire emergency room and surprisingly heavy. A hook of something — curiosity or misgiving — tugged at me.

As I put the box in my car's trunk, I removed the lid and for the second time in two days found myself examining the contents of one of my father's storage boxes. A quick inspection confirmed that this one, too, had duct tape, cable ties, rubber gloves, rope, a box-cutter and a heavy flashlight, but also two bottles of water, a small fire extinguisher, a first aid kit, ice-scraper, rain poncho, several protein bars, a camo-patterned foldable shovel, and a tiny folded space blanket purchased, if I remembered right, from the gift shop at the National Air and Space Museum in DC, when the three of us had visited it at least twenty years ago.

As soon as we were headed back to town, I asked my parents about their accident. Between defensive-sounding explanations from my father and confused asides from my mother, who seemed inclined to blame the incident on Mars being "in retrograde" rather than on icy roads, I gathered that my father had overcorrected on a slide and executed a slow-motion plunge over the edge of the road.

Heart sinking a little, I realized this was probably a preview of forthcoming attractions. As my parents got older, there would be more accidents and illnesses, and I wouldn't be able to take care of them remotely if based in Boston. Whatever I decided about my studies, I did *not* want to return to living in Pitchford. For now, they were still okay to live independently, but it was something I'd have to consider for the future.

"What were you doing out at the Johnson farm anyway?" Yet another J, I realized as I said the name.

"Marjorie wanted a reading, and I obviously can't drive, so your father brought me."

"You offer a mobile service now? Uber Reads?"

"What's that, dear?"

"Why didn't she come to you?"

"Because she's too timid to drive. Even as a little girl, Marjorie had no rambunction. Besides, I wanted to get out of the house. Not seeing all my lovely clients in my store is giving me cabin fever."

"Speaking of your store, when are we going to pack it up and close shop?" I said as we reached the end of the private road and I waited for a lull in the traffic to turn onto the highway.

"We aren't," my mother replied.

"What? Since when?" I demanded, catching my dad's eye in the rearview mirror.

"Your mother thinks that she'll get depressed without the daily stimulation and social contact," my father said.

"Really, dear, I tried my utmost best to retire, but sitting around all day twiddling my thumbs just isn't for me. Besides, your father and I are beginning to get on each other's nerves."

"Are you?" I asked, surprised. I hadn't noticed any friction — well, no more than usual.

"Oh, yes," Dad said fervently, staring out of the window at the snowy forest of fir spires on either side of the road.

"For better or worse, but not for lunch — that's what I always say," Mom chirruped. "Just as soon as my cast comes off and the doctor gives me the all clear, I'll reopen the shop."

"Is there any point in trying to talk you out of this?"

"None at all," Mom said, and Dad gave me such a pleading look in the mirror that I knew he couldn't wait for her to be out of his hair either. What a family we were.

"Fine," I said.

Although I knew reopening the store was a bad idea, a part of me was relieved. If I didn't have to stay and help pack up, I could leave town earlier. Just as soon as I figured out Colby's death. But in the meantime, I needed information to counteract my crazy intrusive thoughts.

"Dad, that emergency box of yours — what's it for?"

"Emergencies," he said in a puzzled tone. "Like today. If we'd been alone, we might have needed the food and water. Dang it, Crystal, we should have used the space blanket to keep out the cold!"

"Now he remembers," Mom muttered.

"Yes, but what about the duct tape and things?"

"What things?" Dad asked.

"The rubber gloves, for a start."

"Those are mine," Mom said. "You never know, when you go visiting, if you might have to pitch in with washing the dishes, and I never, *never*, do that with my bare hands! Ruins the lines and dries the skin. So, I keep a pair in the box for emergencies."

"And do you use a lot of duct tape?" I asked.

"Not really. I don't think I've ever touched that roll in the emergency box," Dad said, looking a little dejected at the realization. "But you never know when it might come in handy to tape up a loose exhaust, or something!"

Not wishing to point out that tape would be of little use in repairing a hot exhaust pipe, I asked, "And the cable ties — what are they for?"

"What's with all the questions about my emergency box?" Dad asked.

"I– I've been thinking of putting together one for my own car."

"Good idea! I found a list on the DMV site and packed according to their suggestions," Dad said helpfully.

"So, the cable ties? And the box-cutter and the shovel?" I asked him.

"Those are all things you might need in a tight spot — to make emergency repairs or dig yourself out of the snow."

"Or if you need to poop in the woods," Mom added.

Well, that was entirely reasonable and plausible. But still... "You have a lot more of that sort of stuff in the basement."

"When I sold the store, I kept aside whatever stock I thought we might be able to use, especially the non-expiring stuff, and brought it home," Dad said.

"Soooo much stuff," Mom murmured.

"It was much cheaper than having to buy more one day when we needed it, Crystal."

"The entire basement was full to the brim with your father's stuff that summer."

"Nonsense. Besides, you're one to talk — all that junk of yours stored down there."

"People shouldn't throw stones at glass houses," Mom said sententiously, and Dad rolled his eyes.

"There was a can of pepper spray," I said.

"I'd forgotten about that! I used to take that with me on walks because the Bernsteins' dog was so vicious. Don't you remember?"

I didn't. "Why've you still got it?"

"Your father never throws anything away if he can keep it," my mother said, and began rooting about in her handbag.

"A case of the pot calling the kettle black, if ever there was one," Dad said.

Interrupting their bickering, I asked about the other question that had been niggling at me.

"When I visited Doc Armstrong yesterday, he—"

"How's he doing, poor fellow?" Mom asked.

"Badly." As I said the word, a cold, heavy dread settled in my stomach. "He said you'd asked him for a copy of Colby's autopsy report, Dad. What was that about?"

My mother turned around in her seat to look at my father. He cleared his throat and said, "Well, we wanted to know how he died, didn't we?"

"Why?"

"Why?" he echoed.

"Yes, why? I mean, the cause of death would have been released, *was* released, to the media, so why did you want all the details?"

"We wanted closure for you, dear," my mother said, extracting a packet of pistachio nuts from her handbag and tearing it open.

"Then why didn't you share it with me?"

"It was just too gruesome. It would've upset you and given you nightmares."

"I was already upset. I was already having nightmares." I met my father's worried gaze in the mirror for a moment and asked, "You didn't maybe get it for yourself?"

"For myself?" he said. "What do you mean?"

"You like that kind of stuff. Murder and court case records and autopsy reports. You're kind of obsessed with it," I said, my voice petering out as another glance in the mirror revealed the growing anger tightening his features.

"If you're asking whether I got a copy of the report on your dead boyfriend's autopsy to fuel my hobby, then no, Garnet, I did not," he said sternly. "I'm deeply offended. I can't believe you think that of me!"

I couldn't either. Or that — briefly, unwillingly, irrationally — I'd thought even worse.

"If you must know, we got it at your mother's insistence. It was for her."

"For *Mom*?" I cut her a glance. "Why did *you* want it?"

She picked out a nut, prized the shell open and popped it in her mouth. Only once she'd chewed and swallowed did she reply. "I suppose I'd better come clean. I can't have you thinking your father's an unfeeling crime *ghoul*. Or would that be a vampire?"

"Mom!"

"Very well! I wanted to know if Colby had bled to death."

Whatever I'd been expecting to hear, it hadn't been that. Yet it rang a bell. "You asked about that before, at the police station when they questioned me. You asked whether he'd bled to death. Why?"

My mother squirmed uncomfortably in her seat and made

a business of eating another nut.

"Why did you want to know about bleeding?" I insisted.

"I don't know if you remember, but the day before his death, Colby popped in before work to visit. While we waited for you to get dressed and come down, we sat in the kitchen chatting and drinking tea. We had cookies, too. Lavender shortbread, I'll never forget. My goodness, I haven't baked that for absolute ages! I must make—"

"*Mo-om*," I said, my frustration stretching the word into two syllables.

"He seemed agitated. Very stressed about something, I thought. That's why I gave him Rescue Remedy and some omega 3 oil capsules. Your omega 3s are very supportive to the nervous system."

"Did he tell you what he was stressed about?"

"No," she said. "He'd also injured his wrist somehow."

"And?"

"And he was in pain."

"*And?*"

"And I recommended he take arnica," she said, in the tone of someone making a serious confession. "In fact, I gave him a whole bottle and told him to take it for a few days. It's excellent for strains and sprains — speeds up the healing process. Even allopathic doctors acknowledge that."

My mother was forever foisting her useless remedies on others — chamomile tea to a friend who wasn't sleeping well, sliced onion steeped in honey to my father when he had a cough, feverfew leaves to me when I had a migraine. Back in my high school days, she'd insist that Jessica and I drank an infusion made from fresh rosemary, swearing it would stimulate our mental functioning during exam time. But what was so bad about giving Colby a homeopathic remedy — something traditional medicine considered a mere placebo?

"I'm missing something," I said.

She sighed. "One of the side effects of arnica is that it increases bleeding. It slows the clotting or increases the blood pressure or something, I forget. Anyway, you're not supposed to take it before surgery."

"So, you worried that when Colby was beaten up, the arnica you gave him might have made him bleed excessively? You thought you might have been responsible for his death?" This was absolutely ridiculous.

"It was a serious dose," she said. "D6 strength. Plus, with the omegas, you know …"

"No, I don't know. What about them?"

"Well, they can also increase bleeding," she admitted.

"Mom, you've got to stop giving people this shit! If it's true that these supplements and remedies can have negative effects, then it could be dangerous."

"It's not dangerous." The face she pulled at me indicated she thought I was being unreasonable. "It's *natural.*"

"So's arsenic. And mercury and lead. And rhubarb leaves. And azaleas and all-natural mistle-fucking-toe!" I yelled at her.

"I get the point, thank you. Now, will you kindly stop cursing and shouting."

I groaned in frustration. "So, did he? Did Colby bleed out?"

"No, he did not. In fact, when I discussed it with Doc Armstrong — this was some months later — he told me I'd have needed to give Colby a wheelbarrow full of arnica to kill him," she said, and resumed eating her nuts.

Was this what Doc Armstrong had been holding back from telling me? I'd been hoping for something more.

"Pinocchio?" Mom said, offering me the bag of nuts.

"Pistachio," I corrected automatically.

"Yes, dear."

The car fell silent. Dad was still sulking in the back seat, arms folded and lip protruding like a toddler's. Mom was munching calmly on her nuts, making a mess of my car with their skins and shells. I stared through the windshield, eyes fixed on the road, thinking. I needed to speak to Doc Armstrong, to persuade him to open up about everything he knew. But he could wait an hour or two — I thought it might be a good idea to speak to Blunt first.

Beside me, my mother was using the shell of one pistachio to open another, wedging it into the slit between top and bottom shells, and twisting the halves apart. I'd do that with the Armstrong father and son. I'd imply to Blunt that his father had already spilled the beans (whatever they might be) on him, and hopefully that would get him to open up. And then I'd use whatever pieces of information I got from Blunt to crack the tough nut that was Doc Armstrong.

One way or another, I was going to find out what he was hiding.

39

Once I'd dropped my parents at home, I called Blunt to set up the meeting and get directions to his place. On the way, I swung by the pizzeria in town to grab a slice of double-pepperoni and jalapeno for myself, and popped into the donut shop next door to buy half a dozen of their best for Blunt. Junkies always have the munchies, right?

Ignoring the low, heavy feeling about Doc Armstrong that still poked at the edges of my attention, I ate my pizza as I bumped along the back routes that led to Blunt's trailer. It was set in a small clearing well back in the trees, behind the perimeter of the golf estate. Two pot plants grew in trash cans placed on either side of the steps up to the trailer door, and a row of beer bottles stuck upside-down in the snow stretched toward the encroaching forest.

My knock was answered by an old man; it took me a moment to register that it was Blunt. Scraggly beard, greasy hair and missing teeth, he looked nothing like his old attractive

323

self. Back when I was still at school, Blunt had been good-looking, the epitome of slouchy, careless cool. Now his thin face, pocked with sores, was crumpled and dragged down into deep lines. Above hollow cheeks, his sunken eyes were dull, even when he cracked a smile at the sight of me.

"Hey. Come in. S'cold out there."

Good thing I had a strong stomach, because a person of a more delicate constitution would have tossed their cookies at the sight and smell of that trailer. It was rank with the sour stench of beer, sweat, unwashed clothes, pot and cigarette smoke. At one end of the interior, a bare mattress was piled high with dirty clothes and a couple of grubby pillows without cases. Did he actually sleep there? Dirty dishes, half-eaten microwave dinners, plastic cups and candy wrappers littered the counter tops. Mugs of half-drunk coffee with discs of green mold floating on their pallid liquid surfaces clustered on the small table top, amongst the paraphernalia of drug use — a stained teaspoon, candle and lighter, aluminum foil, syringes, a glass pipe and several bottles of pills.

"Here," he said, sweeping an old pizza box onto the floor to expose a patch of cushioned seat by the table.

I checked for needles then perched on the cushion and handed him the box of donuts.

"For me? Thanks, man." Sitting down on the other side of the table, he chose a chocolate-glazed donut with colored sprinkles and crammed half of it into his mouth.

"So, Blunt, how are you doing?" I asked.

He swept an arm around as though gesturing to palatial surroundings. "Living in the lap of luxury, as you see," he said, his voice sharp with sarcasm.

I merely nodded.

"I was just about to shoot up. You want in?"

"Huh?" It took a moment to figure out what he meant. "Um, no, thanks. I mean, it's very generous of you and all, but I really just wanted to ask you some questions."

"Oh, yeah? What about?"

"Colby."

"Colby?" His face was blank.

"Yeah, Colby Beaumont. He was my boyfriend in high school, remember?" No recognition. "He died. They found him drowned in Plover Pond?"

"Ohhhh. Yeah. Him."

"Yeah, him."

An image of Doc Armstrong flared behind my eyes.

Sleepy.

What the hell? Now I was having hallucinations about an old man falling asleep?

"He was on your case back then about your dealing," I prompted Blunt.

"I remember. He had a bug up his butt about it. Had a plan to keep this town clean or something." He shook his head and picked up a tiny baggie of brown powder. "Blowing against the wind, man."

"I guess. Um, I remember he told Jessica that you'd been hanging out near the middle school classrooms. Near his sister."

"Uh-huh." Blunt tipped the powder into a teaspoon and then set it aside while he used a narrow syringe to draw up a few milliliters from a bottle of Beaumont Brothers' finest mountain spring water.

"He was pretty upset with you. And he'd hurt his wrist on the day he confronted you. Did you have a fight?"

Blunt's face crinkled with the effort of trying to remember. "Maybe pushing and shoving. I don't think more than that."

"He thought you were dealing to the kids."

"Yeah, yeah, that's right." Blunt rocked in his seat, nodding in recall, while he carefully squirted the water into the teaspoon. "That pissed me off. I would never have sold to kids, man, never." He shrugged. "Didn't need to. Teen market's plenty big enough. Adults, too, these days."

"Right."

Listening to this, watching him invert the syringe and use the back of the plunger to stir the contents of the teaspoon, I wanted to grab all this crap and trash it. And drag Blunt by the ear to the nearest rehab — exactly as his father and sister had no doubt done on countless futile occasions. "So, if you weren't selling to the kids, why were you there?"

He gave me a condescending look. "Kids aren't the only ones at schools."

I thought about that for a moment. "*Teachers*? There were *teachers* at Pitchford doing drugs?"

"More than one." He pointed to the detritus of clothes and blankets beside me. "Hand me those pantyhose, will you?"

I lifted the gray nylon with two fingers and passed it over, watched as he expertly pushed up his sleeve and tied the makeshift tourniquet around his arm, just below the elbow, pulled it tight with his teeth, and slapped his forearm. The exposed skin was a painful-looking patchwork of scabs and spots of raw pink skin.

I averted my eyes. "Was Mr. Wallace one of them?"

"Can't remember who they were. People came and went, y'know? That's life."

"How'd you wind up out here?"

"My father arranged it all. Did some kind of deal with the owners so I could stay so long as I don't deal down there in rich man's land."

"How did he manage to swing that?"

Another shrug. "Paid them. Pressured them maybe. Doctors" — he pointed the syringe at me — "know things."

"Your father's real sick, Blunt. I think he misses you. Do you ever visit him?"

Holding the flame of a lighter under the teaspoon, he moved it around in small circles until the golden liquid bubbled.

"Nah. He doesn't want to see me, not really. Not like this. He doesn't want to know what I'm doing as long as I stay away and don't steal his booze or prescription pads."

"You stole whole pads?"

He drew the liquid in the spoon up into the syringe. "Hey, gotta be some perks to having a drunk doctor for a father."

"And now you're farming pot?" I guessed.

He gave me a lazy smile. "I got a few plantations here and there in the woods."

"I got the idea from your sister that you were doing more than growing weed."

"Fuck her. She never could keep her mouth shut." He held

the syringe up, flicked a dirty finger against the side. "Yeah, I'm cooking, so what? Got a base up the hill." He jerked his head in the direction of the woods on the hill behind the trailer.

"Anybody else know about that?"

"I sometimes see drones flying around out here, so yeah, probably somebody does."

"Hugo's UFOs!"

"What now?"

"Nothing." I waved the word away. "So, someone's spying on you. Do you think it's the government — cops, or maybe the feds?"

As I said the last word, it occurred to me that Colby may have been calling the FBI about the drug situation in town. He wouldn't have trusted Turner to handle it properly.

"Doubt it, man." Blunt slowly pressed the syringe plunger until a single drop oozed out of the needle tip. "They wouldn't care that much about the pot, and if they saw the lab, they'd have raided me by now."

"Maybe they can't see through the cover of trees?"

He shrugged, examined his arm carefully, selected a spot below his wrist and slid the needle upwards into a vein. "That was the idea."

"Who else could it be?"

"Dunno." He drew a little blood up into the syringe. "Maybe my dad. Maybe someone he paid off checking to see I'm keeping away from the estate."

A phone on the table vibrated and rang — a jarring note that made me jump in surprise.

Blunt glanced over at the display and gave a grunt of

surprise. "Will you get that?" he asked me. "My hands are kinda full at the moment."

The phone display read *The Bitch*.

"Hello, James Armstrong's residence," I said.

Blunt threw back his head and laughed.

"Garnet? Can I speak to my brother please?" It was Jessica, and she sounded upset.

I held the phone up to Blunt's ear.

"Yeah?" His fingers stilled as he listened. "What? When? ..." He let go of the syringe, leaving the needle stuck into his arm, and grabbed the phone from me, pressing it against his ear. "How? ... Yeah ... Yeah."

"What is it?" I asked as soon as he ended the call.

He tossed the phone aside. "My father's dead." He released the tourniquet. "And get this, man, it was an overdose."

He pressed the plunger in all the way, steadily pushing oblivion into his veins. His eyes rolled back, his lids drooped, his body slumped. And he was gone.

40

Thursday December 21, 2017

While Blunt tripped on smack inside his trailer, I paced in the snow outside, tripping on guilt.

Behind the trailer, the forest of blue-gray sentinels, limbs sagging under their cold weight of white, stood guard over Blunt's secrets. Mist shrouded the valley and dampened the sound of the highway beyond. Up here, all was silent except for the snow which squeaked beneath my feet. I could already feel the freezing wet permeating my running shoes; I needed new boots. I kicked at a beer bottle, sending it an unsatisfying few feet away. Small flakes of snow drifted down from the heavy, steel sky.

Doc Armstrong was dead. Why hadn't I paid attention to the niggles about him? I'd had a bad feeling, felt him falling asleep — drifting into a death-bound coma, I now realized — but I'd been determined to follow my own nose. If I'd gone to him first, I may have been able to save his life. Admittedly not for very long, but, a selfish part of me pointed out, for long enough to get more information out of him. Now that opportunity was lost.

I picked up the bottle, welcoming the burn of cold on my tender fingertips — I needed to wake up. Or maybe what I really needed was to drift more fully into the dream. Being one leg inside Colby's circle and one leg out wasn't working. I had to choose. Either I was going to be true to myself — the self I had been all my life: rational, logical, scientific, despising all things mystical and spiritual — or I was going to abandon everything I believed and respected, and instead allow the possibility of a whole other world, kiss the person I'd always been goodbye and step into a whole other self. Embrace what I most disdained in my mother.

What did I have to lose? Either I was getting messages from beyond the veil — I rolled my eyes at that phrase — or I wasn't. If I wasn't, if the weird experiences I'd had weren't really paranormal, then I was already crazy and suffering from the symptoms of psychosis. But if it was real, if Colby was trying to connect with me?

I threw the bottle at the nearest tree, hitting a low branch and setting off a small snowfall.

Once, on a family vacation in Maine, I'd gone horse riding with a bunch of older, more experienced teenagers, and I'd known from the start that my mount — an Appaloosa ominously named Tempest — was definitely the boss of our relationship. He'd fought me for control all the way out and all the way back to the resort.

The return route passed alongside a grass airstrip backing a campground. Our guide warned us to hold our horses when we approached this.

"They always get excited here, because they can smell the stables. Do *not* let them bolt!"

I shortened my reins and held them as tight as I could as the horse danced sideways, tossing its head and straining at the bit. My arm muscles bulged and burned as I tried to control the thousand pounds of muscle and defiance beneath me, but there was no way I was going to win this battle of wills, and the horse knew it. There was a moment, magnified into timeless clarity by sheer terror, where I contemplated my options. And chose surrender.

I loosed the reins and gave the horse its head, trusting it knew where it was going. Behind us, the guide screamed something, but the wind in my ears whipped it away. I held onto the pommel for dear life as we galloped down the airstrip, ducked as we hurtled under a low tree branch, hung onto the beast's neck as it jumped a small stream, and yelled in terrified exhilaration as it careened around tents and trailers in the campground.

We charged down a dirt road curving around the resort hotel and entered the stable yard at top speed. I flattened myself on the horse's back as it stamped into its stall, narrowly avoiding decapitation from the doorframe. Amazed that I was still alive and in one piece, I'd slid off the saddle and staggered out into the cobbled yard on trembling legs.

Now, standing in the falling snow outside Blunt's trailer, I again felt like I had back then, when I'd stared down the length of runway, contemplating giving in to a force I'd underestimated and couldn't control. Again, I surrendered.

Even as I wondered if I was psychotic, I opened myself up

and spoke into the cold, quiet air. "Colby, are you there?"

I stopped and listened — with my ears, but also with my body, with my long-frozen heart. A surge of love — warm, intense enough to make my chest hurt, so bright it made me gasp — washed through me.

Real.

Love.

You.

The words and feelings swirled around inside and came to rest in a soft, quiet calm.

I puffed out a breath and spoke out loud again, "Colby? I sure as shit hope this stuff is coming from you, because from now on, I'm going to treat it like it is. I want to solve your murder and bring your killers to justice. You want that, don't you?" A snowflake landed on the tip of my nose. "And to do that, I need your help, okay?"

Silence.

"So, let's cut to the chase: do you know who killed you?"

Nothing. Nothing in my head and nothing in my body. I rubbed my freezing arms and stared hard into a nearby bank of snow — though what I was looking for, I couldn't have said. Perhaps a raven dropping stones on the snow to spell out the name of the culprit? It occurred to me that Colby was as clueless at sending messages as I was at decoding them.

"Come on, Colby, bring it. You've got memories? Send them. Got ideas? I'm waiting. Let's do this so we can solve it, and you can rest in peace, and I can get on with the rest of my life. Let me have it."

For a moment nothing happened.

Then a flood of yellow blinded me, knocking me sideways.

"Yellow? *Again*? I don't know what that means!" I yelled aloud.

Immediately, the mustard saturation was supplanted by scenes from the attack down at the pond.

Again, the hands on my shoulders, the shouts, the dark, hidden faces, the devastating pain.

More than one!

"Two attackers, you can't see who they are, it hurt — I know. You've showed me all that before. Give me something new already!"

An image of a box wavered in my vision. It was just like the box of Colby's stuff his mother had given me, only it was completely empty.

"An empty box? That's very helpful. No, really, thanks for that," I snapped into thin air.

Nothing.

"Sulking, now? You need to do better, Colby."

Shivering with cold, and perhaps madness, I tramped to my car and drove back down the hill to the highway. I needed to buy flowers and pay a condolence visit to Jessica and her mother, and I dreaded the thought of it. No doubt it was going to be super uncomfortable — I was pretty sure they would both still be upset with me and would find no comfort in my presence. But it still needed to be done. I might be taking directions from a spirit, but I wasn't lost to the dictates of convention and good manners. I'd spend the afternoon doing what I could to help out. Maybe I'd follow in another of my mother's footsteps and do the dishes. That way I could be useful and hide out in the kitchen at the same time.

"Further transmissions and investigations will have to wait until tomorrow," I told Colby. "That means you have tonight to hone your skills. Maybe get a few tips from some of the other entities on your side? Because if I have to ask my mother for help, I'll kill you."

41

The next morning, I made a list of all the words and images I'd received from the ether so far. Nothing new had arrived since the visions outside Blunt's trailer; perhaps Colby was still peeved at my less-than-enthusiastic attitude.

I booted up my laptop, opened my browser and typed the word "yellow" into the search bar. *About 7,580,000,000 results,* Google declared. Great, shouldn't take long at all.

The first hit was a song by Coldplay. I let it play in the background while I sifted through the results that followed. Definitions and synonyms, math games, book titles, apps and online courses, videos, student hostels, and a conspiracy theory about the McDonald's arch that would have delighted Hugo. I looked for images and scrolled through pics of yellow things — bananas, splotches of paint, roses, sunflowers, police crime scene tape, emojis, egg yolks, radioactivity warning signs, bell peppers, chrysanthemums and fall leaves. It went on for pages and pages.

Nothing sparked an epiphany.

I clicked on a picture listing different shades of yellow — amber, butterscotch, canary, cadmium, fire, gold, lemon, ochre, sunshine and mustard. I read through the entire entry on "yellow" in Wikipedia — science and nature, history, art, pigments and dyes, minerals and chemistry, symbolism, associations and idioms — and learned more than I ever wanted to know about the color. I read about its wavelength and position on the color spectrum, how carotenoids in plants absorbed light energy and protected against photodamage, that it was one of the first colors used in cave paintings, and that it was associated with Chinese emperors, the pope, the keys to the kingdom (whatever that might be), but also with Judas Iscariot, and that it had been used to mark heretics in early times and Jews in more recent history. Was any of this relevant?

Depending on your religion and culture, the color was associated with health, happiness, warmth and courage, but also with sickness, envy, avarice, duplicity and cowardice. Nothing confusing about that, then.

From metaphysical sites, I discovered that yellow symbolized harmony through conflict — harmony through conflict, what did that even mean? — and that yellow was the color of the third, solar plexus chakra, and was the main hue in the aura of people in intellectual occupations. Professor Perry would've called this a load of buggery bollocks. I would've agreed.

The main yellow gemstones were citrine, tourmaline, yellow jasper, sapphires, diamonds, topaz and garnets. That last one was new to me — I'd only ever thought garnets came in ruby red. Could the yellow refer to my name, to me? Each of the stones had different meanings and uses; if there was a commonality, I sure couldn't find it.

I gave up on trying to figure out what the yellow visions meant and decided to focus on the image of the empty box. Once more I retrieved the container Bridget had given me and dumped the contents onto my bed. I examined the interior and exterior of the box, inspecting every square inch, but found nothing unusual. I closed my eyes and cocked my head, waiting for a signal from the beyond.

More nothing.

Maybe the image of the empty box meant I was supposed to unpack it and then check its *contents* for some clue. I picked up the funeral program with Colby's photo on the front, examined it inside and out, held it tight in both hands against my chest in anticipation of a mystical message, but felt only the old sadness, the bitter consciousness of waste.

One by one, I held each item before packing it back into the box. At the end of the exercise, I was still no wiser than I had been at the beginning. Exasperated, I ran my fingertips over the coverlet, feeling for the catch of a rough nail edge on the fabric. Finding one, I tore a strip off the nail with my teeth and immediately knew it'd gone too deep, right into the nail bed. That would hurt for days.

A new thought struck me: maybe there was something *not* in the box that was supposed to be there? I wracked my brains but couldn't think of anything. Grabbing my phone, I hit dial on Cassie's number.

"Hey, it's Garnet here, how are you doing?"

"Same old, same old. How are *you* doing? Find anything yet?"

"Nothing definite," I hedged. "I wondered, though, whether you took anything else of Colby's back then? Something that maybe your mom would've hung onto if she'd found it afterward?"

"No," she said slowly, "nothing I can remember. He was always accusing me of taking and hiding stuff, but he'd usually just misplaced it himself. Honestly, I only took little things — a pack of gum, maybe, or his lip balm. Do you remember he used to always have that cola-flavored type?"

The memory of the scent came to me as strongly as if I could smell it. For me it would always be the smell of kisses. "I do."

"Oh, wait. I did once steal a bobble-head miniature figurine of Gollum—"

"Who?"

"Gollum — from Lord of the Rings?"

"Oh, right." I didn't read fantasy; I'd always struggled to connect with the far-fetched stories and mythical themes. Which seemed ironic now, given how things had turned out. "And his laptop?"

"No. Honest, the only important thing I ever took was his phone. I'd tell you if there was anything else."

Disappointed, I ended the call, promising to give her an update soon.

I glared at the box on my bed, willing it to reveal its secret. There was something important in or about this box, there had to be, but I was too stupid to see it. My groan of frustration was interrupted by a thought — the boxes in our basement. Some of them were similar to this one. I slipped on a sweater and shoes and ran downstairs.

Dad must have replaced the globe in the basement light, because it was working again. I glanced around, searching for any boxes I hadn't yet checked, and found only two, both of which only contained stacks of old National Geographic magazines. Nothing about their dusty contents or cobwebby exteriors sparked anything in my crowded brain. I was about to leave when my gaze fell on the stack of my father's planners crammed on the shelf above the workbench.

Although I was certain that my dad was not a deranged serial killer who'd also murdered my boyfriend in a rage at him having unprotected sex with seventeen-year-old me, I still reached up and wiggled out the ones with 2006 and 2007 stamped on their spines.

Just then, the light above me flickered for a few seconds, and although it held, the cold around me suddenly intensified. A prickle of primitive fear rippled up my spine. For the first time it occurred to me that if there *was* some kind of life beyond this one, if there were spirits like Colby, then there might also be more malevolent entities.

"Shut up, Garnet. You're a moron." Trying to bolster my flagging courage, I spoke out loud, but my voice came out weak and breathy.

I marched over to the stairs and began climbing. Halfway up, I was overcome by an atavistic urge to run. My careful steps turned to bounding leaps, covering several stairs at a time, and when I got to the top, I slammed the door behind me. Then locked it.

My mother was in the kitchen, perched on a stool in front of the stovetop. "I'm making breakfast for you — pancakes and syrup, your favorite."

"Thanks. I'll be back down soon," I panted.

Back in my bedroom, I opened the 2007 planner at the date of Colby's death. At the bottom of a page of reminders for the store, was a notation written in black: *RIP Colby Beaumont (1989-2007)*. Was my father even now making a similar entry in this year's planner for Doc Armstrong? If Ryan hadn't fished me out of the drink, would there have been an entry for me?

Starting at the beginning, I paged through the planner, meticulously reading every entry on every date. I soon noticed my father had a color-coded system for highlighting different categories of entries — pink for reminders of birthdays, blue for business meetings and deadlines, green for doctor and dentist appointments, orange to highlight financial month- and year-ends, and yellow for his regular fishing trips. I focused my attention on this last category. Otter Creek, Lake Winnipesaukee, Battenkill River, Manchester, Lake Champlain — there was something familiar about the locations of his angling expeditions.

I read the names again, more slowly, and remembered. I was almost sure that Manchester was one of the Vermont towns Ryan had mentioned when he told me about the old serial killings. Quickly, I riffled through the two planners, writing down dates and names. When I'd made a note of every trip out of town, including some supposedly for business purposes, I rang Ryan and asked him if he had a list of the dates and places of the killings back in 2006 and 2007.

"What's this all about, Garnet?"

"I promise I'll tell you everything — just as soon as I figure it out myself," I said. "Can you email me that information?"

"How about I just read them off?"

"Fine," I said, figuring that he'd rather not leave a record of him sharing case information with a civilian.

Five minutes later, I was staring down at the chronologically ordered list Ryan had dictated, comparing it to the place names from my father's planners. My heart gave an unpleasant kick when the very first items on each list correlated. Antoine Marshall, a twenty-two-year-old electrician's apprentice from Meredith, New Hampshire, had disappeared on a weekend in 2006 when my father had been participating in a fishing tournament at Lake Winnipesaukee, just outside the town. Shit.

I moved to the second item on Ryan's list. Sean Walton had been a good student at Huss University. He'd gone missing on August the eighth, 2006, and his body had been found two days later in Bangor, Maine. I checked the list from the planners. No correlation in dates. In fact, there was no mention of Bangor in my father's planners that I'd seen at all.

One by one, I checked the entries on the lists, but found only one more possible correlation. Ewan Grady, seventeen, had been killed in April 2007. He'd been a runaway, squatting in an old hunting cabin just outside Manchester, so no one had been sure of the exact date he went missing. Based on the state of the corpse, the medical examiner estimated he'd been dead around ten days by the time he was discovered in an abandoned building site on the last day of the month. My father had been on a fishing trip to Battenkill River, just northeast of Manchester, on the twenty-first and twenty-second of that month, so there was a possible overlap.

Two matches, maybe only one, out of a list of at least twelve unsolved murders and umpteen out-of-town trips? Mere coincidence. Rolling my shoulders in relief, I headed back to the kitchen.

"Sit," my mother said, pointing to a chair at the table. "Breakfast is the most important meal of the day."

I watched her anoint a stack of pancakes with a generous drizzle of syrup. "I don't think that rule applies when the meal is high fructose on top of carbs."

"Any more visions or messages from beyond?" she asked eagerly.

"Not a one."

"They don't always come spelled out in bright lights on billboards, you know. Although they can, of course." She nudged the plate of pancakes closer to me. "Spirits will talk to you in all kinds of ways — you need to open yourself and keep your peepers peeled."

"I'll be sure to do that."

"Now where's your father at?"

My mother called for him while I tucked into a pancake. It was delicious — light and fluffy and sweet. I'd missed this. I smeared the top of a fresh pancake with butter, realizing as I did so that it was how Colby had preferred them — without syrup. *This one's for you*, I thought as I took a big bite.

A light tinkle to my right had me glancing sideways. Two coffee cups dangling on the mug tree were swinging ever so slightly on their hooks, as if a hand had just brushed across them even though no one was near them.

"Hey, kiddo," my father said as he entered the kitchen.

"Hey, Pops."

Ruffling a hand through my hair, he sat down opposite me at the table. How could I ever have suspected him, even for a moment? He was the kindest, gentlest man I'd ever met.

Helping himself to a stack of pancakes, he asked, "What are my two lovely ladies up to today?"

I had an idea I'd be spending the day in a state of frustration, racking my brains to think of anything I may have missed.

"I'll be at the church," my mother said.

"Preparing for the Armstrong funeral tomorrow?" Dad asked.

"No, Irene's in charge of that. She wants to remove all the Christmas decorations before the service, says it's not fitting to have those up on such a sad occasion. Irene has got a bit of a bedbug about what is and isn't fitting. Of course, everything will just need to be put back up again afterward — you can't have the church bare on Christmas day, now can you? And she'll have to do that herself because I don't have time to be diddly-daddlying."

Dad lifted the two mugs — completely still now — from the mug tree, poured himself and me a cup of coffee, and asked my mother, "So why do you need to go to the church today? I'm assuming you'll need me to drive you there?"

"I sure do. I've volunteered to help with the Christmas packages for the needy. Tomorrow, Reverend Scholtz will deliver them to all the homeless and the old folks about town."

"'All the homeless' — how many does Pitchford have?" I asked.

"It used to be just Lyle Wallace," Dad said. "But now, with the drug problem getting out of hand, there are more every year."

My mother sniffed. "Michelle Armstrong thinks if she plays a blind eye to the problem, it will go away. There's no end to the list of things that woman is wrong about."

My mother rambled on about the town clerk's many faults, but I was no longer listening. Lyle Wallace. His name kept turning up, but he was probably just a sad, harmless guy, as Ryan had said. Thinking about Lyle and the police together fired a memory in my brain. Lyle Wallace had been the homeless guy on the bench outside Chief Turner's office when I gave my statement on the day after Colby's body was found. Hadn't there been something about him wanting to make a report? I remembered how Turner had dismissed him as crazy, but what if he'd been there to report something about Colby, what if he *had* known something?

I swallowed the last of my coffee, wincing at the lukewarm temperature. "I've got to get going."

"Where to?" my father asked.

"I have people to see."

And a promise to keep.

42

NOW
Friday December 22, 2017

I found Lyle Wallace on the corner of Main and Mohegan, near the Methodist church; maybe he'd heard they'd be handing out goody bags for the poor soon. By day, he looked a lot less scary.

I pulled up near him, lowered my window and called out, "Can I buy you breakfast? You and Cat?"

He nodded warily.

"Hop in. We'll go to Dillon's."

He stared at me suspiciously for several long moments, then appeared to consult his cat about the wisdom of accepting a ride from me. Oh God, was I as crazy as Lyle, consulting thin air for guidance on my actions?

"Better I meet you there," he finally said.

"Fine. I'll get us a nice table and order the coffee while I wait."

"Hot chocolate. Not coffee."

"Hot chocolate it is. Any preference food-wise?"

"Hot beef on rye. Toasted. No pickles. And better you get takeout. Pete don't allow … cats inside."

Lyle was waiting outside Dillon's by the time I emerged with his sandwich and drink, and a tuna salad minus the salad. He, or perhaps his cat, again balked at getting into my car and instead led me to a bench in a quiet side street. I perched on the freezing wooden slats, shivering as the icy chill cut through my jeans and began freezing my butt. Lyle, apparently unbothered by the cold, opened the takeout box of tuna and placed it on the sidewalk beside the bench. But the cat — its amber eyes fixed unwaveringly in my direction — didn't approach.

"Not hungry this morning, Cat?" Lyle asked it, tucking into his own food.

Cat hissed. I was pretty sure it was hissing at me, or, more accurately, at the space beside me, but I didn't tell Lyle that. He seemed mistrustful enough as it was.

"I wanted to talk to you about something," I began.

"Figured that."

"Ten years ago, a high school senior by the name of Colby Beaumont was killed in Pitchford."

Lyle stopped chewing for a moment but said nothing.

"You remember?"

He rubbed his fingers across his lips and then rattled off, "2007. Second rainy season. Government seeded clouds. Chemtrails not contrails. Sick cows. Red Sox won the World Series. Meteor shower, Perseid power. Star in the east? Government loosed a shooter at Virginia Tech. Kryptonite. Big blizzard in December."

"Right," I said. "When that storm ended, they found Colby's body in Plover Pond. And when the cops interviewed me the next day, I saw you there — at Pitchford Police Station. It was you there, wasn't it?"

"Maybe. Who wants to know?"

"I do."

He took another large bite of his sandwich, wiped mustard off his mouth with the back of a gloved hand. "I think there's pickle in this."

"They said you wanted to make a report?" I prompted.

"Who said? The CIA?"

"What? No. I think it was Ryan Jackson."

"Because they monitor my thoughts. All the time."

"No, they d– Gee, that must be distressing."

"Got to block them."

"Of course, I see that. So ... *were* you there to file a report that night?"

"Uh-huh."

"Was it about the CIA?"

Lyle shook his head. "Waste of time. Turner was in their pocket."

"Wow. So, what *did* you want to report? Was it something about Colby?"

"Uh-huh. I seen something."

"What?" I asked, trying to hide my excitement in case it spooked him.

"A car."

Just when I thought I'd have to extract the information from him word by single word, like a dentist pulling teeth, Lyle launched into a long, rambling story. On the night Colby was attacked, Lyle had known the weather was about to take a turn for the worse. He could always tell, always. That was one of the reasons the CIA wanted in on his brain. So, he decided to bed down in the bandstand — did I know there was a storage area under it where they kept chairs and banners and things?

I did not.

Well, it was a good place to shelter in a storm. He'd been headed there when he stopped to take a pee against a tree — you didn't want to be stuck with a full bladder under the bandstand with the snow piling up against the access flap — and he was midstream when he saw a figure walk by some twenty feet away, in the direction of the road. No, he couldn't see who it was, but he reckoned it was a man because it was tall, though it was dark and the person was wearing a coat, so he couldn't say for sure. And did I know they wear disguises? And for sure this one would want a disguise because he was up to no good.

How did he know that?

Way he was looking around, checking. But he didn't see Lyle, no sirree. Lyle could disappear when he wanted to. Become invisible. Was I sure I'd told dickface Dillon to hold the pickles?

I was. What about the man?

Well, he, Lyle, had craned his neck around the tree and watched as the figure walked to where his car was parked on Pond Road, got in and driven off. No, he hadn't seen the plates. The headlights hadn't come on until it was some way down the road. What kind of a car? A big one. Expensive. One of those

European types. No, not a Mercedes, or an Audi or a Volvo. A BMW? Yes, he thought that was the one. Lean and mean. And it had carried the man off into the darkness, and that was all he knew and even the NSA couldn't prove otherwise.

"Did you ever go back, tell Chief Turner what you saw?" I asked. "Or Officer Jackson?"

"They weren't interested." He swallowed the last bite of his sandwich and crumpled the wrapping into a tight ball inside his fist. "Gotta go. Can't talk too much, or they'll kill me like they killed Doc Armstrong."

"I heard he'd given himself an overdose."

"That's what they *want* you to believe, but he didn't kill himself."

"What makes you say that?"

He looked at me like I'd asked a dumb question. "He wasn't done drinking yet."

Remembering the pleasure with which the doc had downed his Johnny, I said, "I guess he wasn't at that. So, who do you think killed him? And why?"

The man in the vision had been insistent that Armstrong should keep his mouth shut about something. Perhaps he'd paid the doc another visit later. Dead men tell no tales.

"Done talking, now." Lyle stood up, and as he loomed over me, I was again aware of how big he was. "Can I have some money?"

"Sure, thanks for your help." When I gave him a twenty, he solemnly handed me the screwed-up ball of sandwich wrapper.

I walked down the hill to Main Street where my car was parked, mulling over the new information, wondering what to do with it, questioning if I could even believe it, given its source. At the corner, I turned to give Lyle a wave. He was still standing beside the bench, watching me. Cat was at his feet, eating the tuna.

43

NOW
Saturday December 23, 2017

The church was packed for Dr. Armstrong's funeral. I'd arrived before my parents and been roped in to hand out programs at the door. It seemed the whole town had turned out to pay their respects, even Lyle Wallace, whose cat narrowed its eyes and hissed at me as they walked inside.

Blunt, looking marginally cleaner, but higher than the church steeple, snuck in at the last moment and took a seat in the back row, then slipped out during the last hymn. Michelle Armstrong — clutching her pearls and every inch the distraught, grieving widow — sat up front beside Jessica, in the same pew where the Beaumonts had sat during Colby's funeral. I tried to stop myself thinking about that, but there were too many similarities to avoid it: the same church, the same unconvincing platitudes by the same old minister, the same dreary music, even a framed photograph of the deceased on the table up front. Doc Armstrong hadn't been cremated yet, so at least there was no urn of ashes.

When the service ended and everyone drifted across to the church hall, I stayed behind, trying to ignore the headache I could feel gathering behind my eyes. Jessica, her eyes shadowed and her face pale, was collecting the funeral programs from where they'd been left on the pews.

"Hey, Jess?"

She didn't look up. "Yeah?"

"Did you do this at Colby's funeral? Collect the programs, I mean. They were blue."

"Now that you mention it, I think I did." She gave me a sad smile and picked up another paper. "It must be my thing." She paused, a faraway expression in her eyes, and then let the papers fan and slide from her hands onto the floor of the aisle. A score of Doc Armstrongs smiled up.

"Let's go get something to drink," I said, tugging her to the church hall, where the reception was being held.

"I don't think they're serving vodka," she murmured.

We shared a smile, and for a moment, it was like how it used to be between us.

In the crowded hall, she got herself a cup of coffee and went to join her mother. I grabbed a plate of finger sandwiches and sought out Ryan.

"Have you double-checked the call logs yet? Scrutinized the land development?" I asked.

"I'm fine, thanks, Garnet, and how are you on this sad occasion?"

"I'm sad — happy, now? And since you ask, I'm also vexed at the slow pace of this investigation."

He gave me a lazy grin. "Vexed, is it?"

"Yes, vexed. Very, very vexed," I confirmed. "So please tell me if you've found out anything."

"We're still checking whether any of the numbers with an 802 area code belonged to a person whose name started with a J."

As we talked, we made our way through to where my parents were standing, chatting to the Beaumonts.

"And the land deal?"

"I spent yesterday checking that out, and it's as kosher as turkey bacon."

"But—"

"I investigated it myself, Garnet. And I did a thorough job, because I have a place there — a bachelor unit which I bought off-plan back when it was still being developed."

"You own property there?"

"I do."

"You live there?"

"No, I live in town now, in a bigger place. I keep the golf estate property as an investment and rent it out."

"Hmmm."

If Ryan Jackson owned property there, how willing would he be to investigate any wrongdoing or illegalities that would jeopardize his investment?

"Good investment, is it?" I asked, biting into a cheese-and-tomato sandwich.

"Sure."

My parents were standing with Colby's mother, father and uncle. Roger Beaumont gave me a disapproving look as we joined them, but said nothing.

"How's Cassie doing, Mrs. Beaumont?" I asked. It still felt

strange to address her directly as Bridget.

"Much the same. I'm sure she'd love to see you again when you and your parents come for dinner tomorrow evening."

Roger pinched his lips together. I guess his sister-in-law hadn't told him she'd invited the McGees.

"Sure, okay." I blinked several times, trying to ward off both a threatening yellow haze and my worsening headache.

"Can Ryan come, too?" my mother asked. Clearly she was set on matchmaking the two of us.

"*Mom*," I said, embarrassed by her rudeness, but Bridget didn't blink an eye.

"Of course you must, Ryan," she said smoothly.

"That would be a pleasure, Bridget, thank you."

Someone tugged at my jacket. A little girl wearing smart clothes and a black eye mask with sharp pointed ears looked up at me and lisped, "Batman has no limits."

I crouched down on my haunches. "That's true."

"Anyone can be a hero!"

"Also true. Are you a hero under that mask?"

"I'm not who I am underneath. It's what I do that's who I am."

I gasped as a few million neurons fired inside my brain, making connections.

Of course! The dark faces in the attack — they'd been wearing masks. Or, more likely, balaclavas. That was why Colby hadn't been able to see them. And why would his attackers have covered their faces? The only reason could be so that he wouldn't be able to identify them afterward. *Afterward.* Which meant they'd intended to beat him up, but to leave him alive.

"Sydney, there you are!" A flustered mother scooped up the little girl. "I hope you haven't been bothering the lady. And I told you not to put that mask on here."

I was still gaping at the kid, thinking about faces and masks, and no doubt I looked a little disturbed, because the mother gave me a nervous look and hustled her little heroine away.

Still on my haunches, I allowed the flashbacks to roll like a movie through my mind, recalling the exact words, remembering Colby's message: *more than one.* I'd just assumed he was referring to the fact that more than one attacker had assaulted him, but what if he'd meant there'd been more than one *attack?* What if the thugs had left him bruised and bleeding, but alive, and someone else had come along afterward and finished the job? I strained my brain to remember whether there had been anything in the vision of Colby drowning that gelled with this possibility.

"Garnet? *Garnet?*" My mother tapped on my shoulder.

"Are you alright?" Bridget asked as I stood up. "You look like you've seen a ghost."

"Not quite," I said. Not this time. "I just realized something."

Ryan cocked his head at me. "Something important?"

"Yes. Can we talk privately?" But even as I said the words, his phone rang, and he stepped away to take the call.

Roger frowned at me. "Are you still digging around into Colby's death?"

"What's this?" Philip asked sharply.

"She's checking no stone was unturned in the investigation. *And* she's getting supernatural help," my mother said proudly.

Roger snickered, my father sighed, and Bridget opened her

mouth — no doubt to ask what the hell my mother was talking about — but, thankfully, Ryan returned at that moment, saying, "I've got to go, I'm afraid. Domestic dispute." To me, he added, "I'm not sure how long it'll take to sort out — these things can take twenty minutes, or the whole night. I'll call you when I'm done, if it's not too late."

"Okay."

Before anyone could resume the conversation about my mystically assisted investigation, I bid the Beaumonts and my parents goodbye. Outside, darkness had fallen. The deserted parking lot was illuminated by a single light which flickered briefly as I walked under it. A prickle tightened the skin at the base of my skull. Someone was watching me, I could feel it, but when I spun around, I saw no one.

"I'm not up for the heebie-jeebies, Colby," I muttered under my breath. "If you're going to send me stuff, make sure it's real."

I climbed into my car, turned the ignition, and again glanced around as I backed out of the parking space. A man and woman were hurrying across to the other side of the lot.

"Make it real *and* useful," I clarified as I drove out onto Main Street. "For instance, lotto numbers would be great. You can send those anytime."

The center of town was a cheerful display of jewel-colored lights and brightly lit windows tempting last-minute Christmas shoppers, but I'd already done my gift-shopping back in Boston. A white-bearded, red-suited Santa Claus sat outside Dillon's, ringing a bell and ho-hoing as passersby dropped donations into his kettle. Where would Lyle be spending the night — back under the bandstand as he had on a similar cold night a decade ago? At the bottom of the hill, the Tuppenny Tavern beckoned, promising a strong drink and the possibility of meeting up with Ryan a little later. On impulse, I pulled in and grabbed a seat at the busy bar.

"What'll it be?" the barman asked.

"An extra-hot Irish coffee" — *a very cold beer* — "No! An Irish coffee, please."

I guess he was used to weirdos, because he served my drinks without comment. It was crowded and noisy in the Tavern, but my headache, I noticed, had vanished. I called Ryan and left a message on his voicemail telling him where I was, in case he was able to meet up.

I spent the next hour or two alternating coffees and beers, and working on my phone — slogging my way through the mountain of emails that had accumulated in my inbox. I'd half-expected a note from Perry, asking how I was doing and wondering whether I was any further in committing to psychology as my field of study. But there was nothing. Good thing, because I had no answer for him, even though I was beginning to suspect that not-a-yes was a no.

Several journal articles I'd requested from the main library for my thesis were awaiting my attention, but I had zero interest in reading them. Instead, I found myself diving into the deep end of the web, researching the onset of extrasensory perception after near-death experiences.

Not surprisingly, I found that scientists denied any such thing as ESP existed, while those ranged on the other end of the reality continuum insisted it was a common outcome of

NDEs. I learned that clairvoyance was the ability to see things not accessible to normal vision, while clairaudience referred to hearing the inaudible, and clairsentience to feeling emotions and sensations that were not your own. I figured that if what I was experiencing was real, I must be clair-all-the-things — except claircognizant, because I *knew* nothing for sure, not even why the stool on my left stayed empty all evening, even though every other seat in the place was taken.

I surreptitiously sniffed my armpit and cupped a hand to smell my breath but detected nothing offensive. Perhaps I had a resting bitch face? I checked in the mirror behind the bar, arranged my features into a friendly expression and smiled benignly at anyone who approached the bar counter, but the seat remained vacant. When a young man stood with his back to the stool while his companion perched on an adjacent stool, I tapped him on the shoulder and said, "You're welcome to take the seat — I'm not holding it for anyone."

He glanced at the barstool, looked confused for a moment, and then grinned. "Thanks. I thought it was taken."

Perhaps it had been.

My fingertips rubbed the edges of my nails, unconsciously searching for a rough edge. I picked at the uneven corner of one and then tore off a thin strip with my teeth. The edge was rough on the other side now; I nibbled it, striving for even. It never was.

I checked my phone again, but there was still nothing from Ryan. I relinquished my own seat to whoever wanted it and left the Tavern on feet that were just the slightest bit unsteady.

I drove down Pond Road, aware of the pond's dark presence

beyond the yellow glow of the street lights. The only other car in sight was the one driving too close behind me, dazzling me with its harsh, blue-white headlights. I slowed down, waving the driver ahead of me, but the car inched closer. I flipped my rearview mirror to reduce the blinding dazzle and accelerated, because the car was right on my tail now. In these conditions, it was crazy-dangerous to drive like this. I leaned on the horn, gestured again. But the car didn't back off.

Fearing that it would smash into the back of me if I slowed down enough to take a right at the traffic circle, I plowed forward, bumping straight over the raised center, hearing it grate the undercarriage of my car. The car behind me followed suit. This was no mere drunk or careless driver. I was being chased. I raced along the road curving around the pond, sped past the turnoff to the golf estate, strained to outrace my tail. As we reached the dark wooded section of the park at the far end of the pond, the car behind accelerated hard. I felt more than heard the massive impact.

My car veered across the road. Another impact sent me jolting across the snow-covered grass toward the pond. I braked hard, yanked on the wheel, slammed into a tree. The airbag exploded into my face. Snow, pine needles and cones rained down on my car. Then all was silent.

I checked my side and rearview mirrors. Behind me, I could just make out a low, dark car parked on the side of Pond Road, and a tall figure in a long coat silhouetted against the light of the street, walking in my direction.

A spike of panic stung my fingers and jolted my heart into top gear. I needed to get out. My car was a good hundred yards into the dark park and wouldn't be visible to any passing traffic. The figure stalked closer with every passing second. If I stayed, I'd be a sitting duck.

Fighting the deflating airbag, I pushed open the door and ran.

44

Saturday December 23, 2017

Gasping, heart hammering, flushed with cold sweat, I thrashed through the deep snow. Away from the figure following me. Toward the pond.

The ground fell away beneath me, tumbling me into a hollow filled with a deep drift of pillowy snow. Flailing, I spat out a mouthful of ice, scrambled to my feet, risked a glance behind me. The figure was closing in.

Run! Hide!

The words, as likely my own as Colby's, filled my mind and fueled my headlong flight into the bank of tall reeds at the pond's edge. I splashed into the slushy water. The frigid impact snatched my breath and robbed my will to go further, but I forced myself forward, deeper into the reeds, cursing the noise I made. My running shoes were already soaked, and my jeans were absorbing the frigid water. Where the reeds began thinning out, at the edge of where the pond's frozen surface began, I crouched down and waited. Tried to control my panting. Strained to hear above the bang of blood in my ears.

The loud squelch of following footsteps rent the stillness of the night. What to do? I was trapped between the man and the pond, and both of them were potentially lethal.

There was no help for it. Knowing full well I was risking a repetition of my last time on the pond, I stepped onto the icy surface. My first footstep pushed right through the mushy ice at the edge, sending me knee-deep into the bitter water. The splashing footsteps behind me were closer now.

Move!

I leaned over as far as I could and slid my body onto the ice. Then I pushed myself up onto my hands and knees and began crawling forward. The ice seized me, trying to freeze onto my wet knees and hands. I tugged my hands free, yanked my cardigan sleeves over them for some protection and crawled forward over the creaking ice, wrenching my knees free on every movement until the denim froze and I could slide more easily, ice on ice.

After about twenty yards, I thumped a fist on the frozen surface. It felt solid, and I heard no cracks. I clambered to my feet and made my way across the ice toward the center of the pond. Then I spun around. The figure was a shadow of deepest black against the darkness of the reeds. It stood watching me, then tested the ice with a foot. Fell through, as I had. Tried again. Fell through again.

Suck it! You're much heavier than I am, you bastard.

The ache spreading from my wet feet and legs was brutal enough to make me weep, but I had no time or energy for tears. Breath rasping painfully, I sat down on my denimed rear, lifted my feet off the ice, and folded them tight against my chest. I jammed my hands into my armpits. Shivers pulsed through me in fierce waves as I sat in the darkness, watching the figure watching me.

I wished with every fiber of my slowly freezing body that I'd taken a minute to grab my phone before I'd left the car. Then it occurred to me that he didn't know I hadn't.

"I've called 911!" I screamed across the ice. "They're coming for you."

For a few long moments, the figure didn't move — no doubt debating whether I was bluffing, whether to chance waiting until I died from exposure. Then it turned, pushed back out of the reeds, and strode up the incline to the road. The lights of the dark car were visible for only a second before it disappeared into the night.

Shuddering violently now, I stepped and fell and slid across the ice toward the reeds — toward my car, the space blanket in Dad's emergency box, and the phone in my handbag.

I slept in late the next morning and then stayed in bed for a long time, drinking the coffee Dad brought me, reviewing the events of the night before. The EMTs who'd arrived first on the scene of my "accident" the previous night had insisted on hauling my ass back to the hospital in Randolph to be checked out, but after examining me head to toe, the ER doctor had pronounced me "shaken and stirred, but good to go". Wearing my still wet and muddy shoes, I'd caught a cab back to Pitchford.

I wished I could spend all day in my bed with the electric blanket turned up high, but the night before, I'd promised the two cops at the scene — neither of whom had been Ryan Jackson — that I'd go in to the station and file a report.

Ryan called when I was on my second cup of coffee, his voice a blend of concern and exasperation.

"Am I to understand you wound up in the pond again?"

I sniffed. "Not in, *on*. There's a difference."

"Why did you run *on*to the pond after you crashed your car? Was it just blind panic?" Without waiting for a reply, he continued, "I'm sorry I couldn't come out and assist last night, Garnet. That domestic violence call out kept me tied up for hours, trying to persuade the wife to lay charges."

"Right."

"Should I come over to your folks' house this morning to take the statement?"

"You'll have to — I don't have a working car, and neither do my parents. Eleven-thirtyish work for you?"

"I'll be there. And you're sure you feel okay?"

"Yeah."

Truthfully, I felt wary. My attacker the night before could have been anyone. I thought it had most likely been a man, but it could have been a tall woman; the long, dark coat had disguised the figure's shape.

Had the attempt on my life been triggered by my general investigation into Colby's death, or by something specific I'd said or done? Someone might have seen me talking to Lyle, or discovered I'd chatted to Doc Armstrong before he died. But maybe someone at the funeral had witnessed my moment of epiphany, heard me gasp and say — like the total fool I was — that I'd realized something important and wanted to talk to Ryan about it privately. They could've followed me from the church, waited for me outside the Tavern, and then seized their opportunity on the dark, deserted road.

I thought about who'd been in the group of people in the church hall when I'd put two and two together — my parents, Bridget, Roger and Philip Beaumont, and Ryan Jackson. I discounted Bridget immediately — too short, too frail, no motive — and also crossed my parents off the list. Roger and Philip, however, were likely suspects — either of them would be likely to have a long coat and the sort of newer-model car that had those absurdly bright headlights. But if Ryan was right about the land deal being aboveboard, then what motive could they have had?

Ryan. Had he really still been out on the earlier case when my call had come in, or had he been getting far away from Plover Pond, possibly hiding his damaged car? He could easily have hidden evidence in the original investigation, or dragged his heels this time around, in the hope of protecting his investment. Or his involvement. He appeared to be such a good guy that my mistrust seemed utterly ridiculous, but still, I couldn't exclude him.

Could it have been anyone else?

Michelle Armstrong hadn't been in our group when I'd had my realization, but she was thick as thieves with Roger Beaumont, and he might have told her what I'd said. She was tall enough to look like a man from a distance, and she'd worn pants to the funeral. Or she could have had an accomplice. I couldn't rule out Blunt, either. He'd been well enough to attend the funeral, and maybe in a moment of clarity, he'd perceived some danger in my investigation, borrowed or stolen a car, and taken his shot.

I suspected all of them, yet I couldn't truly believe it of any of them. Couldn't — or didn't want to?

Irritated, I finished my coffee before it cooled and switched to mulling over what I'd finally figured out the day before. Colby had been attacked, and then he'd been drowned *by someone else.*

Who might have wanted to beat him up, but not kill him? Who hated him, wanted to warn him off something — or someone — and would have been coward enough to take along a crony? Which J might have drawn Colby to the pond with the lure of wanting to talk, or — the thought appeared so clearly that I ought to have heard a penny drop — which person might have used a "J" to get Colby to respond?

At once, I knew who I needed to speak to.

45

Sunday December 24, 2017

According to directory services, the address I wanted was a mere six blocks from my parents' house. That was surprising. I would have thought a move to grander accommodations would have happened before now. I walked there, ignoring the protests of my stiff muscles, relishing the brisk air.

The house was a two-story clapboard with a shingle roof, set well back from its neighbors at the end of a cul-de-sac. I climbed the steps to the porch, stepped around the small bike, pink tricycle and plastic two-wheeled scooter stacked against a swing bench, and rang the bell. No one answered. The unmistakable noise of television cartoons blared from inside the house, along with the screams of kids fighting. I rang again then thumped a fist against the door.

Finally, it opened a crack. Though it was a dull, overcast morning, Judy Dillon wore sunglasses large enough to cover half her face, and she seemed both surprised and put out to find me on her doorstep.

"What do *you* want?" she said.

"Is Pete home?"

"He's at the coffee shop."

"Good, I need to talk to you alone."

"What about?"

"About a text message sent from your phone to Colby Beaumont's on the day before he died."

Judy reached behind her for a pack of cigarettes, lit one, inhaled deeply and blew a stream of smoke my way. "I don't know what you're talking about."

"There's no point in denying it. The cops will have detailed records of all activity on Colby's number by this afternoon," I lied. "Then they'll check the number and find out it was registered to you."

"Good luck with that. My phone was an unregistered prepaid," she said, gleeful at having outwitted me, before she realized her mistake. "Fuck," she said dully.

"Yup."

"I'll deny what I just said. It's your word against mine."

"I have a theory about what happened that night. And, I'm guessing that after what happened between you and Pete *last* night, what I reckon has been happening ever since you two were nicknamed Punch and Judy, you're tired of protecting the real culprit."

"I'm protecting the girls!"

"By letting them think it's normal for a man to beat on his wife? You want them to imprint on that, replicate it in their own relationships?"

She sucked on her cigarette, said nothing.

"And what if he starts in on them?"

A flicker of distress contorted her features. It lasted less than a second, but it was enough.

"He's already started, hasn't he? Judy, this has got to stop. You owe it to them."

"Easy for you to say, Miss No-kids, No-husband, Shrinky-dink."

"Yeah," I said. And waited.

When she merely continued inhaling nicotine in silence, I sat down in the middle of the swing bench and played my final card, loathing myself for doing it. "The other night, at the gallery, you know where I found Pete?"

Her gaze snapped to mine.

"In the back room, getting all hot and heavy with Jessica."

Judy let loose a torrent of curses and kicked the scooter from one end of the porch to the other, narrowly missing hitting me.

"Are you going to tell the cops about your *theory?*" she demanded.

"Probably. But maybe not just yet." I wanted to figure this thing out before I told another soul anything.

She ground the cigarette butt under a heel and immediately lit up another.

"How about you come sit here beside me, and I'll tell you what I think happened," I invited. "Then you can just confirm if I'm right."

She sighed but sat down next to me — on my right side, I noticed.

"Even after Colby broke up with you, you still loved him and wanted him back. You hooked up with Pete — maybe you thought that would make Colby jealous." I glanced sideways at her for confirmation.

She waved her cigarette in a *carry-on* gesture.

"But, instead, Colby and I started dating. I loved him, too, you know. I wanted him, too."

"I know. I saw how you were ... afterward," she said grudgingly.

"And I think Pete could feel it, that you weren't really in love with him. He knew that he wasn't in Colby's league" — Judy gave a tiny, involuntary nod — "and it drove him crazy with jealousy. Perhaps he was already hitting you back then."

She didn't deny it.

"That didn't improve your feelings for him, probably made things worse. You felt scared and stuck. And Colby being Colby, I guess he stayed being your friend. Was—" I paused, but I had to know. "Was there more between you?"

She twisted her mouth in contempt at my question. "Colby being Colby, what do you *think*?"

"I think no. He was just being kind to an ex-girlfriend. But Pete didn't see it that way; he wanted Colby to stay the hell away from you. He was simmering with anger and suspicion, and then something happened to tip him over the edge. You threw Colby in his face, maybe, or he saw the two of you together, chatting?"

"Asking advice," she murmured, almost inaudibly.

"You were asking Colby for advice about something?"

"Deanna." She jerked her head back to the screaming voices inside the house.

I raised my eyebrows in question.

"Pete had knocked me up. And I didn't know whether to keep it or get rid of it."

So that's why Colby had been calling counseling services and looking up pregnancy sites online. He hadn't guessed I was pregnant at all. He'd known Judy was.

"You thought Colby could advise you on the decision?" I said around the sudden lump in my throat.

"Maybe," she said. "Maybe it was just an excuse to talk to him. To get some attention, and a hug. Funny how you can be dating a guy so jealous he hardly gives you a minute alone, and yet you still feel lonely."

"And Pete saw you. He blew up?"

"Nah. He went dead quiet — which is always worse, trust me. He took my phone, checked if I'd been calling or texting Colby — as if I'd be stupid enough to leave evidence — and then he sent the text to Colby. Once it went through, he deleted it. Said if I interfered, he'd kill me." She wiped the back of a hand across her mouth, smearing lipstick. "I believed him."

"Then he waited for Colby on Sunday night with one of his friends. I'm guessing Brandon Nugent?"

Judy nodded.

"And they attacked him, beat him up badly. Warned him to stay clear of you. But Pete didn't drown Colby. He and Bran ran off, leaving Colby unconscious by the pond."

"How do you *know* that?" she asked, clearly bewildered.

How to answer that question?

"I– There was a witness."

"A witness who never said anything all this time?"

"There were … special circumstances that made it difficult

for him to communicate what he knew."

"But now he told you?"

"Judy, do you know who came afterward and killed Colby?"

"No idea. Honest to God."

"Could it have been Pete? Could he have gone back to finish what he started?"

"No way."

"How can you be sure?"

Judy made a harsh noise — something between a snort and a sob. "I was the getaway driver. I drove Pete and Bran back to my place, and they hung out there all night, with Bran getting stoned and Pete threatening me not to breathe a word to anybody, or else ... The storm came in fast, and they were stuck there. My old man wasn't too pleased to find them in our kitchen the next morning."

The way she said the last bit made me suspect that, even before she hooked up with Pete, Judy was no stranger to being knocked around.

"I'm sorry," I said, reaching out to squeeze her hand, but she snatched it away.

"Screw you. I don't want anyone's pity. Especially not yours."

"Okay, then."

"Then Colby turned up dead. Pete and Bran said that even though he was still alive when they left him, they'd carry the can for his death if the cops ever found out about the beating." She sighed. "I was pregnant. I wanted to get the hell out from under my father's thumb. So I needed a husband. I needed Pete at home, not in the big house."

A bloodcurdling scream sounded from inside the house. Without another word, Judy stood up and went inside, slamming the porch door behind her. I headed home, chin tucked into my chest, head bowed against the icy wind. I now knew Pete and Bran were the men who'd beaten Colby, but I was no closer to knowing who'd drowned him.

What am I missing, Colby?

I was instantly rewarded with flashes of Doc Armstrong — arguing with the mystery man, swallowing pills, drifting off into a lethal sleep. Was it possible that the killer could have been him? Perhaps, with his mania for justice and his crusade against the spreading scourge of drugs, Colby had confronted Armstrong about Blunt, threatened to alert the cops, to tell them about the fake prescriptions. I couldn't remember whether I'd ever told Colby about those, couldn't be sure that I hadn't triggered a sequence of events that resulted in his death.

Hello, guilt, my old friend.

My visit to Dr. Armstrong, the fact that I obviously still hadn't put my grief behind me, may have filled him with enough remorse to end his life, or he might have done it because he knew that the whole story would likely soon come out. On the other hand, maybe he'd just hastened the inevitable out of a desire to avoid more pain, and it had nothing at all to do with me or Colby.

When I got home, Ryan was already waiting at the house to take my statement. We sat in my father's study with the door closed so my parents couldn't eavesdrop. I'd simply told them I'd had an accident, not wanting to worry them with the fact that the car wreck had been intentional, that there was still someone out there who wanted me dead.

I told Ryan what had happened the night before, keeping my description of the events brief, explaining that I didn't know what kind of car it had been, and insisting that I couldn't guess who might have wanted to hurt me. He seemed genuinely troubled, and though I watched him carefully, I saw nothing to indicate that he himself might have been the very man whose description he so carefully recorded in my statement.

When we finished, he asked me, "What was it you wanted to tell me last night?"

I waved a dismissive hand. "It was nothing, really."

"Garnet, you very obviously thought of something important. What was it?"

"Well, I just realized that whoever assaulted Colby might not have been the same person who drowned him."

He canted his head at me in confusion. "That's it?"

"That's it."

He studied me skeptically for a long moment and then said, "Are you still going to the Beaumonts' for dinner tonight? Can I give you and your parents a ride?"

"Yes, please."

"I'll see you at six."

46

A blanket spread out on a soft, mossy patch of the forest floor was our bed, the fiery blaze of fall leaves in the tree canopy above, our sky. A leaf — ochre and orange with the promise of winter — drifted down and landed on Colby's chest. He lay on his back with his head on the pillow of my stomach, panting and on the verge of drifting into sleep. I was also breathless, and energized, too, in a quivery way. A soft breeze cooled the sweat on my bare body, tightening my skin with its slight bite of cold.

The small clearing deep in the woods on Kent Hill was our eyrie, the place where we'd first made love, trembling with nerves and excitement. We often hiked up there — sometimes because we couldn't get enough of each other's bodies. And sometimes just to get away from the world and to talk — about our exhausting families, and what the lyrics of *Chasing Cars* really meant, and whether God existed. And about our future.

I picked the leaf up off Colby's chest and tickled his face

with it, giggling when his nose twitched. He opened his eyes and snatched it. Then, grinning, he placed it between my legs, like the fig leaf on Eve in an old painting.

He gestured to the colors above and the valley beyond, just visible through a gap in the trees. "Look at that. You won't get this in the city."

"True. But I won't get anatomy lectures in Pitchford."

"So you've decided then — you're definitely going to study medicine?" he said, turning over and pushing himself up onto his elbows so he could see my face.

"Yes. No. I don't know. All of the above."

He captured a yellow leaf from its downward tailspin and laid it solemnly on my left breast, then found another of the same color lying on the ground and decorated my right.

"Do you know how magnificently beautiful you are, Garnet?"

Magnificently beautiful. I smiled and wriggled in pleasure, sending one of the leaves sliding off my chest.

"You're ruining my art," Colby complained, setting it back in position.

"The only thing I know I want for sure is you," I said.

"Good thing you've got me, then."

He sat up, fanned my hair out around my face, and began threading colored leaves into it.

"You're definitely going to do law enforcement?" I asked.

"Yeah. My father and uncle are playing the big disappointment card, but it's my life, so it's my choice."

"What does your mom say?"

"To follow my heart — which will be in Boston." As he

spoke, he arranged a crown of golden leaves around my face. "So that's where I'll be going to school, too."

Keeping my head still, I blew him kisses at this confirmation that we'd be there together. "It's going to be awesome!"

He pinned my hair to the ground with a final scarlet leaf and sat back to admire the effect. "You look like a pagan goddess."

"You're not so bad yourself," I said, shedding leaves as I sat up to claim his lips.

A drop of water hit me on the cheek. Another landed on my back, and then another. As if it had only been holding off while it waited for us to finish, the rain started splashing down in earnest. Laughing, we tugged on clothes, pulled the blanket over our heads and began stumbling down the forest path.

When I turned onto the path leading down to where we'd left the car, Colby yelled, "The bridge — it's closer!"

The blanket was soon drenched in the deluge, and by the time we reached the covered bridge, we were wet to our skin. Colby tugged me inside, laughing and shaking the water off his head.

"I'm c-cold," I said, rubbing the gooseflesh on my arms.

"Come here, you." He pulled me close and held me tight against the warmth of his chest while the rain hammered on the wooden roof above and the river roared beneath us. "Isn't this awesome, being inside the bridge like this?"

"No. It's dark and creepy. This is what being in a coffin must feel like."

"No way! It's the opposite of that. Out there, behind you, it's Pitchford. And out the other side back behind me, it's not.

But in here it's no man's land — we could be anywhere. It's magic."

I pulled back and made a face. "What are you even talking about, crazy face?"

"It is!" he insisted, his face intense with excitement. "We're not on land, or in the water, or up in the sky — it's like we're between worlds. Can't you feel it?"

"All I feel is a strong urge to run and scream."

"Okayyyy," Colby said, grinning. "Well, you *know* how I like to satisfy your strong urges."

He grabbed my hand, and we hurtled through the tunnel, screaming and shrieking, pushing back the dank gloom with our fierce laughter, defying time itself with our youth and our love.

At the other end of the bridge I leapt out into the rain, eager for the open air. Colby stayed in the shadows, just under the cover of the eaves, watching me turn my face up to the sky, inviting the elements. Then he leaned out and kissed me with infinite tenderness.

"I'll always love you," I said.

"And I'll love you forever," he replied.

47

NOW
Sunday December 24, 2017

I spent the afternoon of Christmas Eve in town, replenishing my wardrobe. This had been a very expensive trip home — the estimate from the body shop for my car repairs was extortionately steep, and the insurance deductible would hit me hard, plus I'd ruined my favorite coat and running shoes and lost my boots. And quite possibly my mind, too.

That evening, I dressed for the Beaumont dinner in my new purchases — a pair of black pants, bloodred turtleneck, and flat-heeled, lace-up boots which ended mid-calf — and was just applying a last coat of mascara when my mother yelled up the stairs for me.

I stuck my head out my bedroom room and called, "Yeah?"

"Jesus has brought a message for you, dear."

Sweet suffering son of a bitch. My mother was getting more unhinged by the day. Like mother, like daughter?

"Yeah, alright," I replied. "Just take it for me."

It was one thing getting messages from Colby, but if Christ himself started appearing in my life, then it was time for a padded cell and straightjacket.

When my father yelled that Ryan had arrived, I touched up my lipstick, grabbed my new coat, and ran downstairs to find the two men chatting at the door. Ryan, jiggling keys, looked up and grinned when I appeared. Without meaning to, I found myself returning the smile. His blue sweater brought out the slate gray of his eyes, and the graze of stubble emphasized his jaw line. Too bad I'd sworn off all men, especially any involved in this case.

He greeted me with a peck on the cheek. "Looking mighty fine, Garnet. Ready to go?"

"Sure." I opened the front door and saw a massive police SUV in our driveway. Was there a reason he didn't want us to see his car — like maybe a dented front bumper? "Where's your car?"

"I thought we could use this because it's bigger. And there are a bunch of us."

"Right," I said, all my suspicions about him flooding back.

"I'm calling shotgun," my mother said, limping up to us just then.

Ryan supported her as she negotiated the front steps, then kept a steadying hand out as they headed down the icy front path. But polite and obliging meant nothing; I'd read enough of my father's books to know that a psychopath could act like a regular Prince Charming.

My father was locking the front door behind us when my mother called over her shoulder to me, "Did you see your letter from Jesus, dear?"

"A letter? From Jesus?"

"Yes, a big fat letter. I put it on the table in the hall."

I saw Ryan's shoulders shaking, but I was more bewildered than amused.

"Sorry, Dad, can you open up again? I need to see this."

"Sure, kiddo. I don't think a letter from the good Lord himself can wait."

Sure enough, there was indeed a bulky envelope on the hall table. A thrill of excitement shot through me when I saw that it bore the logo and return address of the Roseacres Nursing Home and had been sealed and addressed to me in shaky handwriting.

"Is this from Doc Armstrong?" I asked my mother as we climbed into the car.

"That's right. Jesus said the doc gave it to him before he died and said he should be sure to give it to you."

"It's *Jesús*," I ground out in frustration. "It's pronounced *Hay-soos*!"

"Yes, dear. But on his nametag it was spelled Jesus, you know," my mother said. "Oh, my goodness, I clean forgot the flowers and the hostess gift for Bridget! Bob, would you mind …?"

"Yes, dear," my father said, with a sigh.

"They're in the kitchen, I think," she called after him.

Ryan started the engine and left it idling so the heater could warm up the car while we waited for my dad. I slid a finger under the envelope flap, tore it open, and extracted the contents: Colby's pen and a stack of papers. There was no covering note. Puzzled, I quickly scanned the papers. They appeared to be test results from a laboratory in Boston. Why the hell would Doc Armstrong have wanted me to have these?

"I made up a bag of crystals for Bridget," my mother was telling Ryan. "Red amethyst for strength, sodalite for compassion, aquamarine for hope, and black obsidian to expel negative forces and open her third eye — because that's always useful, don't you think?"

By the light of my cellphone, I examined the reports more closely. They appeared to be from tests conducted at regular three-month intervals for the last four years; the most recent was dated just three weeks previously. The results at the bottom of every single page were the same: *less than 0.005g/L; within normally occurring range.*

"I'll show her how to lay them out in a crystal grid. That enhances their power, you know. Oh, my goodness, perhaps I should have made up a collection for Cassie, too?"

Mystified, I shone my phone's light on the central section of the reports and read carefully. Saw what had been tested. And for what. And let out a long, low "*Ohh!*" of realization.

"What's that, dear?" my mother asked.

Yellow flooded my vision, but this time I didn't fight it. Finally, I had an idea what it meant.

Ryan shot me a searching glance in the rearview mirror. "What've you got there?"

"Proof of absence," I said, half-smiling in amazement. "Which, as you know, is not the same as absence of proof."

My dad climbed in the car then, looking flustered and holding a large bunch of white lilies surrounded by a swath of feathery fern leaves, and a small cloth bag with drawstring top.

"What took you so long, Bob?" my mother asked.

Ryan turned around to see what I was doing — which was taking photographs of every single page and uploading them one by one to the cloud. I was taking no chances with crucial evidence going missing again.

"They weren't in the kitchen. I had to hunt all over for them," my father grumbled. "Is there a reason why you put them in the guest restroom, Crystal?"

"Hmmm. I suppose there must have been a reason. At the time."

"Can we go now?" Dad asked impatiently.

"Sure, of course," Ryan replied, but he looked reluctant as he turned back around in his seat and steered us down the driveway.

I was already on Google, searching as fast as my fingers could fly over the screen. Making connections. Putting it all together. Clue by clue, fact by fact.

"Yes," I murmured. "Yes, yes, yes."

"Glad you agree, dear. I did have a moment's doubt — white lilies, you know, *death!* Plus they were out-of-season pricey — but the only flowers that weren't past their prime were carnations, which I always consider such a tight-fisted, begrudging sort of flower."

My mother nattered on as Ryan drove us to the Beaumonts, shooting occasional glances back at me. He clearly couldn't wait to find out what I was doing.

It all made sense to me now — the two years of record-breaking rain, what Lyle saw, what his father said in class that day, the sick cows, the missing laptop, and Blunt and his father, especially his father. I could guess who Doc Armstrong had been arguing with just before he died and why he'd chosen not to be around when everything came out. And he'd wanted it to, that's why he'd sent me the information.

"I wonder who else will be there tonight, and what Bridget will be serving? She's a fine cook, you know, but fancy. I remember once …"

The calls and searches on Colby's phone — I'd been wrong about some of those. Now I knew what they'd really been about, as well as the empty box, trying to tell me something was missing, and the mysterious *Itai-Itai*. The call to the MIT professor made perfect sense when I checked what subject was her specialty. I even understood the significance of the exasperating yellow.

"… and turkey can be so dry. But perhaps she'll serve goose. Or a lovely ham!"

I could see how it had happened now, and I knew why. How I wished I was wrong.

48

NOW
Sunday December 24, 2017

I tucked the envelope and my phone into my handbag as we pulled into the curved driveway in front of the massive Beaumont mansion. Ryan opened my door and insisted on escorting me to the front door, leaving my father to take care of the flowers and my mother. None of the three other cars already parked out front showed any damage, I noted, but at the sight of the last car, a silver Chevy Malibu, Ryan suddenly pulled up short.

"Oh. This could get awkward."

"What is it?" I asked, but the front door was already opening, answering my question.

"Hello, Garnet, long time no see!" Colby's older sister gave me a friendly hug. Then her surprised gaze fell on my companion. "Ryan."

"Hi, Vanessa. Home for the holidays?"

"Yeah. So" — she glanced between Ryan and me, as if assessing the nature of our relationship — "come in!"

Bridget arrived to welcome us then, and we were swept into the living room on a wave of greetings, thanks and perfumed hugs. Bridget's "You really shouldn't have," when she received the crystal baggie from my mother, sounded entirely sincere.

Vanessa introduced us to her husband, Rick Torres — a stocky lawyer with a habit of blinking his eyes rapidly every couple of seconds — and said, "Our little girl's upstairs sleeping, and I never mess with a sleeping toddler, so you'll have to meet her another time."

Philip and Roger Beaumont greeted me civilly, but coldly; Michelle Armstrong pointedly ignored me but explained to Ryan that although she felt completely crushed by grief at the loss of her husband, she'd felt it important to come and draw comfort from the support of good friends; and Jessica explained that Nico wouldn't be coming because he was in the middle of painting a new masterpiece from which he absolutely, positively could not be pulled away. Domino, trotting up to greet the visitors, stepped back from me, ears flat against his head and tail between his legs. A sound that was half-whine, half-growl escaped his bared teeth.

"What's up, boy?" Ryan said, ruffling the dog's head and giving me a quizzical look.

I shrugged. Really, there was no way to explain what I suspected the dog's problem was without sounding like a total lunatic.

Roger took my coat and hauled Domino off to the kitchen, while his brother handed me a tiny glass of sherry. I downed it and immediately accepted a refill. Dutch courage would be required this evening.

"May I go say hi to Cassie?" I asked Bridget.

"She wouldn't forgive you if you didn't. Come, we'll go together."

I followed her upstairs and once again admired the lovers' bronze statue on the landing, once again came face-to-face with the picture of Colby in the family photograph gallery on the wall opposite. I kissed two fingers, laid them on his lips, and whispered, "I've almost worked it out."

I was about to follow his mother down the hallway to Cassie's room when my gaze slid to the picture next to Colby's. The hair on the back of my neck stood up, but this time there was nothing supernatural about the sensation.

I was looking at a picture of the Beaumont family — Cassie cradling a black-and-white puppy, Vanessa making bunny-ears behind both her father's and uncle's heads, while Bridget was absent from the shot. Maybe she'd been the one taking it. They were gathered outside their old house near my parents' place, posing for a quick picture just before they set out for a family vacation to judge by the collection of bags at their feet, and the suitcase Colby had paused in the act of putting into the trunk of a car.

A large, charcoal-gray car. A BMW.

Totally engrossed in the picture, I started in surprise when Bridget spoke beside me.

"She's fast asleep, and I'd rather not disturb her. Could we try again later?"

"Cassie — right. Yes, sure, I will." I tapped the photograph. "This picture, Mrs. Beaumont?"

"We were off to spend time at the house in Martha's

Vineyard." She sighed. "It seems like that was the last time we were all truly happy."

"And whose car was this?" I asked, and nodded when she told me.

Dinner — roast turkey, not at all dry, with all the trimmings — was a noisy affair. I sat quietly between Ryan and Vanessa, listening to the chatter around me with half an ear, while I tried to put the final pieces of the puzzle together. Jessica, her face drawn and pale, told us that Nico was entering his own blue period, which was nothing like Picasso's, but that we should expect great things from him. This set my mother off on a tangent about turquoise and blue lace agate which had Vanessa's husband blinking even more often.

Bridget diverted her with an offering of more gravy and regaled us with a story about the fight for the last turkeys in the new grocery store in town. "Why, I thought your mother might snatch this bird right out of my hands, Jessica!"

"I wouldn't put it past her," Jessica said, while Michelle gave her practiced smile and said, "It *was* on the menu for our lunch tomorrow. But we'll make do with a hickory ham."

Then Roger recounted an anecdote about how he'd bumped into his old pal Fred at the garden center.

"He'd brought along a branch from his *Pinus resinosa* to show the experts there, wanted an opinion on why the tree is dying. He had them all scratching their heads, trying to figure out what disease would cause twisted branch tips and browned needles like that. I could have told them, but I didn't want to get old Mrs. Hale in trouble."

"Mrs. Hale?" Philip said. "What's she got to do with it?"

"She's Fred's neighbor, and she's been complaining about that tree of his for years. Says it puts a permanent shade over her yard, kills her lawn, spoils her view, and now the roots are lifting her driveway. Seems she finally got tired of asking Fred to take care of it and took matters into her own hands."

His brother smiled at him indulgently. "I suppose you caught footage of it on your drone?"

My ears perked at that. "Drone?"

"You spy on the people of Pitchford with your drone?" Vanessa asked, instantly outraged.

"I don't *spy*. But I do occasionally get accidental footage of folks around here," her uncle said.

I placed my knife and fork down on my plate. "What's your intentional footage of?"

"People have rights to privacy, you know," Vanessa said. "You can't just do what you want when it impinges on other people's rights."

"Vanessa," her father said, "please don't start."

"But—"

"Clear the plates away, would you, dear?" Bridget asked her daughter. "I'll bring the crème brûlée."

"Talk about Big Brother watching! Soon the clocks will be striking thirteen on a cold day in April," Vanessa muttered as she collected and stacked the plates. Jessica leapt up to help, but I stayed seated, eyes on Roger.

"Do you ever film over the woods on the hill up behind the estate?" I asked him.

"Indeed, I do."

"Why?"

"*Why?*"

"Yes, why?"

"Well, it's a very picturesque spot, isn't it, with the trees and the view."

"I'm sure you must see some very interesting things. And you probably like to keep an eye on your investment."

"Of course. This development didn't come cheap."

Bridget placed the shallow dishes of baked custard with their caramelized sugar tops in front of each of us.

"Get back to the story, Roger," my father said. "What exactly did Grandma Hale do?"

"Well, I hope this won't get her in trouble with our local constabulary," Roger said, waggling his eyebrows at Ryan, "but she's been spraying whatever parts of that tree she could reach through her fence for months."

Everyone laughed politely, except my mother. To her credit, she would never have prioritized lawns and driveways ahead of magnificent trees.

"What did she poison it with?" I asked.

Roger raised his hands in an *I-have-no-idea* gesture. "Some sort of herbicide, I expect. Perhaps a common weed killer."

I nodded, cracking my spoon through the hard sugar topping of my dessert. "So, not something like cadmium, then?"

Roger's smile became fixed. "I don't think cadmium's a weed killer."

"You're right there. It's a heavy metal." I could feel Ryan's gaze on me as I ate a spoonful of the silky custard.

"Cadmium is the name of a paint pigment. Yellow thirty-seven, I think," Jessica said. "It's been used in art since the early nineteenth century. It was a favorite of Monet's."

"Not sure whether it would do any damage to a tree, but it's poisonous to humans," I continued.

"Really, dear?" my mother said. "Did you know that in minute doses, poisonous substances like arsenic and hemlock are used in homeopathy?"

I tuned out the hubbub of hot debate about the safety of homeopathy that followed; I was thinking. It wasn't too late to drop this whole thing. If I went ahead now, if I told what I knew, I'd be destroying a family and initiating a sequence of serious consequences that would cost many of the people around this table deeply. If justice came at such a high price to so many, would Colby still want me to pursue it?

Screw that, I knew what *I* wanted. Besides, I'd promised him. Promised Cassie, too.

49

NOW
Sunday December 24, 2017

Raising my voice to be heard above Michelle's accusations of homeopathic quackery, my mother's outraged defense, and my father's futile attempts to defuse the argument, I said, "I also have a story to tell. And, like Roger's, it's also about poison."

Philip swallowed hard and said, "Bridget, I think it's time for coffee, now."

Roger tossed his napkin beside his plate and pushed his chair back from the table. "Good idea. Let's all go to the living room where it's nice and toasty by the fire, and chat about something more cheerful."

But Ryan leaned back in his chair and folded his arms across his chest. "I'd like to hear Garnet's story."

The Beaumont brothers exchanged a glance, and Michelle said, "Really, I don't think any of us wants to hear—"

"I do," said Vanessa, wriggling in her chair as if settling in for a bedtime story. "Once upon a time ..." she cued me.

"Once upon a time, about eleven years ago," I began, "there were two years of very heavy rains in Vermont."

"I remember it well," my father said.

"Me, too," said Jessica.

I nodded. "Yeah, your senior AP chemistry project was about acid rain, and your test results were affected by the high rainfall."

"Global warming, end times warning," my mother said in a sing-song.

"There was so much water and so little sun that Vermont's dairy cows, including those on Farmer Johnson's farm at the bottom of Kent Hill, developed a bad kind of eczema due to a fungus on the pasture plants. The only thing that worked to treat them was to give them huge doses of zinc — added to their food, and applied to their bodies in a special ointment."

"When do we get to the good part?" Vanessa said.

"When the zinc was excreted in the cows' manure and washed off their bodies by the rain, it was carried deep into the ground by the heavy rains, until it hit the rising water table. And along the way, it collected a toxic chemical passenger."

They were all looking at me now.

"Cadmium."

Yellow threatened at the edge of my vision. *Not now, Colby,* I thought.

Jessica tucked her chin back in surprise. "Why was there cadmium in the soil?"

"Cadmium is an ingredient in organophosphates — the fertilizers our farmers toss so generously on their crops. The ground's full of it. Normally that's not too much of a problem because cadmium binds to the soil and stays there, inert. Even when it rains."

"I bet California wishes it could have some of our rain and snow right about now," Roger said. "Those wildfires are wreaking havoc on their forests."

"You said *normally* it's not a problem. But?" Ryan prompted me.

"But one of the properties of zinc is that it loosens those chemical bonds, so the cadmium, freed from the soil particles, travels down into the water table."

"Dear me, that can't be good," Bridget said.

"It's very bad," I said. "Especially when Beaumont Brothers Spring Water Company draws its water from that very water table."

"Excuse me!" Roger exclaimed indignantly. "But we draw our water from the source of the spring right at the top of Kent Hill."

"You do now. But back then, you took it directly from a well sunk into the water table at the bottom of the hill, on the Johnson farm side. Easier. Cheaper, too, no doubt."

Roger jutted his chin out. "I see where you're going with this preposterous tale, but you're dead wrong. We tested that water, and it was absolutely fine. Pure! There were no contaminants. I can show you the lab reports."

"No doubt you did, when you first sunk the well. But how often did you do it after that? How regularly did you check?" I asked. "Because the FDA only required an initial testing. Of course, responsible companies would've tested more regularly than that, but it wasn't actually a legal requirement."

"I don't understand. Are you saying that Beaumont Brothers' water is contaminated with cadmium?" Bridget asked, her eyes round with shock.

"It was in those two seasons of heavy rainfall, but not anymore. Not for the last ten years, I think. And definitely not for the last four. Do you want to know how I can be sure about that?"

Roger pinched his lips together mutinously. Philip stared down at his untouched dessert. Jessica and her mother gaped at me.

"Well, *I* sure do," Ryan said.

"Doctor Armstrong told me. Just this afternoon."

"*What?*" Jessica said.

"This– this *female* is clearly out of her senses," Roger said.

"Not in person, of course," I said. "Not like he told Roger and Philip, here, many years ago. He sent me a stack of laboratory reports. Turns out he's been testing Beaumont Brothers bottled water every three months for the last four years, and every time it's come up clear."

"Well, there you are then," he retorted.

"Just what is going on here?" Michelle demanded. "And what did my husband have to do with anything?"

"Don't you want to know why he started testing the water?" Without waiting for a response, I hurried on. "I think he'd been puzzled by one of his cases, maybe several. And he'd requested special tests be conducted on a tissue sample from an organ removed from that patient. The findings confirmed the presence of renal cancer, which he'd expected, due to long-term, low-level cadmium poisoning — which he hadn't."

"Kidney disease," Vanessa said solemnly. "Cassie?"

"Cassie," I confirmed.

"Oh my God!" Bridget's face went white as chalk. She raised a trembling hand to her throat. "Cassie's cancer was a result of cadmium poisoning?"

I nodded. "I'm so sorry."

She turned on her husband and demanded, "From your water?" When he didn't reply, she thumped her hand on the table, sending a spoon leaping into the air, and cried, "Philip! What is this? Did you know? Is this true?"

Philip stared ahead blindly, saying nothing.

His brother said, "Of course not. It's utter drivel."

"Doc Armstrong needed to break the news to his patient's parents. You, Mrs. Beaumont, told me that you left all the medical details to your husband, so you" — I pointed at Philip — "went alone and listened to what he had to say, understood what it meant. And then you went home and didn't tell your wife a word of it, am I right?" I turned to Bridget. "You never knew about the cause of the cancer?"

She swung her head from side to side in shocked misery.

"But you did tell your brother," I said to her husband. "Your partner in life had to be kept from the truth, but your partner *in business* needed to know immediately."

"*Philip*," Bridget said, her voice a rough plea.

"Dad? Why aren't you saying anything?" Vanessa asked.

"And Cassie couldn't have been the only case of illness due to the contaminated water," I continued. "Alarm bells must have been going off in the doctor's head as he did his research on the sorts of health problems that could appear years down the line from chronic low levels of cadmium consumption. Perhaps he thought it might be implicated in many other disorders he'd been seeing more frequently in the town's folk — anemia, osteoporosis, prostate and ovarian cancer. So, I'm guessing he called you back in?"

"Both of us," Philip said to his lap in a voice so low, it was almost inaudible.

"Shut up!" Roger told his brother. "Not another word."

"He confronted you two with what he'd discovered. Said the only way so many people could be affected was if they'd consumed it regularly. Cadmium doesn't bind to plants, so that wasn't the source. Pitchford's main water supply came from the public system, which *was* regularly tested. So that left the bottled water."

"It was Cassie's favorite. She drank it all the time. Said soda was bad for you," Vanessa said softly.

"Did you know about this?" Jessica asked her mother, her tone more accusation than question. "Did you hush it for the sake of the town?"

"No! No, I most certainly did not," Michelle said hotly. "Good God, what sort of a person do you think I am?"

"Doc Armstrong would have insisted that the truth come out, but that would have been the end of the Beaumont Brothers company, and the two of you individually. The plant would have been shut down, there would've been civil claims, perhaps even class action suits. I'm no lawyer, but I think there would even have been criminal charges."

Rick Torres nodded fervently.

"You both stood to lose everything if Armstrong talked. But

somehow," I said, "you two persuaded him to keep the secret."

"Dad, tell me this isn't true!" Vanessa begged.

"We needed the money for Cassie's treatment. How could we possibly afford the best medical treatment if we were penniless? How could I take care of her — of this whole family — if I was in prison?" Philip said.

"*Philip*, shut up!" Roger bellowed.

"Besides, there was no point in telling," his brother added.

"No point?" I asked, unsure I'd heard him right.

"There was nothing to be done. Many years previously, we'd built the new factory on the other side of Kent Hill and shifted water uptake to the source of the spring right at the top. So it was uncontaminated. And we'd tested it religiously ever since. What possible good could have come from Armstrong going public when the damage had already been done years before, and the problem had already been fixed?"

"You moron!" his brother snarled at him.

I said, "He would probably still have believed he was duty-bound to tell. It was a public health issue — people needed to be made aware of their exposure and seek treatment, if necessary. And he was a doctor, after all."

"He was a drunken sot," Roger said.

Michelle glared at him. "I beg your pardon!"

"Oh, spare me the indignation. You've called him that — and worse — every time you've spoken of him to me these last twenty years."

Jessica stared at her mother in disgust.

"Then why didn't Armstrong come clean? Why didn't he report what he knew to the police?" Ryan asked.

"Blunt," I said. "They used his son to blackmail him into staying silent. They must have had some kind of evidence of Blunt's drug-dealing and threatened to report him. Blunt had two previous convictions, so another conviction would see him imprisoned—"

"Baseless speculation!" Roger blustered.

"—possibly for the rest of his life. And to sweeten the deal, they allowed him to live in a trailer in the woods behind this estate, where they knew he was farming weed and cooking meth or crack."

"You have evidence of drug manufacture, and you haven't brought it to me?" Ryan challenged Philip.

"Roger visited Doc Armstrong on the day he died," I told Ryan, "and warned him against making a deathbed confession. He said he had hard evidence about Blunt's activities — I'm guessing that was drone footage of precisely whatever it is Blunt's doing in the woods."

"He told you that?" Ryan asked.

"In a way."

"I don't believe you!" Roger snapped. "Now, please leave this house. You are no longer welcome to trespass on our hospitality while you tell these baseless, slanderous lies."

"This isn't your house!" Vanessa yelled at him. "You have no say here."

"Doc Armstrong knew he was living on borrowed time," I continued. "He didn't want to be around when all of this came out, and I think he still felt guilty. So he ended his life, but not before ensuring I got all the evidence I needed. He knew Roger might follow through on his threat, but maybe he figured the cops would be too busy with this case to worry about Blunt's activities, or maybe he was past caring."

"If what Garnet says is correct," Ryan said, "then you've concealed several very serious crimes and engaged in a conspiracy to obstruct justice. And when Ca– And if anyone's death can be ruled due to the effects of cadmium poisoning, then that's manslaughter."

"At the very least," Rick said.

"They've done worse than that," I said. "They've done cold-blooded, intentional, first-degree murder."

50

Philip's head snapped up at that. Roger's face mottled red with rage.

"Murder?" Ryan asked.

Everyone at the table stared at me. I shifted my gaze between two faces, studying them minutely, because I wasn't yet one hundred percent certain which one of them had actually done it, and whether the other had known, or whether they'd acted together.

A wave of deep sadness filled me. Colby hadn't known who'd done it either, until now. And he knew I was right.

"Murder. Because Doc Armstrong wasn't the first to test the water. He wasn't the first to put two and two together and draw a conclusion that pointed at cadmium contamination, was he?" I asked the Beaumont brothers. "That was Colby."

"Colby?" Bridget said faintly.

"Ten years ago, for his AP chemistry project, Colby chose to do an analysis of Beaumont Brothers' bottled water. He

402

tested for a bunch of trace elements — chemical, mineral, even metal. I think he wanted to prove how pure it was; he may not have wanted to join the family business, but that didn't mean he wasn't proud of it. But instead he found something impossible."

"Cadmium," Vanessa said.

"Yeah, cadmium. He couldn't believe his results. He thought maybe Cassie had been fiddling with his chemistry set, so he repeated the test, got the same findings. He researched the FDA standards on bottled water to check permissible limits. He tried to get hold of a professor who's an expert in groundwater pollution at MIT, hoping to find out more about the heavy metal. He studied online sites explaining the connection between zinc and groundwater contaminated by cadmium. He researched the health consequences of cadmium consumption and read about *Itai-Itai* — a mass cadmium poisoning that affected thousands in Japan last century. He realized he'd tumbled onto something catastrophic. Something that needed to be stopped and rectified immediately. He debated who he should tell — the cops, the FDA, or the FBI." I glared at Colby's father. "Did he come to you first? Maybe that Saturday, the day before he died?"

He nodded, his face white as old bones, his lips bloodless.

My anger was growing, solidifying into something cold and sharp behind my eyes. "He'd been distracted about something those last days, but he never got a chance to tell me what about. When I discovered the other day that he'd been sexually harassed at his job and then fired that day by this piece of work" — I cocked a thumb at Michelle — "I wondered why he'd never told me. It was because he was worried sick about what he'd discovered and needed to talk to his father. Did you know about the water?" I asked Philip.

"No! You have to believe me," he said desperately, directing pleading looks at his wife and daughter.

"You would have called your brother immediately to tell him the shocking thing Colby had discovered. Roger was no doubt horrified, too. He called Colby the next morning, the Sunday he disappeared, and talked to him for over twenty minutes, trying to persuade him he was wrong, eventually agreeing to meet that night at the Tavern to talk things over, telling Colby to bring his laptop so you two could check his findings and calculations."

Bridget's horrified gaze was riveted on me.

"The three of you — Colby, his beloved father, and his dear uncle — met at the Tuppenny Tavern that night," I said bitterly, my rage intensifying as I visualized that evening's events, imagined how it had been for Colby. "Why there? Why not at the factory?"

"He said he refused to set foot on those premises," Philip said.

"So you settled for one of the private booths in a quiet corner. Colby would have urged you to come clean. The contaminated water was on shelves across the country — you needed to do a product recall, urgently. He would've insisted you make a public announcement telling people who'd drunk it to seek immediate medical help. Perhaps they could get treatment to prevent further damage. Maybe even stop conditions from developing in the first place. And you two tried to persuade him to keep it quiet."

Beside me, Ryan tensed. His eyes were locked on the Beaumont brothers at the end of the table. Jessica was watching me, wide-eyed, her wine forgotten. Vanessa's hands, clenched in white-knuckled fists, rested on either side of her dessert dish, as though ready to be deployed.

"What did you say to him? That you'd stop collecting water until it could be done safely, that you'd test the water thoroughly and regularly from then on? Perhaps you even promised to recall stock. You," I said to Roger, "would've come up with some spurious reason for the recall that wouldn't alarm the market or hit the press. But Colby would've refused. Maybe he stormed out, taking his laptop with him, and the two of you were left with your fortunes and your futures crumbling down around you."

"I offered him a ride home, but he said he had to meet someone at the pond," Philip said.

"Pete Dillon," I said. "Though he thought he was meeting Judy."

"*Pete?*" Jessica said.

I explained about Pete's jealousy, his ruse to get Colby to meet him that night by the pond.

"He and his sidekick Brandon Nugent beat Colby nearly senseless, warned him to stay away from Judy." I turned to Jessica, possessed by a sudden suspicion. "Did you know? Did Pete ever tell you?"

"No! Never! And I'm finding it hard to believe he'd ever do something like that."

"You don't know him, Jess," I said. "Not at all."

"Why on earth would Peter Dillon confide in my daughter about his sordid romances and thuggish behavior?" Michelle demanded.

"Not now, Mom."

"So, Pete Dillon did it. Pete killed Colby?" Bridget asked. Her eyes were dark with pain, and tears ran unchecked down her face.

"No. Pete and Bran left him unconscious, but alive."

"How can you possibly know all this?" Ryan asked.

"I have it on good authority." On the word of the deceased victim himself. "Ask Judy Dillon. She'll confirm everything. So, either Philip or Roger — maybe both, but my money's on Roger — followed Colby to his meeting at the pond, no doubt hoping for another chance to dissuade him from the course of action he seemed set on."

"No," Philip gasped.

"And watched as Colby was beaten and left behind in the falling snow," I said loudly, my voice tight with fury. "And saw his opportunity to shut Colby up for good by dragging him into the water and holding him under until he stopped moving, stopped breathing." My voice rose higher, until I was almost yelling. "Then dragged him deeper still and wedged him under the thickening ice."

"*You!*" Philip lunged across the table, grabbed his brother around the throat, and throttled him with both hands, screaming, "You killed my boy! You murdered him!"

Michelle shrieked. My father waved his hands ineffectually. But in an instant, Ryan had hauled Philip off his brother.

"You murdered him!" Philip shouted over and over until his

voice grew hoarse, and he collapsed onto his knees on the floor, sobbing. Ryan stood beside him, a restraining hand on the man's shoulder.

"You knew!" Roger spat. "You *knew*. You were just too cowardly to admit it. You knew something had to be done, but you were too spineless to do it yourself. You were *glad* to have the problem solved so neatly without you having to get your hands dirty. Admit it, you were relieved that the truth would never come out."

"Glad? Relieved? I was *broken*! I was dead inside. You killed me, too, that night. You killed this whole family!"

Roger's face contorted in a rictus of contempt. "This is all mere speculation. There is not the slightest shred of proof."

Vanessa grabbed her dessert dish, leaned across the table and whacked her uncle on the side of the head, yelling, "You've already half-confessed, you bastard!"

Her husband tugged her back into her seat and wrapped her in his arms, held her while she wept.

"There's an eyewitness who saw Roger leaving the scene, who can identify his car," I said.

"Who?" Ryan demanded.

"Plus, I have proof of the water contamination."

"What proof could you possibly have?" Roger challenged.

"You're thinking about the missing test tubes from Colby's chemistry set, and his laptop which never turned up." The items that, along with his phone, hadn't been around to be saved in his box of possessions. "You or your brother dumped that evidence someplace it would never be found. But" — I pinned Roger with a savage smile — "you never thought to check his school notebooks. I have those, and the chemistry one is filled with notes, measurements and calculations for his project. I'm guessing there's more than enough proof there for any jury."

Roger stared at me for a split second and then bolted. Quicker than I would have believed possible, my mother stuck out her leg. Roger tripped over the cast and went sprawling. He scrambled to his feet, ran two steps, and then I sailed into him, tackling his legs at the knees, bringing him down and winding myself in the process. He kicked back, hard. Connected with my jaw, sending a shaft of pain shuddering through my body. He clambered upright and dashed out of the room.

Ryan raced around the table and leapt over me to hurtle after him. Ears ringing, and holding onto my jaw as if it might fall off my face, I got to my feet and followed them into the hall.

Roger was already lying face down and motionless on the marble floor. Either Ryan had landed a good one, or Roger had hit his head when he landed — either way, he was out cold. Ryan pulled out his phone to call for backup, but I marched straight over to Roger and kicked him in the ribs.

"*That's* for stealing Colby's phone. And *that's* for wrecking my car, and chasing me onto that fucking *pond*!" I kicked him again. "And *that's* for Cassie!"

Ryan put his hand over the mouthpiece and waved me away from Roger's unconscious form. "Stop that, Garnet!"

"*What*? He was resisting arrest."

I waited until Ryan began speaking into the phone again, then took a little run at Roger and kicked him in the balls. "And *that's* for Colby!"

"Garnet, I'm not kidding — stop that!" Ryan dragged me away from Roger and backed me up against the front door. "Stay!"

His back was to the hall, and the stairs, and the landing above. But I could see everything. The bronze lovers, still clinging tightly to each other in that last moment, plummeted down from above and smashed into Roger's head with a sickening, wet crack before thudding onto the marble floor. One of the bronze heads broke off and skidded away from the blossoming pool of blood. I stared up at the landing where Cassie stood, insubstantial and pale as a wraith, her trembling arms still raised above the rail.

"I stumbled," she said. "I bumped into the statue and it fell. Very sorry."

But she didn't look it, not at all.

Epilogue

Plover Pond had long seemed menacing and sinister to me, but that day, it looked merely pretty. Pale winter sun glistened on its frozen surface, and the reeds and bare winter trees formed a spiky coronet around its edges. Only the small group of people, silently clustered with the Beaumonts near the water's edge, spoiled the picture-postcard-perfect scene.

Bridget and Vanessa stood on either side of Cassie, holding her up while they scattered Colby's ashes onto the water.

My parents and I watched from higher up the embankment. I wanted to be down there with them — I craved the connection of holding a fistful of that gray dust, prolonging a last touch with Colby, even as I shuddered at the thought of it. But when I made to walk down and join them, my mother held me back.

"No, dear," she said, patting the back of my hand. "It's still too soon."

I nodded at the surprisingly sane bit of wisdom. I wanted to offer what consolation I could to the Beaumont women, but they seemed to want only each other. I was a reminder of

Colby's murder, and they were too full of anger at his father and uncle, and surely also at me for bringing the whole thing up again and being the cause of them losing yet more family members, to want to talk to me.

"Rest in peace, Colby," I whispered, the mist of my breath fading in the air, along with my words. "Always and forever."

In the week since the Christmas Eve dinner, a lot had happened. Pete Dillon and Philip Beaumont had been arrested, Roger Beaumont's body had been taken to Burlington to await the chief medical examiner's attentions, and operations at the Beaumont Brothers water bottling plant had been shut down until further notice. The police had yet to decide whether or not to bring charges against Cassie, but it was clear she wouldn't live to see a trial. We McGees had celebrated a subdued Christmas, my mother's plaster cast had been removed, and my bruises and tender-tipped fingers had all but healed.

What had *not* happened, however, was anything remotely spooky. I hadn't had a single vision. No words had fallen into my mind, no surges of foreign feelings had flooded through me, no lightbulbs had blown, and I'd felt no mysterious drafts. Even my bouts of nausea and the incessant headaches had disappeared.

Just as Professor Perry had predicted, all my guilt-induced hallucinations and symptoms had subsided along with my guilt. I hadn't been the cause, directly or even indirectly, of Colby's death. And whatever I may have owed our love, I'd settled it by solving his murder. I was free to be me again. Rational, logical, more-or-less normal me — only with different-colored eyes.

"You need to hurry if you don't want to miss your bus, kiddo," my father said.

My car was still in the shop. I'd promised my parents I would make a long weekend of it when I came to fetch it, probably at the end of January. Right now, I was headed back to Boston; I had a meeting with Perry scheduled for the next day.

Ryan Jackson gave us a ride to the bus stop at the gas station in Main Street, stowed my suitcase in the storage compartment, and kissed me — this time, on the lips. And this time, I didn't pull back.

"Dinner when you come back to get your car?" he said.

"Maybe," I said.

But I said it with a smile and a nod, because it was time to start living and feeling again. Perhaps even — one day — loving again. And Ryan had, after all, brought my heart back to life once. Maybe he could do it again.

I scored a window seat, shoved my handbag under the seat by my feet and wiped a forearm against the window to my right, clearing a circle in the condensation. As the bus pulled away, I waved at Ryan and at my father, who'd given me a murder mystery to read on the ride, and at my mother, who'd pressed a lilac gemstone into my hand as I climbed onto the bus full of folks headed back to the big city after the holidays.

"Lepidolite – for clarity in decision-making," she'd said confidently.

I'd already made my decision. I now knew, as Perry already had, that I was not cut out to be a psychologist. Beyond that, I had no clue what I wanted to do with my life except to sleep for a week. It had been an exhausting trip home, and I was eager to get back to the neighbor-noisy sanctuary of my apartment, to enjoy the quiet solitude of my own mind.

I dropped the stone into my parka pocket, where it clicked against the amethyst quartz I'd found in the shallows of the pond. Opening Dad's novel to the first page, I sighed happily and began reading.

The book was almost finished by the time we reached Boston, and though we made multiple stops and collected even more passengers on the way, the seat beside me, on my left, remained empty.

Dear Reader,

I hope you enjoyed this novel!

If you loved this book, I'd really appreciate it if you'd leave a review, no matter how short, on Amazon or Goodreads. Every review is valuable in helping other readers discover the book.

Would you like to be notified of my new releases and special offers? My newsletter goes out once or twice a month and is a great way to get book recommendations, a behind-the-scenes peek at my writing and publishing processes, as well as advance notice of giveaways and free review copies. I won't clutter your inbox or spam you, and I will never share your email address with anyone. Sign up at my website: www.joannemacgregor.com.

I'd love to hear from you! Come say hi on Facebook (@JoanneMacg) or Twitter (@JoanneMacg), or reach out to me via my website and I'll do my best to get back to you.

– *Jo Macgregor*

Acknowledgements

My thanks to my editor, Chase Night, and to my fabulous beta readers, Emily Macgregor, Nicola Long, Edyth Bulbring, and Heather Gordon, for all their invaluable feedback. You improve my writing immeasurably, and I deeply appreciate each one of you!

Thanks also to technical consultants for this book — Mary Scholes and Tamiru Abiye from the University of the Witwatersrand, and Tyler Arbour for so generously sharing their expertise in heavy metals, biogeochemistry and ecology. Any technical errors are my own!

I'm also grateful to Cameron Garriepy for being my expert Vermont reader — you have a beautiful state!

31208886R00255

Made in the USA
Lexington, KY
16 February 2019